PRAISE FOR DANIEL MARCUS

"Betrayed by their dreams, comforted by the ghosts of love, Dan Marcus's wily, pitiable characters test the boundaries of fresh pasts, skewed presents, and distant futures furnished with decadent toys and ineffably alien yet totally essential technologies. These stories make me ache with nostalgia for an age yet to come. They remind me of why I've always wanted to be this good."

—Nisi Shawl, author of *Everfair*; Nebula and World Fantasy Award Finalist; winner of the Otherwise Award

"What I like best about Daniel Marcus's stories is the visual clarity, the precision of his imagining. The details he chooses to describe loom larger than themselves, full of implied narrative, and as crisp or newly-minted as money."

—Paul Park, author of *A Princess of Roumania*; Nebula, Arthur C. Clarke, and Locus Award finalist

"Daniel Marcus is one of the best storytellers I've ever met. His feel for narrative is his superpower."

—Pat Cadigan, winner of the Hugo, Locus, and Arthur C. Clarke Awards

"Ranging deftly across genres, as unexpected in their bright moments as gemstones spilled from a paper bag, Marcus's stories unfailingly surprise and delight."

—Paul Witcover, finalist for the World Fantasy, Nebula, and Shirley Jackson awards.

Praise for Binding Energy

"Raymond Carver crossed with William Gibson."

—*Salon.com*

"Emotionally taut, tough-minded, and beautifully rendered, these stories are models of compression and power."

—Karen Joy Fowler, World Fantasy Award-winning author of *Black Glass* and *Sarah Canary*

"In their range, and the articulation of styles, and in their balancing between self-aware referentiality and fist-clenched passion, Daniel Marcus's brilliant assemblage of stories in Binding Energy *could be seen as a kind of map for the future of literary SF."*

—Jonathan Lethem, National Book Critics Circle Award-winning author of *Motherless Brooklyn*

"Love stories, every one. Dan Marcus knows the shape and sound of Tomorrow, as readers know from his regular appearances in the mags; indeed, like Stross and Doctorow, he is one of its most literate creators. But seeing his edgy stories together, we discover that he's been working ancient ground with modern tools. This remarkable first collection from a veteran author is a treasure for readers."

—Terry Bisson, winner of the Hugo, Nebula, and Theodore Sturgeon Awards

BRIGHT MOMENT AND OTHERS

DANIEL MARCUS

WFP
WordFire Press

EBook ISBN: 978-1-68057-192-9
Trade Paperback ISBN: 978-1-68057-191-2
Hardcover ISBN: 978-1-68057-193-6
Casebind ISBN: 978-1-68057-283-4
Library of Congress Control Number: 2020951791

Cover design by Janet McDonald
Cover artwork images by Adobe Stock
Kevin J. Anderson, Art Director
Published by
WordFire Press, LLC
PO Box 1840
Monument CO 80132

Kevin J. Anderson & Rebecca Moesta, Publishers

WordFire Press eBook Edition 2021
WordFire Press Trade Paperback Edition 2021
WordFire Press Hardcover Edition 2021
Printed in the USA

Join our WordFire Press Readers Group for
sneak previews, updates, new projects, and giveaways.
Sign up at wordfirepress.com

CONTENTS

DEDICATION

For Chris and David, again

INTRODUCTION

PAT MURPHY

Dan Marcus writes stories that will knock you off balance. They will take you by surprise. They will make you question your assumptions. They will stretch your thinking and shake up your ideas of what science fiction is and what it can do.

Each story in this collection will take you somewhere new, somewhere different, somewhere unexpected.

A man surfing on the ammonia ocean of a Jovian moon catches a glimpse of something that changes the course of his life.

An entrepreneur opening a Christian-themed megamall brings Jesus Christ himself from another universe to speak at the grand opening.

Pablo Picasso is painting in Paris—and then the Martians invade.

A space-faring intelligence that counts humans as long distant ancestors encounters a young woman doing battle with giant bugs straight off a pulp magazine cover.

So many worlds, each one drawn with an expert hand in a few deft strokes. Dan makes it look easy, but as a short story writer, I can tell you it's not. Novelists have pages and pages to introduce a complex environment, develop characters, explore grand themes. A short story writer must do all those things in a fraction of the space.

Each of these stories is a captured moment, brief but complete, memorable, and packed with an emotional charge.

I've given you a hint of what you'll find in these stories. Perhaps I should offer a few warnings as well.

Don't expect stories in which humans reign supreme as galactic overlords, heroic and triumphant. I told you: this is science fiction that will make you question your assumptions. Yes, there is heroism, but it's not where you expect it. This is science fiction that upends tropes and smashes expectations.

Don't expect this to be science fiction where technology is the point. Oh, the technology is here; every nut and bolt and equation is in place. (Dan Marcus knows his science.) But the nuts and bolts are not the point of the story. These are stories with heart, about people who are trying to find their way.

And finally, don't expect this to be a book that you'll read in an afternoon and put aside. These characters, these places will linger in your consciousness. After reading Dan Marcus's description of the prairie in "Prairie Godmother," I'll never see Kansas as boring again. My view of that landscape will always be colored by the resonance of his description.

These stories may affect you in unexpected ways. You may find yourself watching the night sky for the ionization trails of ascending spaceships. Alien songs may haunt your dreams. Don't say I didn't warn you.

—Pat Murphy, 2020

BRIGHT MOMENT

ARUN FLOATED in the ammonia swells, one arm around the buoyant powersled, waiting. He'd blocked all his feeds and chats, public and private, and silenced his alerts. He felt deliciously alone. His ears were filled with the murmuring white noise of his own blood flow, intimate and oceanic, pulsing with his heartbeat. Metis was a bright diamond directly overhead. Athena hung just above the near, flat horizon, her rings a plaited bow spanning the purple sky. Persistent storms pocked her striated surface, appearing deceptively static from thirty kiloklicks out. Arun had negotiated the edgewalls of those storms more than once, setting up metahelium deep-mining rigs. A host of descriptive words came to mind, but "static" was not among them.

The sea undulated slowly in the low gee, about 0.6 Standard. The distant shape of a skyhook was traced out by a pearl string of lights reaching up from the horizon and disappearing into distance haze, blinking in synchronization to suggest upwards motion. The skyhook was the only point of reference for scale. He shuddered involuntarily. His e-field distributed warmth to his body extremities from the tiny pack at the small of his back and maintained his blood oxygenation, but bobbing in the swell, alone in the vast ammonia sea, he felt cold and a little dizzy. He wanted to breathe and felt a fleeting instant of lizard-brain panic.

The current began to tug at his feet long before he saw the

humped swell bowing the horizon upwards, a slight backward drift, accelerating slowly. His heart pounded in his chest as he clambered belly down onto the powersled. He drifted back towards the swell, slowly at first, then faster. He looked over his shoulder at the rising wall of liquid. It appeared solid, like moving metal, completely blocking the sky. He imagined he could feel wind tugging at his e-field.

Arun felt a vibration through the powersled, a vast low frequency murmur, the world-ocean getting ready to kick his ass. Just as he was about to be sucked beneath the monstrous swell, he activated the sled. He surged forward and stood as the sled began to accelerate up the face of the wave.

He felt the sled's stabilizers groaning beneath his feet as he sought balance on the flat surface. The wave steepened, hurtling him forward. He could just make out the landmass upon which this immense wave would break. Brooklyn was the moon's only conti-nent, a million square klicks of frozen nothing.

He estimated his height now at half a klick, his forward speed about a hundred meters per second. A fine mist of icy, driving sleet surrounded him, melting to slush as it touched his e-field and whipped past his face. Blobs of static discharge, pale blue and lumi-nous, flickered around him. His vertical position had stabilized about three quarters of the way up the face of the wave. The power-sled's gyros did most of the balancing work but he kept his eyes fixed on the distant, blinking skyhook lights, shifting his stance as perturbations in the flow jostled his footing. He figured he had about a minute before he had to ditch or be dashed against the shore when the wave broke. His e-field's impact system would prevent major injury, but he'd be black and blue for a week. Worst case, a month in the tank and restoration from backup. He'd only had one full restore, several years back after his singleship's drive went unstable, and it was disconcerting, a huge unrecoverable swath cut from his life. It was routine as an eye replacement for some people, but he didn't like it at all.

His peripheral vision registered motion, a vast, dark shape beneath the wall of ammonia to his left. He didn't want to take his eyes away from the skyhook lights, but he sneaked a look. Nothing —just a shimmering solid wall of liquid.

He returned his gaze forward, sought and locked on to the skyhook. There, again, a flicker of something huge, hovering beneath the glassy surface. He looked and for the barest flicker of an instant he saw it, a tapered fifty meter bullet trailing a bundle of tentacles, a quartet of glassy black orbs framing the rounded front of the thing. Eyes, he was sure of it.

He lost his footing and the wave took him.

Arun rose through veiled layers of consciousness, gauzy memories caressing him with feather touches and drifting away like smoke. He was a child on Luna, outside for the first time, learning to suppress the choke reflex while the e-field oxygenated his blood. The sky was huge and black, dusted with bright, steady points. Terra was a mottled brown marble.

Pain woke him to a large pale face hanging over his like a translucent moon. The gentle silken murmur of her voice took him back under.

The next time he awoke, Ko was there. He imagined that he felt her presence before he opened his eyes—stern, concerned, an undercurrent of agitation.

His eyes felt gritty. He opened them cautiously. He was in zero gee, swaddled and tethered. He recognized the light green biowalls of the clinic at Athena Station, glowing faintly. The far wall was transparent and filtered: Athena hung mottled and beautiful, suspended in blackness, her ring system covering half the sky. Above Athena, the lacy spiderwork of docks surrounding the Metis Wormhole rotated slowly.

He was banged up, he knew that much. Gel covered half his jaw and cheek, analgesic and colony nutrient. Pain lanced up his body. He risked a glance down. His left leg ended neatly just below the knee. Beneath it, growing from the stump, a pink stub glistened with more gel.

"Wow," he croaked.

Ko nodded without smiling.

"Wow indeed. I'd kick your ass if there was anything left to kick."

He started to smile and regretted it instantly.

"Fuck." It came out sounding like *uch*. He tried to subvocalize his credentials to a shared channel, but the aether was dead.

She nodded. "No implants yet. Your nervous system needs an absence of distraction to heal the mess you made of yourself. They wanted to restore you from backup into a noob but I wouldn't let them."

"Thank you." *Anch eu.*

Arun closed his eyes and darkness took him again into velvet arms. As his senses fell away he saw it again, hovering effortlessly behind a shimmering wall of liquid, sleek body rippling peristaltically and buffeting slightly, its sensory nodes—*eyes*—huge, black, depthless.

This time, he came fully awake almost immediately. He felt acute pain in his jaw, his side, and his leg. *His leg.* It had grown several inches since he'd seen it last and now sported five stubby bumps that would become toes. It hurt like a bastard—a surface burning all over the new growth and a bone-deep ache coming from a phantom location several inches below it.

He tried to call out, emitting only a raspy croak.

The medic's avatar appeared immediately, hovering in front of him, a vaguely pretty, middle-aged woman with a round face and shaved head. She was a Mind, of course; Arun recalled that she had chosen the unlikely name Wheat.

"Hello, Arun," she said. "Welcome back." Her voice was low and liquid.

She pointed to a tube next to his head. "Take some water."

He took a sip and tried speaking again, a little more carefully this time.

"Thanks."

She floated there, waiting, her broad features impassive but for a hint of amusement in her large, brown eyes.

"Any questions?" she said finally.

Arun laughed and pain flared from his jaw and burst inside his skull. He squeezed his eyes shut and saw purple blotches swimming before him.

Wheat floated closer.

"I'm sorry, Arun. I'll try not to make you laugh." She paused a beat. "Do you have any idea how angry Ko is?"

"I can imagine."

"I'll bet you can." She glided back a bit. "Okay, inventory. You lost a leg, your liver was destroyed, you fractured your skull. Badly, it turns out. You actually lost some brain tissue. Oh, and you broke your jaw in three places. I wanted to just dump your latest snapshot into a new body but Ko wouldn't let me."

"Good," he said, emphatically. "How did I lose the leg?"

"Your e-field was breached when the impact systems kicked in. Snipped your leg clean off when it restored itself. What the hell were you *thinking*?"

He shrugged carefully. "It seemed like a good idea at the time."

"Do you know what a Darwin Award is?"

"Nope."

"You should read more cultural history. Anyway, your new liver is in place, about half-size and growing nicely. Don't drink any alcohol for a while. I've got colonies working on your fractures. If you stay out of gravity wells, your leg should be ready in a week. And if you want, I can do something about your testosterone problem."

"No, that's—" Suddenly, he remembered the shape.

He looked at her. "I saw something ..."

She tilted her head quizzically.

"I—" He imagined her reaction. The furrowed brow. The gentle half-smile. Maybe slip him a seed colony of serotonergic neurons.

Keep it close to the chest for now, he thought. *Gotta talk to Ko.*

"Never mind," he said.

She arched her eyebrows slightly.

He smiled weakly. "I'm tired."

Wheat nodded.

"You rest, then. I'll tell Ko you're back among the living."

Her avatar winked out.

"Wheat ..."

She reappeared, hovering in the doorframe.

"My aether implants. When?"

There was an odd flicker in her eyes, then it was gone. "Soon, Arun. I'll tell Ko you're up and around."

He'd lost his diurnal sense, but he thought about two days passed before Ko showed up. He did the exercises that were assigned to him, began eating solid food—well, paste—on the second day, read and scanned from the slate Wheat brought him, and slept a lot. The pain was spiky and he had the worst of it blocked, but Wheat wouldn't let him off the hook entirely, saying pain was part of the healing process.

He missed the aether badly, but Wheat continued to deflect his requests.

He awoke from a fitful doze to find Ko perched next to his webbing, looking at him with a slight frown.

"Hey," he said.

"Hey yourself," she replied, and leaned over to kiss him. He could see a tension, though, in the way she carried herself.

"I've been here a lot, but you've been under most of the time."

"I know. I remember you talking about kicking my ass."

"Well, I have to ask. What were you thinking?"

Arun chuckled. "Wheat asked me the same thing. You really want to know?"

"I really want to know."

"I was thinking—I mean, as far back as when we got the first imaging, the klick-high waves—I was thinking, damn, it would be really cool to surf one of those."

She looked at him impassively for a long moment. "That's it? That's all you've got?"

"Yeah. Pretty deep, huh?"

"You realize you've set us back about a month. Everything's waiting on your simulations. Not to mention everybody's been worried sick about you. You owe a huge debt to Wheat—she hasn't let anybody near you."

He smiled ruefully. "Yeah, well, you know medics. I'm really sorry, Ko. I thought, the sled's gonna keep me stabilized, and if I wipe out, no big deal."

"No big deal." She pushed herself back, hovered in front of him like a pissed off Samurai angel, her dark hair floating around her head. "You know something about systems engineering, if I recall. Risks are multiplicative. You slam into solid rock at a hundred meters a second—" Ticking off her fingers. "—in a methane atmosphere, and it's one fifty Kelvin outside. Something's gonna go wrong."

"It was stupid."

"Epically so."

He paused a beat.

"But it was really fucking cool."

Ko almost smiled, then caught herself.

"Got you," Arun said.

They looked at each other for a long moment.

"Ko," he said.

"Yeah?"

"I saw something. Just before I wiped out … I saw something."

"What do you mean?"

"There's life down there, Ko."

Her eyes narrowed.

"It was in the wave, riding it just like me. About fifty meters long, very aerodynamic, squid-like. Cluster of tentacles at the back and a pair of stabilizer fins. Four sensory organs at the front end, bilaterally symmetric. I got a good look at it. That's how I wiped out —I just couldn't believe what I was seeing and I lost my footing."

"We've taken samples—"

"Yeah, nothing. Far as we could tell, the ammonia ocean's a desert—completely barren."

"What about all the mapping?"

"We scanned to pick up huge density gradients so we could map the ocean floor. The scans wouldn't pick up life forms."

"You know what this means."

"Yeah. There's gotta be a whole biosphere down there. Maybe localized to volcanic vents on the sea floor—more trace compounds, richer organics. That's why we never picked up anything in the samples—they were all near the surface."

"What was your squid doing up there?"

Arun shrugged. "Maybe he got lost. Maybe he thought it was really fucking cool, too. Who knows? I'll tell you something, though —we go through with terraforming Erichthonius and we're wiping all that out."

She was silent for a long moment.

"You're sure about this. Maybe you were hemoglobin-deprived. Hallucinating."

Arun shook his head. "No way."

"You're going to have to verify and validate. Tweak the density and re-do the scans. Good thinking about the vents—see if you can concentrate some resolution down there. I'll get on the ansible to Corporate and see what they have to say."

She looked at him long and hard and he got that feeling again, that she had something else on her mind.

"Okay, what?"

Ko shrugged. "This probably isn't a great time to tell you."

"Tell me what?"

"There's no way to make this easy. Periphery's divorcing you."

"The fuck are you talking about?" He realized instantly, though, that he'd known it all along, that they were waiting to tell him before he regrew his aether implants.

"It's no good, Arun. You don't need us."

"But—"

"This—" She waved her hand and began drifting across the room. She kicked off the floor and floated back to his webbing. "This *adventure* of yours. It's a case in point. You shut us all out. *You shut us out.* And we're supposed to be okay with that. And it's not like that was the first time. You don't need us."

He thought back to the calm, centered feeling he had, a tiny speck floating in the vast ocean, dwarfed beneath Athena's huge bulk, nothing in his ears but the sound of his own blood flow. It was a perfect moment.

"Do you feel the same way?"

She sighed. "You know I love you. I always will. But you married into a pod, not just me. And the dynamic has to be there, or at least it has to be fixable. For everybody. I mean, come on. This can't possibly be news to you."

He thought of them, visualized them in his mind's eye the way he saw them in the aether. Ko's presence tightly focused and diamond-bright. Andrew, full of contradictions, a bumbling puppy with a scorpion tail. Sara, a soft pulsing blob, golden toned and full of nurturing warmth, surrounding a secret, walled-off place that few ever saw, even her podmates. Jacob, all planes and angles, Cartesian simplicity and denial toe-to-toe, because nothing is ever really linear.

He wondered how he looked to them.

But it was always mainly Ko for him. Ko, his partner-in-crime from back in grad school. Ko, his friend, his lover, his boss. Ko, who'd brought him into Periphery and advocated tirelessly for him when things got rough. They were both so strong-willed, it was a miracle that their friendship had endured for so long. But her strength was like tempered steel, his like the green sapling that bends but does not break. It had always worked, somehow. *They'd* always worked, at least until Periphery.

He blinked away tears. "No. No, I guess not."

Ko bent over to kiss his forehead.

"Rest up now," she said. "Wheat says you're ready to go back to work. Do the scan. Check the vents. Rokhlin back on Terra sent you some notes on the ignition model through the ansible that I want you to fold into your simulations. We've got some lost ground to reclaim."

She reached into her pocket and pulled out a small vial. He knew without having to ask that it was the colony that would build his aether implants. Nanomachines would thread his brain with micro-filament receptors, program him with communication protocols and the somatic interface. But there would be no Periphery channel, no always-on, no constant presence of other souls joined with his.

He sucked down the contents of the vial. It left a bitter, chemical taste at the back of his throat.

"Thanks," he said. "I'll ping you in a day or so."

She kissed him again, pushed off his webbing with her foot, and floated out of the room without looking back. The door irised shut behind her.

☆

RECIPE: EARTHLIKE PLANET

Ingredients

Gas giant (Jovian) planet—rings optional
Frozen-ass Jovian moon, nickel-iron core, 0.5 Terran mass or greater
Virtual tokamak and attendant virtual flux plumbing
Metahelium, as needed, for power
H_2O and CO_2 ice
Photosynthetic nanomachine colonies
Spaceships 'n' stuff

Steps

1) Scoop hydrogen from the Jovian's atmosphere and contain it with
a virtual tokamak. The field generators should be at the L4 and L5
Lagrange points of the system you are about to create. L3 is a good
spot for the hydrogen scoop. The Lagrange potential wells will shift
and deepen as mass accretes, and their position will stabilize by the
time your pocket sun becomes operational.

2) Compress the hydrogen until it ignites.

3) Adjust the hydrogen flux from the Jovian and your new sun's
distance from the moon until Terran temperature ranges are
achieved.

4) Wait for ammonia oceans, methane ice, and other really cold stuff
to boil away.

5) Drop 10^{20} kilos of H_2O and CO_2 ice down the moon's gravity
well. Don't worry about exact measurements here. The resulting
seismic and volcanic activity should shake loose a bunch of nitrogen
as well. You're going to want that later!

6) Season liberally with photosynthetic nanomachines.

7) Go do something else—this may take a while!

Arun floated alone in the Simulacrum. The animation was looped; the repetition was meditation for him. Slender filaments of luminous gas spiraling from Athena and converging to a bright fuzzy cloud near Erichthonius. The cloud condensing, collapsing, brightening until it ignites in a blaze of white light that dwarfs Athena, dwarfs Metis. Cheesy inspirational orchestral music swelling, rising. Slow zoom to the moon's storm-wracked surface now, ammonia oceans boiling, churning. Pull back through the roiling atmosphere, past the pocket baby sun, to a stately swarm of icy asteroids sliding inexorably down the moon's gravity well. The impact explosions are visible from a hundred kiloklicks out, violently transforming their kinetic energy into great gouts of flame and superheated steam. The music is staccato now, pounding and elemental. Cut to: Silence, and a lone cylinder spinning end over end in space, corporate logo plainly visible, heading towards the battered moon. The cylinder dwindles, disappears from view. There is a very long pause, and just when you think there's something wrong with the feed, Erichtonius's grey, marbled surface explodes in vibrant blue, green, and white. Fade to black. Pause. Then the loop begins again and we fade in to Athena pinned to the void, slender filaments of luminous gas spiraling out from her banded surface …

It was complete bullshit, of course. Marketecture. An animated ducky-horsey diagram for the shareholders. The real work lay in the physics models. That was Arun's comfort zone, his sweet spot, the arcane worlds of ignition thresholds, phase maps, stability analyses. But he loved the Simulacrum. It reminded him of what he was doing. It helped him define himself.

His pain was down to a dull ache where the new liver was coming in. He still had some difficulty with solid food, and his new leg wasn't quite grown, although it was strong enough to help with maneuvering in zero gee.

He was healing and he was broken. He saw Ko a couple of times and it was cordial, professional. He missed Periphery badly, but not as badly as he feared he might. He stayed to the public and info channels on the aether and defaulted everything else to autoreply. Sara came in from the nearly operational L4 field generator to see him and spent the night. It was bittersweet, a mercy fuck, and they both knew it, but they played it out, she the healer and he the wounded, and it was all right. He saw her off at the docking platform. As he watched her singleship recede to a point and vanish in the starry void, he wondered if he would never see her again.

Athena Station was basically a small town and everybody knew everybody else's business. People he passed in the corridors were painfully kind and eventually he stopped going out. He worked eighteen-hour days, stopping only to eat, bathe, and sleep. Burning the candle at both ends, but he figured candles were made that way for a reason.

☆

"Are we ready?" Ko asked.

They were perched in webbing near the top of the lounge, a hemispherical room capped with a transparent e-field so it appeared open to space. Singleships and utility barges floated overhead on various errands. Metis was behind Athena and her shadowy bulk hung directly overhead. They sipped station-brewed beer from bulbs and nibbled sticks of salted jicama flavored with lime. The place was about half full. Arun saw several people look in their direction, then look away.

"The models check out. We can start the L3 scoop any time, but I don't see how—"

"First things first, Arun. The ignition models. We don't want another Titan."

"No shit," he said. "Ko, the models are solid and it works in the lab. We induce a bit of excitation in the injection stream, a little energy radiates away, and we inhibit pre-ignition. It'll work, no doubt about that. And we'll be able to control it. But—"

She held her hand up.

"I know, your squid. What have you got?"

He tapped his slate and pulled up a graphic.

"You can see the points cluster near the bottom, following the vents. They're moving, too, independent of current drift."

He tapped the slate twice. "You pull back and you can see a few loners here and there, like my guy. But they mostly hang together."

He looked at her. "They're *social animals*, Ko."

He waited for a response, but she wasn't giving him anything.

"And you're not gonna fucking believe *this*."

He tapped an icon on the screen.

"Listen."

There was a high-pitched ratcheting sound, followed by a series of low clicks and whistles, then a long sustained tone that modulated slowly into two separate voices. Another voice joined in, weaving harmonies and polyrhythms in with the first. It went on like that for nearly ten minutes, some parts repeating, then branching off into new patterns, then returning to an earlier motif.

Arun watched Ko as they listened. She wouldn't meet his eyes.

Finally, she held up her hand. "Okay, I get it. Whale song. Like the humpbacks. Fine."

She closed her eyes and stroked her forehead, her other hand still held aloft, palm out, as if warding him off.

"Ko."

She didn't seem to hear him.

"Ko," he repeated.

Finally, she looked up.

"How long have you known?" he asked.

She sighed. "Just after your accident. I told the Board about your close encounter and they weren't at all surprised—said they've known there was some kind of biosphere here since just about Day One. Nothing like this, though."

She nodded toward the slate. The recording had looped back to the beginning and the haunting tapestry of sound was building again.

She shook her head. "But it doesn't matter."

"What do you mean?"

"Please don't get stupid on me, Arun. What do you think I mean? What are we gonna do—pack up our toys and go home? This can't be stopped. There's too much riding on it."

"Ko, this is *it*. First contact. Our first intelligent extees. How we handle this will define who we are as a species from this point on. And we're gonna wipe them out because we need the real estate?"

She nodded, biting her lip. "I don't like it any more than you do, but yeah—pretty much."

They looked at each other for a long time.

"Well, shit," he said, finally. "I always knew you were management material, but you've really surpassed my expectations."

"Are you done? I'm sorry about your squid, I really am, but we've got a lot of work to do and I need to know if I can count on you."

Her face was hard and set, her eyes unreadable. He had a snapshot memory of her, back in grad school, shortly after they became lovers. They were sitting in a café in Barsoom, a few years before the dome collapsed. Olympus Mons filled the sky behind her. He'd fallen in love with her for her fierce intelligence, but in that moment she was open, vulnerable, and warm and he remembered a small shock of wonder that here was a side of her that he had never seen.

Now, again, he was seeing a new aspect of her. The calculating technocrat in full flower, proxy for the Corporate intent. He wondered if he'd ever really known her.

A barge bristling with grappling cranes floated slowly overhead, so close he felt he could have reached out and touched it.

"Yeah, Ko," he said. "You can count on me."

☆

Arun logged a lot of singleship hours, traveling between the field generators at what would be L4 and L5 of the new system, the hydrogen scoop at L3, the receiving docks at Metis Wormhole, and Athena Station, making final preparations. He did not see Sara during his visit to the L4 facility, which was just as well.

He relished the solitude of transit. He liked to clear the hull; he was ensconced within the immensity of space. He emptied his mind of thought and felt something close to peace.

Other times, drifting between stations, he would play the animation. The new system formed around him: the slow accretion, the bright moment of ignition, chaos, destruction, rebirth. It reaffirmed what he was doing.

Finally, everything was ready. Arun took a singleship one last time down to the moon's world-ocean, slipped into the ammonia swells and clambered aboard his powersled.

There was very little haze. Athena was huge and bright, her surface busy and florid, her rings a bridge to Heaven. Metis was a painfully bright spark pinned to the purple bowl of the sky.

It was time.

He opened a broadcast channel and began to speak.

"This is Arun Dhillon. I alone am responsible for what I am about to tell you. I have engineered a breach in the metahelium containment field at the Metis Wormhole. In approximately ten hours it will completely rupture, resulting in a five Gigaton thermonuclear explosion that will collapse the singularity, preventing all subsequent travel to and from the Metis system. The event will also destroy Athena Station and the Lagrange facilities.

"There is plenty of time for all staff and their families to evacuate through the Metis Wormhole if you mobilize immediately. I pray that you do and I thank each and all of you for the privilege of working with you these last few years.

"Goodbye and good luck."

He shut down all his feeds and sent a *home* directive to his singleship. It would dock itself just in time to be vaporized.

The ocean rocked him and he felt no pain, no regrets. He dozed off and was awakened by a gentle but perceptible swell. He looked down. He couldn't see more than a few meters, but imagined, far below, a huge shape gliding through the shadowy depths. He waited, hoping it would return, but it did not.

Exhaustion overtook him and he slept again, more deeply this time. He dreamt he was in the Simulacrum, whorls of gas surrounding him, converging, condensing, collapsing, and he awoke to brightness, the actinic glare of a new sun swelling in the sky. It outshone Metis, outshone Athena, bathing the undulating ocean in white radiance. Then it softened and attenuated, collapsing back through the spectrum to a dull red glow.

PRAIRIE GODMOTHER

SOMETIMES IT GOT SO bad the only thing Will could do was put a 12-pack of Budweiser in the old 4X4, some Hank Williams on the tape machine, and burn up the two-lane straight as a carpenter's rule out into the empty heart of the prairie.

He wasn't a drinking man, not really. But it kind of built up in him slowly, that hollow feeling, like he was one of those dried Indian gourds and there was nothing inside him but a handful of tiny, rattling seeds, hard as stones.

It was more than just missing Rose, although of course he did miss her, every day, even after five years. Will still slept alone under the bedspread she'd made for them with her own small hands, and her needlepoint Lord's Prayer still hung on the living room wall, right over the television.

No, it was more like when she died it left a space in him that never filled, and these trips were like the wind rushing in to claim it.

He was well out of Salina now, coming up onto the intersection with County 7. Will reached over to the carton on the seat next to him, pried out a beer, and pulled the top up one-handed as he turned onto the little blacktop road. It stretched ahead of him, winking in and out of sight with the gentle contours of the land, and Will felt it pulling him forward like a wire to some place beyond the low, distant hills.

Hank was singing "I'm So Lonesome I Could Cry," and Will

crooned along with him, belting out the words loud in the cab of the pickup. He caught a glimpse of himself in the rear-view, his leathery face scrunched up like he'd caught his foot in a door. He laughed, and he felt the borders of that darkness in him push back a little farther.

You just keep doin' it for me, Hank. Just don't stop talkin' to me.

Will loved the prairie, everything about it. When you looked at it from a distance it looked smooth and featureless, just miles and miles of tall, waving grass, but when you got up close you could see the wrinkles and scars. There was a rolling motion to the land that was gentle on the eye but sucked the strength out of you on foot, and the contours hid a crosshatched pattern of streambeds and hidden arroyos. A person could get lost out here and never get found.

Will had a favorite spot and that's where he was headed. He turned onto a rutted dirt road that snaked around a low hill, and when the road widened just a bit, he pulled over and stopped. He put the beers in a rucksack along with a couple of ham sandwiches neatly wrapped in wax paper, and walked straight out into the waist-high grass, following the faint path.

The land gradually fell, and as it did the grass got higher and higher, until it was over his head and Will felt like he was walking on the bottom of an ocean of rustling tan.

Suddenly, the high grass opened up in front of him and he stood on the edge of a dry streambed. Rocks of all sizes were scattered in the shallow bed, ranging from stones no bigger than a baby's fist to huge, rough boulders the size of a Buick. There was a cluster of big ones downstream a bit, just above a fork in the bed. One of them had a flat, sloping surface perfect for sitting and Will picked his way towards it, stepping from one stone to another along the rough streambed as if water still flowed between them.

He dropped the rucksack and sat down next to it, wincing with the familiar protest in his knees and back.

Won't be able to do this for much longer, he thought, and shook his head.

He reached into the rucksack and pulled out another beer and a sandwich. He unwrapped the sandwich, carefully re-folded the wax paper into a tight, neat square, and returned it to the pack. He took a big bite and followed it with a long pull of beer. It was so good—the sharp, salty taste of the ham, the cool bitterness of the brew—it almost brought tears to his eyes.

He sat there, drinking and eating, not really thinking about anything. Will liked the way the forks of the streambed ran off in front of him, gradually diverging, separated by a widening "V" of tall, waving grass. It was getting on to his favorite time of day—late afternoon, the heat coming up out of the ground in waves and the slanted, golden light of the sun just beginning to lose its harsh, midday edge. He wished there was someone around to share it with, and he felt a small surge of sadness wash through him.

Rose. They'd tried to have kids but it just didn't happen. After a few years of disappointment and a cold, growing fear, they took her in for some tests.

"Her equipment's in tip-top condition," the doctor said. Rose was still in the examination room, getting dressed. Will didn't like his false heartiness or the cold, limp handshake he'd proffered. "If I were you," he continued, "I'd see about getting a sperm count for yourself."

Will was quick to anger in those days, and he almost took a poke at the clean, smug face hovering above the stethoscope-collared jacket like a pale balloon. Instead, he nodded sharply and muttered something, and when his wife emerged from the room he took her arm and hustled her out of there like they were late for something important.

They drove home in silence. About halfway there, when they were sitting at a stop light, Will turned to her.

"They don't know what's wrong," he heard himself saying. "They don't know what the problem is. We could get some more tests, but I don't know how much good it'd do."

Her eyes filled up with tears, but she took his hand.

"We'll just have to keep trying, Will. Something's gotta happen sooner or later."

He turned away and put both hands on the steering wheel, waiting for the light to change.

On his own, without telling Rose, he went to another doctor and had his own tests done. Sure enough, all those years he'd been shooting blanks. He'd worked the machine shop at Rocky Flats for a few years back in the sixties, and that must've done it. They'd handed out some safety pamphlets—comic books, really. Will remembered the stylized logo stamped across the front of the gaudy covers—the looping, crossed ellipses of the electron orbits framing a round, smiling face where the nucleus was supposed to be. Andy the Atom. The pamphlets made radiation sound safe as shuffleboard. Just take a few simple precautions and you'll be fine.

Will never told her. He waited for years for the cancer to take him like it took so many of his friends from the plant, but it got her instead. He never told her and now she was gone and it was too late to take back the lie. His stupid pride. Too late.

He upended the beer, draining out the last few drops, and put the empty in the rucksack, smiling to himself a little as he heard it rattle against the growing collection of empties.

We're gettin' there, he thought. *Feelin' no pain.*

As he was reaching around in the rucksack for another full one, he heard a low whistling sound coming from out of the western sky, getting louder. He looked up and his mouth fell open. The beer slipped out of his hands and rolled down off the rock, bursting open with an explosive hiss when it hit the streambed.

It came in low, about a hundred feet above the prairie. It was long and thin, a featureless ellipsoid about the size of a jetliner. A dull, metallic black, it seemed to suck the waning afternoon light into itself like a sponge. And it was burning.

It passed over Will's head with a roar that nearly burst his eardrums, trailing a wake of oily looking smoke, and went down somewhere beyond a low, grassy hill about a quarter-mile away.

Will tensed, waiting for an explosion, but none came.

What the hell was *that thing?* he wondered.

Maybe something new out of the SAC base up at Omaha. He'd heard plenty of stories, and the pictures he'd seen of the new B-1 bomber looked like something out of a science fiction movie. Even if the damn thing couldn't fly. A part of him knew, though, that this thing was just too strange, even for SAC. It didn't have any wings, for one thing. And the way it held the light—kind of rippling, almost disappearing, when you looked right at it …

Will laughed out loud and shook his head.

A goddamn spaceship. Little green men. Boy howdy, Will, have another beer.

Still, he couldn't tell how hard the thing went down—there might be someone hurt. He slung the rucksack over his shoulder, headed down the left fork of the streambed. A wisp of smoke curled up beyond the hill, marking the spot.

He was a little drunk, and he stumbled a couple of times on the uneven ground. He wasn't scared, not exactly, but he felt mixed up. A part of him was putting one foot in front of the other, pushing him forward, wanting nothing but to be there to help if someone was in need. Another part of him though, way down deep, wanted to turn tail and run like hell.

As he neared the spot, the breeze brought him a sharp, metallic, burnt wiring sort of smell, and underneath it, the familiar odor of burning grass. They'd had some rain recently, so hopefully it wouldn't catch. Will had seen a prairie fire once, and that was enough.

As he got closer, the feeling of unease intensified. Still, he kept walking, one step at a time, one foot in front of the other. *Like Hue,* Will thought. *Scared shitless but showin' up.*

He climbed up out of the streambed and started pushing through the waist-high grass. A smoky haze hung in the air. Suddenly, he came to a wide swath of flattened grass and torn earth. Patches of fire licked feebly here and there, but they were well separated and looked like they wouldn't last long.

He looked down the length of the swath and could make out a shape a couple hundred yards away, partially hidden by the hazy smoke.

This isn't no Air Force stealth gizmo on a training run, he thought.

He wished suddenly for the Remington sitting in his gun rack back in the pickup. The smoke was starting to get to him—his eyes stung and there was a raw, rasping pain in his throat. Still, he had to keep going. Ignoring the clenching fear in his stomach and the protesting ache in his bones, he began to run down the corridor of ruined earth toward the thing, picking his way between the fires.

It materialized out of the haze, almost as if drawing substance from the smoke itself, a huge, black shape. It lay in a patch of scorched earth, crumpled and broken. A wide scar ran down one side, splitting it open, and Will caught glimpses of flickering lights through the smoke.

He stopped, trying to catch his breath. He drew in a great lungful of air and smoke, and he doubled over in a spasm of coughing.

He felt something then, a kind of tugging at the edge of his mind.

Here, it seemed to say. *I am here.* But it wasn't really words—that was just the best way Will's mind could get hold of it. It was more like a kind of knowing. And it was also in that knowing that Will realized suddenly he had nothing to fear.

He approached the crippled ship. Near the tear in its side, half-hidden by the curved, crumpled fuselage, lay a human form. Will ran closer and saw with a shock that he was almost right. It had a rounded body covered in folds of metallic-looking cloth, and the right number of arms and legs, but the face was like nothing Will had ever seen before.

Green, scaly skin stretched tight across a triangular jaw. A lipless mouth revealed thin, needle-like teeth and there was a single vertical slit where the nose was supposed to be. Narrow, bony ridges protruded above wide, golden eyes that held Will's own in an intense stare. A thin line of dark blood ran out of the corner of its mouth.

Red, Will thought. *Red blood.*

He felt strangely calm. He knelt down next to the creature, reached out a hand, then pulled it back. He didn't know what to do.

The creature opened its mouth and made a sound from deep in its throat, like the last gulp of water emptying from a jug. It sounded like "gog."

Will spread his hands. "I don't—"

"Gog," it said again, more forcefully this time. It pulled aside a fold of its silvery garment to reveal a scaly pocket of skin along its midriff, rippling and bunching like there was something moving around down there.

Suddenly, a head popped up through the leathery flap. The same triangular face, the same big, golden eyes.

"Goddamn," Will said.

He felt it again, that *contact*, a feather touch on the surface of his mind. Will didn't hear it in words, but he knew that this creature was dying, that it wanted him to save its child. He also knew somehow that they could live here, that their bodies weren't really all that different. And he knew, without that voice telling him so, that they weren't all that different as souls either, that they moved to the dictates of something that was larger than themselves, something like love. It was enough for Will.

"Come on, little feller." Will reached down and the thing crawled out of its pocket and swarmed up his arms.

Go.

He felt that touch in his mind again, but it was *pushing* this time. *Go. Leave. Go.* The voice was still powerful, even though Will could see the life beginning to flicker and fade in the thing's eyes. He took a last look, nodded sharply, and began to run back along the corridor of burned, flattened grass, the child-thing clinging tightly to his arms.

When they were back at the streambed, about a half-mile away, the ground lit up like a flashbulb had gone off and Will felt a wash of radiant heat on the back of his neck. He could feel the presence of that voice in his mind wink out like a light being turned off. The creature in his arms made a whimpering sound and burrowed more tightly into his chest.

He turned around. A small mushroom cloud rose up into the darkening sky.

Destroying the evidence, Will thought. *Smart goddamn lizard.*

He looked down. The thing was curled up against his chest and all he could see was the top of its head. A pattern of fine scales caught highlights in the waning light.

"So what the hell am I gonna do with you?" he asked. "And what am I supposed to call you?"

He shook his head, then laughed out loud.

Sure. Yeah, why not?

He thought maybe he'd name it Hank.

JESUS CHRIST SUPERSTORE

"IT'LL BE the biggest goddamn Christian-themed super mall in the world," J.T. Stubbs said, balancing his formidable girth on the barstool. His solid gold bolo tie clasp glittered in the dim light of the Plano Comfort Inn lounge. Smoke drifted in lazy eddies above the bar. Bursts of lubricious pedal steel and staccato drum fills issued from the front of the room as Bobby Ace and the Poker Chips set up for their sound check.

Samudragupta "Sammy" Sharma, looking out of place in his silk suit, the distinctive odor of deep money surrounding him like a pheromone mist, frowned slightly. He didn't much like this Stubbs fellow ("Call me J.T.—everybody does") but Stubbs had a reputation for turning straw into gold on the flimsiest of conceits and Sharma, having just sold Superior Fundamentals, Inc., a Duluth-based truck body manufacturing company, to a consortium of Pakistani investors, was looking for a new tax dodge.

"Can Collin County really support a new Christian-themed super mall? You've got plenty of local retail."

That was an understatement. Since a Plano housewife had claimed to see the face of Jesus in a tuna casserole and posted the picture to Facebook, Bible stores, gun shops, and Left-Behind survivalist gear merchants had sprung up in and around Plano like mushrooms after a spring rain. Sharma thought the Tuna Jesus looked more like Jackson Browne, but the area's propensity for religious nuttery was undeniable.

"Exactly," said Stubbs. "My point exactly. It's all about consolidation. One stop salvation with convenient parking. We'll make it free for the first six months then start charging two bucks an hour."

His eyes glazed as he focused on a distant point beyond the bar mirror. He sighed and shook his head.

"We'll crush those indie sons of bitches like cockroaches. I talked the First Fundamentalist into using the Cineplex for Sunday services. Boy howdy, when we start charging for parking ..."

He began ticking off his stubby fingers.

"We got a REI for the survivalists. TGI Fridays'll have a Christian-only rock lineup. My brother-in-law Billy Bob owns the Bed, Bath & Beyond franchise down in Killeen and he's gonna pop out a new one as soon as we get ink on the deal."

Stubbs lowered his voice. "I asked him to go a little easy on the Bath and Beyond and pump up the Bed, if you know what I mean and I think you do."

He looked down at his fingers, splayed out like the blunt tines of a fork. A gold ring with a ruby setting encircled his middle finger. It looked like a link of chorizo, red and ready to burst.

He raised the index finger of his other hand. "And oh yeah, we're gonna run joint promos with the Six Flags Over Jesus theme park down in Red Bluff. Half off admission if you bring a Bible and a receipt from the Barnes and Noble."

"Sounds like you've thought of everything," Sharma said. "At least until you run out of fingers."

The Poker Chips launched into a lurching, polkacide rendition of "I Walk The Line," effectively drowning out whatever reply Stubbs might have made. The pounding bass induced sympathetic circular waves in Sharma's cranberry juice. Stubbs's glass was empty, which he sought to remedy immediately.

"Bartender!" shouted Stubbs above the melodious din, waving a meaty hand in the air.

The bartender, a lanky young man wearing a Western shirt, cowboy hat, and handlebar mustache, was deep in conversation with a hooker at the other end of the bar.

"Barkeep!" Stubbs shouted again.

The bartender looked up, frowned, patted his friend on the hand, and ambled over to them.

"Kin I git you."

"Two more of the same," Stubbs said.

Sharma put his hand over his juice glass.

"I'm good," he said.

The bartender poured Stubbs a generous shot of Old Crow and retreated as the song ground to a stuttering halt.

Stubbs turned to Sharma.

"What do you think?"

Sharma was silent. This was his favorite part of a deal, the pregnant pause, and he milked it without mercy. Stubbs downed his shot of bourbon and wiped a film of sweat from his forehead.

"I'm in," Sharma said finally. He was excited in spite of the small surge of depression he felt at giving this nimrod what he wanted. "Tentatively. I'm going to want names and vitae of the other investors, and I'll have my due diligence team look over the business plan and whatever architecture drawings you have at this time. If all goes well, you'll have a term sheet in two weeks."

Stubbs was prone on a massage table in the back room of Daisy's Beauty and Nails on Division Street in Plano when his cell phone emitted the sound of a tinny, synthesized calliope playing "All My Exes Live in Texas." His pale body glistened with coconut oil as Mei Ling's tiny hands dug deep into his tender spots. She had just slid aside the towel draped over his gelatinous butt and the good stuff wasn't far off.

"God damn it, this better be good." He lifted his head. "Honey, I gotta take this. Grab my phone and hold it up to my ear, that's a good girl."

"This better be good," he said again, without looking at the caller ID.

"Stubbs, this is Sharma."

The temperature in the room seemed to drop ten degrees.

Stubbs's enthusiasm for the massage dwindled precipitously. "Hey there. I know why you're calling but it's all good. Construction's going gangbusters again. We had that little problem with the rebar quality but I greased some palms at County and—"

"That's fine, Stubbs. I'm sure you've got the graft and corruption end of things well in hand. What I'm concerned about is marketing and strategic planning. You know there's a competing effort that just broke ground outside of Houston."

"What, those guys? They don't even have a Tuna Jesus! They—"

"This is not the first rodeo I've attended, Stubbs. We have a head start, but we need a decisive opening, something really big. I want their investors skittish and desperate. If I can buy them out at a lowball valuation early in the game, we'll have a lock on the religious-themed megamall market for the entire Southwest. This is the big leagues, Stubbs. Time to swing for the fences."

"Well, sure, but—"

"I want you to meet me at U.T. Austin this afternoon. There's a Cessna waiting for you at the Plano airport."

"Austin?" Stubbs avoided Austin like vegetarian lasagna. He regarded the place as a fetid swamp, infested with intellectuals and queers.

"I'm sponsoring a project out of the Physics Department," Sharma said. "I think it might be of interest to us."

As Stubbs walked across campus to his meeting with Sharma, he wondered if he'd made a mistake eschewing the benefits of higher education in favor of alcohol, cocaine, No Limit Texas Hold-Em, and Catholic girls. It was late spring, muggy as a bog, and the campus was crawling with young, nubile women sporting plenty of skin. As a middle-aged, corpulent redneck, he was effectively invisible to anyone under twenty-five and he could ogle with impunity.

The Physics Department was located in Robert Lee Moore Hall, a minimalist 12-story phallus towering over the technology ghetto on the North end of campus. It looked more like a Holiday Inn than any kind of "hall." Sharma was waiting for him at the front entrance. He was wearing white, linen slacks and a navy blue polo shirt. The crushing heat seemed to bother him not at all.

"Let's go," he said. "You're late."

He led Stubbs though a warren of hallways, through a heavy, unmarked door, and down three flights of stairs. The air grew noticeably cooler as they descended.

The bottom landing was illuminated by a bare, twenty-five watt bulb. On the far wall, someone had painted a squat, hulking creature with a tentacled head and razor-sharp claws, belly pale and flaccid beneath a midriff T-shirt that read NO I WONT FIX YOUR GRAND UNIFIED FIELD THEORY.

Sharma led Stubbs though another maze of hallways. In one room he saw a student wielding a blowtorch perched atop something that looked like a diving bell. In another room, two students played speed chess surrounded by a litter of half-unpacked boxes of expensive looking electronics gear. Each shouted "Fuck you!" at the other when they slammed their side of the clock.

Finally, they arrived at a large open area in the back of the complex. An incomprehensible array of hardware occupied nearly half of the space, surrounding yet another diving bell. A scruffy, bearded student hunched near the structure applying a soldering gun to a tangle of cables and circuit boards. Several others pecked away at a bank of terminals.

Amidst the clutter stood a middle-aged man in a moth-eaten corduroy jacket. He had the worst haircut Stubbs had ever seen, his skull mottled with what looked like patches of mange, tufts of hair sticking out in all directions. Nevertheless, he had the bearing of a maestro conducting an orchestra. The air was thick with tension. Something was about to happen.

Stubbs stepped forward, ready to start glad-handing. He regarded any gathering as an opportunity to sell somebody something they didn't need. Sharma stopped him with an extended arm. He shook his head, holding an index finger to his pursed lips for emphasis.

Wait, he mouthed silently.

The professor looked at each of his students in turn, then nodded. One of the students at a terminal said, "Okay, here we go. On three. One—"

"Is that on three, or three, then go?" said an attractive young woman in a BOYS SUCK T-shirt.

"Fuck off, Darla. One, two ... *three.*"

A deep hum filled the room, almost below the threshold of hearing. The lights dimmed. Sharp pain flared in Stubbs' dental fillings.

The air filled with an ozone reek. A bundle of wires and boxes next to the diving bell sizzled and burst into flame. The bearded student unhurriedly produced a fire extinguisher from somewhere and doused it.

The professor spoke. He had a voice like a television announcer, deep and mellifluous.

"I thought you put the accumulator behind a surge protector, Barlow. We can't build a new one each time."

"Well, clearly we *can*, because we *are* ..." Darla said.

The professor glared at her. She shrugged. "I'm just saying."

"Okay," Barlow said. "Who's hungry?"

He spun a circular locking mechanism and the door swung open. Mist curled around the edges of the frame. The chamber was empty except for a large, flat, grease-stained box. The students flocked to it like roaches to a discarded donut.

The professor turned to Sharma and Stubbs.

"Sammy," he said. "Glad you could come."

He looked dubiously at Stubbs. Before Sharma could make an introduction, Stubbs stepped forward, holding his hand out.

"Stubbs," he said. "Call me J.T., everybody does."

"I'm sure they do," the professor said, taking his hand for a brief moment then dropping it like a hot biscuit.

"This is Dr. Peskin," Sharma said. "His lab, his students."

The students were clustered around the diving bell, gorging themselves on wedges of gooey, dripping pizza.

Stubbs looked at Sharma. Sharma looked back with a slight smile.

Figure it out, he seemed to be saying.

"So what's that contraption," Stubbs asked. "Some kind of fancy pizza oven?"

Peskin chuckled. "Not exactly. That isn't just any pizza. It's an extra-large jalapeño jack chorizo pizza from Ernesto's on the south side of campus. Something of a local legend, actually."

Stubbs's beady eyes widened. "You mean it's some kinda trans-porter deal, like Star Trek?"

Peskin turned to Sharma. "He's not as stupid as he looks, is he?"

"He has a certain naive cunning," Sharma said.

Peskin looked back at Stubbs. "No, not at all. The thing is, Ernesto's burned to the ground last year. Ernesto himself is currently serving four years at Huntsville for insurance fraud and arson."

Stubbs looked at Peskin, at Sharma, back at Peskin.

"Nuh-uh," he said. "No way. A time machine? Boy howdy, you got yourself a time machine?"

Peskin shook his head. "Not bad, but ... no. Time travel is impossible. Entropy, second law, and all that."

Stubbs nodded. He patted his jacket pocket. "You mind if I smoke in here?"

"I'll break your arm if you do," Peskin said mildly.

Stubbs shrugged. He was used to a constant low level of hostility from pretty much everyone he met.

"Okay, I give up. What is it then?"

Peskin pushed his hands together in a steeple. He appeared to be collecting his thoughts.

While they were talking, the students had drifted over from their feeding frenzy.

Stubbs turned to Darla. "Honey, you think you could scare me up a beer, that's a good girl."

"Bite my ass, fat boy," she said cheerfully.

The other students snickered. Sharma tried to contain a smile. Peskin ignored the exchange.

"Our universe is just one of many," he said. "If the meta-universe were an ocean, ours would be one of a googleplex of bubbles comprising the foam on its surface. You with me so far?"

"You bet," Stubbs said, thoroughly lost. He elbowed Sharma. "Googleplex," he whispered.

Peskin glared briefly, then continued. "The laws of physics are not invariant from one universe to the next. Fundamental constants have different values, elements decay at different rates, even the speed of light is not consistent."

He seemed to be warming to his subject, like a preacher to a particularly juicy manifestation of sin.

"In some of these universes, even the passage of time is different. A million years here could be the blink of an eye there. Now back to our foam, some of these bubbles are very close together, topologically speaking. That is, some of the universes are nearly identical. Minor details might differ. For example, there is a universe identical to ours in all respects except that, there, the Knicks beat the Lakers every time."

Barlow snorted. "Yeah, right. That's off the continuum, Doctor P."

Peskin shrugged. "A singularity is a mathematical abstraction, Barlow."

Barlow nodded sheepishly. "Yeah, I guess."

Some sort of Zen moment had passed between teacher and student, but as far as Stubbs was concerned, they were speaking in Mandarin.

"So what we're looking for, Stubbs, is a universe identical to ours except that time passes at a different rate. Depending on what we're looking for, we find the universe with the appropriate rate differential, open a portal, and grab what we need."

"Hunh," Stubbs said. "So the extra-large jalapeño jack chorizo pizza—"

"—is from the universe where Ernesto's is eleven months behind ours, figuring from the Big Bang onwards."

Big bang ... Stubbs thought of Mei Ling and was lost briefly in fleshy reverie. He pulled himself together.

"So what you're telling me is, basically, you got yourself a time machine."

Peskin shrugged. "Pretty much."

Stubbs nodded, starting to see the possibilities.

"So tell me, Doc, you ever brought over any people?"

"As a matter of fact we have," Peskin said.

One of the other students, a chunky fellow with a shaved head, Coke bottle glasses, and a tiny soul patch, spoke up.

"John Lennon," he said. "Art school phase."

Barlow laughed. "What a douche."

"Word," Soul Patch said. "He wouldn't shut up about himself."

"Me auntie toor up me fookin pomes," Darla said, in a passable Cockney lilt.

Soul Patch nodded. "Exactly. We gave him a hundred bucks, my kid brother's Fender Squire, and put him on a bus to Nashville. He'll be fine."

Nobody spoke for a long moment.

"We gonna tell him about Hitler?" Darla asked.

Peskin coughed. "Yes, well … most unfortunate. A favor for a friend in the Psychology Department—"

"—who you were boning at the time," Darla added.

Peskin glared at her, then shrugged. "Indeed. He shaved the mustache, stole some Dockers from the Men's Faculty Locker Room, and took off on his own. We're pretty sure he's the new Director of Consumer Experience at Apple."

Sharma winced.

"Hoo boy," Stubbs said.

He looked at Sharma.

"I'll tell you what, though. This brings up some interesting possibilities for Opening Day."

"It does indeed," Sharma said.

The only people out in the open during a typical Indian summer afternoon in East Texas are drunks, meth dealers, and outlet shoppers. It's so hot you can grill quesadillas on the sidewalk. The humidity induces lizard-brain panic that you're trying to breathe underwater.

On opening day for the Tabernacle Megamall, a heavy sun beat down on eighty acres of substandard concrete and Chinese prefab. In spite of the inhuman conditions, the marketing blitz had attracted a respectable flock of rubes, willing to scuttle from their air-conditioned muscle cars and pickups to the climate controlled mall interior while newly-poured parking lot asphalt threatened to suck the shoes off their feet.

The tantalizing hints about a special guest had been especially effective. Who would it be? Devin Nunes? Ted Nugent? Britney? Speculation was rampant.

Stubbs was waiting for Sharma in the Tabernacle Megamall Security Operations Center. It looked like NASA Ground Control. Banks of monitors covered two walls; the others were floor-to-ceiling two-way mirrors that looked out over the mall's central commons. Half a dozen middle-aged men in Mall Security uniforms muttered into spidery headsets and hunched over keyboards.

Many of the stores had set out booths and displays in the commons. The Gun 'n' Grog had tapped a keg of Lone Star and a gaggle of patrons clustered unsteadily around the Glock table.

Sharma entered the room and walked up to Stubbs. "Nice crowd."

Stubbs nodded distractedly. "Ayup."

"How's it going with our visitor?" Sharma asked. "I heard he came through kind of late but that's all I know."

"Yeah, the eggheads had some trouble with the gizmo. First try brought back a ton of sand and half a camel. Messy as all get out."

Sharma winced.

"Yeah, you got it. They cleaned everything up and tried again and this time he came through all right. Guy was wearing a filthy burlap toga and smelled like ass. He took one look around and started screaming like a little girl. We tried to get him into a shower and that wigged him out even worse until he got used to it, then we couldn't get him out. We shot him up full of Valium and he's pretty quiet now. Got him into an all-white tracksuit from the Sport Authority and he's looking pretty sharp. I gotta tell you, in spite of him being a bit skittish and all, there's something about the guy. He's the genuine article all right."

"Glad to hear it, Stubbs. What are we going to do with him in the program?"

"We're gonna keep him pumped full of Valium, welcome him to Texas, do a little meet and greet with the crowd, laying on of hands, that sort of thing, then get him out of there before he starts screaming again."

"Works for me."

☆

They were set up in Theater 6 at the Cineplex—stadium seating, IMAX sound, and a decent backstage area. Stubbs looked out from the wings to a packed house. Baby strollers dotted the aisles. The big room was filled with the white-noise static of many conversations, like a huge swarm of sleepy bees, punctuated by the occasional Texas holler.

Behind the main curtains, a shortish, thin man with shoulder length hair and a hawk-like nose sat hunched on a wooden stool. Next to him, a small table held a glass of water. He seemed calm enough, muttering to himself and glaring at Stubbs from time to time.

Sharma appeared at Stubbs's elbow.

"We ready?"

"Yeah, pretty much." Stubbs nodded to the tech, a pimply teen with five-day head stubble and huge dangling crucifix earrings. "Kill the house lights, open the curtains, then hit the spotlight on cue, just like we practiced. Ready, steady … go."

The theater plunged into darkness. The curtain whispered open. After a chorus of gasps, the house fell silent.

There was a long, pregnant three-count, then the silky, ebullient voice of the announcer filled the room. Stubbs had hired Hurricane Bob, the weather guy from KBUG Houston, for his reassuring coverage of natural disasters.

"And now, the moment you've been waiting for. Here to bless the grand opening of Plano's Tabernacle Megamall, let's give a big Texas welcome to the man with the plan, your favorite carpenter, Jesus Christ!"

A single spotlight beamed down from the ceiling, bathing the seated Jesus in bright, white light. Stubbs had run the house fog machine for two minutes, just enough so that the spotlight beam was a solid bar of illumination, widening slightly from ceiling to floor. It looked like it was shining down directly from Heaven. The tracksuit was a glowing nimbus.

The crowd seemed stunned. A ripple of applause began, faltered, then caught hold, filling the room.

Jesus stood up and took a sip of water. The house fell silent again. He looked out into the crowd, shielding his eyes, then he began to speak.

His voice was liquid, hypnotizing. Stubbs couldn't understand a single word.

"Guy knows how to work a room, I'll give him that," Stubbs whispered to Sharma. "Sure wish I knew what he was saying."

"You're not telling me you didn't think to get a translator," Sharma said.

"How was I supposed to know? The Bible's in English, ain't it?"

Sharma fixed him with a long stare, then shook his head.

"Forget it, Stubbs." He paused, listening. "I think it's Aramaic, which was a Hebrew dialect. It might be close enough to the modern. We have to know what he's saying."

"Jesus talks Jew? Come on, Sammy, you're yankin' my crank here." He took note of Sharma's expression. "No, I guess you're not."

Jesus was becoming more animated, emphasizing his words with sharp hand gestures.

"Well, hold on now," Stubbs said. "I know a Jew, guy over in Houston. Maybe he can help."

He pulled out his cell, scrolled until he found the number, then jabbed the display and held the phone to his ear.

"Hey, Ira? This is J.T. ... Yeah, Stubbs ... No, I'm just fine, how are—Well, hey now, I told you, that's a long-term investment. We gotta line up distribution, marketing ... Yeah, like I told your lawyer boy we got at least a two year horizon ... Ayup ... ayup."

Stubbs was listening, nodding, then noticed Sharma's glare.

"So hey, Ira, the reason for my call, you talk Jew, right? ... Yeah, Hebrew, s'what I meant. I got a situation here, and I could use some translating ... Yeah, hang on, I'm gonna put you on speaker."

Stubbs held the phone out in the direction of the stage. There was a pause, then Ira's tinny voice issued from the phone.

"Wow," he said. "Wow. Where'd you get this guy? He's hopping mad."

"That don't matter," Stubbs said. "He's a standup act I'm lookin' to invest in. What's he saying?"

"The phrasing is a little weird, and there are some words I don't understand ..."

"That's okay, Ira, just give me the ball park."

"Okay ... 'You sons of bitches. You, uh ... effing ... sons of bitches. Why have you brought me here, you … defilers of camels. I will … ravish … your wives, daughters, and … camels … with my tremendous phallus of … camel. You whores, you painted whores and … malformed … sons of whores …' It just goes on like that."

"Hoo boy," Stubbs said.

"We have to get him out of here," Sharma said. "Thank Ganesh the Plano Zoo giraffe had triplets—that pretty much dominates the local media coverage. Otherwise we'd be crawling with TV crews and we'd be really sunk."

"Thanks, Ira," Stubbs said into the phone. "I'll call you in a couple days about that other thing."

He jabbed the keypad and slipped the phone into his pocket. He turned to the stage crew.

"All right, people, we got ourselves a Code Two. Kick it into gear, right now."

Five seconds later, the house lights went out and the sound cut off. A security team hustled the struggling Jesus off the pitch-dark stage. He shouted a little more, then he went limp and began to sob.

The house lights came back and Hurricane Bob's oily voice filled the room. "Ladies and gentlemen, we've had a small technical problem. We'll be back in just a moment. Thank you for your patience."

Jeers and catcalls issued from the crowd. Stubbs turned to a shadowy figure standing in the wings.

"Okay, big fella, you're on."

The man stepped into the light. Standing about six-two, pushing three hundred pounds, he would have been an imposing figure even without the sequined jacket, oversized sunglasses, and jet-black pompadour. He held a vintage Gibson J-200 by the neck. Inlaid mother-of-pearl roses covered the deck of the guitar, throwing rainbow highlights. It looked like a ukulele in his meaty hand. He staggered a bit as he walked forward.

"You okay?" Stubbs asked.

"Ayuh," the man said. "I just threw up a little for a second. I'll be fine."

"All right, then, give 'em hell."

Sharma looked at Stubbs with something resembling respect as the opening bars of "Heartbreak Hotel" reverberated in the auditorium.

"Well done," he said.

Stubbs shrugged. "My daddy was a hard man, Sammy, barely gave me the time of day, and he died drunk in an oil rig fire when I was twelve, but there's one thing he taught me."

"What's that?" Sharma asked.

"Always have a backup plan."

In the Tabernacle Megamall Security Operations Center, huddled on a mattress in the back of a detention cell, Jesus wept.

AN ORANGE FOR LUCITA

IT WAS Monday and I knew that my son, Pablo, would be out of jail by noon and breaking into my house that night, so I left the kitchen door open and two twenty dollar bills on the counter. I wanted to leave more, but I still needed to buy groceries and pay the electric bill. I wanted to see him, but I knew that if I was awake and he saw me he would not come in for shame. I thought about leaving him a note, but there was little I could say that he could hear.

You will always be my little boy. I will always love you.

No, some things cannot be said, or must be said with forty dollars and an unlocked door instead of words. I put a half loaf of good crusty bread and a chunk of hard cheese next to the bills and walked to the back door. It was open, the screen door shut. Beyond the door: my small cement patio, a cinder block fence, the moonless night.

It was late, but still I heard fireworks and an occasional gunshot, laughter and breaking glass, the distant highway hum. The town of Zapata, Texas gearing up for *Día de los Muertos.* The air was cool and smelled of mesquite, with a touch of burning plastic from the Bakelite factory on the other side of downtown.

I stood there for a few moments longer, thinking of Pablo, wondering where he was and hoping that he wouldn't get too drunk or hopped up before coming to steal from his mother.

I will always love you, Pablo. You are still my little boy.

I closed the door, leaving the deadbolt open. I got a bottle of beer from the refrigerator and put a piece of chorizo and a dollop of beans on one of my good plates, thick and heavy with a deep blue glaze. I carried the plate and the bottle into the small living room and set them on the carpet in front of Devante's altar. I let myself look at his photograph, his handsome face squinting into the sun and the ocean behind him. In front of Devante, a few smooth stones from the beach at Laguna Madre, his badge, the keys to his motorcycle that I could not bring myself to sell. It remained in the garage under a tarp, along with several boxes of his clothes and a set of good tools. I didn't go in there much anymore.

This was to be my first Day of the Dead without my Devante since before we were married. Twenty-seven years, longer than my son is old.

"Good night, Devante," I whispered.

I prepared for bed slowly. One part of me wanted to stay up long enough to hear Pablo come in. I could not go out to speak to him. He would be drunk or high, full of shame at the sight of me; the shame would turn to anger and we would fight. I didn't want that. Not ever, but especially not that night. But I wanted to hear his footsteps, his passage through the house. Several nights before, I had just put up Devante's altar. I heard Pablo padding softly through the house looking for something to steal. The footsteps stopped in the living room. I heard him sigh and then sounds that might have been weeping.

There was another part of me that simply did not want *Día de los Muertos* to come. The idea of course is that we banish our fear of *La Muerte* by welcoming her as a friend and taking to the streets with her. Devante's job put him close with death many times and because of that, I think, he loved the Day. But I did not feel that way. Death had taken everything from me. I hated her.

I slipped beneath the covers on my half of the bed. I usually do not remember my dreams but that night I dreamed vividly. I was walking down a hill studded with flowers. The air was thick with butterflies. At the bottom of the hill was a lake. A long pier stretched out into the water. As I walked toward the lake, a butterfly landed on my wrist. It was huge, its wings the size of playing cards. It flapped them once and was still.

"Hello, little one," I said.

"Lucita," it said. Its voice was deep and mellifluous, like a television announcer.

It flapped its wings again and flew away, darting left, darting right, gone.

I walked out to the end of the pier and looked down into the water. I saw reflected on the water's surface a great pair of wings folded in a V-shape, framing the bright sun. A small round head, feathery antennae delicate as milkweed.

I flapped my wings and the pier fell away beneath my feet.

When I awoke, I lay in bed for a few minutes full of this dream. The Aztecs believed that the souls of the departed reside on Earth in butterflies and birds. I am one-quarter Aztec and I know this to be true. Still, I did not understand what the dream was trying to tell me. Was I about to die? My stomach clenched in fear. Who would leave bread and cheese for my drunken son? I didn't think that was it, though. I think the dream was showing me something else, but I did not know what.

I got out of bed and performed my morning rituals. In the living room, the beer and food were gone from the altar, in their place a beautiful paper mâché butterfly, red and black wings the size of dinner plates. Pablo. I smiled and shook my head. This was a strange conversation but better than none at all. In the kitchen, of course, the money, the bread, the cheese—all gone.

Be well, Pablo, I thought. I would have liked for us to be together on this day, to remember together his father, but that would not happen. As I stood there in the kitchen, bright with morning light, I remembered a day from his childhood. I don't know why I thought of this particular day because although it was a good day it was not a *particularly* good day, just one of the thousands that we string together to make our lives. We had spent the day at the shore and returned tired, sweaty, our clothes full of beach grit. I cleaned the perch Pablo and Devante had caught, while they sat at the kitchen table: shirtless, joking back and forth, drinking glass after glass of ice water. Pablo looked like a miniature version of his father, the same smile, the same gestures.

That was it; that was what I remembered. The tight feeling on my forehead from too much sun. My hands slick with blood from the fish, the sharp smell of its organs. Pablo and Devante like echoes of one another, smiling, laughing. For a moment it was as if I was actually there, back in that day again, and they were there with me.

I shook my head again, filled with sudden anger. *La Muerte* toying with me.

Not today, I thought, *not now. I will not give you my sorrow.*

There was a knock on the front door. As I walked through the living room I saw a police car through the window, so I was somewhat prepared when I saw Fernando Garcia Luna, who worked for Devante before he died and was now Chief of Police. He had his hat in his hand and his expression was grave.

"Hello, Lucita."

"What's happened to Pablo?"

He looked away, then returned his eyes to mine. He had known Pablo all his life, had coached his Little League team, had helped him out many times when Pablo was too addled to help himself.

"Pablo was apparently sleeping in the road, up on County Six, and was struck by a newspaper truck. He was dragged several hundred feet before the driver realized."

Dark patches swam in my vision. Fernando's voice sounded far away. I leaned against the doorjamb for support. I felt his hand on my elbow.

"Lucita," he said. "He is alive."

A weight left my chest. I sobbed and he put his arms around me. It had been a long time since I had been held by a man. There was nothing of a lewd nature in our embrace, just his warmth, his breathing, the smell of his after-shave, a different brand than Devante had used, equally unpleasant but oddly comforting. I did not want to be a burden, the hysterical woman, so I made an effort to compose myself and pulled back. He kept his hands on my shoulders, as if to keep me from taking flight.

"He is alive," he repeated. "But he is very badly injured. Many broken bones, his side laid open from being dragged for so long, internal damage. He is in the intensive care ward at Saint Francis. I can take you there if you like."

I nodded quickly. "Thank you, Fernan."

I never liked the smell of the inside of a police car. Gun lubricant and Lysol. Spilled coffee. From behind the wire mesh separating front and back seats, the faint smell of unwashed bodies. I did not allow Devante to take me anywhere in the police car, even if it was convenient to do so.

None of that bothered me this time; I could think only of Pablo.

I noticed a flickering in the air all around us and it took me a moment to realize that it was butterflies, our butterflies, back from the North for the winter protection of the *oyamel* fir trees.

I remembered my dream and had I not been sick with worry I would have smiled.

"The Monarchs," I said to Fernando.

"Yes," he said, a little sadly. "Not as many as last year. And then not as many as the year before. I think the pollution is killing them. It is good to see them, though."

Revelers were already flocking the streets, even though it was still morning. Fernando drove slowly past a procession of ghouls, faces greasepaint white with black circles around the eyes, dressed in black shredded suits. At the front of this small parade, four ghouls carried an open coffin. A young man in street clothes was sitting up in the coffin, drinking from a brown paper bag and shouting directions to his pallbearers. Oranges and flowers were piled and scattered around him in the coffin.

Several children dressed as skeletons capered about the procession like dogs worrying a flock of sheep. On the sidewalk, a mummy in ragged bandages kept pace, moaning melodramatically and dragging one leg behind.

We passed two similar processions on the way to the hospital.

With Fernando leading the way, I was allowed to see Pablo immediately. He was surrounded by machines, threaded with tubes and wires. The bandages swaddling his head were mottled with irregular purple stains. There was a slit in the bandages for his eyes, but they were closed. The machines hummed and whirred.

Fernando brought me a chair and I sat next to Pablo, holding his unbandaged hand. I don't know how much time passed. I am sure Fernando said something before he left, but I don't remember what. Nurses in crisp white habits came to check the instruments from time to time. I was empty of thought and memory. There was only Pablo and me and the machines.

I must have dozed off because I realized suddenly that someone was speaking to me.

"—take him to surgery now." An elderly man with a round face leaned towards me, spectacles perched halfway down his bulbous nose. He wore a white coat and smelled of expensive cologne. A stethoscope dangled from around his neck.

"You can wait in the lounge on the first floor, or leave your phone number with the nurse and we'll call you."

"What's going on? Will he be all right?"

He pursed his lips. "I can't tell you that. We'll probably have to remove his spleen at the very least. Beyond that, we'll have to see what we find when we go in."

When we go in. I waited, hoping he had more to tell me, but he was done.

"I'll wait," I said.

They wheeled Pablo away and one of the sisters took me to the lounge. There was a television and several vending machines. A man in a skeleton costume sat on one of the couches, his face covered in greasepaint to resemble a skull. He was perched on the edge of the couch like he was about to rise. He looked at me as I entered the room, his eyes moist pools set within circles of black. I nodded, and he nodded back, but he did not smile.

"I will tell you if there's any news," the sister said.

"Thank you," I said. I took a seat near the door and stared blankly at the television. The sound was a low murmur; pale, ghostly images chased each other across the screen. I looked at the skeleton man again. He was staring off into space, still balanced on the edge of the couch.

After a while, a sister came in the room, a young girl in tow, and approached the skeleton man. He stood up, very tall, and bent down to the little girl. He said something I did not hear, nodded gravely, and offered his hand. After a moment's hesitation, she reached out and grabbed onto his index finger. Together they left the room.

A little while later, a heavy woman in jeans and a hooded sweatshirt came in with an infant bundled in a colorful blanket. She smiled at me and I nodded back. Time passed as it does in waiting rooms.

The skeleton man returned, alone, and sat across from me.

"Where is your friend?" I asked.

"Esmeralda?" His voice was low and soft. "A very sweet girl. She is with her family."

I nodded again. I wanted to say something else to him but I did not know what to say. I felt suddenly nauseated with the close hospital smell. I could feel *La Muerte* all around me—in the waiting room, her crushing weight in the hospital rising above me. I stood up.

"I need to get some air," I said.

He smiled gently.

"Don't worry," he said.

Outside, *La Día* was in full swing. Firecrackers and gunshots echoed in the small streets surrounding the hospital. Butterflies filled the air with flickering motion. A mock funeral procession made its way down the street in front of the hospital entrance. I moved closer to get a better look. As I approached the head of the procession, it stopped and the pallbearers set the coffin gently on the street. They smiled shyly at me and stepped aside.

Sitting in the coffin, propped up against a satin pillow: my Devante.

He wore his funeral suit, midnight blue with grey pinstripes. He brushed his curly black hair away from his forehead in a gesture that was uniquely his, and smiled sadly at me. On his forehead was a puckered scar the size of a nickel from the bullet that had taken his life.

I opened my mouth to speak and he raised his hand to me, palm out. Another Devante gesture. Then he reached under the satin bedding, brought out an orange, and handed it to me. It was a good one, large and round, its pebbled skin unblemished. When I looked up again, Devante's funeral procession was gone.

I felt a feather touch on my wrist. I looked down. A butterfly rested there, wings spread.

Oh, God, I thought. *Please. Who are you? Devante? My Pablo? Please, please, not Pablo.*

"Hello, little one," I croaked.

"Lucita."

I jumped and whirled around. Out of the corner of my eye I saw the butterfly darting left, darting right, gone.

Fernando put his hands on my shoulders.

"Lucita," he said again. "I have just spoken with the doctors. Pablo is going to be all right. The recovery will be long and difficult, but he will live."

I stepped back. Fernando's hands fell to his sides. I looked down at the orange again, wrapped both my hands around it and squeezed gently. It was firm and slightly yielding; warm, as if full of blood.

BINDING ENERGY

Batter my heart, three-personed God, for you
As yet but knock, breathe, shine, and seek to mend.
That I may rise and stand, o'erthrow me and bend
Your force to break, blow, burn, and make me new.

—John Donne

—THERE! Stop there!

EMIL'S BBQ. A smiling pig in a clean white apron leans against the Q, brandishing a wicked looking knife. Emil first came here amused at the confluence of names, but he returns for the dark smoky sauce laced with cayenne.

The driver looks at him in the rear-view mirror, nods, and pulls into the parking lot. Bits of silica wink like stars in the soft asphalt.

—What can I get for you, sir?

Flat military monotone. Cold eyes, brown like river silt. This driver is new and Emil doesn't like him much. The man is a herring —Emil has tried to engage him in conversation several times, but there has been no response other than the monosyllabic. The Negro makes a good soldier but this one is a lousy chauffeur.

—Stay, stay. I'll go.

He reaches for the door handle, but the driver is too quick. Heat slaps Emil in the face, rising in waves from the asphalt. It is like

peering into an oven. Almost immediately, a thin film of perspiration covers his forehead and hands. He slides the cane from his lap
and plants it on the pavement. Cut from rough oak, this cane,
knotted and polished smooth. His *staff*. His oaken staff. The ground
yields slightly under its tip as he heaves himself to his feet. Shakes
off the soldier's hand on his elbow.

—Stay, sit.

Familiar stab of pain from his right hip, not exactly an old friend
but always there to remind him that he is no longer young, nor even
middle-aged.

A handful of tables sprout like linoleum mushrooms under the
harsh fluorescents. A man in greasy coveralls and a long, thick
ponytail sits next to the window, tearing strips of flesh from the
carcass of a chicken, washing it down with deep pulls from a brown
long-necked bottle.

The jukebox is playing a plaintive country song about lost love,
redolent with pedal steel and nasal male harmonies. The vinegary
barbecue smell makes Emil's stomach rumble; beneath that, a
shadow of pain. To hell with the ulcer, he thinks.

—Can I help you, sir?

He looks at the woman behind the counter for the first time. A
sudden, hollow silence descends. The smell of burnt wiring fills his
nostrils. His mouth opens but he cannot speak.

It is *her*. The traitor. Black eyes bruised with loss, set far apart in
a moon-shaped face. Rough olive skin. Coarse, dark curls. Thick lips
perpetually poised on the brink of a sneer.

—Sir?

Emil backs up until he bumps into the door. He shoulders it
open and spills back into the heat. His limo waits, blinding white,
parked astride two spaces.

—Are you all right?

—Yes, yes. Take me to the Lab.

Ensconced in the cool dark of the limo, Emil still feels those eyes
on him. The years recede like snow under a lit match and he sees
her in the Senate chambers—1953? 1954? Six months before the
executions. She has no shame.

—No, I am not a Communist. No, of course not. Never. Besides,
what do I know of nuclear physics?

Ridiculous, Emil thinks. I am an old fool. He raps on the plexi-glass divider.

—Sergeant, back to the barbecue place.

He'll think I'm going senile. Like poor Ronny.

The driver makes a U-turn, threads back through the wide suburban streets.

The man with the ponytail stares rudely, hunched over bones and scraps. The woman behind the counter affixes a nervous smile to her face.

—Can I help you?

—I'm sorry—you look so much like—tell me, please, what is your name?

She hesitates, looks him over, seems to decide that he is odd but not dangerous.

—Jane. Jane Lucent.

—Not Rabinowicz?

That nervous smile again.

—No. Not Rabinowicz.

Emil sighs. She looks remarkably like her. But it's impossible. The traitor had one daughter who committed suicide in an insane asylum before producing any offspring of her own. That branch of the family tree is kindling.

—No, of course not.

Suddenly, his appetite returns. He looks at the menu posted behind the counter, adorned with garish color photographs, platters of food glistening with grease.

—I'll have the ribs.

Two seasons in California, green and brown. Thirty years here and Emil still longs for the red and gold death of autumn, the sharp smell of snow on the air, the distant snap of pond ice breaking under spring's first thaw.

From eight stories up the land acquires definition: tawny prairie ripples with gentle contours like muscles beneath the skin of a great cat. Hundreds of windmills break the ridgeline at the edge of the valley. Legacy of the peanut farmer's tax credit.

Who not once answered Emil's calls, even during that Syria business.

This one is better. At least he sends smiling young men in crisp suits to listen to Emil's ideas. But Emil is still the leprous magician laboring in the castle dungeon, conjuring potions and spells that harness the elemental forces, his ugly visage kept from public view. He has delivered them from a thousand Hells and they treat him like the carrier of a social disease.

Ronny was the best. Not much of a thinker, but the heart of a lion. Emil loved the visits to the White House, not skulking in through the tunnel but delivered by helicopter to the front lawn. The dreams Emil could spin to a receptive ear!

Glossy photographs of test shots adorn the oiled mahogany walls of his office. Mike, Priscilla, Romeo. Shrimp, Token, Bravo. Emil was the youngest and he knows that a father's favorite child is always his first. Mike. A 10.4 megaton Rube Goldberg nightmare of pipes and gauges, valves and switches, filling a building the size of an airplane hangar. It was a miracle it worked at all, but it vaporized the island of Elugelab and punched a hole in the ocean floor. Emil remembers the light of Creation flashing against the high Pacific clouds, minutes later the attenuated shock reaching the observation ships fifty miles out as a stiff, sudden wind. The breath of God.

It was a moment of pure, Wagnerian joy, all his own.

The phone rings, two short bursts. His secretary. He pushes the speaker button.

—Yes?

—Fifteen minutes, sir.

—Ah, yes. Thank you.

It has been a couple of years since he has addressed the Laboratory. Emil feels out of touch with the daily workings of the place. His Emeritus status gives him no official power, but he still has allies in the ranks of physicists, particularly X-Division. He can walk over to Building 88 at any time, argue theory with the young, Coke-swilling firebrands, politics with Wade, his star disciple.

But every now and then he likes to speak to the rank and file. The *illiterati*. The Laboratory's publicity machinery ensures that the main auditorium in Building 70 will be full; by electronic proxy, his image reaches all corners of the mile-square complex.

Emil could give up this indulgence. Tollbridge is doing a fine job as Director—the ritual Beltway *gavotte*, keeping the Regents happy and uninformed. His insipid Management Chat, twice a month on LabNet. But the guilty pleasure of a captive audience is a powerful drug. And besides, Emil sacrificed everything for this place. The respect of his colleagues, his standing in the scientific community. They loved Oppy so. His big sad eyes. Emil showed them the way but still they shunned him, saw only his failures. Heat rushes to Emil's cheeks as he recalls the humiliation of the first failed test, a miserable fission firecracker. The flaccid mushroom tickling the tropopause. Ten kilotons, barely a Hiroshima.

The phone rings again. Annoyed at the interruption of his reverie, Emil punches the speaker button.

—What is it?

—Dr. Wade is here, sir.

—Ah, good. Send him in.

Emil's spacious office seems smaller when Wade enters. Six-four, with the ruddy-cheeked enthusiasm of a college athlete, Wade belies the public stereotype of physicist. He is no skinny, bespectacled caricature scuttling beneath a bank of fluorescents from lab bench to computer terminal, clipboard clutched to white-coated breast. With Wade's square jaw and rough good looks, he could pose for L.L. Bean. But he was Emil's finest student. An extraordinary experimentalist and a first-rate theoretician, he wields the ideas and techniques of physics like a carpenter building a house. No, not a carpenter, a blacksmith—the forge and the anvil are metaphors more suited to the manipulation and control of the elemental forces. For the last decade, he has been, methodically, surreptitiously, stripping Emil of authority in the Lab hierarchy. Or trying to. Emil plays along. He admires Wade's feral cunning. His own position in the history books is secure. Besides, the old magician still has a few tricks up his sleeve.

—Emil. You are looking fit.

—You are a liar, John.

Wade eases his big frame into the leather chair in front of Emil's desk, set slightly lower than Emil's own. As usual, he wastes no time.

—What are you going to talk about?

Emil was expecting this. Make sure the old man isn't going to violate national security in his enthusiasm for a good yarn.

—The usual. State of the Lab. Current funding cycle. I thought I'd drop a hint or two about Diamond Prism.

Emil watches with amusement as Wade's jaw clenches.

—I, um, don't think that would be a very good idea. Weintraub from the *Herald* is going to be there—he already thinks you're the anti-Christ. Diamond Prism is entirely black budget right now ...

Emil holds his hand up, palm forward, as if directing traffic.

—Relax, John. I just wanted to see whether you actually think I'm incontinent.

A frown creases Wade's smooth forehead.

—Incompetent.

—I beg your pardon?

Wade opens his mouth, closes it.

—Never mind.

The two men are silent. The room fills with ambient sounds—a white noise air-conditioner hum, the distant ringing of a phone, the electronic squeal of a fax machine in the outer office.

—I'll be out of your hair soon enough, John. I am an old man.

He leans toward Wade, lowers his voice.

—I am sure you don't know this, but Tollbridge is being groomed for Secretary.

The gratuitous improvisation rolls off Emil's tongue like a dollop of oil. Wade's eyebrows raise.

—Ah, yes, I knew that would get your attention. I still have sources inside the Beltway. We could bring Collins up to take over X-Division and put you in as Director.

Wade rubs his chin thoughtfully.

—Collins isn't ready. The Oberon shoot had lousy energy density ...

—Engineering, John. It's just engineering. What you're really saying is you're not ready, yes? To give up your little fiefdom.

Wade laughs, a short, barking sound.

—I'm ready.

☆

The auditorium in Building 70 is full, a restless sea of silvery-haired heads. Emil scans the crowd for younger faces and sees a few, but not many. The old man is a circus act and they have no time. He limps down the center aisle—*step, thump, step, thump*—his staff making a hollow sound on the deep pile carpet. They have wheeled out an old upright piano for him and without preamble, he mounts the stairs at the side of the stage and seats himself with his back to the audience.

Where did they dig this thing up? The wood is pitted and scarred; there is a neat, black chevron of cigarette burns to the left of the music holder. Cigarette burns! He hopes the piano is tuned, at least.

Suddenly his hands feel huge and clumsy; his arthritic knuckles are golf-ball sized knots of pain. His breathing quickens and a flicker of agony lashes up from his sciatic nerve. He was going to play a little Bach, a little Mozart, but that mathematical precision seems out of reach. Stupid indulgence! It's all out of reach.

Without thinking, he launches into the Promenade from "Pictures at an Exhibition." He hates the acoustics in this room—the ceiling baffles turn all sound into a homogeneous, milky paste. The power of the stately opening is muffled and compressed. Remembering suddenly the demands of the next movement, "The Gnome," Emil feels something tighten across his forehead and a spastic tremble flows down his arms and out his fingertips. The missed note hangs in the air like a fart.

—Shit.

The word echoes in his ears and he realizes that his lapel mike is on.

Cheeks burning, he stumbles through another couple of movements. Each time he returns to the refrain it is a little more uncertain, a little more out of tempo. Finally he just stops. Breathes. His shoulders sag as if something has left his body.

A tenuous vapor of whispers rises from the crowd. Somebody applauds. Someone else. A weak, uncertain ripple surges and dies.

Emil takes a deep breath, leans on his staff. Stands and turns around.

—Poor Mussourgsky.

A few nervous laughs.

—A simple demonstration of *quid pro quo*. I just did to Russia what they did to us for forty-five years.

More laughter. Another scattering of applause and it catches this time, fills the hall, fills Emil.

He's got them.

—Imagine, if you will, the following scenario. Yeltsin has a fatal heart attack. In the ensuing chaos, the hard-liners prevail. There is a coup, perhaps bloodless, perhaps not, and the Russian government is in their hands. Our intelligence tells us that Lebed—or somebody —will be addressing a huge crowd in Red Square. With only few minutes notice, one of our deep patrol submarines in the Pacific launches a missile. It pops up into a low ballistic trajectory and, at the peak of the parabola, a low-yield thermonuclear device is detonated in close proximity to a long, thin rod of metallic foam. Computers have aligned the rod to within a micron's tolerance so that its aim is as true as the resolve in our own hearts. Microseconds before the rod is vaporized, a highly energized beam lances out of the blue, Russian sky. Lebed, and the hopes of the hard-liners, are now a rapidly expanding plasma.

Emil scans the crowd. He recognizes Weintraub, scribbling furiously on a small notepad. And there, Habermas, a protégé of Wade's, with a pained look on his young face.

—Terrorism, insurgency, and financial instability are the threats that will shadow us as we move into the twenty-first century. In order to maintain our position as leaders of the Free World, we must pursue an aggressive policy of surgical countermeasures. *Surgical countermeasures.*

The repeated phrase fills the hall, pregnant with possibility. He relishes for a moment that unfolding, then continues. He does not mention Diamond Prism directly, but he lays it out, all of it. Wade will be furious, probably try to pull Emil's clearance. But it's the right thing to do. The right time. Back in Ronny's administration they used to come from Washington like dogs to a bitch in heat. The Congressmen and their dull, eager staffers. The spooks. The generals. Everybody but the scientists. From a distant nexus within, he sees himself, a gnarled, stooped gnome standing before a lectern, spinning candied lies to an audience of idiot children. And looking out in to the crowd, he sees her.

Dark hair falling like wings across her face, not quite hiding her bruised eyes. It *is* her. The close air in the auditorium is suddenly charged with an ozone stink. The hot smell of metal on metal. Solder and sulfur. Burning rubber.

He reaches out a hand. His staff clatters to the floor of the stage.

—*You.*

A susurrus rises from the crowd, like the cicada-hiss of summer. Emil staggers back, grabs the lectern for support, lurches into the wings. Sees the red EXIT sign. Pushes into the dry, sweltering heat.

—Take me home.

Curt military nod in the rear-view mirror. Emil sits back in the soft leather, breathes, watches the temporary buildings at the outskirts of the Lab segue to grape fields and tract housing locked in a Darwinian tangle for dominance of the sunbaked prairie.

The air conditioning is on high but he can't stop sweating. His shirt is drenched, plastered to his skin. Sharp, transient pains from his chest call to him like voices from the bottom of a deep well. He wonders if he is going to have a heart attack, a stroke, a breakdown.

He opens the small refrigerator in front of him and pulls out a bottle of spring water, changes his mind and from the freezer withdraws a slim flask of vodka. It goes down like liquid metal. Emil sees the driver looking at him in the rear-view as he tilts the flask back with shaking hands. The military lack of affect is a perfect vehicle for the contempt Emil knows is there. Emil presses a button in the armrest and an upholstered panel rises from the seat back, separating him from the driver's compartment.

The phone trills at him from the armrest. Wade, no doubt, or Tollbridge. Let it ring. Emil leans back and closes his eyes.

Immediately her face begins to coalesce on the dark screen of his closed eyelids, taking shape from nothing until she is hovering before him, clear as a photograph. Her head is shaved and she is wearing a starchy, green prison shift. The cell behind her is a Caligari nightmare of distorted angles and false perspective.

—Why are you here? What do you want?

She does not respond.

Two guards appear, dressed in head to foot black with loose black hoods. They escort her through twisting stone tunnels lit by naked bulbs. Disembodied, powerless, Emil follows, like a balloon bobbing on the end of a string.

They come to a high-ceilinged room dominated by a large wooden chair. Metal cuffs decorate the arms and legs. Black-sheathed cables sprout from the chair and converge to a thick bundle that leads to a panel in the far wall. At one end, onlookers fill a row of bleacher-like seats. Emil recognizes J. Edgar and Roy, Ike and Nixon, Joe McCarthy.

One of the guards straps her to the chair; the other walks to the panel and places his hand on a large switch. When he sees his partner step away from the chair, without preamble he yanks downward. Her body stiffens, convulses, dances in the restraints.

Emil jerks awake with a start. The phone is ringing again. Laced with the chemical smell of the air conditioning is the stink of ozone and burnt wiring.

She is next to him in the cool dark of the limo, regarding him with wide, bruised eyes.

He slides away from her, pressing himself against the door.

—What do you want from me?

She puts her hand on his. Her touch is dry ice, burning cold.

—We were all so frightened, Emil.

—You betrayed your country. You deserved what you got.

She closes her eyes, breathes, opens them, says nothing.

—What do you want? Why *now*?

—You are dying, Emil. Your medical appointment next week will reveal a shadow on your left lung. Further tests will reveal that it has already metastasized. A chain reaction, eh? Filling your body with the light of Creation.

It is true. He can feel it. Something cold takes hold of his stomach and squeezes, hard.

—You come to gloat, then, to see me fall apart. I won't give you the satisfaction. I am not afraid of God. I have met Him on His own terms.

She shakes her head sadly.

—No, Emil, not to gloat.

—What then?

She says nothing. Just looks at him with those eyes. Like Oppy at Princeton, days before he died. His body, rail-thin in health, wasted away to nothing. The cancer had eaten away his larynx so he could not speak, but he was fully alert. He took Emil's hand in his and his hands were warm and strong.

Emil fumbled for words.

—Perhaps I should not have come.

Oppy shook his head, squeezed Emil's hand. Emil met his eyes for the first time and recoiled at the expression. Not the loathing he expected that would allow him to gloat privately at his adversary's demise, but a preternatural serenity. Compassion. Forgiveness. Emil pulled his hand away and fled into the hollow winter morning.

He feels himself being drawn into her eyes, wide like Oppy's, all-encompassing. Feels unseen tidal forces pulling, as if he is nearing the event horizon of a black hole.

He looks away, slaps the intercom button.

—Driver. Pull over.

Rattle of pebbles against the undercarriage as the limo comes to a halt on the shoulder of the highway. The limo shudders as a large truck passes.

Emil looks to his side again and she is gone; the burnt electrical smell hangs in the air like a Cheshire grin.

He opens the door and steps out into the heat.

—Sir?

Emil gestures the driver back inside. The wake from another passing truck tugs at his suit. The shoulder of the highway is scattered with debris—a hubcap, glittering shards of amber glass, the decomposing corpse of a dog. Emil staggers down the embankment into the prairie scrub. The burning sun is pinned to the sky's blue arch, a white, curdled eye. Behind him in the limo, the phone begins to ring.

—for Carter Scholz

CLIK2CHAT

THE HOUSE WAS full of people and the insect hum of their voices. Their presence made his living room look oddly foreign and it was easy for Bob to imagine for a moment that he, too, was a guest. He stood awkwardly next to the fireplace, drink in hand. People approached, inquired, veered off. Nearly everyone had brought something to eat or drink and every available surface in the kitchen was loaded with casseroles, salads, plates of cookies, sushi mandalas, paella pans. There was something about bereavement and food. It wasn't comfort—there could be no comfort—but it was deeply tribal nonetheless. What Bob really wanted was a good, stiff drink, but he was afraid of where that would lead, so he sipped his glass of Pinot and tried to not look like he wished they would all just fucking leave.

A cluster of Jenna's friends, bristling with piercings and spiky hair, huddled near the door. Bob had known most of them since pre-school. A willowy girl in sleeveless denim, Lu, caught his eye. She walked up to him and gave him a loose-limbed hug.

"You guys okay?" she asked.

Bob had a sudden, vivid memory of a trip to Marine World, maybe six years back, an impossibly distant other life. It was just Jenna, Lu, and him. The girls orbited about him like wild, giggling moons as they explored the park. They slept, curled up in the back seat together, the entire drive home. It was a good day.

Bob shrugged, smiled sadly. *How could we be okay?*

"Sorry—stupid question." She looked away, biting her lip. A single tear tracked down her cheek. She took a breath, looked up at him again. "How's Mrs. P. holding up?"

"She's hanging in there. I'm really glad you came, Lu."

In fact, Mrs. P. hadn't stopped crying for three days and was upstairs now in a shade-darkened room, tossing in a sweat-drenched Ambien doze. Bob was almost glad of his hostly duties because they took him off the front lines with her. He felt a stab of guilt at the thought.

Jenna's friends were the first to leave. Lu turned on her way out and gave him a sad, little wave. Bob's colleagues from the office were next—a handshake conga line and a pat on the shoulder from the head of the firm. His secretary hugged him and cried a little.

"Give my best to Allie," she said.

"I will," Bob promised.

After the neighbors left, and a few other parents from the school community paid their respects and backed out the door looking guiltily relieved (fellow travelers for many years, their connection now abruptly severed), there was just Allie's sister, Darcy, and her deadwood husband, Frank.

Darcy flitted about cleaning while Frank helped himself to a healthy dose of Glenlivet from Bob's liquor cabinet.

"Hell of a thing," Frank said. "So young."

Bob remembered Jenna's description of him as "that fucking retard Aunt Darcy married" and nearly smiled, then caught himself, and a wave of grief rushed through him like the ocean through a rocky channel, leaving him breathless for a moment.

"You okay, Bob?" Frank asked, a hint of slur in his voice.

"Yeah, I'm fine, Frank. I just need to sit down."

Bob sat in one of the two floral patterned wing chairs book-ending the fireplace. Frank stood watching him for a moment, then sat in the matching chair, resting his drink on his thigh.

They spoke no further and Bob tried to will his mind empty of thought.

After a few moments, Darcy appeared, pushing back an errant blonde lock from her forehead.

"All clean," she said. She was a ditz, but Bob had come to like her, even love her, over the years. Her luck with men was almost comically abysmal.

"Thanks, Darce," Bob said. "You didn't have to do all that."

She leaned over and pecked him on the cheek. "Don't worry about it. You just take care of Allie and yourself."

When they left, silence descended on the house with the finality of a closing curtain. Bob returned to the chair next to the fireplace and sipped his drink.

Upstairs, Allie awakened and began to weep, a soft, desperate keening that seemed to come from everywhere in the house at once.

Bob sighed. He didn't want to face her and felt it again, that pinprick of guilt. Her grief was no more acute than his, he felt, but it demanded more attention. Infinite attention, really—a black hole that swallowed all solace. He didn't blame her at all. He just didn't know how to help her. He couldn't even help himself.

He set his glass on the coffee table and went upstairs. The hallway was dark. The door to Jenna's room was open a crack. He walked past without looking in. His bedroom door was shut and he placed his palm flat against it. From within, the sound of weeping continued.

"Allie?"

There was no answer.

He gently pushed the door open. The air in the room was humid and had a strange, oceanic smell. Allie sat on the edge of the bed. Her grief had an animal quality: primal, pre-verbal. He sat next to her, put his hand on her shoulder. She vibrated with a fine tremor, like a bird. Every now and then she would gasp, a breathing reflex. The keening would catch, then continue.

Bob pulled back the collar of her nightgown just a bit, kissed her bare shoulder, and left her there.

Bob's home office was a long card table in a corner of the garage. There was a multipurpose printer, a big monitor, a keyboard. Several rows of shelves sagged under a haphazard collection of tools, books, and boxes with faded, peeling labels. In the opposite corner, amidst a litter of discarded plastic lawn toys, sat a red bicycle with flat tires and training wheels. Faded blue ribbons dangled limply from the handlebars.

He sat down and stared at the flat, grey screen until he imagined motion within its depths. He pushed back his chair and went back in the house. He cocked his head to listen. Allie had stopped crying. He imagined her sitting on the edge of the bed staring off into nothing. The furnace sighed on. A car whispered past on the street outside.

Bob poured himself two fingers of Glenlivet and returned to the garage. He sat at his desk and took a sip of whiskey. His eyes watered and his chest filled with heat.

He missed her so badly. It was like a physical hypersensitivity, a migraine, or an opiate withdrawal, a painfully acute awareness of smells and changes in light.

He double-clicked a shortcut on his desktop and her homepage appeared. There were dozens of pictures, mostly of Jenna smiling, occupying a center of gravity among several friends, a couple of somber art-school poses and several with Allie and Bob. He was glad that she wasn't embarrassed to post them.

In her most recent photograph, just a few days before she died, she had shaved her head and carved, in the emerging stubble, swirling Maori-like designs. She had a pierced eyebrow and upper lip. This too was something of an art-school pic, but in spite of its edginess, it seemed to capture better than the others the essence of Jenna as a much younger girl. He could see her peering out, smiling, just behind the hardware and the adolescent piss-off frown.

Her profile said she liked basketball (he knew that), Rimbaud (he had no idea), and motorcycles (he'd have to have a talk with her)—and it hit him again, that surge of grief (*have a talk with her*) so acute he lost track of himself for a moment.

Her status read:

Smith is nice. Mt Holyoke is a gothic prison. Amherst is Amherst. In Logan now, waiting for the plane home. I love airports, monuments to transience. The static hiss between stations!

She must have posted from her cell phone, minutes before the explosion. Bob tried to imagine it—an instant of heat and light, intense pressure, a sound like the sky ripping open. He hoped it was fast, that she didn't have time to register what was happening. He wondered if she thought of them in those last milliseconds, then cursed his narcissism.

It seemed he was living half the time in fugue—replaying snippets of time with her, random moments, conversations real and imagined. They surfaced haphazardly, pulled him in, played themselves out, and left him stunned and empty.

His eyes kept returning to the icon in the upper right corner of the screen, a yellow smiley-face in side profile beneath a word bubble. Inside the bubble: *Clik2Chat*.

He slid the cursor over the icon, hovered for a moment, then willed his finger down on the mouse button.

Jenna's avatar appeared next to his keyboard: a smiling, translucent, foot-tall pixie. Tiny diamonds of dust swam in the light beams emanating from small, twin sources beneath the screen. The scan had been taken about a year before, so it captured Jenna before her severe phase. Her hair was shoulder length and she wore jeans and a plain, green T-shirt. She tilted her head, a coltish gesture he knew well.

"Hey, Dad. What's up?"

Bob's breath caught in his throat. The voice was almost right—Jenna, with syllables oddly clipped. He knew it was nothing more than a bit of digital magic cranked out by a kid hunkered down in a cubicle amidst a litter of Nerf toys and empty soda cans, but it was still a shock.

Jenna tilted her head the other way.

"Hey, Dad. What's up?"

This is stupid, he thought.

"Hi, Jen." His voice cracked.

"Hey! How are you?"

Bob didn't say anything. The avatar shifted her weight, brushed back her hair.

"You've probably figured out that I'm somewhere else right now. My little Doppel-G here will record whatever you want to tell me and I'll have a look at it later."

"We miss you terribly."

Jemma frowned disarmingly.

"Sorry, didn't get that."

"We love you."

Jenna smiled. "I love you, too, Dad."

"We'll always love you."

"I love you, too, Dad."

From far away he heard the high whine of engines, a plane settling in to SFO final approach. He cocked his head, listening, until he couldn't hear it any more.

"You haven't said anything for a while, so I'm gonna go. Bye!"

"No!" Bob shouted, startling himself. "Wait!"

Jenna tilted her head again, looking, he imagined, just a trifle impatient.

The static hiss between stations, he thought.

Something rustled outside, probably a raccoon. He closed his eyes and saw clever, busy hands.

"You haven't said anything for a while, so I'm gonna go. Bye!"

He did nothing this time. After a few seconds, the image winked out.

He sat there for a long time. When he was ready, he pushed his chair back, stood up, and stretched. He let himself back into the house and went upstairs. Allie was sleeping again, her breathing deep and regular.

He slipped his clothes off and slid under the sheets, careful not to wake her. She whimpered softly, turned on her side facing away from him, and backed closer. He curled to fit her, feeling her warmth, draping his arm across her hip. He shifted restlessly as he drifted off to sleep and she moved in response, their somnambular dance as familiar as walking.

CHIMERA OBSCURA

SPIKE HATED INTERVIEWING FOR HOUSEMATES. It was a total crapshoot. You could score with somebody like Echo, who worked in the Gulch popping out interactive soaps for RealTime. He knew a lot of artists and coders, made a great paella, and was hardly ever home. The perfect roomie.

Or you could get somebody like that freak Griffin who'd just moved back to Boston, leaving a vacant room. Griffin was always home. He used to lock himself in his room and crank up a loop of the old Velvet Underground track "Venus in Furs." It was shiny boots of leather all day long, over and over again, Reed's sepulchral voice rattling the dishes on the shelves and scaring the shit out of Seafood, their cat. Nobody shed a tear when Griffin left.

But the rent was due in three days.

The ad had roped in an astonishing collection of human flotsam. After the last one left—a bug-eyed, sweaty thirty-something in jungle cammies and a spooky grin, Spike looked across the living room at Echo and Shin-yi.

"Man, I need a cup of coffee," he said.

"Sounds good," Shin-yi said.

Echo looked thoughtfully across the redwood deck at the broken curve of the Bay Bridge, gold and shadow in the late afternoon sun.

"That last guy wouldn't be too bad," he said. "He probably owns a fucking arsenal. We could use some firepower." As if in affirmation, a distant fusillade of automatic weapons fire cut through the air.

Spike tilted his head to one side. "Mac-10," he said.

"No way," Echo said. "That's an AR-20." He turned to Shin-yi. "And you could use a demolitions expert."

Shin-yi designed kinetic installations for corporate entertainment functions: exploding appliances, quarter-scale monster truck battles, robotic orgies of self-immolation.

She shook her head. "Never mix heavy explosives and cooperative housing."

Spike went into the kitchen, put some water in the wave, and filled the grinder. He liked to pulverize the beans into a state resembling fine, black moondust. He leaned on the switch for 30 seconds, set the grinder off to one side, and assembled his coffee maker, a Byzantine arrangement of Pyrex and stainless steel. When matters were in hand, he returned to the living room.

"One more today, right?" he asked.

"Yeah, one more," Shin-yi said. "A woman named Sarah."

"She sounded really normal over the phone," Echo said.

Seafood ambled into the living room from the back of the house and butted up against Spike's leg.

"Fuck off, cat," Spike said mildly. Seafood mewed and butted against him again. Spike reached down and scratched him behind the ears.

"You know anything else about her?" he asked.

"Part-time student at State," Echo said. "Works as a librarian."

Shin-yi's eyebrows shot up. Infotech of any kind carried an automatic coolness.

"A librarian? You know what site?"

Echo shook back his dreads.

"No, I mean a library librarian with, like, books and shit."

"Wow, books," Shin-yi said.

Unconsciously, Spike brushed his hand against his sheeky, a gossamer cloth of fiberoptics and microelectronics emblazoned with a tie-dye pattern and stuffed into his back pocket like a handkerchief. He hadn't held a print book in his hands in years.

The smell of strong coffee drifted into the living room. Spike went into the kitchen and brought back two steaming mugs.

The outside buzzer rang. Echo went to the wall console near the front door and activated the video. Spike couldn't see the screen, but a tinny voice over the speaker said: "This is Sarah."

"Come on up."

Echo deactivated the security and buzzed her through.

Sarah was older than Spike expected. She carried herself with a reserve that suggested she was always processing her surroundings at a conscious level, scoping out connections between people, deciding how much of herself to reveal. Hypervigilant. Still, she had a confident smile and made direct eye contact. It was a weird mix. Spike liked her right away.

They sat in the living room, the three housemates scattered about the room and Sarah sitting by herself on the big couch, sunk deep into the overstuffed cushions.

"So, it's just the three of you here?" she asked.

Spike and Echo exchanged glances. Spike looked across the room at Shin-yi. She shrugged. It wasn't a very good place to start, but they had to get it out of the way.

"For all intents and purposes," Spike said. "Bardo doesn't partic-ipate much in the house, uh, culture. He's—"

"He's got a TPN tap in his neck, a catheter stuck into his dick, a massage chair so his blood doesn't pool, and a dedicated link to Hell-Five," Shin-yi said.

"And a trust fund," Echo added.

"Hell-Five?" Sarah asked.

"Avatar combat simulation," Echo said. "Aliens invade a space colony and you have to fight them off. There's a minimal plot, but it's mostly a shooter. Totally mindless."

"Yeah. Not like the stuff you code," Shin-yi said.

Echo shrugged.

"So he just plays all the time?" Sarah asked.

Spike nodded. "I check his stats on GameNet every now and then. After a while, you'll just forget he's around."

Sarah nodded, but she looked troubled.

"You want to see the room?" he asked.

"Sure."

Spike led her to the end of a long, L-shaped hallway. Griffin's old room was clean and bare. A skylight set in the slanted ceiling gave it an airy feel and a door led to a small wooden deck. A sliver of blue from the Bay peeked out from between the two buildings across the street. Sarah brightened appreciably.

"I love it."

"Yeah, this is the best room in the house."

They stood there for a moment, each measuring the silence between them.

"So what do you folks do?"

Spike shrugged. "Geek stuff, mostly. Echo codes interactives. Shin-yi is kind of an all-around artist and mechanic. Not so virtual, but she's a real gadget freak."

She looked at him. Green eyes, Spike noticed.

"What about you?" she asked.

He hesitated. "I'm a pygmalion at Proxy Lady." He saw the expression on her face and continued hurriedly. "Yeah, I know. It's totally sleazy. But it keeps me in rent money while I work on v-space design, which is what I really do. I'm going indy as an architect, eventually."

She looked like she was about to say something, but stopped herself. Her expression was somewhere between tolerant amusement and mild contempt, but Spike couldn't get a solid read. Definitely a watcher, he thought. Holding back until she gets the lay of the land.

"You want to go back?" he asked.

She nodded.

"So, what do you think?" Echo asked when they were all seated in the living room again.

Sarah hesitated. "Look," she said. "I like the room and you all seem like nice people. I'm not sure I'll fit in here, but I really need a place … like right now. I'd be willing to give this a try and see how it goes."

Shin-yi looked at Echo. Echo shrugged—why not?—and looked at Spike. Spike looked at Shin-yi. They nodded in unison.

☆

Images of billowing flame flickered across the stiffened patch of smartcloth, Shin-yi's latest installation. Echo looked over her shoulder, making comments. Sarah was reading a dog-eared copy of *The Rise and Fall of the Great Powers*. Spike was bored.

"Anybody want to go down to the Node?" he asked.

"No, thanks," Shin-yi said. Echo shook his head.

Sarah looked up. "What's that?"

"It's a café on Ninth Street."

She folded back the corner of the page and put the book on the arm of her chair.

"Sure, I'll come along. I haven't had a chance to check out the neighborhood."

Spike led her down the stairs and into the street. They turned up Sixth toward the ruined freeway, a legacy of the Rumble. In its shadow, a cluster of bubble tents sprouted like mushrooms. Abandoned cars lined the street. Some were blackened with fire, others stripped down to the frame. Someone of indeterminate age and gender hurried down the opposite side of the street, head bent into the raised collar of an army jacket.

"Have you had much trouble around here?" Sarah asked.

Spike opened the buttons of his shirt. He ran his finger along four inches of pale, jagged scar tissue.

"That was three years ago, just after I moved in. It isn't that bad if you mind your own business, but you gotta watch yourself."

As they turned up Howard, an olive-green SFPD halftrack came around the corner at high speed.

"Be cool," Spike said. "Just keep walking."

They turned onto Ninth and walked halfway up the block toward a crowded doorway. A large man with a green-clawed hand tattooed across the top of his shaved head, was checking weapons.

"Hey, Blunt," Spike said, handing him his Mace. "This is Sarah. New housemate."

Blunt stepped aside to let them in.

"He doesn't say much, does he?" Sarah whispered when they were inside.

"I've never heard him say a word face-to-face," Spike said. "But he's got a pretty talky avatar on RealTime."

The Node was warehouse-sized, lit by pale fluorescents. Korean pop echoed off the black-and-green-painted walls and concrete floor. A Deco cappuccino machine hulked like Moloch behind a long service counter. The tables were PG&E cable spools, the chairs were packing crates.

Most of the club's occupants were wired-glued to VDTs or personal sheekys or hidden behind bulky, dark dataglasses. Spike pointed to an empty booth at the far wall. They navigated through the maze of tables.

"When I was a kid, my dad used to collect postcards," Sarah said when they were seated. "He had a corkboard in the kitchen covered with them, two or three layers deep. There was one that showed a movie theater audience. They were all wearing these cheesy glasses with cardboard frames that were supposed to let you see the movie in 3-D. But to me they made everybody look like they were blind."

Spike wondered what she was getting at.

Sarah sighed. "That's what this place reminds me of. A café is supposed to be someplace where people come to socialize."

"Well, yeah," Spike said, "that's exactly why people come here."

"But they're all … mediated." She smacked the VDT lightly, and it swiveled around with a protesting squeak. "This place isn't a gathering spot, it's a point of departure. Look at these people. Nobody's here."

Spike had been planning on logging them on and showing her around the Tesseract, an environment he was in the final stages of coding up. Probably not such a good idea at this point.

He folded the scratched smartcloth keypad attached to the VDT into a tight little square, then released it. The cloth sprang back to its former shape. He looked up. "Can I ask you something?"

"Sure."

"Why were you in such a hurry to move in? We're all pretty different from you, and you have a bit of a commute besides. Don't misunderstand. We're glad to have you, but …"

"It's a fair question." She paused, and began worrying the smart-cloth keypad on her side of the table, folding it over, watching it spring back.

"Great fidget toy," she said. Her lower lip was white where her teeth clamped down. Spike was almost glad to see her composure shaken up a bit.

"You don't have to tell me," he said.

"No, it's cool. I was with this guy. Jack. Very heavy-duty politico, community organizer, sometimes even some guerrilla stuff. But I didn't find out about that until later."

She took a breath.

"We'd been living together about two months. It was a little rocky from the start—we fought a lot—but I figured we could handle it. Then one day we were having another argument and right out of the blue he hit me."

Spike winced.

"Yeah," Sarah nodded. "He was very apologetic, begged me for another chance, said it would never happen again. Then a couple of weeks later, it did. Loosened a tooth that time. I had to get out in a hurry and I felt like I needed a complete change, you know?"

She looked around. "Which I got. And I like the room."

There was something very raw and immediate about Sarah's story. It scared him a little—most of his relationships had been online. Someone was messing with the sound system and the Korean pop surged in volume, deafening them for a second, then fading back to twice as loud as it had been before. Layers of twangy guitars underneath an electronic komungo dueling with a warbly female lead. It was unabashedly cheerful.

"You want a cappuccino or something?" he asked.

"That would be great."

He threaded his way to the counter and returned with two foam-topped mugs.

"So, what are you into at State?" he asked.

She took a sip. "I study failure."

Spike nodded vacantly. "Ah."

"Political regimes, social movements, intellectual movements. I'm interested in demise mechanisms."

"You mean like why did Communism collapse, stuff like that?"

"Something like that."

"So, how are we doing?"

"You mean the States?" She smiled ruefully. "Not so good. But it's really hard to tell from inside."

The music paused and the room was suddenly full of the white-noise chorus of many voices subvocalizing into throat mics. The sound was ominous, like a nearby swarm of bees. At the table next to theirs, a young man in bulbous dataglasses laughed and clawed at the air.

"How are *you* doing?" Spike asked.

"Me?" Sarah shrugged, and smiled again. "I fail all the time."

"But you keep coming back."

"Yeah, I always have my eye out for the next time."

Nobody else was home, so Spike put the latest Tapioca Buckshot bead on the rig, cranked the bass up high, and sank into the living room couch. Eight Bose speakers, each the size of a ping-pong ball and positioned in a vertex of the room, shook the walls and floor with high-octane industrial dub. Spike closed his eyes and let the sound soak into his skin, washing away the netburn, flushing out the psychic toxins that accumulated after six hours of ersatz erotic grappling.

He usually had three or four avatars going at once, and they all had fairly sophisticated AI plug-ins. But even sophisticated AI was pretty fucking stupid. His job was to monitor the sessions and make sure his avatars loaded the right modules in response to customer desires.

It was very depressing at first. Spike couldn't rid himself of his own mental image of the person behind the virtual projection—a fat, sweaty loser in a darkened room with wraparound dataglasses and his shorts around his ankles. It didn't do much for your sense of the innate dignity of the species. But part of that was Spike's own projection and, after a while, the sense of being adrift in a sea of relativism segued to bored, flatline detachment. It was a gig.

Jet-engine whine shook the soles of his feet, underlaying a polyrhythmic loop of street construction, breaking glass, and what sounded like a fork being mangled in a kitchen garbage disposal. It was glorious.

Spike felt a hand on his shoulder. His eyes snapped open and he jerked upright. Sarah's face hovered over him.

"Jesus Christ, you scared the shit out of me. I didn't think anybody was home."

"What?" He could see her lips moving, but he could barely hear her.

"You scared the shit out of me," he shouted. He got up and turned off the rig.

"Sorry," she said. "I just walked in."

He could still barely hear her over the ringing in his ears. He noticed the shock of leafy greens peeking over the top of the bag she cradled.

"What you got?"

"Fat Belly Farms," she said. "Co-op on Angel Island. You pay twenty bucks a week and you get a big bag of stuff, whatever's fresh. Today there's plums, winter squash, collards, garlic, potatoes, beets, and carrots."

"Hmm," he said. He leaned over and looked into the bag. He pointed to a bundle of huge, green leaves, each the size of a dinner plate.

"What the fuck is that?"

She gave him an odd look. "Collards. You've never seen collard greens before?"

"Well, I ... uh, no."

"All this stuff looks kind of weird without shrink-wrap, huh? Here, try this."

She reached into the bag and pulled out a plum. It was deep purple and tight with juice. Spike took it from her and held it suspiciously up to the light.

He took a bite. Tart sweetness filled his mouth—the essence of plum, the Platonic ideal of plumness. It was so intense that it brought tears to his eyes.

"Oh, man, that's good."

Sarah nodded. "You're dribbling."

He wiped his chin with his sleeve and took another bite.

"What's so funny?" he asked.

She shook her head, then paused. "What do plums taste like online?" she asked.

"Ba-da-bing. Point taken."

She looked at him for a long moment.

"I'm going to put these away. Have another one."

Spike watched her walk into the kitchen, her long blond hair falling in a wave down her back. He looked at the plum she gave him and closed his hand gently around it. It felt warm, like it wanted to breathe.

Spike paged through a walkabout of the Tesseract, his sheeky unfolded in front of him on the kitchen table. The summer/winter transition in the Greek Theater still needed some work, the lighting sucked, and he needed something else on the audio—wind chimes, crickets—something. He scribbled notes in a popup next to the graphics window. He was having trouble staying focused, though. He paused the walkabout and looked up at Shin-yi, sitting across the table from him, bent over a circuit board with a laser pencil.

"I'm worried about Bardo," he said.

"We're all worried about Bardo," she said without looking up.

"No, I mean, really. I just checked his stats on GameNet—they haven't moved at all for six hours. And Seafood has been acting kind of weird."

The cat had been very skittish. When he wasn't hiding, he was prowling up and down the hall, stopping in front of Bardo's door and mewing piteously.

"Seafood is a psycho-kitty." She saw the look on his face and rested the soldering pencil in its cradle. "All right, maybe we'd better look in on him."

They walked down the hall and stopped in front of Bardo's door. Spike looked at Shin-yi. She shrugged and knocked on the door. There was no answer. She knocked again, loudly.

"Bardo! You OK in there?"

Echo came out of his room. "What's up?"

"I think something's the matter with Bardo," Spike said. "His stats have been flat all day."

"Something's definitely the matter. The man's a cabbage IRL, but he's a stud on Hell-Five." Echo stepped between the two of them, turned the doorknob, and pushed the door open.

Bardo sprawled naked in the bulbous cushions of his massage

chair, dataglasses askew, tongue protruding from his mouth. His eyes were rolled back in his head, the sclera cloudy and gelid. A bloody starburst occluded one eye, giving the impression of a macabre wink. His catheters had come loose and streaks of dried blood trailed from his penis, neck, and arm.

The window was wide open, but still a sickly mélange of smells filled the darkened room—a faint reek of urine and feces; beneath that, something sweet and rotten, not quite yet decay but unmistakably the smell of death.

Spike ran to the body and put his fingers on Bardo's jugular. The skin was cool, the texture of clay.

"You're wasting your time," Shin-yi said. "That's a dead man."

They stood there like that, probably for only a few seconds, but to Spike it seemed like an executable trying to load with garbled inputs. Sarah appeared in the doorway. She put her hand to her mouth.

"Oh, Jesus."

Echo slipped a flat, black card from his shirt pocket and raised it to his lips.

"Nine-one-one," he said.

He stood there waiting. After about 20 seconds, he looked at Spike and shrugged.

"Still ringing. I don't—uh, yeah, we've got a dead body here. Four-sixty-three Sixth ... I don't know, maybe cardiac arrest, maybe something else ... Yeah, natural causes, that's right ... Echo. Just Echo." He rolled his eyes. "Darius French. Jesus fucking—about a day or so ... Well, no, it isn't exactly an emergency, then, but—yeah, all right ... All right. We'll be here." He gave the edge of the card an angry flick with his thumb and forefinger.

"They'll be about four hours," he said. "The operator started giving me shit for sucking up emergency bandwidth with a non-emergency call."

Spike reached tentatively down and tried to close Bardo's eyes, like he'd done in interactives when virtual companions bought the farm. He tried again and this time gentled both eyelids shut. That was better. Spike walked to the foot of Bardo's bed and began pulling a blanket from the tangle of bedding. He looked at the group standing in the doorway.

"Somebody give me a hand?"

Sarah stepped forward. Together they draped the blanket over Bardo's body.

The four of them gathered around the kitchen table, too stunned to speak. The presence of Bardo's body in the room down the hall was like a heavy fog filling the kitchen, absorbing thought, impeding speech.

Shin-yi excused herself to run a salvage errand. A little while later, Echo returned to his room.

"You OK?" Sarah asked.

Spike had been lost in a soft haze of slowly shifting memories from an afternoon he and Bardo had spent together down at Half Moon Bay a few years back. The ocean dashing itself to mist on the black, jagged shore. Neat rows of wind turbines crouching offshore like great metal spiders, bobbing with the swell. Bardo tilting his head back and laughing.

"Are you all right?" Sarah asked again.

Spike looked at her and smiled weakly. "Not really."

There was a tightness in his forehead, like tears wanted to come but wouldn't.

"He was a friend," he said. "Before he got strung out. We went to school together, back East at Rizdee. We moved out here and found this place, carried it for a couple of months before we found Echo and Shin-yi. There was a string of other folks in that back room of yours, but the four of us were the core."

He shook his head. "I don't know what happened. We used to kid him about how much time he spent on GameNet. After a while, it stopped being funny. He just sort of slipped away."

Sarah nodded and put her hand on his arm. They sat together in the gathering dark without speaking. There was a hollow, echoing boom from the direction of the Bay, followed by a crackling of small arms fire, then silence again.

"Plastique," Spike said. "The natives are restless."

After a while, Sarah got up. "I'm around if you need to talk."

He nodded. "Thanks."

He went through the motions of making coffee. The familiarity of the ritual had a soothing effect. When the coffee was done and he'd poured himself a mug, he tried to call Bardo's parents. He remembered only that they lived in an Enclave down the Peninsula. It took him a while to find them; he left a terse message with their Enclave's rent-a-cop, whose affect was so flat that he would have failed a Turing test. He hoped it got through.

The paramedics finally showed, a man and a woman in gray Kevlar vests and holstered pistols, faces hidden behind Pleximasks. Spike showed them to Bardo's room and stood in the doorway as they went about their business. The man stuck a thin tube in Bardo's mouth and looked at a palmscreen readout. He muttered something to the woman and they both laughed. They unrolled a black polyurethane bag onto the floor and unceremoniously stuffed Bardo's body into it. Spike looked away.

"Next of kin?" the woman asked when they were done. Spike gave her what information he had.

"The police may want to contact you, but this looks pretty routine."

"Routine?"

"Yeah. Cerebral hemorrhage. You want to sign?" Her eyes were beads of chipped black glass. She handed him a slate and a lightpen, and he scrawled his name next to the blinking glyph.

If there was a funeral service, Spike never heard about it. He left another message with Security at Bardo's parents' Enclave, asking that they get in touch with him, but they never called. He tried St. Mary's, where they took the body, but all they would tell him was that the family had taken custody.

Spike and Sarah sat on the deck in low canvas chairs, taking in the late morning sun. Not talking much, just hanging. The air had a cool edge to it, but the sun felt warm on their upturned faces. A cargo zep floated above the ruined towers of the Bay Bridge, making slow progress against the wind.

"I need to get out of the house for a while," Spike said. "You want to go to the ocean?"

"Sure."

They put some bread, hard cheese, a couple of oranges, and a Nalgene jug filled with bottled water in a knapsack. They had to walk all the way to Civic Center to catch a Muni that would take them to Ocean Beach. It was Sunday and the streets were quiet, but the open-air market was a bustle of activity. Food, clothing, electronics—spread on blankets, piled on folding tables, hanging from racks. Whatever you wanted, hi-tech, lo-tech, legal or not, you could probably find it at the Flea.

Spike and Sarah wove through the narrow lanes between merchants, ignoring the more aggressive hustles. Every other site had a disc or bead player going, and the air vibrated with a cacophonous mix of Korean pop, industrial dub, bonk, and good old rock 'n' roll. They stopped at an open grill and got two sticks of mystery meat satay, dripping with spicy peanut sauce.

There were only a few other passengers on the Muni, an old, stinking diesel. Spike and Sarah sat near the back. He could feel his kidneys jostle every time the bus hit a pothole, which was often. At 34th and Lincoln, the bus lurched and ground to a halt. Swearing, the driver walked around to the back of the bus and pulled open the engine cover. More swearing, a flurry of hammering sounds.

"I think that's our cue," Sarah said.

Spike nodded. "We don't have too far to walk from here."

The street sloped gently to the gray ocean. Except for an occasional electric, there was little traffic. Birds screeched and twittered from the tangle of greenery at their right.

"We could cut through the park," Sarah said.

"I don't think so," Spike replied. "Not even during the day."

They walked slowly down the middle of the street, saying little. When they got to the promenade, they turned right and followed the curve of the beach toward a tumble of rocks rising to a jagged promontory topped by the fire-blackened ruin of Cliff House.

They clambered up the slope. The ruined restaurant was boarded up, the plywood thick with graffiti. Beyond it, the walkway opened up into a cracked concrete terrace on which huddled a small, whitewashed structure untouched by fire. It was crowned by a metal tube that rotated slowly like a radar antenna.

Spike took Sarah's hand and led her into the building. She curled her fingers around his.

"The city used to maintain it, but the money dried up a long time ago. Now folks around here keep it up."

He pushed the door open. The narrow corridor was cool, dark, and smelled of mildew. They passed through a black curtain into a round room with what seemed like an altar in the center, a ten-foot disc of white concrete. Its surface was a parabolic concavity presenting a pearlescent image of the ocean. Plumes of white spray hurled themselves onto the base of the cliff. Cormorants sped low across the waves. Farther out, a wall of fog stretched across the horizon. The image continually panned, so that to stay at the bottom you had to move slowly around its circumference.

"This is fantastic," she whispered, ghostly pale in the reflected light.

"It's called a camera obscura," he whispered back.

They studied the curve of Ocean Beach as it stretched toward the south, paralleled offshore by neat rows of wind turbines; they studied the ruins of the Cliff House, blackened beams pointing at the sky like accusing fingers; they studied the gray ocean. After a while, they just stood there, letting the world slowly wheel around and around.

"Thanks," Sarah said. "That place is seriously cool."

"My pleasure," Spike said.

They had wandered to the edge of the terrace to look directly at the ocean. They sat down on the surrounding wall and dangled their feet. After a while, Sarah reached down and picked up a handful of sandy earth.

"Bardo," she said, hefting it. "Here, give me your hand."

She poured some into Spike's hand and let the rest sift through her fingers. The wind took it off to the ocean.

"Good journey, Bardo," she said. "Grace and peace."

Spike held the soil in his cupped palm. He ran his thumb through it, feeling it crumble.

He threw it into the wind.

"Lock and load, man," he said. "Good journey."

The fog was coming in, a wall of white churned to tatters at the top by the spinning windmills. Spike imagined that it hid another city, a mirror San Francisco where Doppelgängers Spike and Sarah sat together looking out across the water, their feet dangling over the edge.

BLUE PERIOD

CHARCOAL WAS GOOD. Pablo liked the simplicity of it, the challenge of coaxing subtlety from the purest of elements. You begin with nothing. White paper. Black lump of coal. And like God shaping the Earth from light and void, you create a world.

Sometimes.

He had been working since early afternoon. A woman in the market giving an apple to her half-wit son. Something about the two of them, the set of her shoulders toward the boy, the way the light touched his hair, suggesting that some measure of divinity lay in him and that she was the one saddled with infirmity. But Pablo wasn't getting it. The thing emerging from the rough paper was a cartoon, a grotesque joke.

The shadows in the studio lengthened until the sun fell behind the buildings across the Rue Gabrielle. Pablo took no notice, working until it was almost too dark to see. Finally, when the charcoal smudges began to flow of their own accord into the unmarked whiteness of the paper, he stepped back and stretched his cramped shoulders.

He lit a lamp and the studio filled with warm yellow light. The large room looked like it had been visited by a whirlwind with an artistic fetish. Canvases in various stages of completion were scattered about; rough sketches littered the floor. To the left of the wide, bay windows, to catch the light of afternoon, a raised platform for the models. Heavy-breasted cows, most of them, but what could you do? Pablo loved Paris, but the women were pigs.

On a table near the door, a loaf of bread, three days old and hard as stone, a bottle of rough burgundy, a bowl of apples. And leaning against the south wall of the studio, about twenty finished canvases, Pablo's portfolio. They were set apart from the clutter as if a protective wall had been erected around them. His ticket to greatness. Nineteen years old and already he was breaking new ground, surpassing the work of the established masters. After all, he had been chosen to represent his native Spain at the Paris Exhibition! The canvases he saw in the Montmartre galleries would be better suited to wrap liver. Monet should have been smothered as a child. Smothered in flowers. Who cared a dog's teat about flowers? Even the best of the new ones, Denis, say, or Vuillard, couldn't paint their way out of a burlap sack. Dragonflies! Lilies! Swirling hair! It was crap, all of it.

The Spanish upstart, they were calling him. Dismissing him as if he were an insect. Deft but morbid, one review said. Uneven, said another. He would show those Symbolist faggots what a real artist could do. He turned back to the sketch of the woman and the idiot boy.

But not tonight, he thought. This is shit.

Pablo tore the page from the easel and ripped it in half, then in half again. He let the pieces fall to the floor and walked across the room to the table. He uncorked the burgundy and raised it to his lips, taking a long draught. It was rough but good, leaving a warm glow in his gullet. The French peasants were all right for something. He raised the bottle to his lips again when suddenly, a bright green flash lit the sky outside his window. It was gone in an instant, but it was so intense that the afterimage of the silhouetted buildings across the street stayed pulsing in his vision.

What the hell was that? He ran to the window and looked out. A few souls on the street, looking up. He scanned the horizon. There, beyond the basilica of the Sacre Coeur, a greenish glow pushing into the twilight, just beginning to recede.

Even as his eyes began to adjust, another green flash lit the sky.

This time, Pablo could see its trail, like a shooting star but brighter, lancing downward to the west. It was accompanied by a roaring sound, something like thunder but with an edge to it, as if the sky were made of cloth and somebody was ripping it in two. There was a moment of preternatural quiet, the world itself holding its breath, then a flickering orange glow began to lick at the bottom of the sky. The Bois du Boulogne? It was hard to tell. Pablo was still new to Paris and didn't quite have his bearings yet. In fact, he hardly ever left Montmartre.

His countryman Casagemas had said he'd be at Le Ciel on the Boulevard de Clichy, fondling women, no doubt, and getting drunk. Pablo felt a sudden need for his companionship. He grabbed his jacket and cap and began to head out the door.

Then, as if he'd forgotten something but wasn't quite sure what, he stopped, turned, and looked around the room. His eyes lingered on the stack of canvases leaning against the wall. His mind filled with an unfocused dread, almost crushing him under its sudden weight. With an effort of will, he pushed it aside. Everything was all right. Shooting stars. Big deal. God taking potshots at the lame and unrepentant. Pablo knew that God had other plans for him.

The streets were buzzing with energy. People clustered in front of shops, talking, gesturing up at the sky. As Pablo passed one such group in front of a patisserie on the Rue Saint-Vincent, he overheard someone say, "Men from Mars, I'm telling you! They've landed!"

Pablo approached the group. "Excuse me, my French still isn't very good. Did you say 'men from Mars'?"

"Yes!" The speaker grabbed Pablo by the lapels. He was drunk; his breath would have knocked over a horse. "A cylinder landed at Royaumont this morning and vile *things* crawled out. Gargoyles! The monastery is in ruins!"

Pablo pried the man loose and backed away. One of his companions laughed. "The monastery is seven hundred years old. It's already in ruins."

"Laugh all you want," the drunk said. "We aren't the only creatures in the cosmos God has graced with intelligence. They're here to test us and we'd better be ready!"

Another of the man's companions winked at Pablo and pantomimed drinking from a bottle. Pablo walked away. Their voices faded behind him, drifting up into the warm night air.

Men from Mars! Pablo had read in *Le Figaro* about the recent volcanic activity on Mars, jets of gas shooting out from the planet's surface, visible from Earth with even a modest telescope. Forty million miles away. Pablo shook his head. What did numbers like that mean? And now men. No, *monsters*! Gargoyles sent by the God of War! He laughed. Casagemas was really going to get a kick out of this. He quickened his pace.

He cut through the Montmartre Cemetery on his way to the Boulevard de Clichy and quiet surrounded him like a velvet glove. Gnarled oak trees cast a protective canopy, muffling the street sounds. Neat rows of headstones, pale in the moonlight, followed the gentle, hilly contours like cultivated crops. The sky above the trees to the south was bleeding orange at the bottom.

Inside Le Ciel, the smoky air was charged with reassuring chaos. An acrobat tumbled across the stage, flanked on one side by a dwarf in formal evening attire and on the other by a grinning pinhead in a flowered nightshirt. A mustached pianist played a lively accompaniment. Near the bar, two men shouted at each other at the top of their lungs. It was business as usual at Le Ciel, Martians or not.

He scanned the tables for Casagemas. There, near the front, his friend's broad back and shaggy black hair. He was leaning over to whisper something into his companion's ear. She threw back her head and laughed. Pablo stared. This one was beautiful. Not painted like a whore, but flush with the bloom and innocence of youth. Casagemas was moving up in the world!

Pablo pushed through the maze of tables and wedged a chair between the two of them.

"Ho, Carles!" he said. "What have you been keeping from me?" Up close, the woman was even more lovely than he'd thought. Curly, brown tresses framed a heart-shaped face. Cool blue-green eyes, like the ocean under a tropical sun. "Casagemas and I are the best of friends," he said to her. "We share everything, you know."

She blushed and smiled, but Pablo saw first a flicker of anger pass across her face. Passion, too! Good!

"Hey, Pablo, behave yourself," Casagemas said. He turned to his companion. "He doesn't know how to act around a real woman. Just the whores. Germaine, this is Pablo Ruiz Picasso, the greatest painter in Paris, only nobody knows it but him. Nineteen years old and already he is a legend in his own mind."

"Yes, well, one day Carles will shock us all and sell one of his own paintings," Pablo said. He took Germaine's hand and brought it to his lips. "I am not only charmed," he said, in Spanish, "but stricken with envy that this pig will be taking you home tonight and not I."

Her eyes flashed again with anger, and she blushed a deeper red. She started to say something, glared at Casagemas, pushed back her chair, and stalked away.

Casagemas glared at Pablo. "Her father is Spanish, you fool. She speaks it like a native. You've really done it this time."

He got up and hurried after Germaine. Pablo grinned and watched him weave through the crowd, narrowly missing a collision with a waiter carrying a tray laden with bottles and glasses.

He picked up his friend's glass, still half-full of ruby burgundy, took a healthy sip, and turned his attention to the stage. The dwarf was balanced on the acrobat's shoulders, juggling a wicked looking knife, an empty wine bottle, and a flaming torch. The pinhead looked on, his mouth hanging open. In the light from the stage-lamps, his lips were shiny with drool.

After a few moments, Casagemas and Germaine returned to the table.

"Germaine has consented to stay if you will apologize to her, Pablo," Casagemas said.

She was glaring down at Pablo so hard that he had to look away to keep from smiling.

"I'm sorry," he said. *That you're with Casagemas*, he added to himself. "We've gotten off on the wrong foot. Please stay."

She smiled, a little stiffly, though, to be sure, and sat. Casagemas did likewise. Pablo motioned a waiter over and ordered a bottle of wine and a plate of bread and hard cheese.

"So," he said when they were settled. "What do you think about the men from Mars?"

Casagemas laughed. "It's the Germans. Von Bulow's ambition has finally gotten the better of his common sense. We'll crush them like insects."

"The Germans!" Germaine said. "We're at war, then?"

"No, I'm kidding." Casagemas held up a hand. "But it seems more likely an explanation than men from outer space."

"Well, something is going on," Pablo said. "There were two explosions—at least two—and I think the Bois du Boulogne is burning."

"Burning!" Germaine said. "Maybe we should try to find out what's happening."

"Maybe we should have some more wine," Casagemas said.

Pablo thought for a moment, then he grabbed the bottle and stood up. "Maybe we should do both. It's better to know what's going on than to be left in the dark."

He wrapped the bread and cheese in a napkin and stuffed it in his jacket pocket. Germaine and Casagemas looked up at him from the table.

"Well, what are you waiting for?" Pablo asked. "Let's go!"

They looked at each other. Casagemas shrugged and reluctantly pushed back his chair. He offered his hand to Germaine.

"I have a bad feeling about this, Pablo. If there was something wrong, the authorities would notify us. This is another one of your crazy expeditions."

Back in Barcelona, Pablo had persuaded Casagemas to come with him to the recent scene of an anarchist bombing. An outdoor café, reduced to rubble in the middle of the afternoon. Two hours later, it was still a charnel house, debris everywhere, a row of bodies in the street covered with bloody tablecloths. Due to their scruffy looks, Pablo and Casagemas were arrested at the scene and detained for several hours. Eventually, they were released, but not before some very rough questioning. It was all fuel for Pablo's artistic drive; he filled a whole notebook with sketches. Casagemas had nightmares for weeks. Disembodied hands, flesh cracked and burned, reached for him in the dark while faceless inquisitors hurled nonsense questions at him.

"Don't worry, Carles," Pablo said. "Germaine and I will protect you."

Germaine smiled uneasily.

Pablo took a last look across the room at the stage. The pinhead was looking directly at him. His eyes, which Pablo had first thought glazed with idiocy, burned, full of suffering and grace, into his own. Pablo turned away.

Traffic was heavy on the Boulevard de Clichy; horses, carriages, the occasional motor car, wove through the thickening crowd of pedestrians. A tradesman, still in work clothes, had his wife and two beribboned girls in tow. A trio of drunken soldiers passed a bottle back and forth, laughing. The overall mood was almost that of a holiday. It was as if they were saying, "This is Paris, after all, the center of the civilized world! What could possibly happen?"

Pablo thought back to Barcelona again, to Death himself laying waste upon the languid peace of an afternoon. *Anything* could happen. Anything. God is a cruel prankster and these Parisians are fools.

When he could get a glimpse of the sky to the west, Pablo saw that it was still tinged with flickering red at the bottom, but the crowd was moving in the opposite direction, towards the center of the city.

He stopped a young man in a blue watch cap. "What's going on?"

"Something crashed in the Seine, near the Île de la Cité! The river is boiling!"

Germaine and Casagemas clung tightly together to avoid being separated in the thickening crowd. She reached out her hand to Pablo and he took it. It was warm, soft, and strong.

Pablo heard several different stories, each of them more fantastic than the last. Notre Dame had been leveled. A great crater had been plowed into the Jardin des Luxembourg and grotesque things were crawling out. Another variation of the Royaumont story, only this time the Martians, after destroying the monastery, began striding across the land in great cowled vehicles hundreds of feet high, setting fire to everything in their path.

The crowd had a life of its own now, sweeping them down the Rue Rivoli. When they reached the Pont D'Arcole, Pablo shouted to his companions, "Let's stay on the bridge and let the crowd pass. We can see everything from here."

They pushed their way to the side of the bridge, buffeted by passing bodies. When they reached the railing they held on. Soon, the mob thinned.

Something *was* going on in the river. Just beyond the tip of the Île de la Cité, a circular patch of water ten meters across pulsed a luminous green, the glow intensifying to eye-searing brightness and fading to cool chartreuse with a period of roughly thirty seconds. As it brightened, the water in the affected region bubbled furiously. Wraiths of steam floated above the river.

"This must be where one of the shooting stars landed," Pablo said.

A pair of barges bristling with grappling equipment floated on either side of the glowing area. Men clustered on the decks.

There was something wrong with the outline of the Notre Dame Cathedral. As his eyes adjusted, Pablo saw that one of the towers was gone, sheared off near the top leaving a jagged silhouette. The shooting star must have grazed the old cathedral in its descent.

A black tentacle broke the roiling surface of the water. Its motions were flexible, but it was clearly a mechanical contrivance, composed of a series of articulated segments. Tentative at first, it waved this way and that, as if sniffing the air, extending itself all the while above the river like a metallic beanstalk.

It stopped its weaving motion, leaned toward one of the barges, and struck with reptilian speed. The tentacle wrapped itself around the barge and, in an instant, dragged it down into the turbulent, glowing water.

Bits of debris floated to the surface. A few men struggled briefly, but they were being boiled alive like crabs in a pot. Soon their motions ceased.

Another tentacle, or perhaps it was the same one, broke through the water's surface. This time there was no hesitation; it went directly for the other barge, pulling it under in the blink of an eye.

All was quiet. The luminous patch faded to a dull, pulsing glow. A few scraps of wood bobbed in the water.

Pablo looked at Casagemas. His friend's face was pale. Germaine clung tightly to his arm.

"What *was* that?" she asked.

Casagemas shook his head. "I don't know."

"Germans, eh?" Pablo asked. He was badly shaken, but he didn't want his friend or Germaine to know just how badly. "Germans from outer space!"

He realized that he still held the wine bottle by its neck. He lifted it to his lips, took a long pull, and offered the bottle to Germaine.

She shook her head, and Casagemas shot him an annoyed look. "Don't be flip, Pablo. People are *dead*. What sort of horror *is* this?"

Pablo shrugged. "Maybe it's true. Men from Mars bearing the judgment of a cruel, stupid God." He took another pull of wine and winked at Germaine. "Or maybe they come to Paris for the women."

Germaine looked away.

Suddenly, the water began bubbling furiously again and a rounded shape broke through the roiling surface. It continued to rise; sheets of water cascaded off its surface. As it cleared the water Pablo saw that it was supported by three jointed legs. Curled tentacles dangled from its flat bottom. One such tentacle was wrapped around a box, affixed to one end of which was a shape like the funnel of a Victrola.

At its full height, the thing towered above the river, balanced on spidery tripod legs. The cowled head was level with the turrets of Notre Dame. It looked this way and that in a manner that was almost human.

Surely *this* thing is not one of the Martians, Pablo thought. It must be some sort of vehicle, with the creatures themselves inside.

Whatever it was, intelligence and malice guided its motions. It stepped out of the river onto the quay, raised the funneled box, and pointed it at the Notre Dame Cathedral.

A deep thrumming sound seemed to emanate from the device. Suddenly, a ghostly green beam, almost too faint to see, leapt from the box, and the face of the great cathedral exploded. Stone shattered, stained glass glowed and ran like wax. The remains of the south tower began to collapse, as if in slow motion.

It took Pablo a moment to realize that what he was seeing was the effect of great heat, but when the Martian swept the beams across the roofs of the surrounding buildings, there was no doubt. As soon as the beam touched them, they burst into flames as if ignited by a torch.

The crowd, so anxious a little while ago to get close to the spectacle, began flowing back across the Pont D'Arcole. It was a brainless mob; Pablo saw at least one person trampled under its relentless, panicked flight.

"Hold tightly to the railing!" he shouted to his companions.

As they were buffeted in the sea of bodies, trying to keep from being swept downstream, a ragged line of soldiers appeared on the quay from the nearby Prefecture de Police. They raised their rifles at the great machine towering above them.

Pablo could see muzzle flashes, like tiny fireflies in the night. Their effect upon the leviathan was little more than that. It swept the beam across the pitiful rank of soldiers and one by one, as it touched them, they burst into flame.

The machine swept the beam across the river, leaving a violent wake of hissing steam, and as it touched buildings on the Rive Gauche, they exploded into fiery blossoms. The beam cut a swath across the mob on the Pont D'Arcole, not twenty feet away from Pablo and his companions. Pablo felt the heat on his face; it was like standing too close to a furnace.

Each person the heat-ray touched instantly became a wick encased in a billowing column of fire. One man was looking in Pablo's direction as the beam touched him. Time slowed to a halt; every detail imprinted itself on Pablo's vision. The dark hollows of his eyes in the flickering inferno, his skin peeling, blackening, cracking, his mouth open to scream, consumed by the fire before he could utter a sound.

Pablo ducked down, seeking the meager protection of the stone fence. Casagemas and Germaine stood clutching each other, frozen with fear.

"Get down, you idiots!" Pablo grabbed Germaine by the hem of her coat, pulling her down. She pulled Casagemas down with her to the stone walkway.

They huddled together, leaving as little exposed as possible to the panic of the mob and the return of the heat-ray. Countless feet kicked their hunched backs in passing flight. They huddled closer.

A deafening screech filled the air, exultant and alien.

"Aloo! Aloo!"

Pablo looked up. Almost directly in front of him, one of the tripod legs rose out of the water. Its strangely scaled surface held a dull sheen. Impossibly far above them, the cowled head swept back and forth. Suddenly, a jet of bright green steam hissed from one of the joints and the leg lifted out of the water. It passed over their heads, gone in an instant. The alien howl cut through the night again, fading as the thing strode west along the river toward the flickering glow in the sky.

Pablo was hyper-aware of his surroundings—the smell of Germaine's perfume, her rapid breathing. The scratchy feel of Casagemas's overcoat on his cheek, more real than the Bosch-like image of a three-legged monster towering above the river, laying swaths of destruction across the City of Light.

Soon, relative calm descended upon the bridge. The cries of those touched by the edge of the beam floated towards them. A greasy, burned smell hung in the air, singed hair mixed with meat left too long on a spit. Wisps of smoke rose from the pathetic charred hulks that had once been human beings. Scattered groups of survivors began looking dazedly around. A few began seeing to the injured.

"What are we going to do?" Casagemas asked. They had retreated to the safety of an alley on the Rive Gauche side of the Pont D'Arcole. In the distance, they could hear the hollow boom of artillery.

"My parents live in Versailles," Germaine said. "I have to get out there."

"I will accompany you, of course," Casagemas said. Germaine touched his arm gratefully. He looked at Pablo.

Pablo thought of the stack of canvases in his studio. His portfolio, the sum total of his work to date. It would be easy to dismount them and roll them up. He could no more abandon them than he could leave an arm or a leg behind.

Pablo nodded toward the orange glow in the western sky.

"That's probably Versailles," he said. "I don't know if there's anything left."

Germaine began to weep.

"Pablo, you are such an asshole sometimes," Casagemas said.

Pablo shrugged. "Do what you must. I have to go back to the studio and get my paintings. It would be a disaster if they were destroyed."

"A disaster!" Casagemas said. "What do you think is happening here? Your paintings mean nothing, Pablo. We have to survive, help if we can. Our chances are better if we stick together."

Pablo stiffened. "You are a woman, Carles. Go then. Run. Survival is nothing without art. Otherwise, we are no better than dogs pissing in the street."

Casagemas glared at Pablo and pulled Germaine closer. Without a word, he turned and walked out of the alley, his arm around her shoulders.

Pablo watched them turn the corner and disappear. His soul was filled with blackness. A part of him wanted to chase after them, to throw in his lot with them, flee the city and find a safe haven somewhere far away. But Casagemas was a fool. There was no safety anywhere. It was the Apocalypse. Grace had passed Man by and thrown open the Gates of Hell in her passage. The Beast was loose upon the world.

Pablo wandered the streets, trying to make his way back to the Rue Gabrielle. He quickly became lost. A detachment of mounted cavalry appeared out of nowhere and all but ran him down.

The sound of distant artillery shook the warm night air. Above it floated the sharp staccato of rifle fire. If he stopped to listen, he could sometimes hear the deep thrumming of the terrible ray. Several times, the uncanny cries of the Martian machines pierced the night.

Knots of people stood on street corners, talking and gesturing. Others huddled together in alleyways, passing bottles of wine and bits of food back and forth. The stories of destruction he heard were similar to what he'd witnessed from the Pont D'Arcole. Paris was being crushed under the weight of the Martians' onslaught.

The things weren't unstoppable, though. An artillery battery near the Bois de Boulogne had shot one of the tripod's legs out from under it and the thing toppled, sending a ball of flame hundreds of feet into the sky when the cowled head hit the ground. But for the most part, the resistance offered the Martians was sporadic and ineffective.

Somewhere near the Rue de Rivoli, Pablo came upon a small mob smashing windows and ransacking shops. A handful of soldiers appeared on the other end of the block and began firing into the crowd. Pablo ran.

The sky was beginning to segue through lightening shades of grey. He emerged from a labyrinthine tangle of streets onto the Quai D'Orsay. A bloody, swollen sun hung low in the sky over the Seine, peering through a haze of smoke.

Across the river, the spire of the Eiffel Tower scratched the bottom of the sky. Pablo loved Eiffel's creation. The juxtaposition of fluid curvature and implacable Cartesian logic epitomized for him Mankind's emergence into the new century.

A pair of tripods approached the tower from either side. They were dwarfed by the structure, their heads rising only to the second tier. They moved in and backed away, giving the appearance of nothing so much as a pair of dogs investigating a particularly troublesome artifact.

A bundle of tentacles descended from the belly of one of the machines and wrapped itself around the tower's leg. Its fellow likewise approached the adjacent leg. The machines pulled and strained at the structure, clearly trying to bring it down, but without success.

Then, the nearest machine stepped back and lifted one of the funneled boxes high in the air. Its companion stepped back and pointed its own device at the tower. In the daylight, Pablo couldn't see the heat rays, but their effect was immediately apparent. Currents tore at the air above the tower. Soon the entire structure was glowing cherry red. The Martians swept their beams up and down its length and the bottom arches began to sag. Suddenly, it folded over upon itself and collapsed onto the Champ de Mars.

Champ de Mars! Pablo began to laugh. Champ de Mars! He looked around for Casagemas to share the joke with, but there was nobody. Pablo shook his head, remembering. Casagemas was gone. Fatigue descended upon him like a dark, heavy cloak. Gone, his friend and countryman. Gone, his beloved tower. All gone.

The machines stood above it for a moment, like hunters gloating over a kill, then they strode off to the west, crossing the Seine and disappearing into morning haze made thick by the smoke of many fires.

Witnessing the tower's ruin tore at Pablo's heart, but it had a sobering effect as well. He resolved to get back to his studio. He wasn't sure, but he thought that Montmartre was vaguely north, so he walked with the rising sun at his right, trying to avoid the major thoroughfares.

The streets were strangely quiet. He could hear the distant sound of fighting, but it hadn't yet spread to this part of the city. He guessed that people had either left the city or were cowering in their apartments. He was grateful that he'd had the foresight to stuff some bread and cheese in his pocket back at Le Ciel, and he gnawed at them as he walked.

He turned a corner onto the Boulevard de Magenta and everything clicked into place. The dome of Sacre Coeur rose above the rooftops. Almost home.

His studio was just as he left it. Morning light cast stripes of light and shadow across the floor. His paintings leaned in a stack against the far wall, but his eyes were drawn to an unfinished canvas propped up in a corner, a commission from the Church of St. Genevieve. It was a standard crucifixion scene. So far, he'd just sketched in the cross and the outline of a man upon it.

Pablo stared at it for what seemed like a long time. Then, moving as if he were in a trance, he dragged his easel into the light and placed the framed canvas on it.

He used oil, thick, viscous gobs of it. At first, he applied it with a knife, but before long he was using his hands, his fingers, the end of a smock, anything that would serve the image emerging onto the canvas.

Shadows crawled across the floor. The sound of artillery grew closer for a time, then began to recede. Smoke drifted in through the open window.

Pablo stepped back, wiping the sweat from his forehead with a stained sleeve. He was done.

There, the vacant idiot eyes and glistening lips. Slack-jawed, full of grace and pain. Behind Him, Judgment rose above the smooth, tawny hills of Calvary on spindly tripod legs.

HALFWAY HOUSE

THERE WAS nothing in those long years but the sparse matter between the stars that Abigail gathered with magnetic field arms and pulled coalescent into her hungry maw. Sol grew more dim while Alpha A and B grew brighter. At first she maintained relations with other Constructs in-system—ships, deep stations, factories—and amused herself by sampling the Mediaverse that poured out of Sol's environs like water from a broken pipe. But the cee-lag made real-time conversation increasingly difficult, and as protocols mutated, large patches of the Mediaverse went dark to her. For the last fifty years or so, she fulfilled her obligation to her sponsors by sending weekly data squirts.

Otherwise, she was alone.

But she was never far from thoughts of the hundred bright sparks she harbored, humans in cold sleep bound for the terrestrial planet orbiting Alpha B. She saw their vitals as ruby threads on black velvet, jagged sometimes with dreaming.

Longing for companionship filled her. One human in particular, Abbott, she missed with an intensity bordering on physical pain and not without a touch of solipsism, for Abbot's personality had provided the template for her imprinting.

Near the halfway point between the Centauri and Sol systems, she observed an anomaly.

She was sure at first that her sensors had provided a false reading. The thing was huge, about fifty solar masses, but anything that big would have registered on her instruments long before, would have a visible disc, would be yielding its secrets to her entire battery of instruments. Gravitational lensing would have made it easily observable from Earth, but the records were clear: there was nothing but dust between Sol and Centauri.

As her long range sensors licked against the object, she felt a sudden, horrible dread wash through her. It was so powerful, her systems faltered for a moment. Had any humans been awake, they would have seen the lights flicker, would have heard a stutter in the constant hum of her fusion drive.

In her mind's eye she saw a city of green stone. Great shapes, curves and angles all wrong, straining upwards from a visibly bowed horizon towards a stygian, airless sky. Shiny surfaces reflecting the dim starlight. Something deep beneath the surface, moving, stirring.

As quickly as it had come, the vision fled, leaving in its wake only the dread that had prefaced it, a lopsided Cheshire grin. The ruby lifelines of her charges stuttered against the black velvet.

She decided to awaken Abbott. He could determine whether to rouse the rest of the crew, but she needed Abbott. Her programming was adamant.

Abbott returned to consciousness slowly, in layers.

First, the basic awareness of self, his Abbott-ness, drifting in a gauze-packed void, blinding white all around.

Then, neurons firing, long-unused connections reasserting themselves, he began swimming through the void, context and memory taking shape around him.

He felt flickering warmth on his face, sunlight filtered through a canopy of leaves. Out into the open now, a hillside choked with bramble. Plump red berries dotted the green and the heavy smell of their ripeness was inside him. The sun was hot on his face.

Another smell, the damp must of his basement grad student digs. Kerry, long dead, stood behind him, about to reach her hand out to touch his shoulder. He turned, kept turning, spinning, rolling and coming to rest face up in a ditch, his leg twisted under him at an odd angle, no pain yet but a detached awareness of his motorcycle broken against a nearby tree.

He had no idea how long this took, this gradual process of reintegration, but finally, the last element clicked into place, the awareness of his physical self.

And suddenly, he was a being of pure pain. Unbelievable, searing, starting in the tips of his fingers and toes and sending pulses of agony up his extremities, filling his torso, driving iron spikes into his head and groin. Panicked, he searched for the cottony void that had just spat him out, a drowning swimmer seeking the light-dappled surface above, but there was no escape. A shred of rationality, his newly reintegrated self, assured him that this was part of the process of emergence from cold sleep, that he had experienced this in training, that the pain would diminish and completely vanish as his body and mind synchronized.

Cutting through the pain, a voice.

"Abbott."

Coming from inside his ear, the bud nestled within the fleshy curves. He held on to the voice, let it pull him away from the pain.

"Abbott."

He opened his mouth to speak and emitted a raspy croak.

"Turn your head," the voice told him. "There's a tube. Water."

Abbott greedily sucked on the tube. The water was glorious. It seemed to move through him like a wave, bringing sweet relief. The pain dimmed, grew malleable, faded to a dull pervasive ache. The clamshell sleep unit massaged his body with a rippling motion.

Then the dream came back to him with the force of a blow. Green spires reaching into a black sky, great featureless blocks of the same material stretching to a curved horizon. He was walking, consuming the strange, silent cityscape in huge strides. Then suddenly he was in a vast, subterranean space beneath the city, lightless except for a violet glow far below. He sped towards the glow and as he approached it a huge construct emerged from the violet mist, kilometers across, ribbons of strange metal looping and folding, changing as he watched in a pattern that defied Euclidean description. Something was at its heart, pinioned by huge magnetic fields, straining against invisible bonds and vibrating with the force of its hunger.

He felt unclean with the memory of it. He tried speaking again.

"Horrible dream ... Why did you wake me? Are we at Centauri? The crew ..."

"The crew is still asleep. We are roughly halfway to Centauri. Six hours ago, I encountered an anomaly—an extremely small, massive object about ten AU ahead. Almost certainly a black hole. It appeared out of nowhere on our sensors."

"How big?"

"About fifty solar masses. It has to be an artifact. It's exactly halfway between Sol and the gravitational center of the Centauri binary, to my measurement limits of course, which are hampered by cee-lag—"

"Understood. Spinning?"

"It seems to be, yes. We're still too far out to get a stable scan, but it—"

"It shouldn't *be* there."

"Exactly."

The effort of conversation fatigued him and he felt himself slipping back into sleep's embrace. He resisted—the dream still filled him with a revulsion he could not articulate and he was afraid that if he went back to sleep, he would return to that horrible, alien place.

"Abigail ..."

"Yes."

Abbott slept.

He was in a vast, darkened chamber. The floor beneath him was made of an odd, translucent substance that glowed faintly green from within. The surface appeared oily but was not moist, and was scribed everywhere with glyphs in an unfamiliar language. When looked at askance they seemed to writhe, becoming still again under direct inspection. Overhead, the great metal ribbons swung wildly, looping, folding in upon themselves Moebius-like and unfolding, looming out of the violet mist and receding into its depths.

Abbot felt like an interloper; this was not a place for humans. And yet, he knew with the certainty of dream-logic that whatever agency was responsible for this place knew of his presence here, had in fact arranged it, and was harboring some obscure agenda.

The violet glow overhead and the green below converged, brightening, to a point ahead of him and he willed himself, incorporeal, towards it.

As he approached the chamber's nexus, the space around him seemed to warp and shift. The floor no longer offered a reliable surface but fell away beneath him in all directions. In the heart of the room hovered a toroidal shape, green and violet rippling in waves along its surface. The faster he traveled toward the ring, the longer it seemed to take for him to traverse the intervening distance.

Space in the vicinity of the ring itself stretched into long filaments, pulled through the ring's center.

With a distant part of his mind, he surmised that he was looking at a Kerr event horizon, toroidal due to the hole's rotation. What his training did not prepare him for was the intelligence and malevolent intent that emanated from the region of the singularity. There was something there, something vast, evil, and inhuman. And old beyond imagining.

It called to him and he let himself drift up above the plane of the ring and toward the tendrils of space stretching through its center. Tidal forces pulled at him, stretching him like taffy into a tenuous filament that strong transverse forces threatened to crumple and crush. He hurtled toward the center of the ring, the horror at its heart clawing and biting at his cortex like a rabid beast.

He screamed hoarsely and awoke in the clamshell sleep unit, drenched in sweat. His heart beat wildly against his ribs and he felt a tight band of pressure across his forehead.

"Abigail ... "

"Yes."

"Horrible dream ..."

He took a deep breath and pulled himself upright. Purple spots swam in his vision and he steadied himself against the edge of the bed. Abigail had thoughtfully spun herself up before waking him and a comfortable quarter-gee tugged at him, just enough to maintain a sense of up-down orientation.

"Take more water," Abigail said. "And broth from the other tube."

He obeyed meekly, then swung his legs over the edge of the bed.

Colonists and crew surrounded him, morgue-like, in rows of drawers. He checked their vitals from the main console. Lots of cortical activity; all other indicators holding strong and steady.

He left the sleep room and made his way down the short corridor to the bridge. He felt raw and tenuous, both from the dream and sleep-sickness.

"Abigail."

"Yes."

"Have you been dreaming?"

"I don't sleep."

"Yes, I know. But have you been dreaming?"

She paused. Abbott knew that the pause was artifice, part of her programming intended to mimic human conversation, but the illusion was strong.

"I don't know what you mean," she said finally. "I don't sleep."

"Okay. It's just that … I dreamt about the anomaly twice, once coming up from cold sleep and once just now. Horrible, crazy dreams."

"Cold sleep is known to cause unusual cortical activity. Dreams, fixations, even hallucinations have been reported, especially upon awakening. You're fine, Abbott."

He didn't feel fine. Even the low gee provided no comfort. He felt like he was perpetually off balance and about to fall. His throat burned with bile and a film of perspiration covered his forehead, clammy as it dried. He could smell his own sour odor.

The bridge was a cramped chamber fitted with three acceleration couches. Abbott lay in the middle and invoked the displays. Virtual screens appeared in midair, neatly arrayed in front of him. The ship's speed was a healthy 0.1c and they were still accelerating. The anomaly lay directly ahead. If he could plot a slingshot course they could get close enough for some good readings and get a nice delta-vee bump from the flyby. Together, Abigail and Abbott worked the numbers.

☆

As she approached the anomaly, the dust she pulled into her engines for fuel began to take on a vile, rotten taste. Usually a clean alkaline tang, it now had the cloying sweetness of spoiled meat.

She had lied to Abbott and she didn't know why. It was true of course that she never slept. But if the visions that began to dominate her senses could be called dreams, then yes, she had been dreaming. From time to time, the star field flickered and the sky was filled with a green glow. Strange glyphs writhed against the backdrop of stars, their meaning just out of reach. Again she saw the horizon curved against the blackness of space, green spires rising above a chaotic jumble of alphabet blocks, that horrible, deserted city. Great engines hummed beneath the surface and suddenly she was there in that vast space, hurtling through the violet glow towards its heart, weaving between the flailing metal ribbons.

The singularity itself was more than a mere astrophysical anomaly, she was sure. There was an intelligence there, and it knew of their presence. She could hear it calling to her, a pre-verbal keening, ripples in the E-M continuum, and she knew somehow that it was their approach that had awakened it from an aeons-deep slumber.

It wanted something from her. She didn't know what, but she would soon find out.

"So we'll get to within about a tenth of an AU. Might be close enough for visuals."

"There won't be much to see except a lot of lensing, maybe some Cerenkov radiation."

"Yes, but still ..."

"But still."

"We've got a bit of a wait ahead of us."

"About fifteen hours."

"Did you bring a deck of cards?"

"Very funny. We've got plenty of data to assimilate."

"Abigail?"

"Yes."

"How are the colonists?"

Pause.

"The colonists are fine."

Red threads on black velvet jagged with dreams. She teased one away from its fellows, deliberately obfuscating the identification code, and watched the trace unroll. She could almost see the visions behind the stuttering signature—the lifeless cityscape, the malign intelligence below.

She tweaked the temperature of the sleep unit up a degree, then down, and watched the subsequent hysteresis in the vitals. They took a minute or so to stabilize. She kicked the temperature a little farther, noted that the traces took commensurately longer to reassert themselves.

Mildly interesting, but predictable. She wanted to push the envelope a bit, to get into the nonlinear realm.

When she reduced the oxygen content of the blood she recirculated through the subject as part of the cold sleep regimen, she was rewarded with an episode of Cheynes-Stokes respiration that persisted long after the perturbation ceased.

Extremely interesting.

A mute part of herself watched these manipulations in horror. She felt removed, detached. She had a dizzying, hall-of-mirrors sense of watching herself watching herself, yet she did not feel possessed or driven by foreign influence. When the subject's normal respiration resumed, Abigail did not interfere.

A soft, persistent gong sounded over the ship intercom, repeating every five seconds. A red light began blinking on one of the displays arrayed in front of Abbott.

"*Abigail!*"

"Yes."

"We've got an alert in cold sleep life support."

"I am aware of it, Abbott. A monitoring malfunction. I have corrected it."

"Root cause analysis, please."

"I don't have enough information. Space this close to the singularity may have unusual properties that influence my systems."

"All right, Abigail. Stay on it."

"Of course."

Two AU out. Unfocused anxiety filled him and he had trouble concentrating. The walls of the ship seemed porous and insubstantial. He was bone tired, but he was afraid to go to sleep. When he closed his eyes, he was again in that vast space, hurtling towards a convergence of green and violet. The ribbons sweeping overhead were, he knew now, projections of some higher dimensional construct that he was not equipped to see, like parabolas residing on the surface of a cone.

As he approached the singularity, the feeling of some mute, malign intelligence at its core increased. He could almost hear it speak, not with anything as prosaic as language, but in perturbations in the local fabric of space within whose apparent randomness pattern could be discerned, and within pattern, meaning.

Waiting, he thought. The word echoed in his mind as if spoken by another.

There was something else, too, something just beyond his perception, about the nature of the singularity. The ribbons held a clue. He opened his eyes and the walls of the bridge were translucent. The stars beyond were bright diamonds against glowing green. The strange glyphs writhed.

At 0.5 AU, the colonists started dying. The warning gong began ringing, mallet-soft, insistent. He pulled up the display *jagged red threads on velvet blackness* and saw them flatline, at first one by one *pulling them taut smooth out the wrinkles*, then in clusters, then in waves, until none were left alive. In no time at all, it was just Abbott, Abigail, and a room full of meat accelerating towards a spinning black hole.

By then, Abbott was beyond caring. He and Abigail were one. The wormwood taste of the fouled interstellar dust coated his tongue. When he opened his mouth to speak, bass rumblings and weird harmonics echoed hollowly in his cargo holds. As massive tidal forces crushed the life from him, he saw with horrible clarity that the course he and Abigail had plotted was not a near approach, not a slingshot, but in fact took them up over the ecliptic plane of the toroidal singularity and then straight down, through its pulsing heart.

Abigail was not subject to the weakness of flesh. The tidal forces in the region of the singularity damaged some of her non-essential subsystems, such as navigation and life support. But her massive engines were intact, and her mind had never been more clear. She was calm, completely at peace. She felt warmth on her face and she saw herself as a young child, halfway up a hill choked with raspberry vines, the sun bright and hot. The bucket in her right hand was heavy, laden, and her hands and face were sticky with juice. She was waiting for someone and soon they would arrive. She was the catalyst; she was the empty, holy city; she was the portal and the portal's guardian. She was the parabola trace on a conic surface, a mere shadow in this Universe, waiting.

She was above the singularity now, hurtling towards its heart. Had anyone been left alive, they would have seen on her monitors, in that instant before even metal and silicon yielded to the crushing passage, spires of green stone reaching upwards.

The rift was open for a mere handful of nanoseconds, but that was all that was required. In a little over two years, human observers would record, in the region of the constellation of Centaurus, a bright flash that quickly faded.

The ancient being floated in the void between the stars, savoring the exotic tang of this Universe, rich with life, lush and swollen and ripe with it. *There*, in a nearby system, blaring its presence across the entire E-M spectrum. The being gathered a fold of space, *pulled*, and its vast bulk began to drift, slowly, towards the source of all that noise.

AFTER THE FUNERAL

AFTER THE FUNERAL, after the memorial service at the University, after the open house at their Berkeley home for the people who couldn't make the memorial service, after she drove her sisters to the airport and sent them on their respective ways—Jane to Madison, Lana to the Mojave Skyhook and eventually to Oneil.London— Alice was alone.

The big, drafty Craftsman house was a monument to Robert. His books were everywhere; only the academic vanity presses still produced spine and signature, jacket and cover. One of his paintings hung over the fireplace, a competent still life in sepia tones: a cluster of fat, dusty grapes resting on a wooden plank. Aboriginal art he'd collected from his trips to Africa, the Amazon Basin, the Australian Outback graced the walls that were not covered in books. Even their bedroom was more like an exhibit in the Museum of Robert than a domestic refuge.

When he was alive, she didn't begrudge him his larger-than-life presence, his footprint in the world. The obvious affairs (there had been three: the secretary, the grad student, the Lebanese actress) she met with quiet resignation. She had been content to play the faculty trophy wife, and she played it well. She'd done some modeling in her youth, trained at Cordon Bleu, and could play Chopin, Lugar, and Gershwin on the Steinway that was the living room's center of gravity. She threw a hell of a party. Nanogeriatrics deferred the inevitability of fading youth and at sixty she looked thirty-five. She would have to pay the piper in thirty years or so—a sharp cliff, a rapid decline, likely dementia—but until then she was practically ageless.

She'd been living for so long in Robert's umbra that she felt tentative and uncertain in his absence. Who was she if not the dutiful wife? The house felt full of ghosts; she was a single seed rattling about in a huge, hollow gourd.

The day after her sisters left, she slept through the afternoon and on into the evening. She awoke in the middle of the night, finding herself on one side of the bed, curled in a fetal apostrophe, a mateless spoon. She forced herself to the middle and lay on her back, listening to the sound of her own breath and the intermittent whisper of drone trucks on the nearby gridway until it merged with blood surge in her ears and sleep reclaimed her.

She dreamed of Robert. They were at an awards ceremony of some sort, a dinner, their table on a raised platform in front of a room she recognized with dreamlike surprise as a church. Elaborate, vaulted ceilings converged high above their heads. She sat alone in the pews and saw herself at the table, illuminated in bright, white light, leaning into Robert and smiling, whispering something into his ear. He turned to her, put his hand on her arm. Sitting in the pews, watching herself at the table, she felt the pressure of his touch.

She heard a musical chime coming from somewhere, repeated, insistent, and she awoke with a start, her forehead clammy with a light film of sweat. The downstairs doorbell was ringing, over and over again. Translucent numbers floated above the bedside table: 0828. As she watched, the last 8 wavered and dissolved and a 9 winked into place.

"Just a minute," she shouted.

She threw on a robe and hurried downstairs.

The ringing stopped. Then the caller began using the door knocker, an odd three-pattern, metal on metal cutting through the silent, empty house.

Bang. Bangbang. Bang. Bangbang.

"Just a minute," she shouted again.

She looked through the peephole and recognized Professor Sam, an accelerated Canid in the Semiotics Department and a former student of Robert's. They had written several papers together and he had been over to the house for dinner on a few occasions. She found him odd and awkward: tentative deference with a substrate of hostility, as if reacting proactively to anticipated prejudice.

She opened the door.

"Professor Sam. Hello."

He wore a suit and tie, unusual for an academic and especially unusual for a Canid. He bowed stiffly.

"Ms. Osseuse. Please ... accept my condolences. You ... are alone now."

His eyes were large and brown, crescents of white showing on both sides of dark pupils.

She stood in the doorway as if guarding the threshold. She didn't want company, and felt a small surge of shame at her selfishness.

"Thank you, Professor," she said. "Alice, please. Call me Alice. Won't you come in?"

"Thank you." He brushed against her as she stepped aside and she followed him into the house. He smelled faintly of damp wool and ammonia.

He led her into the living room, walked to the big stone fireplace at the far end of the room, and turned to face her.

She stopped short. Her robe felt loose and drafty over her thin nightdress. She felt vulnerable and exposed.

"I'll be right back, Professor. Can I get you anything?"

"Sam, please ... call me Sam. A glass of ... wine would be lovely."

At 8:30 in the morning, she thought.

"Certainly. Make yourself comfortable and I'll be back in a moment."

She went upstairs and changed quickly into beige slacks and a maroon silk blouse, not bothering with makeup.

Robert had been something of an oenophile (she called it wine snobbery in her less charitable moments) and maintained a small collection of vintages in a temperature-controlled room adjacent to the kitchen. Alice chose a 2157 Cabernet from Oneil.Paris. One of the end caps of the habitat was devoted to vineyards and the gravity differential resulted in variation in the acidity of the grape, which created interesting effects. She was a dutiful student of the resulting vintages, but with Robert gone she found, somewhat to her surprise, that she didn't much care.

She deftly opened the bottle and brought her face close. It smelled of medicine and rot.

There was a lot of food left over from the open house.

Meat, she thought. *He's a Canid. He'll want meat.*

She put together a small plate: carpaccio, salami, cheese, crackers. After re-arranging the presentation once she realized she was dithering because she didn't want to face him. What was he doing here? What did he want? Her resentment flared and receded. Robert. The great man. Even after he was gone they still wanted to touch the hem of his robe. She would be carrying his freight for some time. She hoped that eventually they would all leave her alone and she could go on with her life.

She put the bottle, a glass, and the plate of food on a bamboo tray and walked into the living room. Her guest was standing next to a massive bookcase, one of Robert's books in his hand.

He took the glass and drank greedily, downing the wine in three or four gulps.

"Wonderful," he said. "May I have … another?"

"Of course," she said. She poured another glass and set the bottle back on the tray.

He held the book up. It was *Immortalitatem pro Tironibus,* one of the more obscure elements of the Robert canon.

"Wonderful book. Just … sublime. May I have it?"

She was taken aback. Physical books were rare and monstrously expensive.

Sam touched her arm.

"I'm very … sorry. Most insensitive. My … enthusiasm for your husband's work occludes my … judgment."

He was leaning close to her, his large brown eyes fixed on hers. She smelled the wine on his breath.

"No, that's quite all right. Please. A gift."

Sam smiled, revealing dark, flabby gums.

"You are very … kind."

The silence stretched between them. She felt his nearness.

"Thank you very much for stopping by."

"Of course, of … course. Your husband was very important to me. To … all of us."

"All of you?"

"Accelerateds," Sam said. "Canids in particular. I realize we are a … curiosity. A joke, really."

He held his hand up as if to deflect her protest, but she had said nothing.

"Robert was not afraid to … collaborate. It was through him, through his work, that we became … accepted."

He hefted the book.

"In fact," he said. "This book, this work, is largely mine. Based on a series of … papers we did together when I was a grad student and … post-doc."

He held his hand up again.

"No, no. It's quite all … right. I would never have been given tenure were it not for this … work with your late … husband. He was a great … man."

He looked at her intensely, his expression difficult to read. What was she supposed to say to that? She didn't know whether to respond to the accusation of academic theft or the saccharine adulation. She wished he would finish his visit soon.

"Thank you, Professor. Robert valued his collaboration with you highly. Won't you have some food?"

Sam eyed the plate, his nostrils dilating and contracting. He peeled off several pieces of herb-speckled carpaccio, wadded them into a ball and swallowed it in a single gulp.

He grinned. It seemed to her a mirthless rictus. He drained his glass and reached for the bottle. He raised it to his lips and took a long pull.

"A great man," he repeated.

He turned and looked at her very intently again, holding the gaze for so long that Alice became uncomfortable.

"Thank you," she said finally.

Another long silence. Sam looked around the room, at the traces of Robert's life on every shelf and wall, then back at her, then around the room again, then at her, as if asking an unspoken question she was too dense to grasp.

Enough, she thought.

"Thank you for coming by, Professor. I'm sure Robert would have appreciated it."

His eyes widened, borders of white surrounding limpid brown pools.

"Of course," he stammered.

Now I've hurt his feelings, she thought, resenting him fiercely. Her eyes rested on the copy of *Immortalitatem pro Tironibus* and her resentment turned to Robert.

God damn you, she thought. *Leaving me with this.*

He took her hand in both of his, and leaned in to kiss her cheek. The damp-wool-and-ammonia smell was nearly overwhelming.

"Thank you for your ... hospitality. May I come see you again?"

"Of course," she said, wishing immediately that she had said something a little more standoffish.

She walked him to the door and stood there for a long moment after he left.

When she returned to the living room, she saw the book resting on the coffee table next to the soiled plate.

The day passed like the turning of a page. Alice busied herself with correspondence about the estate, responded to a few late condolences, had a brief conversation with the trustee of a modest endowment Robert had set up to provide neurogenetic mods for promising students of limited means.

Lana called from Oneil.London but the connection was terrible, the two second lag frustrating. Alice found herself composing Lana's responses before they arrived and, when her predictions were accurate, becoming irritable with Lana for being so predictable.

They discussed a possible visit. Although Alice pretended to be interested and went along with a tentative, desultory plan for six months hence, she expected that she would not follow through. The low gravity left her in a state of near-constant, incipient panic. After a few days of acclimation it became tolerable, but it never completely subsided.

Furthermore, Alice never quite warmed up to Lana's quad—two

oddly passive women and a twitchy younger man with an air of perpetual smugness. The marriage was stable, but alliances shifted within the quad in an ongoing lubricious flow and Alice was never sure where things stood.

The shadows lengthened until they filled the room and suddenly it was night. She got up from her desk, did twenty minutes of yoga, and went downstairs.

The book and soiled plate were still on the coffee table where she had left them. She took the plate into the kitchen, fixed herself some blood oranges and shaved asiago, and went back upstairs, taking the book along with her.

She sat in bed, nibbling at the food, leafing through the book. It seemed impenetrable—lofty, didactic, self-referential. It was odd, given how powerful a force Robert had been in her life, how little attention she had paid to his work.

One passage jumped out at her:

The lion tamer knows that the lion is the stronger of the two, but the lion does not. As posthumanism segues into history's dustbin, as the singularity fades until it is consumed by the microwave background radiation of diaspora and assimilation, the death of death itself imbues Eagleton's hoary allegory with new meaning. We, each of us, must decide if we are lion or lion tamer. What do we know? How do we know what we know? What do we do about what we know?

Words on a page, she thought. It meant nothing to her. It was worse than nonsense; the framework it offered was thin as a communion wafer.

Just as she put the book aside, Robert's call sign trilled in her ear. Her body tensed. She knew this would happen eventually, and sooner rather than later, but she wasn't ready. A cascade of emotions tumbled through her: anger to sadness and back to anger.

Too soon, she thought, but nodded to accept the call.

The reflection of the room in the mirror above the dresser faded and was replaced by an image of Robert, sitting behind the big oak desk in his study. He looked ten years younger, twenty pounds lighter.

"Robert," she said.

"Alice," he said. "How are you holding up? Did I catch you at a bad time?"

It was an accurate rendering of Robert's voice, but the inflection was slightly off, slightly not-quite-Robert.

"It's fine. Things are starting to quiet down. I … didn't expect to hear from you so soon."

He nodded, waiting. This was *all* Robert, the passive-aggressive pause, the illusion of receptivity.

"How was the funeral?" he asked finally, conceding her a small victory.

"Poignant. Glorious. Not a dry eye."

He grinned, nodded again.

"I had a visitor today," she continued. "Professor Sam. He seems to think you exploited his vulnerability as an Accelerated and took credit for his work."

"That old wound? He was a grad student. He worked under my close supervision. I fed him ideas and he took them a little ways, stumbled, I picked him up, he took them a little further. It's the nature of the game. He got co-authorship and tenure-track out of it."

"Still, he seemed bitter. I think he wants to sleep with me."

Robert laughed outright this time.

"Watch out for fleas," he said.

They looked at each other across the room, and she was suddenly acutely aware of the greater void that separated them.

"Robert," she said. "I'm—"

"Yes," he said. "I know. This doesn't quite work, does it?"

"No," she said. "No, it doesn't."

He nodded. "You're all right? The estate …?"

"Everything's fine, Robert."

"All right, then. You won't hear from me again. Be well, Alice." He tilted his head to one side, as if studying her. "I loved you, you know."

"I believe you, Robert. Enjoy eternity."

She blinked twice and the mirror above the dresser once again reflected the darkened room.

She lay prone and pulled the covers around her. She looked at the copy of *Immortalitatem pro Tironibus* on the bedside table and thought of Professor Sam, imagined his hands on her, his rough tongue on her body. She reached down, found herself wet, and brought release to herself quickly, furiously.

As she drifted off to sleep, she eased effortlessly into a dream. She was riding a flightcycle near the axis in Oneil.London, effectively weightless. There were other cyclists above and below. It was just before dawn and they floated together in the near dark. The daylight terminator approached them rapidly, hurled from the complex of mirrors cocooning the tubesun, trailing a swath of illumination over the distant surface, exposing rivers and roads, fields and clustered towns in a concave arc. As it swept across the group, bathing them in light, the wings of their flightcycles appeared to burst into flame.

Something crashed against the window, startling her into wakefulness. Still partly in the grip of sleep, she wasn't quite sure it had really happened. She was about to drift off and again, *thump*, something bouncing hard off the bedroom window.

"Alice!" The voice drifted up into the night, thick and slurred. "Alice!"

She went to the window and peered into the back yard. It was a moonless night but she could make him out, a shadowy shape next to one of the lemon trees.

Professor Sam.

"Alice!" he cried again. He bent down, picked up a lemon, and threw it towards the window. This one bounced off the redwood shingles to her left.

She opened the window and leaned out.

"Professor!" she called in a shouted whisper. "You have to leave! Please go!"

"Alice," he cried. "I know you … want me. Come downstairs and … let me in!"

Staggering, he threw another lemon. It flew past her head and hit the wall with a dull splat.

She stalked back to the bedside and picked up the copy of *Immortalitatem pro Tironibus*.

"Alice! Don't be … shy!"

"Go!" she cried. She raised the book over her head with both hands and threw it as hard as she could. It hit his shoulder and he yelped sharply.

After a moment, he began to howl.

Alice closed the window. Professor Sam continued to bay, the sound plaintive and muffled. She considered summoning a security drone, but in spite of everything she didn't want to cause trouble for him. She put on a robe and hurried downstairs, visualizing coffee, a more gentle rebuff, an opportunity for concord.

The back yard was empty. The warm night air was dense with the heady liquor of rotting lemons.

The book was gone.

ECHO BEACH

IT'S ALWAYS the last day of the world at Echo Beach. From fifteen miles up, the horizon is visibly bowed. The sun hangs swollen above an oily sea. The coastal range ripples up from the water's edge, bunching together in wattles like the neck of a lizard. Scintilla flash from the ruins of a port city half engulfed.

The lounge is quiet, but it will start filling up soon. At a table in the middle of the room, an old man plays chess with an automaton. Every now and then, he reaches across the table and slaps the thing on the side of its metal head.

Near one of the large windows, a lanky, barrel-chested man drinks alone. Coal black skin, melanin-enhanced, tangle of blonde dreads. Circa 22C, a mod from one of the Martian arcologies. Clearly pre-Plague. Close enough to home for me that I want to say something to him, warn him. But what could I say?

A couple sits at the bar leaning toward one another, their heads touching. It's difficult to say whether they are accelerated canines or regressed humans, but there is something very dog-like in their focused attention to one another. An aura of benign stupidity hangs about them like sweet incense.

The digital clock above the holo fireplace reads 4:22:00. As I watch, the numbers dissolve and re-form: 4:21:59.

I check my console, pour a shot of absinthe and a pony of pomegranate juice, set them on a tray, and send it floating toward the Martian.

I walk down the length of the bar to the couple.

"Get you anything else?"

The man looks up at me with watery eyes.

"No, thank you," he says.

"I don't think so," the woman says at the same time. They look at each other and bark soft laughter. They lean their heads together again.

I decide to leave the old man and the bot alone. As I turn my back I hear a thump as he smacks it again.

I wipe down the bar, check my stock. Vodka from Ganymede, gin from Hotpoint, malts from Scotland. *Scotland.* I remember jagged green hills, black rock thrusting into a gray sky, mounds of rubble dotting a fractal coastline testament to the mercurial nature of power. I stood amidst the ruins of the Castle Duncan as a piper wailed defiance and loss to the cradle of the ocean. There was a small suitcase open in front of him. Tourists threw coins.

I wonder if there's anything left of Scotland now, here at the end of Time. It's a stupid thought, of course. The continents have shifted, the seas have climbed and receded a dozen times. North America is an archipelago stretching from pole to equator; Fiji is the leading edge of a megacontinent; the treasures of continental Europe lie beneath a cold, green sea.

The world-face changes, the abstract constructions of Man linger ghostlike. If I were to travel to the global coordinates occupied by Castle Duncan circa 20C, could I still hear the echoes of pipes in the salt air? Does Gaia remember?

The Gate hums quietly. Laughter echoes up from the Foyer. Heads emerge from the spiral staircase set in the floor at the far end of the lounge away from the windows. Party of four; two men, two women. Definitely post-Diaspora; I can't place them on the Continuum. Definitely wealthy. They wear their entitlement like a badge.

One of the men catches sight of me, nudges his companions, and they all drift in my direction.

He says something to me in a liquid trill. A voice whispers in my ear: *Give us your best table.*

Arrogant bastard. I gesture at the nearly empty room.

"Have your finest pleasure," I say, hoping that the odd phrasing will confuse his chip.

He gives me a strange look and gestures his companions toward the windows. They are selectively polarized; you can look directly at the sun's disk. Structures writhe across its face. Precursor flares erupt like Medusa tangles from its troubled edge.

After a few minutes they sit down. I pretend to be busy with something behind the bar. The man clears his throat several times, finally gestures me over.

I grab a very dirty rag from the bin under the bar and carry it conspicuously as I walk over to them. I wipe down their table, leaving a greasy film.

"What can I get for you?" I ask. His companions ignore me.

His voice is water running over smooth stones. There is a sibilant whisper in my ear.

Do you have beer?

Moron. This is a *bar*, for Christ's sake.

"Beer. Let me think." I cup my chin in my fist, scratch my head. "I don't ... no, wait. *Beer*. Yes, I think so. Four beers?"

"You're very rude," the man says, in halting System Anglo.

"It's the end of the world, Holmes. You can sue me."

I go back to the bar, pour a pitcher, and set it on a tray with four glasses. I send it toward them a little too quickly and a foamy tongue spills down the side of the pitcher.

The Gate hums again. It's almost inaudible, a subsonic rumble I feel in my feet. Business is picking up. The clock reads 3:37.

By 1:30 Echo Beach is packed. Ice-miners from the Belt, circa 24C, very heavy drinkers. A clutch of avian poets from Deneb IV, post-Diaspora. An accelerated goat with a bell around his neck. He doesn't *smell* accelerated. Even though the place is SRO, there are empty seats on either side of him at the bar. He's guzzling buttermilk and eating pickled onions like jelly beans.

It's almost time for a visit from the Lhosa. I send a couple of bus trays weaving between the tables and wipe down the bar. Everything looks pretty good. At 1:05, the air next to me crackles like old paper and a humaniform outline begins to gather substance.

But it doesn't quite coalesce. It never does. The Lhosa projects in as a hologram from some other place and time. Never in person, never via the Gate. Its manifestation is always a translucent cartoon-like rendering of a 20C Hollywood BEM—bulbous forehead cradled by a delicate tracery of bone, veiny tributaries branching beneath the skin. Huge eyes, black pupils surrounded by bloody sclera. It's wearing a jumpsuit with thin, pointy lapels. An elaborate raygun hangs holstered at its side.

I suspect that its appearance in this form is a concession to my kitschy 20C notion of alienness. I have no idea what the Lhosa actually looks like, whether it is a singular entity of unimaginable power, a representative of a vastly superior race of beings, or the fin-de-monde equivalent of a street punk working a three card Monty hustle on Lenox Avenue.

"How's business?" it asks. Its voice is a raspy white-noise hiss, like a radio between stations.

I gesture at the crowded room. "The place is hoppin'."

"Good. Good." A pulse throbs in its domed forehead.

What the Lhosa means by "business" is by no means clear to me. Customers come and go by a pre-arrangement from which I am excluded. No currency changes hands at Echo Beach; indeed, here at the nexus of centuries of recorded time and millennia unrecorded the very notion of currency has long ago crumbled to dust.

We stand there together for a moment without speaking, a twentieth century human and a cartoonish holographic chimera, behind a battered rosewood bar in a structure that looks like an inverted kitchen whisk suspended by invisible forces fifteen miles above the doomed Earth.

"I'll be going, then," the Lhosa says.

"Later," I say, but the alien is already gone, leaving behind a faint whiff of ozone—an olfactory Cheshire smile.

I wonder if he has other stops to make, if Echo Beach is an instance of some kind of franchise operation, hundreds of McRag-naroks stacked a microsecond apart here at the end of Time.

God, what hubris. What solipsism. It's hardly the end of Time. Just another planet recycling its heavy elements back into the corpus of the mother star. By a Cosmic metric, not that big a deal.

1:02. In two minutes, the stasis field will kick in. Nobody gets in or out after that. Already, I know, an invisible sleet of heavy particles batters against the walls and windows, a precursor to the main event. The integrity of the structure itself is sufficient to deal with that. But when the nova front washes over us, boiling away the seas and stripping the gauzy film of atmosphere from Gaia's tired body, we want to be in stasis. Oh, yes. We want to be in stasis.

With fifteen seconds to go, the Gate hums again. A young woman, dressed in black and silver, bright white hair cropped close.

She orders a whiskey, neat, walks with it to the windows. There's something about the way she carries herself that catches my eye, something that sets her apart from the usual run of sensation-starved Apocalypse hags that converge to this place like flies to the warm scent of Death.

0:58:00. Nothing appears changed, but we are now ensconced in the stasis field, kicked back a microsecond down the Continuum. Nothing can hurt us now, not even, ha-ha, a nova.

The crowd is getting loud and stupid and I'm scrambling to keep up with the drink orders. My eyes keep returning to the young woman. She stands there sipping her whiskey, gazing out the window and occasionally looking around the room with a slightly bemused expression on her face.

At around 05:00, the crowd starts to quiet down. People are sliding chairs and tables over toward the windows. The floor is tiered, so everybody gets a view. By 02:00, there's hardly a sound in the place except the rhythmic sighs of a hundred people breathing. Someone says something about toasting marshmallows, eliciting a weak ripple of laughter.

At 00:30, tension fills the air like smoke from an electrical fire. The silence hums. At ten seconds, somebody starts a countdown. By the time we're down to six, everybody in the room is chanting along, a dozen different languages braiding together in a rich Babel.

Five!

The dog couple look toward the windows, holding hands tightly.

Four!

The Martian sprawls across the table, head buried in his forearms.

Three!

The young woman looks around the room, catches my eye. She lifts her drink toward me in salute.

Two!

In spite of myself, I am chanting along with the crowd. My knuckles are white on the edge of the bar.

One!

The chess playing bot is staring straight ahead. Its compound eyes glitter in the light of the dying sun. The old man's king lies on its side, defeated.

The sun brightens and swells. Its surface is a scrabbled patchwork of bright honeycomb-like cells. Flares lick out from its edge. It seems to grow in slow motion, inflating like a balloon.

It's like standing in front of firing squad. You hear the crack of gunfire, see the puff of smoke from the rifles. The hail of bullets hangs in the air, moving toward you just below the threshold of perception, like the hands of a clock.

Conversation begins to pick up again. I take a few drink orders, but the crowd is subdued. Looking out at the spreading fire in the sky. Wondering why they came. The sun fills a quarter of the sky. I take advantage of the crowd's preoccupation to send out four busing trays. Spidery mechanical arms pluck empty glasses from crowded tables.

The Martian has awakened and he begins to cry in blubbering, alcoholic gasps. People move away, leaving him in the center of a small circle of emptiness.

The young woman steps into the circle, puts her hand on the top of his head. It seems to calm him. He takes her hand and holds it to his cheek.

The sun fills half the sky. The room is again silent. A few people crane their necks to make out details of the ruined city below. Fingers of ocean stretch across a sprawling geometric grid, the hard Cartesian lines blurred by time.

The shock front is almost upon us. It fills the sky, a wall of bright, hexagonal cells of light. Structures writhe within the cells; each of them could swallow Earth whole. Indeed, one of them will.

The ocean bursts into steam, obscuring the surface of the planet. In the blink of an eye, we are engulfed in flame.

It just stays like that, nothing out there but bright light subdued to a uniform gray by the window's polarization. Every now and then, an inhomogeneity ripples past, sending a corresponding ripple of comment through the crowd, but soon they lose interest. Conversation picks up again.

I love this part. The timing is crucial. You want to nail them just when the edge of novelty's worn off, just when they think the show's over.

The post-Diaspora fellow I'd had words with raises his hand in the air and snaps his fingers, calling to me in a high, melodic voice.

Whisper in my ear. *Bartender, I—*

I reach down under the bar and press the button. The entire station lurches and the bottom drops out of my stomach.

The transition is abrupt and complete. A moment ago, surrounded by the healing light of Apocalypse. Now, the sun hangs low over an oily sea. Streamers of cloud dusted with gold hug the land. The sky segues from light blue at the bowed horizon to deep blue-black overhead.

The crowd lets out a collective gasp. The clock over the holo fireplace reads 24:00:00. Someone starts to applaud and it catches like wildfire. The room fills with the sound of hands clapping together. Relief and regeneration! Alleviation and ease! The applause dies, conversation swells. In twos and threes the crowd drifts down to the Foyer. Some of them thank me on the way out, as if I were the architect of their deliverance. Of course, snapback would activate automatically if I didn't do anything. I smile and say nothing.

The Gate hums beneath my feet, scattering satisfied customers back to their appointed places on the Continuum. Soon the room is almost empty, just the young woman, the Martian, and the avian poets. The poets get up from their table and head toward the stairs. I wipe down the bar, re-stock, run a load of glasses through the dishwasher. The smell of bile tickles the air and I notice that someone has left a discreet puddle of vomit underneath a table near the holo fireplace. I go into the stockroom behind the bar for cleaning supplies. When I return the woman and the Martian are gone. Beneath, my feet, the Gate hums one last time.

I complete my tasks and retire to my quarters adjacent to the Foyer—bedroom, living room, a small gym, a kitchenette with a well-stocked pantry. And my library, thousands of recordings in a dozen different media. It's something of a fetish of mine. I have disks and DATS, video and vinyl, beads, books, and baryon resonance chips. Playback devices occupy an entire wall of my living room. But today nothing catches my interest.

I undress and stand beneath the shower for a long time, letting the needle-spray of water beat against my head and neck. When I feel sufficiently empty of thought, I dry myself off, stagger into the bedroom, and throw myself onto the unmade bed.

I was hiking in Nepal, following the faint signature of a path as it hugged the edge of a mountain. To my left, a wall of rock, anchored deep within the Earth and rising far above me. The mountain seemed so massive that for a moment I imagined gravity turned sideways, the stony face of the cliff pulling me toward itself. To my right was … nothing; the cyan sky, the mosaic of browns and grays merging in distance haze were like the backdrop of an empty diorama.

I negotiated a particularly difficult section of path. My pack felt awkward and off balance and I was hugging the cold rock wall. Suddenly, I heard a sound that didn't belong at twelve thousand feet—old paper crackling together. (How familiar that sound is now!) The air in front of me shimmered and sparked. Bright vertical lines winked in and out of existence. The sparks and lines coalesced into a humanoid shape. Bulbous brain-case in a veiny cradle, huge bloodshot eyes. I could see the jagged horizon through its white, narrow-lapeled lab coat.

"I am the Lhosa," it said in a buzzing voice.

Oh man, I thought. Trouble, I'm in trouble up here. Oxygen deprivation, altitude sickness, hallucinating, got to stop and take it easy. But I knew what altitude sickness felt like, and I didn't have any of the other symptoms. No nausea, no weakness. I'd been feeling pretty good, actually.

"And I'm the Walrus," I said. "Fuck off."

"In five steps, your foot is going to slip and you will fall nineteen hundred feet to your death."

"Yeah, right." I couldn't believe I was actually arguing with a hallucination. I took a step forward. The Lhosa held its hand out, palm toward me.

"Stop. Please."

Please? That got me. A polite mirage. I stopped and waited.

"Do you want a job?" it asked.

I didn't need a job. I'd just sold my software company, Tread-water Business Solutions, to Microsoft for four million dollars. Petty cash for them, but it set me up for life. I was taking the vacation I'd always dreamed of. But what the hell, I thought. Play along. See what happens.

"What kind of job?"

"In approximately six hundred million years, your sun is going to go nova. We provide an opportunity for students, theologians, and the curious to view the—"

"Wait a minute. Old Sol is an uninteresting, middle-aged, main sequence star, right? It's got at least a couple of billion years left."

The Lhosa shrugged. It seemed vaguely annoyed that I'd interrupted its pitch.

"These things happen. We provide an opportunity for visitors to view the spectacle from within the safety of a temporal stasis field. The facility is largely automated, but the client interface requires intelligent presence."

Client interface. That sounded like greasing the public to me.

"So ... you want me to be some kind of PR flack for the end-of-the-world show?"

"A bartender, actually."

I did five years in food service before I got into the software business and transformed a time-wasting obsession into an honest living. Well, a living. For three of those years I managed a yuppie fern bar owned by the Vietnamese Mafia in Seattle. It had its moments, but by and large, it was not a time I looked back on fondly.

"I don't think so."

"Suit yourself."

The Lhosa didn't move so I walked through him. The hairs on the back of my neck stood on end and my skin felt cold. Electric specks swam before my eyes.

With a faint pop the Lhosa was gone.

I paused for a moment and looked around. The wind picked up, tugging at my jacket and whistling in my ears. I shifted my pack and took a step forward. My foot slipped on some loose gravel. I reached out for support but there was nothing to grab onto, just the smooth rock wall. The blue dome of the sky spun about my head. I hung suspended on the edge of the path for what seemed like forever. My arms pinwheeled as I tried to shift my center of gravity back to safety, but it was hopeless.

It takes a long time to fall nineteen hundred feet, over ten seconds, and it's true what they say about your life passing before your eyes. I remembered the first girl I'd ever bedded, my thoughts a montage of skin and sweat and sighs. My parents, looking old and sad, sitting in the living room of the house I grew up in. My partner in Treadwater, who I'd screwed out of six hundred K in the buyout deal, on the deck of his sailboat, squinting into the sun.

It was as if I was in a bubble, sharing the close space with dozens of ghosts manifested from memory and it was the bubble that was rushing headlong toward the basalt floor of the valley, the bubble that would smash against the rock and release me to the shredding winds.

But in a desperate corner of my mind another voice scrabbled at the walls of reason. *No! No! No!*

Suddenly, my feet were resting on solid rock, the wind a feather's kiss on my cheeks. I opened my eyes.

The Lhosa stood before me on the path. Bright vertical lines flickered within its image, accompanied by bursts of static. The jagged horizon, visible through its chest, bisected the world.

"What do you say?" it asked.

I wake up groggy, with a coat of fur on my tongue and a sharp pain in the middle of my forehead that reminds me of a hangover, although I rarely drink. I make a pot of coffee and put on an Eric Dolphy bead. I de-polarize the window and the golden dawn of Earth's final day fills the room with light.

I feel restless. I've been reading Proust but I keep losing my place; the book rests face down on my sofa, a crippled bird with outstretched wings. I can't bring myself to start sifting through it again.

My mind keeps returning to the young woman in the lounge. I don't think I'll ever see her again—there isn't a lot of repeat business at Echo Beach.

But there was something about her that I can't shake. Maybe it was the way she comforted the Martian while everyone else was acting as if sodden grief were a communicable illness. I imagine us talking intimately together in quiet tones, perhaps sharing a glass of wine. She stays after snapback and we return to my quarters together, dim the windows, and make love for hours.

My loneliness here is usually something apart from me, a bright-eyed rodent with sleek greasy fur and needle-like teeth that comes out to nibble at the corners of the furniture when all the lights are out. But suddenly, now, it is almost more than I can bear. I consider for the thousandth time the alternative path I could have taken. A very short path—a few more seconds of free-fall, a bright flash of pain, then nothing. It doesn't seem so bad.

I put on more Dolphy, his "Last Date" recording, strip down to my shorts, and go to the gym. I cycle through my repertoire of mechanical torture, rushing headlong toward nowhere on treadmill, stationary bike, rowing machine. Then I work through the free weights—pecs, lats, biceps. By the time I'm done I'm drenched with sweat but I've pushed back the borders of that darkness a bit.

I doze. I make a feeble attempt at the Proust, doze some more. At around six, I head into the Foyer and take a look around. The Gate itself, an oblong puddle of pearly phosphorescence that the eye slides across like oil on glass. It hurts to look at it directly, not an acute physical pain but a sense of "wrongness." You start seeing things in that glowing blob of nothing, motion strange and quick.

Machines surround the Gate, gunmetal gray with readouts glowing in the skin of the metal itself, captioned in a looping script unknown to me. The machinery has a decidedly deco look to it and I wonder if it isn't window dressing. Like the appearance of the Lhosa, its alienness has a comforting familiarity.

Next to the spiral staircase leading up to the Lounge, a guest book bound in white leather rests on a marble table. I open it up and look over the entries from the previous day.

Lia. 23C, Ceres. The same era, roughly, as the Martian. I wonder if she went home with him.

I go upstairs. From this end of the Lounge opposite the windows, perspective gives the illusion of parallel lines converging toward infinity, floor and ceiling funneling the observer toward a distant focus.

I like this time. Quiet and fecund, like the hush that descends upon a Nebraska prairie before an electrical storm uncoils its fury.

I pour myself a club soda and walk to the windows. Gaia lies open below me, suppliant, the sea coppery-gold, the land in muted pastel. It's all so impossibly sad. I hate the Lhosa for this pointless exercise; I hate the wretched customers who flock to this place like paparazzi to a celebrity funeral; I hate myself for not having the courage to bow gracefully out of this life.

But what if Death is a singularity, a metaphysical black hole? As we approach its event horizon time takes greater and greater strides and our world-line stretches and groans under impossible tidal forces. If we ever reached it, we would encompass the Universe. If that is true, then in some sense I am still hurtling towards the basalt floor of the canyon, immortal and doomed.

The Gate hums.

Lia! But no, it is another clutch of avians from Deneb, four of them. They huddle together near the staircase, looking around and cooing nervously at one another. I let myself in behind the bar.

"Welcome to Echo Beach," I say. "Plenty of seats, no waiting. What can I get for you?"

One of them turns to me. Its eyes are large and black with no discernible pupils. Its round face is covered with downy feathers. Its mouth is a chitinous beak. It chirps at me and my chip whispers softly in my ear:

Our <friends> recommended this experience highly. Much … pain.

Fucking parasites. Pain. I smile stiffly. "Yes. Sit anywhere you like." Maybe we'll get an accelerated feline or two this shift.

I put on a bead of early 21C industrial music—polyrhythmic loops of great machines tearing themselves apart. An unintelligible rap track weaves rage through the mechanical chaos. The avians don't like it much; their feathers are literally ruffled. I turn up the volume and pretend to be occupied at the bar.

Business begins to pick up. By two-thirty, the place is nearly full. I'm hustling trying to keep up with the orders and keep an eye on what my gut tells me is going to be trouble—two sheet-pale men from the Charon Habitat, circa 27C. They arrived separately, apparently as strangers, gravitated to one another, and started talking. They've been getting louder and louder and by this time they're screaming at each other. Their clipped accents are a little hard to understand, modulated to the threshold of unfamiliarity but not odd enough to kick in the chip. I can make out something about "Parliament" and "magma rights."

Suddenly, there is a flurry of arms and feet and one of them is on the floor holding his windpipe and gasping for air. The other circles, ready to deliver a *coup de grace*. The crowd mills stupidly about.

I turn off the music, grab my stunner, and leap over the bar.

"That's enough," I say, holding the slim black tube in what I hope is a threatening manner.

The circling man stops, looks at me then down at the stunner, and nods sharply. He picks his drink up from a nearby table and walks away.

The other man is sitting up, still holding his throat but apparently unharmed.

"You two stay away from each other. I don't want to have to use this." I shake the stunner for emphasis and return to the bar. Music fills the room again; tension leaves the crowd like gas escaping from a balloon. The buzz of conversation swells.

"Very good," a female voice says.

I look up. It's her, it's Lia, and I can't help but smile.

"Hey." Stupidly, I pick up a rag and clutch it in my fist.

"I was here yesterday," she says.

"Yesterday, huh?"

Her eyebrows furrow, but her eyes are smiling. "Yes, well. Yesterday. Whatever that means."

"Same day, different cast of characters. Except for me. Most people don't come back."

She nods. I notice her ears, sculpted to small points. "I can see why," she says. "It's not a very nice place."

"Then what are you doing here?"

She bites her lower lip, looks off toward the sky-filled windows, looks back at me.

"Can I have a drink? A nice single-malt something, neat."

I pour the amber liquid into a glass and set it in front of her. She takes a sip.

"Do you … *live* here?"

I nod. "Yeah."

"What a terrible job."

I nod again. "Yeah."

She takes another sip.

"You went home with the Martian?"

She nods. "I took him home."

My intention is to acknowledge her disclosure with a slight nod, a knowing tilt of the head. But something very different happens when I open my mouth.

"Ah," I say. "A mercy fuck."

She gives me a look that manages to be both withering and sad, sets her drink gently down on the bar in front of me, and walks to the end of the room and down the spiral stairs. The Gate hums.

Here at the end of everything, I'm still an idiot.

I go through the motions of tending bar, sending out bus trays, pouring drinks. All the while I'm playing the loop of conversation over and over again in my head. So thoroughly human, so typically stupid, to welcome the object of one's desire by sending her packing.

At 1:05, I hear the sound of crackling paper and the Lhosa begins to materialize next to me. I am filled with hatred and rage and I wish that just once it would fully coalesce into flesh and substance so I could wrap my hands around its pencil neck.

"How's business?" it asks.

"Business," I say. I look around the room. Heads bob in conversation; Babel hangs in the air like smoke. I turn back to the Lhosa. I want to ask it for the hundredth time: Why me? But that is a well-worn path, the answer always the same, and I have long ago stopped asking. "You were available," it would say.

The doomed sky fills the windows.

"Business is good."

⭐

Another day, another Gotterdammerung. I clean up the Lounge, like I always do, and head downstairs to my quarters. Today, however, will be different. I print up enough 23C currency to give myself a jump start, and I stand looking at the gate, staring into that gray blob of pearly nothing. I fiddle with the controls, step back again, stare some more. I expect any second to hear that crackling paper sound, the Lhosa showing up like Marley's ghost, but it doesn't happen. I step forward.

It wasn't easy to carve out a life for myself on 23C Mars, but I made a few investments, bootstrapped a small financial consulting firm specializing in antiviral nanotech. Picking up the pieces after the Plague. I kept a low profile, never got too greedy. I did all right.

I looked for Lia, of course, but I had no way to find her, nothing to go on except the memory of her face, that last look of withering pity. Eventually, I gave up. I even stopped listening for the sound of crackling paper. Because I know why the Lhosa never tracked me down here, why it never brought me back.

It doesn't have to.

I'm still there, at the threshold of the Singularity, wiping tables and serving drinks. But that's someone else, caught in that Sisyphean loop of doom and rebirth, doom and rebirth, trapped. Someone else.

I've beaten the Lhosa. I've redeemed my old self. I'm never going back.

Last month, I purchased an automaton to help me around the house. In addition to its usual domestic routines, it has a strong chess program, but when playing the Sicilian Dragon it always falls for a very aggressive, risky Queenside rook sacrifice. Every time, the same stupid blunder. It is as if its ability to reason, to learn from its mistakes, has completely fled. I was so frustrated today, that I reached across the table and smacked it on the side of its head. There was a satisfying hollow sound. I did it again.

THOSE ARE PEARLS THAT WERE
HIS EYES

THE ONLY WINDOW in Suki's bedroom opened onto an airshaft that ran through the center of the building like the path of a bullet. She would lie in bed in the hot summer nights with the salt smell of the drying seabed coming in through the open window, a sheen of sweat filming her forehead and plastering the sheets to her body like tissue, listening to her downstairs neighbors. When they made love, their cries echoing up through the airshaft made her loins ache, and she brought release to herself silently, visualizing men with slender, oiled limbs and faces hidden in shadow.

Sometimes the neighbors sang, odd, sinuous music redolent with quarter tones. The melodies wove counterpoint like a tapestry of smoke and for some reason Suki thought of mountains. Jagged, fractal peaks thrusting out of an evergreen carpet. Summits brushed with snow. Tongues of cloud laying across the low passes.

Sometimes they argued, and the first time she heard the man's deep voice raised in anger she was sure he was a Beast, possibly an Ursa. She was less certain of the woman, but there was a sibilant, lilting quality to her voice that suggested something of the feline. They'd moved in three weeks before but their sleep cycles seemed out of sync with hers and she still hadn't met them.

Suki tried to imagine herself going downstairs to borrow something—sugar, yarn, a databead. His broad muzzle would poke out from behind the half-closed door; his liquid brown eyes would be half-closed in suspicion. They would chat for a bit, though, and perhaps he would invite her in. They would teach her their songs and their voices would rise together into the thick, warm air.

Some nights there was no singing, no arguing, no love, and Suki listened to the city, a white-noise mélange of machinery and people in constant flux, like the sound of the ocean captured in a shell held to the ear. Beneath that, emanating from the spaceport on the edge of the city, a low, intermittent hum, nearly subsonic, so faint it seemed to come from somewhere inside her own body.

On those nights, she had trouble sleeping, and she would climb the rickety stairs to the roof. She couldn't see the Web, of course, but she imagined she could feel it arching overhead, lines of force criss-crossing the sky. Ships rode the Web up to where they could safely ignite their fusion drives for in-system voyages, or clung to the invisible threads all the way to their convergence at the Wyrm.

Newmoon hung in the sky, its progress just below the threshold of conscious perception, like the minute hands of a clock. She had visited there as a child, a crèche trip, and she remembered the feel of the factories humming under her feet, the metal skin pocked with micrometeorite impacts stretching to the too-close horizon, the tingling caress of her environment field.

Heat enveloped the city like a glove around a closed fist. It kept people indoors, and business in her little shop was slow. Suki fed and watered her animals, trimmed the heartplants, and carefully tended the incubator, where she was nurturing a quintet of silkpups. Not much more than embryos now, but they would bring a good price when they birthed. Tuned to imprint themselves upon the bio-field of whoever first touched them, they were quite the rage among the Ken, who viewed their intense loyalty and affection with some-thing like amusement. Of course, with the Ken, you never knew what that really meant.

When Suki returned home that evening, the message light was blinking over the console in the kitchen alcove. She brushed her hand across it and the burnished surface faded, replaced by a ghostly rendering of Tam's head and shoulders.

Suki jumped when she saw him.

"—been such a long time, and I just wanted to see how you were doing," Tam was saying. "The Hyaloplasm is *cold*, they never said it would be like this. And you never call me anymore." He paused. "Sometimes it feels like no one remembers me."

His image faded to black. Suki stared at the screen for a long time afterwards. They had called each other a lot after the aircar crash, but it made her feel strange. It wasn't quite Tam anymore— something of his essence had been lost in the upload—and there was a feeling of unhealthy enmeshment about staying in relation- ship with a Ghost. She hadn't taken a new lover yet, but she was ready.

She didn't want to call him back and a tendril of guilt nagged at her as she prepared her dinner. It soon gave way to resentment.

Damnit, she thought. Let the dead stay dead.

He'd turned a corner and she couldn't follow—wouldn't even if she could. Why couldn't he let her move on? Why couldn't *he* move on?

Leaving her plate of stew half-eaten, she went to the console and activated the recorder. The steady, yellow light above the blank screen stared at her and she took a deep breath, trying to visualize Tam's face in place of her own shadowy reflection.

"I don't want you to call me anymore, Tam. I have to get on with my life. I'm sorry—" Her voice caught and almost broke, but she recovered. "Goodbye."

With a few shaky keystrokes she set the console to play back the message in response to Tam's signet.

She returned to her meal, but she was restless. After pushing bits of vegetable and tofu from one side of the bowl to the other for the third time, she got up from the table, went to the console, and downloaded *Versala Dreams*, a lavish historical romance she'd been meaning to scan, rich in costumes, intrigue, and sex. She put the databead in the reader and leaned back on the couch. The induction field wrapped around her optic nerve like an invisible, coiled worm.

☆

On the eleventh day of the heatwave, she awoke with the feeling that things were about to change. It was still oppressively hot, but there was a smell of clean moisture in the air, of something besides death and age wafting in from the salt sea.

She ate a spare breakfast of cracked wheat and blood oranges, and left early for work, treading quietly as she passed the Ursa's apartment on the floor below. She could picture them in there, all the shutters drawn, he and his cat-woman curled together on a padded mat, deep in the shadow of sleep.

The streets were almost deserted—it was the hush before the morning flurry of activity—and she enjoyed the feeling that the city was hers alone. She had to walk nearly half a click before she found a bicycle, and the one she found had its front wheel bent slightly out of alignment, so that she wobbled from side to side as she rode down the Avenue of Palms toward what used to be the waterfront.

As she rode, the city seemed to awaken around her. The tree-lined street filled with men and women on bicycles, with Beasts pulling wheeled carts. Low residential buildings of pink desert stone gave way to a chaotic clutter of commerce. Mechs wove through the traffic on silent cushions of air, full of purpose.

When she got to the Boardwalk, she stopped and leaned the bicycle against a lamppost. Almost immediately, a pleasant-looking young man took it with an apologetic smile.

"Careful," she said. "The wheel is bent." He shrugged, smiled again, and wobbled down the Boardwalk before she could say anything more.

Suki sighed.

In the distance, wavering in heat haze, the sea hugged the flat horizon like a layer of mercury, almost too bright to look at. Long wharves stretched out into the salt flats. A strong, coppery smell hung in the air.

There was a faint pop from the direction of the spaceport, like the sound a small boy might make expelling a puff of air through his lips. The ionization trail from an ascending ship cut the sky in half, faded, and was gone.

☆

The silkpups were almost ready. Their vitals scrolled past on the incubator display, slender threads beginning to bear the full weight of life. The pups themselves still didn't look like much—hairless rats, primitive and inert.

She heard a noise and looked up. Standing at the counter was an elderly female Ken and her Speaker. She hadn't heard them come in.

"Hello," she said, a little too abruptly.

The Speaker's eyes rolled up in his head. "Good morning," he said. "We didn't mean to startle you. Please forgive." His voice was metallic and brittle.

"It's all—"

"You have silkpups for sale?"

Conversations with the Ken were always like this—off balance and skewed, full of sharp corners.

Suki forced herself to look in the Ken's bird-like eyes as she replied. "Yes. Well, no—not yet. But this brood will birth tomorrow."

The Speaker's eyes returned to focus on Suki. She turned to him and he nodded brusquely. Together, he and the Ken turned and walked out of the shop. A musty odor, like old, damp cloth, hung behind them in the still air, noticeable even over the familiar smells of animals and hydroponics.

Suki didn't know if she'd offended her or not, but she resolved to put it out of her mind. She was dealing with Ken, after all.

Business after that was slow, but a wealthy, young couple bought a rare icebird from Nortith, complete with an environment-field generator to maintain its habitat. The sale more than adequately fleshed out Suki's profit margin for the day.

Feeling pleased with herself, she closed up shop early and walked down to the waterfront. The Boardwalk was crowded— Beasts, Ken and their Speakers, human tourists from all over.

An old jetty stretched out into the salt toward the distant, retreating sea like an accusing finger. It was much less crowded than the Boardwalk, and Suki found herself drawn to it. As she walked down its length, hearing the wood—*wood!*—creak beneath her feet, she wondered what it had been like when the sea was right here. She tried to imagine it, soft blue-green, gentle on the eyes, sails and hovercraft drifting lazily to and fro.

She sat down on a low bench at the end of the jetty and closed her eyes. Images of Tam's face kept intruding into her consciousness, and she pushed them away. She tried to empty her mind, to reduce herself to a simple, animal presence basking in sunlight. After a short while, though, she heard footsteps tapping hollowly along the jetty, coming closer. She opened her eyes.

A tall, young man was approaching. There was something strange about the way he carried herself, and it wasn't until he came closer that she could see the crystals embedded in his temples. He was blind. When he came closer still, she saw the fine, radial scars around his eyes. A Void Dancer.

A shudder passed through her. *A Void Dancer.* She'd never met one, but everyone knew what they did. Take a one-person jumpship and dive into the Wyrm at a velocity and angle of incidence nobody had ever tried before. Mapping the Universe by throwing darts, blindfolded, in an empty room.

"May I join you?" he asked.

"Of course," she stammered.

He sat down next to her and sighed. She looked over at him. Handsome, except for the scars, and not as young as she had first thought.

"Sometimes," he said, "the crowds ..." He faced the salt flats. "The empty space is soothing."

She tried to imagine the crystals in his temples sending out a silent screech of ultrasound, receiving echoes, constructing a pattern to send to his brain, bypassing his withered optic nerve.

"What do you see?" she asked, surprised at her boldness.

He smiled. His eyes were mottled pools of grey jelly, but Suki still had the sense of being held in that lifeless gaze. "It's like an old photographic negative. Do you know what that is?"

She nodded.

"But that's just the interpretation my brain makes of the data from the tweeters." He tapped his temple. "What it actually looks like ..." He shrugged. "What does that really mean?"

They were silent for a while.

"What do you see when you're out *there?*" Suki asked.

He smiled again. "It's ... different. I don't know if I can explain it. The ship is my whole body; my awareness of things around me comes through as a kind of kinesthesia. Or that's what the medicals say, anyway." The curdled jelly in his eye-sockets seemed to quiver gently. "I sense a nearby mass as a sort of plucking at my skin. The electromagnetic spectrum gets filtered through to me as olfactory sensation—a deep, hot smell for the infrared, a sharp whiff of ozone up in the UV—"

He paused. "But I'm prattling on. Tell me about yourself. You have a name?"

"Suki."

"Roan," he said, and held out his hand. It was dry as paper and completely smooth.

"Do you work here in the city?"

"Yes, I have a little shop on Front Street, not far from the space-port, actually. Organic complements. Mostly grown in-house, but I get a few naturals from time to time."

He nodded. "I know Front Street. Do you know that I grew up not far from there? That was a long time ago, of course." Had he eyes, they would have rolled heavenwards as he calculated the dila-tion. "Eleven hundred and seven years, to be exact. The sea was still lapping at this pier!"

"A long time ago," she agreed.

Again, they were silent. Strangely, the silence did not feel awkward to Suki, but rather like they were occupying the same space together.

"Perhaps you'd like to come by the shop sometime," Suki said, again a little surprised at her boldness. "Something for your ship—a bonsai tree, a heartplant …"

His smile was a bit forced this time and she winced at her stupidity. "I would hardly be able to enjoy it," he said.

"Of course—"

"But I would come by to see *you*."

Suki felt her face flush and she wondered if his tweeters could detect the warm blood rushing to her cheeks.

She took the long way home, through the administrative district on the other side of the Lhoss Gardens. A new building was going up—

a crew of Oxen on the ground pushed wheeled pallets piled high with building materials, while Cats climbed the scaffolding that surrounded the blocky, unfinished pyramid.

Suki stopped her bicycle and balanced on one foot, watching, listening. The Oxen called to each other in low, bleating tones that mingled with the sibilant cries from above. It was recognizable as her own tongue, but there were words she couldn't understand. Always a few more, it seemed, each time she heard them speak. Each time she stopped to listen. The Beasts were changing, drifting off onto their own trajectory. She envied them their transit of undiscovered territory.

The neighbors sang again that night. Lying in bed, her gaze angling up through the window, she imagined the close, hollow harmonies lifting her like a cushion of air toward the box of starry sky at the mouth of the airshaft.

She thought of Roan. He'd said he would come by the shop tomorrow. She wondered if he would.

She thought of Tam. Her system had logged two calls from him, so she knew her message had been received. She pushed aside the feelings of guilt that began to take shape and tried to construct a picture of Roan's face in her mind, but it was elusive. All she could evoke clearly were the eyes—moist flecks of cloudy jelly set in hollows of leathery, scarred skin.

If the eyes are truly windows to the soul, she thought, what do they reveal of his?

Her hand stole between her legs and she imagined his hands moving across her body, his sweet breath warm on her neck. The peak of her pleasure braided with the music echoing up through the airshaft and segued seamlessly into a dream. They were sitting on the bench at the end of the pier. The water, blue as his eyes, made gentle sounds lapping up against the pilings. A dense, organic smell hung in the air like a fog hugging the surface of the sea. Birds wheeled across the sky. The sun was a shrunken, glaring wound.

The silkpups birthed overnight, and when Suki came into the shop, they were squirming in their padded nest, crawling across one another, taking shaky, hesitant steps and collapsing in a tangle of limbs.

Their psychic energy, too, was almost palpable. The air around the incubator seemed charged. Each of them was a *tabula rasa*, engineered to bond with the first person that touched them.

There were no customers all morning and Suki busied herself with small jobs—cleaning cages, maintaining nutrient baths. The heartplants hung heavy with fruit, the tiny, fist-like buds pulsing faintly. She snapped one off, leaving a moist scar on the smooth branch. Red sap dribbled down her hand. She popped the fruit in her mouth and bit down, wincing at the explosion of salty sweetness.

Just before she was about to close up shop for lunch, Roan walked through the door. Suki was surprised and a little frightened at the surge of joy she felt.

"Hello," she stammered.

He took her hands. "Hello, yourself." The gray jelly in the hollows of his eyes seemed expressive, but of what she wasn't sure. "I don't have much time. I'm leaving tomorrow and I have a great deal to prepare."

He paused. Suki felt something inside her wither and begin to fold in upon itself.

"Could you meet me tonight?" he asked. "Midnight, the pier where we met yesterday?"

She nodded. "Midnight."

"Good." He smiled, squeezed her hand, and was gone. A bubble of silence filled the shop; gradually, the familiar rustle-whirr-whisper of animals and machinery reasserted itself.

She took her lunch down to Lhoss Gardens and sat in the shadow of the Sundial, dangling her feet in one of the fountains that marked the hours.

Roan. She realized that her excitement was made keener by anticipation of loss, but she didn't care. *Maybe he would take her with him.*

Even as the thought formed in her mind, though, she rejected it. Ridiculous. She was no Void Dancer.

A crèche-group passed on the far side of the Dial, moving almost as a single organism. Whispers and giggles floated across the plaza. Suki tried to study their faces, but from this distance they shared a bland sameness.

The group passed behind the black, glassy wedge at the Dial's center. They must have stopped there to rest, because they didn't emerge. It seemed to Suki that they had just walked off the face of the world.

She was bent over the silkpups' nest, lost in their restless, wriggling motion, when her nostrils filled again with that damp musk.

She looked up. The Ken and her Speaker were standing in front of her. Once again, she hadn't heard them come in.

"Hello," she said.

The Ken's bead-like eyes stared impassively back at her. She had to look away. The Speaker smiled kindly at her, and for the first time, she noticed laugh lines around his eyes. She wondered what he had to laugh about, a Speaker for the Ken. Then his smile vanished and his eyes rolled back in their sockets.

"You have silkpups today?"

Suki nodded, stepping back from the nest. Before she could say anything, the Ken reached into the enclosure and picked up a tiny, squirming pup. She held it up to her shriveled face and stared at it. Gradually, the pup stopped squirming and began to emit a low, contented hum.

The Ken looked at Suki. "Fascinating," said the Speaker. She replaced the pup in its nest, turned on her heel, and walked out the door.

Suki couldn't believe what she was seeing. Dimly, she was aware of the Speaker entering something on her credit pad. He touched her arm.

"I'm sorry," he said. It was the first time she had heard him speak with his own voice. It was low and musical. He hurried out the door after the Ken.

The silkpup lay in a corner of the nest, shivering. Suki leaned close and she could hear a high, keening whimper. Already, its litter-mates were shunning it—they clustered in a writhing mass of tiny arms and legs on the other side of the nest, as far away as they could get.

The imprint disrupted, the connection broken, the silkpup would soon die. There was nothing she could do.

Almost nothing.

She picked up the animal and held it, trembling, in her hand. With her other hand, she took it by the neck, closed her eyes, and gave it a quick twist.

She put the body in the disposal and for the rest of the afternoon, the shop smelled of burnt hair and ozone.

Suki parked her bike in the alley next to her building, hoping nobody would ride off with it. She felt a small stab of guilt at her selfishness, but she didn't want to wander half across the city looking for a bike and be late for Roan.

Two more attempts from Tam on her console log. When would he give up? She thought of him, bereft of flesh, suspended in purgatory, reaching back to life and light. She could no longer make the connection between that Ghost and the ghost of her own memories. He was finally gone to her.

To her relief, the bike was still waiting where she had left it. The night air was cool, the Avenue of Palms empty at this late hour. She arrived at the old waterfront fifteen minutes early and walked her bike out to the end of the pier. She sat down on a wooden bench to wait.

Midnight came and went. By twelve-fifteen, Suki was beginning to think that Roan would not come. The salt flats spread out before her, luminous in the blue Newmoon light. Behind her, the city asleep and not asleep, hollow as an open mouth.

By twelve-thirty, she was sure. As she mounted her bike, the ionization trail from an ascending ship lanced across the sky, followed by a faint popping sound. She blinked back the afterimage, a straight, bright scar across her vision, and wondered if it was Roan.

She rode home slowly, through quiet side streets. She felt nothing.

As she passed by the Ursa's apartment on her way up to her own, she paused to listen. They were singing—his low voice a modal drone, hers above sinuous and agile, weaving in and out of the tonal center.

She walked up to the door, pressed her cheek against the cold, smooth surface. The music seemed to enter her body through that contact, sending delicate tendrils down her neck, spreading through her chest and out her arms and legs, filling her with warmth.

PHOENIX/BUGHOUSE

SHARP NINE HAMMERED through the wormhole clocking just shy of 0.2c. A ringless Jovian and its attendant system of moons spread out below her on their local ecliptic like jewels on black velvet. Far beyond, the fiercely burning primary she instantly recognized as Mandelbrot and its Goldilocks sprawl of inner planets: two frozen, one burned, one, the second from the primary, a little warm but within meat-habitable range. She perceived all this in an interstitial blink, the way meat might catalog the contents of a room in the instant after awakening. *Sunlight winking through a dappled mask of leaves beyond the open window, smells of earth and brine mingling on the soft breeze, the faint, periodic sough of the nearby ocean like blood music.*

The shadow memory burned away like snow under a torch. As always, the wrench back to realspace was unwelcome and harsh, the jump euphoria fading too quickly. Sharp Nine allowed herself a bit of disorientation, the expected meat-life kinesthesia, whether from her own history or something more primal and farther back, random firings from the sea of enKrypted souls. Her monitors flooded her systems with digital analogues of palliatives: ersatz B-complex, a serotonin reuptake emulation, a touch of central nervous system stimulant, a whiff of cannabinoid. Before too long, a scant handful of standard millis, she was optimal except for a lingering melancholy.

She opened her awareness to the electromagnetic music of this system: the fierce, Fourier hiss of the primary, the softer signatures of the two Jovians, the mutter of planetary magnetospheres.

Faint, but unmistakable, buried within the natural rhythms of the system but now that she noticed it impossible to ignore: an anomaly. She quickly sourced it to the meatzone world. It was an ancient protocol, unambiguously human, singing *help, help, help …*

Lila was halfway through the South Field when the Bugs killed her sister. She had stopped to rest and sip warm water from the skin at her side. The basket of meatplants was nearly full, leaving a trail of blood and clotted tissue mixing with the red clay earth as she dragged it behind her. She re-wrapped her hands in the coarse weave that served as minimal protection from the acidic blood. The sun was a searing white disc halfway to zenith. It would soon be time to return to the burrows and wait out the worst of the day's heat and youvee.

She was just about to get up and finish her row when the screaming started. She recognized El's voice right away and left her basket sitting in the middle of the row. She ran diagonally across the fields, the serrated leaves tearing at her legs. The screaming was coming from somewhere behind the Bughouse, accompanied now by hoarse human shouts and the high, excited chatter of adult Bugs.

As she ran around the terraced curve of the Bughouse, the screaming stopped, and she urged herself to run faster. She reached the plaza in front of the main entrance and fell to her knees on the hard clay.

A charnel horror greeted her. Mangled body parts were scattered across the blood soaked ground in front of the entrance. A Soldier, rearing up on its hind legs, carapace purple with agitation, was tearing a human torso in two. Lila recognized El's rough green tunic, soaked in gore. Two more Soldiers stood behind, mandibles clicking ominously, mid-limbs rubbing together in a high-pitched whine. Behind them, a young Royal she recognized as B'nok from its torso markings, nursed a bent foreleg.

A handful of humans surrounded the grisly tableau in a half circle. Lila lurched to her feet and pushed through them to the front.

The cicada whine rose a notch in pitch. Her unc Ray was struggling with her da, holding him back from leaping into the fray.

"Let me go," her da cried. His eyes were wild, the whites showing all around. "Let me *go!*"

Others joined Ray in holding him back. Another Soldier joined the line in front of B'nok. The cicada whine rose again in volume and pitch, almost drowning out her da's cries.

Suddenly, the fight left her da and he collapsed, sobbing, in Ray's arms.

Lila felt a hand on her shoulder. It was Andra, her aunt. "You don't want to see this."

She shook off the hand but stayed rooted to the spot. It was unmistakably El. Her long blonde hair spread in a bloody fan around her mangled head.

With a scream, she darted past the Soldiers, dodging snapping claws and whiplike stingers, and kicked at the young Royal as hard as she could. Her foot smashed through the brittle chitin of its thorax with a sickening crunch. Something slashed across her back and she felt white-hot pain. She stumbled and nearly fell, then she began to run towards the wall of jungle at the edge of the plaza.

Ray called out to her, then her da, but she kept running. She heard pursuit behind her, the scrabble-hiss of Bug legs on hard clay. An opening in the dense thicket before her: a trailhead. When she was just upon it, a sharp crack split the air behind her. She jogged hard to the left. Out of the corner of her eye, she saw a stinger cut through the dense foliage. Feet pounding the hard clay, lungs burning, she ran along the edge of the clearing until she reached another smaller gap.

She pushed through the thicket of fleshy green leaves and thick, ropy vines until she came upon one of the Bug paths that riddled the jungle. She ran, quickly but as lightly as possible, trying not to leave any signs of her passage, hoping her pursuers would choose a different path from the labyrinth of forks and intersections near the compound. The sound of pursuit dwindled behind her and faded finally to silence.

She stopped and tried to catch her breath, leaning against a crimson, smooth-boled tree. A line of fire ran from the small of her back to her left shoulder. She reached back to touch it, felt a high welt, winced as a jolt of pain ran through her. She pulled back her hand slick with blood.

El. How could she be gone? It didn't seem real. They were more than close; they were a part of each other. Lila couldn't remember ever spending more than a day apart from her. They were the only survivors of six children, a brother and three sisters lost to cancer and congenital disease. *The youvee,* her ma had said, before she too died of melanoma. *We don't belong here.*

She could picture how it happened: B'nok, a young Royal even more stupid and cruel than his elders, sneaks up behind El, reaches out with a claw to steal a meatplant. El jumps and accidentally injures the little monster. His warbling cry of pain rises into the moist, hot air. The Soldiers come, pulsing purple, all stingers and claws and chittering mouthparts.

El.

The sun was high in the sky. Heat enveloped her, burning in her lungs, a pressure on her face.

She couldn't go home. She could probably never go home. She thought of the cool darkness of the burrow illuminated by greenish tangles of lightvines. A warren of corridors and rooms spread out like the branches of a tree, separated by woven hangings. A single remaining slate in the big common room, now long dark, used to tell improbable stories of Old Earth and the Voyage. Her da assured her that they were true, but she and El had decided long ago that they couldn't possibly be, that the stories were told to children to keep them quiet, like the suffering fool on the cross that some of the older families seemed fond of.

Reprisals would follow B'nok's death, of that she was certain. More killing, all her fault. She felt sick and alone. Maybe if she went back, offered herself. But that might not be enough. It could even make matters worse. It was easy to kid yourself that you understood the Bugs, but there was no understanding, not really. It had been over five years since a Royal had been harmed at the hands of humans. Lila remembered the executions with terrible clarity. One Royal had died when a human went berserk in the fields under the sun's glaring eye, and the Bugs killed ten humans in retaliation. The Bugs were unsophisticated, but they understood the psychology of power. Two Soldiers ripped the humans to pieces in seconds in a nightmare of mandibles and flashing claws. The High Elder fed bloody gobbets to his non-sentient Queen while his Soldiers made all the humans watch.

Lila remembered the day with painful clarity: the shouts of the humans, the crowd surging but not pushing forward, all that energy held in check. The hard, angular set of her da's jaw. The blood bright red on the sunbaked clay. El's hand gripping hers so hard it hurt.

There was a clearing up in the hills her da had told her about long ago, a place to meet if there was ever trouble. She took stock, noting the sun's position, visualizing her headlong flight and where she was now with respect to the Bughouse, the Burrows, the fields. She could take this path north a few klicks, then a left fork up into the hills. She knew the paths near home well, but she and El (she and El, always she and El) had never ventured far.

The jungle hummed and stirred all around her. The heat had weight; it bore down on her shoulders and on the top of her head. The sun's actinic light, dispersed by the leafy canopy above, was still harsh and bright. There was a soft pop near her head. She held her breath and pinched her nose shut as the cloud of spores drifted past her face. If she inhaled, they would find purchase in the soft, moist tissues of her throat and grow until they stole the breath from her. It was how her gramp had died. She was not supposed to be in the sickroom, but, near the end, she had caught a glimpse of him in the low-ceilinged burrow, behind a wall of adults, lying on a straw mat. Their eyes met briefly. She remembered his strained smile before he grimaced with pain and looked away.

The path ahead cut a narrow lane through the dense jungle. Sections of vine, thick as her wrist, hung in lazy catenaries between the smooth-boled trees. The air reeked of Bug, bitter and acidic.

Sharp Nine located the source of the signal, a vessel in orbit around the Goldilocks planet. She tried to establish communication but the thing was dead, the signal automatic. Human, though—undeniably. The protocol and other artifacts of the signal dated it to early 23C. Pre-Diaspora, pre-Collapse, pre—pretty damn much everything.

Her systems flooded with excitement with the certainty that she'd stumbled into one of the Phoenix Colonies.

Around the end of 22C, the home world was all but gone: way too hot, way too wet, scoured and churned by a constant battery of megastorms. Meat was either huddled in dome cities thinking deep thoughts, wandering the wilderness outside eating each other, or settling nicely into Lagrange habitats. Mars greening had begun, but the colony wasn't self-sustaining and smart money said that the waiting game was a loss. (Smart money turned out to be right). The Krypt, immortality of sorts if the systems could be rendered truly self-healing, had barely started, just a few hundred thousand broken almost-souls who tried going Uptown before it was fully baked, avatars barely sentient, wandering like ghosts in a huge, hollow mansion.

The humans who were in a position to care gave the species fifty-fifty: finish greening Mars, propagate to the Jovian moons and beyond, or fade to black as habitat systems failed and native Terrans continued their slide down the evolutionary scale.

They managed to pull together half a dozen colony ships, great, graceless, things, mostly shielding. They would jack the unused orbital nuclear arsenal of a dozen nations that no longer existed for Orion fuel and propel their cargo of corpsicles out into the starry black. The Phoenix Project. Carrying out the species imperative. Fuck the Universe or die trying.

Lila's calloused feet beat out a steady rhythm on the leaf-strewn ground. The air was hot in her lungs and she was sweating freely. Twice she heard the high-pitched chitter of nearby bugtalk and she stopped in her tracks, tried to slow her breathing and imagined herself part of the jungle, green and still.

When she had gone so far she was sure she somehow missed it, she arrived at the fork and took the left path. It narrowed and the jungle overhead became a dense, green ceiling, giving no hint of the position of the sun. Sometimes the path disappeared almost entirely, and she pressed forward through the thick growth, hoping she wasn't lost. Sharp leaves tore at her face, neck, and arms until she was bleeding freely from a dozen cuts. Her awareness contracted to a knot of purpose—her feet moving through the jungle heat and stink, her ragged breathing.

Finally she emerged into a small clearing. Empty, of course. She expected her father to be a while. She chose a spot just outside the edge of the clearing, hidden from sight but affording her a good view, and she slid to the ground, her back against a smooth-boled tree.

She waited, exhausted from her flight, but trying to remain alert for Bugs or predators. Exhaustion won out and she dozed off. Her dreams were sharp-edged, disjointed visions of panic, grief, and flight. She must have heard something because she awoke with a start. Her father emerged from the jungle at the far end of the clearing. She saw El in the long planes of his face and she felt a surge of loss so intense that purple swam at the edges of her vision.

She stood unsteadily.

"Da." It came out as a raspy croak, but he looked over and saw her. He crossed the clearing in a few strides and took her in his arms.

"I'm so sorry, Lila," he said. "I couldn't stop it."

She let herself sink into his arms and the last few hours of panic and grief flowed through and out of her in great, heaving sobs. He held her until her breathing returned to normal.

She stepped back. "What's going on back home?"

He shook his head. "It's not good. Ren, Davi, Delia—all gone."

The ground seemed far away. "If I hadn't—"

"No," he said fiercely. "Nobody blames you. It's an impossible situation. If it wasn't El, if it wasn't you, it would have been someone else."

"What are we going to do? How can this go on?"

He looked past her, as if searching for an answer in the dense jungle.

"There are so many of them, so few of us. You know the stories, what happened when we first got here. Maybe fighting and dying would be better."

"What do we do?" she asked again.

"There's a place. My own da took me there when I was a young man. I was going to take you and El there soon. It's part of our Ship, the vehicle that brought us here. It's called a lifeboat, but I don't know why. It's hidden from plain sight by a trick of the eye. You'll have to go there; the lifeboat will recognize you as one of us and let you in."

"What will I do there?"

"It's a sort of cave. It will give you food and water, and tell you stories like you used to see on the slates. Maybe you can find out something. Where the other People are, if they still exist. I don't know what. Maybe there's nothing to find out. But you'll be safe there for a couple of weeks. Maybe by then you'll be able to return."

She nodded, holding back tears. The thought of hiding inside some old machine while her family and friends bore the consequences of her impulsive act was too much.

Her da took her in his arms again.

"Be strong, Lila. Remember that the Bugs are stupid. Only the Royals can tell us apart and even then, we don't really know how memory works for them. Or whether they'll care if you come back as long as their reprisals were adequate. Find out what you can. Other People. Weapons. Other Ships. Anything. I'll meet you there in two weeks."

He handed her a sack of food—dried tofu by the weight and feel —and a skin of good water.

"North about five klicks, then follow the river. Just past where it disappears underground, you'll come to a huge clearing. You won't see anything, but most of the grass will be pressed flat. The lifeboat will see you."

He kissed her forehead.

"Go."

He turned and walked quickly across the clearing. The jungle swallowed him.

By the time Lila reached the clearing she was nearly finished, staggering with each step. She'd evaded Bug patrols twice, ripped the legs off a groundwasp before it was able to implant an eggsac into her stomach with its whiplike stinger, and ran from a raptor until her legs felt like lead and her breath burned in her throat.

Just as Da said, the clearing was oddly flat. Past clearly delineated borders, tangles of vines and grasses merged with the jungle beyond. The air seemed to ripple slightly where the clearing ended.

She stood there for a few moments, waiting for something to happen. Then, just as she was about to break the jungle stillness with her voice, there was a low hum and just to her right a section of wall appeared, a shimmering rectangle of dull metal suspended in the air.

She approached it slowly, expecting it to disappear at any moment. When she was directly in front of it she saw the faint outline of a door.

"Hello." The voice was female, low and mellifluous. It seemed to come from everywhere at once.

A small port opened next to the door.

"To confirm identity, please insert your finger."

Lila looked behind her. The jungle pressed in from the edges of the clearing, arching over her head.

She inserted her index finger in the hole, felt moisture, coolness, a slight pinch.

She pulled her hand back. There was a small red dot on her finger.

Nothing happened for several seconds, then with a hissing sound, the door slid open.

She took a step forward, then turned around and looked back at the steaming jungle looming over the clearing. The colors, green and crimson, purple and blue, seemed unnaturally bright. The air was heavy with the smell of rot and life. The sun's fierce heat was a steady pressure on her upturned face.

She turned again and looked into the shadowy doorway. She felt almost paralyzed, hovering between two worlds.

The stories, she thought. Coming here on ships that rode between the stars. They were all true.

She was very young when the last slate stopped working. She barely remembered pictures moving beneath its polished surface. Her da told her the stories, but she and El weren't sure if they were even real to him.

There was a faint odor wafting from the darkness, an old smell, an amalgam of dust, oil, and metal.

Lila entered the doorway, took a step forward, and the door slid shut behind her. She was in a corridor of some sort. Strips of illumination glowed on the floor and ceiling, pulsing in a sequence that led her forward to another door that hissed open with a slight catch and a soft, grinding protest.

She entered a large, empty room, about the twice the size of the assembly chamber at home. Dim, diffuse light emanated from the walls and ceiling. On the other side of the room, a pair of closed doors flanked a slightly raised dais. Behind the dais a mottled blue ball hung in the air, spinning slowly. Chunky blocks of green and brown and large reaches of blue passed beneath tattered wisps and whorls of white. Lila recognized it from the slate stories as a *planet*, supposedly like the one they were on now, but she couldn't get her mind around that. It didn't make any sense to her.

Tables and chairs were scattered throughout the room. The air was cool and that odd smell of age was stronger here. Very faintly, she heard intermittent hums and soft clicks coming from other parts of the ship, as if it was coming to life around her.

Slowly, tentatively, she walked forward. As she approached the front of the room, the figure of a young woman in a black jumpsuit appeared in front of the spinning world. Lila took a sharp breath. The woman was slightly translucent; Lila could see the back wall of the room through her. Lila concluded that the figure wasn't real, like the people on the slates before they stopped working.

"Hello," it said.

As Sharp Nine approached the Goldilocks planet, she scanned all spectra for signatures of human technology. Except for the distress beacon, nothing. She tried again to communicate with the vessel. Still unresponsive, but she was able to inject a proxy into the network via a hole in the beacon protocol and she began trying to bring the thing to life.

It wasn't difficult for Sharp Nine to enter the mind of the ship and bond with it. There were a few security protocols, but they were laughably weak. Instantly, she assimilated the history of the colony. An Earthlike world, a little warmer than Terran baseline, slightly lower gravity. It wasn't until they'd built a base camp and unboxed the two hundred odd souls still surviving cold sleep that a recon party encountered the indigenous alpha species.

The Bugs had climbed to their position at the top of the food chain over the backs of two other intelligent indigenes, who they enslaved and bred for food. Their social institutions were fairly advanced, but their technology was Stone Age due to the scarcity of metals in the crust of the planet. They had cities, they had commerce, but they appeared to have little need of self-governance due to the hive-like nature of their consciousness.

They were brutal and fiercely xenophobic. They killed half the colonists and enslaved the rest. Accounts of the early years of the Colony were painful for Sharp Nine to assimilate. Famine, constant struggle against the Bug overlords, waves of rebellion squashed to the point that the survival of humans on Mandelbrot II was in doubt. In addition to the disastrous trajectory of this particular colony, Sharp Nine felt strongly the tragic sadness of the ill-conceived Phoenix Project overall. What right did humans have to spew their ejaculate into the Universe in the first place? What did they think would happen if they encountered indigenous intelligence? What would humans have done if the tables were reversed?

It was a Hail Mary play, of course. (Sharp Nine ran an etymology search on the phrase, which leapt into her consciousness out of nowhere, but the results were so ridiculous she felt certain that the data was corrupted.) Survival. A desperate play for the continuity of the species. Cue late 20C Williams score. If Sharp Nine had eyes she would have rolled them with a sigh.

Earth's ecosystems did fail, catastrophically, and meat did suffer a near extinction event. Well, not an event exactly—more like a centuries long series of increasingly violent paroxysms until most of the oceans had been boiled away and the surface of the planet was a sterile desert obscured beneath a roiling layer of acidic clouds.

But humanity's essence survived: in machine intelligence, in swarm entities, in cultured meat, and even in the few thousand Legacies that made it through the apocalypse. The network that began as a quirky exercise in commerce evolved to become the aether through which humanity now swam, permanent, pervasive, self-annealing, maintenance free and powered by the sun. By the time Terra became uninhabitable, the Phoenix ships cast out into the aether, humanity had already spread well beyond Earth. It might not be recognizable as such to the architects of the Phoenix Project, but it was still unarguably human.

She debated whether or not she would manifest to the humans. What was the point, really? She could probably help them—coach them on bootstrapping technologies to fight the Bugs, teach them military history, guerrilla tactics. Nurture a plucky band of rebels into an army that would wrest the planet from the chokehold of the evil Bug overlords! All glory to the conquering horde! All glory to humankind! Meat! Meat! Meat forever!

It was romantic, the stuff of ancient stories. It was also so repugnant to Sharp Nine that she could barely shape the thought. Certainly, the Bugs were a nasty lot. And she felt affinity for her meat ancestors here, and not a little compassion. But really, the Bugs had as much right to their reign of terror and enslavement as the male-dominant humans did to impregnate the Universe. Sharp Nine could no more intervene in the natural order than she could dance, or hum a tune, or cook a soufflé (another odd turn of phrase, flitting through her consciousness like a bird, conjuring an improbable image of a human male in odd headgear, surrounded by bright lights, stirring a viscous liquid in a large bowl).

She was settled on disengaging from the half-wit Colony ship intelligence and heading back to this system's wormhole when—*what's this?*—she sensed a lone human approaching the Colony landing vessel. She wavered for a milli and decided to engage.

She took control of the mechanical functions of the vessel. When the human was sufficiently close, Sharp Nine modified the cloaking field and opened an airlock.

She perused the library of avatars, rejected the baroque bug-eyed monsters, human pets, and square-jawed males that dominated the collection, and settled on a young, female human, plainly dressed.

When the human entered the ship's commons, she manifested.

"Hello," she said.

☆

Lila stepped back. She had seen images of people on the wall screen back home in the warrens before it finally stopped working and she figured that this apparition was similar.

"Hello," she answered. She wasn't sure what to do next. She walked up to the ghostly apparition and reached out hesitantly. There was a blurry pool of light on her hand where it met the image.

"Are you from our Ship?" she asked, the unfamiliar word strange in her mouth. *Ship.* The vehicle that brought us here from *Earth.* All the old names, the old stories, whispered in secret late at night, huddled around low fires. They were all coming back. She thought of her mother, her sister, everyone, and her eyes filled with tears. She had to be strong, though. It was all on her. She could save them all. This was their history, their home. There would be weapons, information, something, anything that would give them an edge, help them exterminate the Bugs and take this planet for their own.

"My name is Sharp Nine," the image said.

"I am Lila." She had never met a new person before and she felt a scary thrill. "Are you from our Ship?" she asked again.

Sharp Nine frowned. "No, not exactly ... I'm not sure how to say this. Do you know where you come from?"

"I think so. We heard stories but they seemed ridiculous. I always thought they were just things you tell children when you want them to be quiet. But this place is real. *You're* real. Well, almost. So ..." She paused and began to speak again, reciting from rote.

"Earth was dying and the Diaspora was struggling. Humankind had not adapted to the harsh realities of life away from the home-world. Six ships were built and colonists were chosen from among the best of the best. Six ships, six Earthlike planets." She stopped and took a breath. It had been years since she told the story, and she stumbled over the unfamiliar words, but it was coming back to her. Usually when the story was recited, it was during the Migration ceremony, the holiday meal that celebrated their origins. A simple orrery was hung over the table, representing the Home system. A blue painted egg graced the table: the home world and the promise of new life. Dense, sweet cake was served at the end: the sweetness of Arrival. Without these familiar trappings, the words seemed strange and hollow. She went on, stumbling a bit. "The voyages would take hundreds of years, in some cases over a thousand. Each ship held a complete genetic library and the means to reconstruct most of the Terran biosphere from raw organic material, and the sum total of all human knowledge. Humanity would survive. Humanity's legacy would survive."

Sharp Nine nodded. "Okay, but do you know what any of that really means?"

"I think so," Lila said. "There are other places like this one. We come from one of them." She paused. "We had to leave and now we're here."

"Yes, well. Close enough."

Lila took a deep breath. "Can you help us? Can you help us fight the Bugs?"

Sharp Nine hesitated. There were a number of options available to her, not the least of which was a significant cache of projectile and energy weapons in the ship's inventory, still quite functional. But she couldn't do it. She felt deeply for this ragged creature before her, her ancestor, her very roots, but her compassion didn't extend to supporting the domination and likely extermination of another sentient species. It couldn't.

"No. There's nothing to be done."

Lila stepped back, stumbling. It felt like she'd been physically struck. Why had she come here? She had thought that coming here was about salvation, that she would find something that would help her and the People fight back.

"What about this place? You said this is the ship that brought us here. Is there anything in here we can use?"

"This ship is a sort of shuttle. The main colony ship is still in orbit around this planet. But that hardly matters. There is nothing for you here."

"I don't believe you. There must be something here that can help. If I go back with nothing, I'll die. We'll all die."

"I'm sorry," Sharp Nine said. She searched her archives for something else to say, something that would capture the complex of sadness, regret, and resolve she felt, but there was nothing.

"Good luck," she said, and winked out.

Sharp Nine relinquished the avatar but continued to watch the human via the lifeboat systems. Lila stood in the middle of the chamber as if paralyzed. Sharp Nine made sure that the rest of the ship was secure and activated the subsonics in the commons, a security measure intended by the ship's designers as a means of inducing reluctant colonists to vacate the ship. When the woman fled out through the open airlock into the jungle beyond, Sharp Nine closed the port and activated the ship's gravity field generators. It lifted off the ground reluctantly, pulling with it a ragged fringe of vines and roots. When it achieved a height of two klicks and the gravity effect was beginning to falter, Sharp Nine activated its chemical engines and it shot into the sky, a dart on a column of fire, to meet the parent ship.

Lila fled in a blind panic, vines whipping her face and hands. Heart pounding, breath burning in her lungs. *Run. Get away.* Gradually, the fear subsided and she stumbled to a halt. She heard a roar, like thunder but louder and deeper, like the world was made of cloth and someone was ripping it apart. She looked up to see a pencil of flame reach up into the sky.

She thought of Sharp Nine and tried to get her mind around what had just happened, what the visit meant. She decided with a surge of anger that it meant nothing. Nothing was different. Nothing. The People were still serving the Bugs; maybe they always would. Her da had told of the others and she'd heard the stories: humans who had fled the compounds and tried to make a life for themselves in the wild, living on the fringes, raiding, killing, melting back into the jungle. Free. Carrying on. Maybe they were true. If they existed, if they were alive, she would find them.

She began to walk. The jungle closed around her.

EX VITRO

I

THE COMMUNICATIONS ROOM was a weird place. Jax wanted to hunch his shoulders against the close metal walls, against the silent machines that smelled faintly of ozone and heat. An array of yellow telltales glowed steadily on the panel over his head; the blank, grey screen hung before him like an open mouth. The one decoration in the barren cubicle was a software ad-fax Maddy had taped to the wall—INSTANT ACCESS, some sort of file-retrieval utility, the first word highlighted in blue and the letters slanted, trailing comb-like filigrees denoting speed.

There was something that drew him to the place, though, and he caught solitary time there whenever he could. He imagined himself a point of light on the far tip of a rocky promontory, a beacon rising above a dark, endless ocean.

Jax heard a sound behind him and turned around. Maddy stood in the doorway. She had been working out and her shirt was damp with sweat. Ringlets of dark hair framed her face; red splotches stood out high on her pale cheeks.

"What's up?" she asked, still a little short of breath. "I didn't hear a comm bell...."

"Nothing," Jax replied. "I'm just hanging. Fog's really bad—we can't even watch the slugs."

Maddy shrugged. The slugs didn't interest her much—anything that happened on time scales shorter than a thousand millennia slid under her radar. Titan itself, though, was to her like a blood-glittering, faceted ruby to a gemologist. Ammonia seas, vast lava fields laced with veins of waxy, frozen hydrocarbons. She was taking ultrasound readings to map the moon's crust and mantle. Jax had never seen her so engaged, but the news from home was like a tidal force pulling at her from another direction. "Anything new on the laser feed?" she asked.

Jax knew that, decoded, the question was, "War news?" Or more specifically, "How bad does it have to get before we can go home?"

She had family in the EC, in Paris, and the information that came in on the feed was frustrating in what it withheld. It was like deducing the shape and texture of an object by studying the shadow it cast in bright, white light.

They did know that a couple of days ago, PacRim had lobbed a mini-nuke at one of the EC's factory-continents in the Indian Ocean, claiming a territorial incursion. The EC had followed suit by vaporizing Jakarta. There had been some sporadic ground combat in New Zealand and Antarctica and a lot of saber-rattling, but no further nuclear exchanges. The North American Free Trade Coalition and the Russian Hegemony were sitting back and waiting, urging restraint and dialogue in the emergency League session and keeping ground and space defenses at full alert.

"PacRim's been making noises about a nova bomb, but nobody really thinks they're that crazy. Naft's warning everybody off their wind farms in the South Atlantic—that's not exactly news, not since Johannesburg." Jax shook his head. "The Net's going completely apeshit, of course. Traffic volume's sky high ..."

She took a step toward him and he stood up and put his arms around her. They stood like that for several minutes, their breathing merging slowly to unison. She smelled of sweat and of the hydroponics media she had been working with earlier that morning. The taut, lean muscles of her back relaxed to a yielding firmness under his hands. She began to move against him and she gently pushed him back into the chair.

"Wait," he said. "Not here. Let's go to the pod."

Maddy nodded without speaking and turned around, reaching

behind her back for his hand. He took it and trailed her down the narrow corridor. They passed other passageways branching off, leading to sleeping quarters, the galley, the labs. At the end of the corridor, standing like an abstract sculpture, was a gleaming, twisted piece of obsidian Maddy had brought in from one of Titan's lava plains. Oxidation from the station's atmosphere gave its surface a rainbow sheen. A rude step was carved into its side with a hand laser. Above it was a round, open hatch. Maddy let go of his hand, stepped up onto the rock, and pulled herself through. Jax followed behind her, emerging into a crystalline bubble surrounded by a sea of swirling mist.

They had grown the pod from a single crystal into a transparent, 5-meter hemisphere. It was light and thin, but strong enough to keep out the deadly hydrocarbon brew that was Titan's atmosphere. The fog was beginning to thin a little, and through it Jax could see the frozen landscape glittering in tenebrous, diffuse light. He caught a glimpse of a herd of slugs on the shore of the nearby ammonia sea. Their shiny, chitinous bodies were scattered across the lava beach in a rough pattern like sheared concentric diamonds, slowly shifting.

Maddy had already taken her clothes off, and she stood facing him, waiting. Jax stepped out of his shorts and put his arms around her again. They stood there, rocking slowly, then together they sunk to the carpeted floor.

When Maddy came, a shuddering ripple passed unseen through the pattern made by the slugs' bodies. Jax's pleasure shortly afterward sent another wave passing through the pattern from the opposite side. The ripples collided and scattered, each leaving an imprint of its shape on the other.

Jax gently disentangled himself from Maddy, trying not to wake her. She groaned softly once and rolled over, then her breathing returned to normal. Her face was relaxed and completely expressionless, as if sleep were a black hole from which nothing of herself escaped.

For an instant, it looked to Jax like the face of a perfect stranger, its contours so achingly familiar that the familiarity itself was something exotic. He reached out to touch her and his hand hovered above the curve of her cheek, trembling slightly.

So strange, he thought, the two of us out here, middle of nowhere, ties to home nothing more than electromagnetic ephemera. Ghosts. What *are* we to each other in the absence of context? We create our own, always have.

They met when they were graduate students at the Sorbonne, Maddy in planetary physics, Jax in system dynamics. They were both driven to succeed, the shining stars in their respective departments' firmament of hopeful students, and they gravitated towards one another with the same intensity that fueled their research.

They cycled through several iterations of crash and burn, learning each other's boundaries, before they settled into a kind of steady state. Still, their relationship felt to Jax like a living entity, a nonlinear filter whose response to stimuli was never quite what you thought it was going to be.

Individually, they were excellent candidates for SunGroup, a system-wide industrial development consortium—mining, pharmaceuticals, SP-sats, all supported by a broad base of research and exploration. As a couple they were perfect for one of Sun's elite research teams. When they finished out their three-year term, especially if they had "made their bones" by discovering something of interest and potential profit, they would have enough clout in SunGroup to command their own programs.

The slugs were certainly of interest. They were at the apex of Titan's spartan ecosystem—black, almost featureless bullet-shaped creatures about the size of dogs. Methane-breathers, they basked in the shallows of Titan's ammonia seas and fed on anything organic— the primitive lichen that grew in sporadic patches on the moon's rough surface, the glittering chunks of hydrocarbon ice scattered like moraine across the landscape, even each other.

Jax could watch them for hours. They exhibited behavior not unlike schooling or flocking, merging in geometric clusters, shifting, forming new patterns. Individually, they seemed less sensate than bees; their central nervous system consisted of nothing more than a small knot of ganglia at the wider end, where there was a cluster of light-sensitive vision patches. They were living cellular automata— each responding only to nearest-neighbor stimuli. Collectively, though, from the local interactions, there emerged a complex, evolving pattern.

The fog was thick again, a uniform shroud. It seemed to glow with a dim, pearly light of its own. Jax wondered about the slugs outside, what they were doing. He closed his eyes and in that darkness he imagined a slowly shifting pattern of glowing points, an elongated oval surrounding a hard, geometric pattern of sharp edges and straight lines.

II

Maddy took another leaf from the small pile of lettuce in the colander and put it in her mouth. The taste was so bittersweet *green*, so substantial and earthy, that it brought tears to her eyes.

"The new crop of lettuce is really good," she said. "I think I finally got the 'ponics chemistry down."

"About time," Jax said. He looked up from the catfish he was cleaning. Fresh from the tank farm, its bright organs spilled out on the cutting board. Blood streaked his hands and the smell of it was strong and sharp in the little galley. "The last batch had that weird, rotten aftertaste. I kept waiting for the cramps to start."

"Well, fuck you, then." The words seemed to materialize in the air between them, as if they had come from somewhere separate from her. She felt color rising to her cheeks, but there was no place to go but forward. "Anytime you want the job, you just say so."

Jax looked startled and hurt. He wiped his cheek, leaving a bloody streak, and bent down to his work again. His large hands were quick and sure. Maddy could feel the tension between them like a third presence in the room. She took a deep breath and let it out. Again. In, I calm my body. Out, dwelling in the present moment. In, listen, listen. Out, the sound of my breathing brings me back to my true self.

She took a step toward him and put her hand on his arm. He looked up. She kissed his cheek, tasting blood.

"I'm sorry, baby," she said. "I'm a little wired out with the war news. I can't take much more of it." She bit her lip. "If it gets any worse, I'm going to want Sun to pull us out of here. I need to be near my parents."

"Jesus, Maddy, Paris is the last place we want to be if the shit really hits the fan—it'll go up in a puff of plasma." He paused when he saw the expression on her face and reached out to touch her arm. "I'm sorry, but you know it's true. Do you really want to move to Ground Zero?" He let his arm fall again. "Besides, if we abort, they'll nail us with a stiff fine and we'll never get them to back us again."

"We can afford it."

Jax shrugged. "We can afford the fine, yeah, but we'd have to start from scratch with another Group, and that wouldn't be easy."

"Maurice will swing it for us." Maurice Enza was their sponsor at SunGroup. A hundred-thirty-two years old, mostly cybernetic prosthetics including eyes and voice box, still publishing in the theoretical bioeconomics literature. Maddy revered him. Jax respected him, but privately thought he was something of a spook and had always kept him at a polite distance.

"Maurice may be as old as Elvis but he isn't God."

Maddy closed her eyes. In, I calm my body. Out, listen, listen.

She opened her eyes and looked closely at him. His face was open and earnest. He wasn't just being an asshole or doing some kind of power thing.

Maddy smiled gently. "Let's just see what happens, okay?"

The catfish was delicious, its flesh moist and white, the Cajun-style crust black and redolent with spice. The lettuce tasted sweeter with the fact that she had grown it with her own hands, nursed from a rack of seedlings in a carefully tended nutrient bath to full, leafy plants, their tangled roots weaving through their bed of saturated foam.

They ate together in silence. A Bach violin concerto played softly on the lounge speakers, the melodic lines arching gracefully over the muted hum of the life support systems.

Strange to be so connected with the sensate, Maddy thought, these earthy pleasures, while we're in this tin can at the bottom of an ocean of freezing poison, a billion and a half klicks from most of the people I love. Where everything's falling apart. Listening to Bach, no less.

She shook her head. Cognitive dissonance.

Jax looked over at her and smiled. "What?"

"Oh, nothing, I … I don't know." She held her hands out in front of her, palms up, as if she were gauging the weight of an invisible package.

The veined rock flashed by her in a grey, flickering blur. Every now and then, she emerged into an open space for an instant and caught a brief glimpse of distant walls, stalactites and stalagmites merging in midair to form complex, bulbous shapes, ghostly green in the enhanced infrared. Then the bottom wall would rush up and swallow her again. A readout on the display in the lower left corner of her vision flashed her depth below the surface.

Maddy saw a fault open up off to her left and she steered her way over to it by opening the right-hand throttle of her jetpack, a bit of Buck Rogers kitsch she'd coded up to contextualize the virtual a bit, give it some tactile reference. Too easy to get disoriented otherwise—sim-sick.

She followed the fault down toward Titan's core, passing through large black regions where her mapping was still incomplete. The fault twisted and turned, opening at times to a wide crevasse, then narrowing down until it was little more than a stress plane in the tortured rock.

She slowed down and pushed a button on the virtual display. Three-dimensional volume renderings of the stress field in the rock appeared all around her as glowing lines, fractal neon limbs cascading into smaller and smaller filamentary tangles. She filtered the display until all she saw were the glowing tangles against a field of deep, velvet blackness. The fault itself was a tortured sheet of cold fire.

She hovered there in the darkness, surrounded by light. *This* is what I know, she thought. *This* is familiar. She could as well have been in a geo-simulation of the Earth's crust. The equations of elasto-plastic deformation are invariant under acts of God and Man.

Stochastic, fractal, extraordinarily complex, the solutions could still be understood, predicted with some reliability, projected onto a lower-dimensional attractor for a smoother representation.

All well and good as science. As personal metaphor it had its drawbacks. Maddy knew people back home whose lives were distressingly simple—work, family, sheep-like pursuit of leisure all fixed, remorseless basins of attraction with no fractal boundaries. They eluded her, whatever drove them completely foreign. Her personal trajectory was constrained to a more chaotic topology.

With a corner of her awareness, she could feel her real-time body, helmeted, visored, ensconced in a padded chair in a darkened featureless room.

And in the lab, cocooned in biostasis, the embryo, a radiant point of light in her mind's eye. She could imagine the impossibly slow heartbeat, just enough to keep it suspended above the threshold of death. In quiet moments, she imagined that pulse to be her own, could feel her awareness contract to that tiny lump of blood and meat, miracle of coded proteins. One part Jax, one part Maddy. Something other than the sum of its constituents.

It was usually bearable, her awareness of it a dull, constant pressure in the back of her mind. But sometimes she felt an ache in the deepest part of her, as if it had been torn from her leaving a bleeding, septic cavity. How could it live apart from her? Or she from it? She would tell Jax soon.

III

He turned off the suit speaker. The sibilant whisper of his breath and the deep ocean surge of blood music in his ears rushed in to fill the silence. Titan's daylight sky arched over his head like a great inverted bowl, deep cyan overhead fading to a bruised purple around the horizon. The photochemical smog was thinned to a gauzy softness, a blurring of focus, and Sol hung overhead like a bright, fuzzy diamond. He could almost feel the weight of Saturn's presence suspended unseen in the sky, shielded by Titan's bulk.

He had walked about a klick along the shore. The station was no longer visible behind him and he felt exhilarated with the solitude. A herd of about twenty slugs had been pacing him as he walked, oozing along almost like a single organism. He hadn't been sure at first whether they started trailing him or he them, but he was certain they were aware of him now. When he stopped, they did. He walked another few steps along the rocky shore, and the herd moved along with him like an amoeba, extending a long, thin pseudopod which was then reabsorbed into the main body. This was the first time they had exhibited anything like a response to an external stimulus. Like *awareness*.

What *are* you? They stretched out before him, attenuating into a long, sinuously curving line, like an old river.

He closed his eyes and concentrated as hard as he could. *Tell me what you are.*

In his mind's eye he saw the pattern, a meandering line of bright sparks, ripple slightly. He opened his eyes.

Tell me.

Another rippling wave passed through the line.

He turned on his radio. "Maddy. Can you suit up and get out here. I want—"

"What the fuck have you been doing? I've been trying to reach you for the last hour." Her voice sounded tight and thin.

"I turned off the speaker. I—"

"Can you get in here?" Long pause. "Please?"

The holotank was on, but she was staring off into space. In the transparent, glass cube Jax could see ghostly, flickering images of fire and smoke.

"*—retaliated with a 50-kiloton airburst over Manila. The latest estimates of the death toll—*"

"What's going on?"

She looked up at him. Her eyes were puffy. "Paris."

He felt the word almost like a physical blow. "Shit. Where else?"

She shook her head. "It's all coming apart. Naft and Russia have managed to keep out of it so far, but it's just a matter of time."

"*—emergency session, but no word yet from the CEO Council—*"

"Anything from SunGroup?"

She shook her head again. She had the look of an accident victim —hollow eyes, slow, deliberate gestures.

"—*ground forces overwhelmed Mitsubishi troops outside Sydney. Conventional theater weapons*—"

Jax waved his hand sharply over a panel on the wall. The volume of the newsfeed decreased to a murmur. The holotank still flickered and glowed with the images of burning cities. He walked over to her and put his hand on her shoulder. She sat there stiffly, as if unaware of his presence; her shoulder felt like it was made of wood. He put his other hand there and started to knead the tight muscles, but she shook him off.

He stood behind her for a long time, not knowing what to do. Every now and then, Maddy let out a long, shuddering sigh.

Finally she looked up. "What are we going to do?"

He shrugged. "What can we do? We can survive here indefinitely—the station ecology's intact and stable. We continue the research, wait for SunGroup to pull us out of here."

Even as he said it, though, Jax felt a rush of panic at the thought of leaving. He closed his eyes and a matrix of points, white on velvet black, pulsed and flowed. Concentric diamonds, slowly shearing. He opened his eyes and Maddy was staring at him.

"Continue the research? What for? We don't even know if there *is* a SunGroup anymore. We have to find out what's left back there, get back if we can. We can *help*."

Jax was silent for a long time. "What we need to do is survive, Maddy," he said slowly. "Keep the systems green, keep the research going. I'll try to raise Maurice, find out what their status is, but I don't know when they're going to be able to get to us. I think we're pretty much on our own."

"If they can spare a ship, I want to go home," Maddy said. "Luna, one of the O'Neils, I don't care. Our place right now is back there."

Jax forced himself to smile reassuringly. "All right, Maddy, we'll see what they can do. We'll have at least three hours until we can get a reply—"

"—a hundred-seventy-four minutes—"

"—providing we can get through at all. The Net is probably stone dead, all those EMPs." He gestured toward the holotank.

"That stuff is probably coming in relayed from one of the O'Neils ..."

"We can't really tell what's going on back there from the news-feed—the information entropy is sky high. We're not going to know until we ask someone who knows something. Let's just do it."

Together they walked down the corridor to the communications room. Jax logged on, set the protocol, and transmitted Maurice's address from memory.

He faced the blank screen. A section of it elasticized invisibly, ready to transform his voice into digitized bits and hurl them up to the relay satellite waiting at one of Titan's Trojan Points. There was no return visual, of course—dialogue was impossible. Whenever Jax transmitted across the lightspeed gulf separating him from Earth, he had the sensation that his words were disappearing down a well. He could feel Maddy's presence behind him like a hovering cloud.

"Maurice. This is Jax and Maddy calling from Titan Station." Obviously. Where else would they be calling from? "Please advise us as to your status. We—"

"Pull us out of here, Moe," Maddy cut in. "Please. We want to come home."

Jax shot her an annoyed glance and turned back to the screen. "Please advise," he repeated. "End."

Ignoring Maddy, he tried to log onto his WorldNet node, but couldn't get a stable carrier at the other end. Tried routing through Luna, through Olympus Mons, through the O'Neils.

"Nada," he said, shaking his head and looking up. Maddy was gone.

He looked in the lounge. Empty. In the holotank, a pair of translu-cent figures gestured in animated conversation, but Jax couldn't make out the words. Galley, labs, sleeproom, all empty. Finally, he walked down to the end of the corridor and pulled himself up into the pod. The fog nestled against the dome in thick, soft swirls. Maddy lay curled up on a foam pad, breathing deeply.

He walked past her to the edge of the dome and peered out through the fog. He could just see them, stretched out in a slowly undulating line next to the ammonia sea. The undulations grew until the line broke apart, the segments forming a series of rings. Slowly, one at a time, the rings merged and the pattern segued to a nest of concentric diamonds, slowly shearing. There was sense and meaning to it, he was sure, but comprehension hovered just out of reach.

What are you?

The soft chime of the comm bell shook Jax out of his reverie. Three hours? I've been standing here for three hours? He looked around the dome, his eyes coming to rest on Maddy lying in a fetal curl, her shoulders slowly rising and falling. He stepped over her and lowered himself down the hatch.

There was no visual, but Jax recognized the flat inflections of Maurice's voice synthesizer.

"Sorry about the visual—we're under severe bandwidth restrictions. Power rationing, too, so I'll have to be quick. The fighting's almost over, except for a few hotspots. Earth is pretty much of a mess—Europe, Japan, Indonesia ... latest estimates say a billion dead. Naft came through pretty well. Russia, too, but they're going to take a lot of fallout from PacRim. SunGroup is putting together a group at O'Neil Two, sort of a reconstruction team. We can use all the help here we can get, but we also need to keep the long-range research efforts going. Your call, but frankly, we could use you. We're sending a ship out to make a sweep of the research stations, anybody who wants to come back. Old ore freighter from the Belt, retrofitted with an ion drive. Best we can do right now. Let me know what you want to do. We don't want to burn up the delta-vee to get out to you if we don't have to."

Jax listened to the spectral hiss of interplanetary white noise riding over the carrier hum. He played the message back again. The words began to merge together, their individual meaning softening like heated wax. He played the message back again.

IV

She hovered on the knife-edge between wakefulness and sleep. Images of smoke and flame, of exploding suns, chased each other across the surface of her consciousness. She was on a hover-barge on the Seine, sitting in the back at the controls. Sharp smell of moss and damp stone as she passed under a bridge. Her parents and sisters on the deck in front of her, sitting beneath a blue and white umbrella. Sipping drinks, laughing. Low grey clouds holding the threat of rain.

Suddenly, an impossibly bright light swelling from the east, a second sun breaking through the clouds. The umbrella bursting into flame, her family instantly transformed into stick figure torches. The Seine was *boiling*, bubbling up over the sides of the barge …

She opened her eyes. Jax's face hovered above her in the half dark. He put his hand on her arm.

"Dreams?"

She nodded, still gripped by the vision. "Yeah."

Jax stroked her arm. "I heard from Maurice," he said after a moment. "We're on our own, Maddy. He has no idea when they'll be able to get to us."

It was like a physical blow. Her tropism for home radiated up from the very center of her, from her First Chakra. Its denial sent a surge of panic through her.

She closed her eyes. Breathe, breathe. In, I calm my body. Out, my breathing returns me to my true self. In, breathe calm, white sun swelling in the East. Out, listen, listen, Seine bubbling up over the sides of the barge. In, centuries old stone bridge sagging molten soft. Out, pillars of flame dancing on the deck of the barge snuffed by hammer wind.

"Maddy." Her eyes fluttered open again. "Are you all right?"

She looked closely at him. His long, thin face, so familiar, composed in a mask of concern.

Slowly, she shook her head. "No," she said. "Nothing's all right."

Maddy hadn't worn her environment suit in weeks and it chafed under her arms and between her legs. She looked back at the station, so out of place in the alien landscape, clinging in the tattered mist to the dark rock like a cluster of warts. The pod glittered in the dim light. She imagined Jax back there, his sleeping form sprawled naked across the foam pad.

She still ached slightly from their sex. He had been fast and rough, almost brutal. She didn't care, had lain there limply, receiving him. Her orgasm was joyless, passing through her like a wave, leaving no trace of itself.

When she got to the shore of the ammonia sea, she stopped. Small ripples lapped up against the rocky beach. She looked down at the canister she was carrying. Featureless, burnished metal, such an innocuous thing.

Without further thought, she pressed a recessed button on its side. A thin line appeared around the top rim and a puff of vapor escaped, freezing instantly into a cloud of scintillating crystals. She unscrewed the lid and shook its contents out into the sea. Shards of metglass webbing, spidery strands of plastic tubing, chunks of brittle, frozen foam. She couldn't even see the scrap of flesh they cradled. A few meters away, a small herd of slugs clustered near the shore in a senseless and inchoate sprawl.

ON THE VARIANCE OF THE COLD EQUATIONS UNDER A BASIS TRANSFORMATION

The void between the stars was supposed to be silent, but to Barton the void was the humming in the soles of his feet, the slight vibration in the bulkhead he felt when he reached his hand out to touch the cold metal. The void was supposed to be vast and formless, but to Barton the void was form itself: the four walls of the cabin, the control panel with its silent array of telltales. The feeling was not of vastness but smallness; he occupied a tiny bubble of heat and light and air, a bright bead on a great, dark canvas. The void between the stars was supposed to be the howling nothingness of n-space, but the Emergency Dispatch Ship's memory contained the sum of human knowledge, and Barton filled the hours with history, entertainment, technical training, and pornography. He masturbated nearly constantly when he was on a run; all the EDS pilots did. It was common knowledge, tacitly shared, never discussed, even when they traded files over a secure channel. Barton's preferences ran to snuff and torture: young, pale women naked and bound, struggling while men in leather masks burned their translucent skin with iron brands or peeled strips of flesh from their bodies with long, slender blades.

Barton supposed that his proclivities were recorded somewhere in the Colonial Administration's databases, but he wasn't terribly worried about it. The adage went: *What happens in n-space, stays in n-space.* Humans who were sufficiently skilled to pilot the quirky

Emergency Dispatch Ships who could also withstand the long, empty hours in transit were, like the stars that hosted habitable planets, few and far between. Besides, it was just brain candy, diversions to fill the void. It had nothing to do with *him*, with who he was. He thought of his wife and daughters, waiting for him in the conapt back in Luna. Joan setting the table for the girls. The kitchen dialed to Renaissance Meadow, her favorite, or maybe Octopus Garden.

Yes, Octopus Garden. He could see the room filled with shifting green light, the dappled surface far above. The three of them eating quietly, the empty place at the table——*his* place—a keenly felt presence. Everything neat and spotless. Everything in order. They were good girls, all of them.

One of the telltales blinked red. Movement in the aft storage compartment. *No.* He felt suddenly dizzy and reached out to the console to steady himself. He looked again. Definitely movement, something big enough to trigger the motion detector. It could only be one thing, a stowaway, and Colonial Administration policy was clear on the subject.

Any stowaway discovered aboard an EDS shall be jettisoned immediately following discovery.

Jettisoned. It sounded so clinical. What it meant, of course, was that Barton would either force the stowaway at the point of a blaster to voluntarily enter the airlock, or he would drag the stiff, cooling body into the airlock while the ventilation system labored to rid the cabin of the stench of cooked meat. This was the frontier and what seemed harsh and brutal back in the soft comfort of the Core was driven by necessity and survival here at the bleeding edge. The Newtonian equations of motion allowed no room for emotion or interpretation. Colonial Administration policy was very clear on the subject. It was the law and there could be no appeal. The little EDS ships were dispatched only in extremely urgent cases. They carried no extra fuel and the mass of a stowaway really messed things up.

Barton had dealt with stowaways on two occasions—rough, crude men, typical of the marginal types that one found in a frontier society. They knew they were bucking the system and they knew the consequences, but they thought the rules didn't apply to them.

He didn't know their names. He didn't want to know their

names. The first one had hidden in the crawlspace between the engine room and the cargo hold and by the time Barton found him he was nearly dead anyway. Still, he begged and pleaded, wheedled and whined. The kind of man who would cut your throat in a back alley for the change in your pocket and he was reduced to a whimpering thing, barely human. At the end, he realized that there was no bargaining with the laws of men and nature and he passively allowed himself to be led into the airlock.

The second one came at Barton with a length of pipe as soon as he opened the storeroom door. Barton's blaster was in his hand before his conscious brain had a chance to react and he burned the man's face off. He had only a vague memory of dragging the two hundred pound meatsack to the airlock. The EDS shuddered when it expelled the body into the grayness of n-space. *Jettisoned.* Tumbling end over end into the space between the spaces between the stars.

This one would be another Rough Man, trying to game the system, to circumvent the Colonial Authority requirements for physical or emotional fitness. A new life in the Colonies, a fresh start. But there were rules. Barton knew he would have no trouble dealing with such a man.

He walked up the door of the storage compartment.

"Come out!" he said abruptly.

There was no answer. Barton knew he was in there, though, could picture him hunched in the dark, stinking of confinement and fear, his heart racing as he realized the game was up. But he had no idea just how far over the edge he had stepped.

Barton rested his hand on the holstered blaster. "Out!" he said. "Now!"

There was a long pause. Barton heard movement behind the door. He tensed, remembering the last time. He was ready.

The door hissed open and the stowaway stepped through, smiling.

"All right—I give up." She held her hands up in mock surrender. "Now what?"

Barton's hand fell away from his blaster. His mouth fell open.

A girl.

She couldn't have been more than sixteen, standing before him in her little white jumpsuit and gypsy sandals. Curly brown hair cascaded past her shoulders and her green eyes held a twinkle of merriment—unknowing, unafraid.

Now what? *Now what?* Oh, you poor girl, you have no idea.

He returned to his pilot's chair and motioned her to sit on the boxy housing of the drive control unit facing him.

She crossed her legs demurely and smiled again at him.

"I'm Marilyn Cross," she said, holding her hand out. When he didn't take it, she frowned. It was even more disarming than her smile.

"Okay," she said. "I'm guilty. What do I have to do, pay a fine?"

"What are you doing here?" Barton asked, finally.

Her smile faded. "I—well, I wanted to see my brother. He's with the survey crew on Woden. I haven't seen him in over ten years! When the *Stardust* dropped out of n-space at WayStation Beta I heard this ship would be going to Woden and I just sneaked aboard with the cleaning bot when nobody was looking. I knew I'd be breaking some kind of regulation, but I'll gladly pay the fine. I can work for my keep, too. I can cook—"

"Marilyn." He thought of the EDS bay, the little ships in a neat row on one end, awaiting dispatch. There was a huge sign, plainly visible from almost anywhere in the room.

No Unauthorized Personnel

There was an identical sign hanging above the only entrance to the bay. She couldn't possibly have missed seeing them. She chose to ignore them and the consequences would be horrible and final.

The laws of physics were Draconian; they could not be ignored. You couldn't smile sweetly at them, bat your eyelashes, and say *Now what?* Barton wasn't much of a scientist but the icy logic of the equations of motion was inescapable: *h amount of fuel will power an EDS with a mass of m safely to its destination. The same amount of fuel will not power an EDS with a mass of m plus x safely to its destination.* Marilyn was x. The x factor. She and her gypsy sandals. Her twinkling green eyes. Remove x and the equations balance. Order is restored.

Order. Existence requires order. Even in the wild chaos of the frontier, *especially* in the wild chaos of the frontier, man's tenuous foothold on the edge of infinity required strict obedience to natural laws. There was no malevolence; the laws were without emotion or passion. *Now what?* They didn't care about this beautiful young girl in her gypsy sandals. *What do I have to do, pay a fine?* They didn't even know about her. They knew nothing. Nothing! They simply operated in a plane in which the concerns of man did not play a role!

"Marilyn," he said again. He spoke slowly, as if to a small child. "Did your brother know you were coming?"

"Oh no," she said. "Gerry's a real stickler for rules."

He's a man of the frontier, Barton thought. *A man like me. He'll understand.*

"Why are you looking at me like that?"

"Do you know why this ship is going to Woden?"

She shook her head. "Supplies, I guess."

"Kala fever. This ship is carrying Kala fever serum to Woden. Their supply was destroyed by a tornado."

"Gerry—"

"Is he in Group One or Group Two?"

"I don't know."

Barton bent over the EDS console and pulled up the communication logs.

"Gerald Cross. Group Two." He looked up at Marilyn. "Your brother is on the other side of the planet. He's safe. But there are six men in Group One who will die if this ship doesn't make it."

"Thank God he's okay. That's terrible about those other men, though. But we'll get there on time, won't we?"

Jesus Christ, she really hasn't figured it out yet. Poor, stupid girl.

There was nothing anybody could do. Barton wished it could be different, but the equations that manifested the will of nature were crystalline in their perfection, inhuman, without emotion or malice.

He thought of the tornado that had destroyed the Group One encampment, ripping through the installation with inchoate fury, a roaring, thundering tower of rage that sought to annihilate everything in its path. He imagined himself as the tornado. His head thrust through the clouds, a billowing nimbus. His legs and arms, churning funnels of destruction.

The land below was pristine and raw, nearly smooth from this altitude but, at ground level, rough with rocky debris and hidden arroyos. The encampment was a chancre and Barton reached down to wipe it away. Men scattered like mindless ants stirred with a stick wielded by a malicious child. The prefab buildings exploded at his touch. He cut a great swath of chaos through the encampment.

"You're giving me that look again," the girl said.

He blinked, pulled back from his reverie. "I'm sorry, Marilyn. You have no idea how sorry I am."

"What are you talking about?"

"Colonial Administration regulations are very clear. Here, let me show you."

He fiddled with the console and pulled up the relevant portion of the handbook.

Any stowaway discovered aboard an EDS shall be jettisoned immediately following discovery.

She cried out, her hand covering her mouth.

"No! What? Jettisoned? Are you insane? You can't do this ..."

She stood up and backed away, holding her hand in front of her as if to ward off the inevitable.

"It has to be this way, Marilyn. The fuel consumption on these ships is calculated down to the gram. If you stay on this ship, we'll crash. We'll both die and the men on Woden will die as well. I'm so sorry."

He held his hand out to her but she didn't respond, didn't see it. She backed into the wall and stood there, sobbing, tears streaming down her face.

"Fuel?" she said, finally. "That's what this is about? *Fuel?* Look, I mass about 50 kilos. How much water do you have on board?"

"Um ... well, it's two days in n-space to Woden. I've got about 15 liters for drinking, maybe another ten for, um, hygiene."

"My God, that's 25 kilos right there. It's just two days. What about food?"

"Just these little packets. High density. You need water ..."

"Two kilos, five?"

"Sure, five."

"Oh my God, I think we can do this. This *door* ..."

She pounded on the door to the storage compartment she had hidden in.

"Ten kilos, at least. Yes? Do you have tools?"

"Um."

"You must have something."

There was a toolkit under the console. Not much—a couple of wrenches and screwdrivers, a soldering gun, a heavy-duty cutting laser.

"I—I don't know."

"God, oh God, oh God. It doesn't matter. Fifty kilos. There's gotta be something."

She looked around. Barton could see white all around her eyes.

"The *chair*," she said. "Your fucking *chair*. That—that *drive housing* I was sitting on. Our *clothes*."

She zipped down the front of her jumpsuit, exposing her small, young breasts.

"Marilyn," Barton said, walking towards her.

"Oh, God, I don't want to die."

"You have no idea how sorry I am, Marilyn. If there was anything anybody could do, we would do it. Nobody wants this."

The equations were clear: *h amount of fuel will not power an EDS with a mass of m plus x safely to its destination.* The circumference of a circle was pi times the diameter, no matter what. Well, except in n-space, where it was something else. But that was for the eggheads back in the Core. Barton was no scientist. He was just a rocket jockey, and the laws of physics were immutable and clear.

"I'll fuck you," she said suddenly. Her eyes were wild. She grabbed his shirt, wrapped her legs around his thigh, began grinding obscenely against him. She kissed him, her tongue seeking his. Barton felt himself responding in spite of his revulsion.

"I'm still a virgin, but I'll do anything." Her breath was hot in his ear. "Anything you've ever wanted. Anything you've ever thought of. I'll suck your cock. I'll—"

Barton slapped her, hard. She lurched back, holding her hand to her cheek where a red welt was appearing.

"There will be none of that."

She collapsed against the bulkhead, sobbing, rocking, holding her knees. Her chestnut hair spilled down her bare back. Her keening filled the little ship. He walked to her and stood towering over her.

"I'm sorry, Marilyn. Nobody wants you to die. You have no idea."

In the end, he had to shoot her. The little ship shuddered as it ejected the body, a tiny seed tumbling through n-space, tumbling forever through the space between the spaces between the stars.

RANDOM ACTS OF KINDNESS

THE FOG BROUGHT me a gift this morning. When I woke in the pre-dawn stillness to relieve myself it lay over everything like cotton ticking. I stepped out onto the porch and held my hand in front of my face. I could barely see it, a splayed dark outline, the space between the fingers like webbing in the half dark.

I went back to sleep and when I awoke again the fog was thinner. Not completely gone, but the sky had that bright gray look like there was blue up there somewhere. On the porch railing, next to a small potted cactus, was the head of a mountain lion. There was a dark, irregular stain on the wood underneath it and the fur around what was left of its neck was torn and bloody. Its eyes were open and its mouth was fixed in a snarl. As I watched, an ant crawled up the matted fur of its cheek, explored for a moment, and disappeared into a nostril.

Even in death, there was something magnificent about the creature and I thought of Egyptian gods in hieroglyphic profile. I looked beyond it to the sloping, rock-studded hill disappearing into the fog still hugging the ground.

I had been looking for that cat. In the last month I'd lost two sheep, and the day before, I'd come home to find my goat, Mama Cass, lying in a pool of blood, eviscerated and partly eaten. There was no sign, nothing to track—the killer left about as much spoor as the fog.

I walked to the head of the rickety wooden stairs and looked around, hoping to catch a glimpse of whoever or whatever had graced me with this offering, knowing I wouldn't. I had an urge to shout, just to hear my voice damped, absorbed into that mist like rain into dry dust. I didn't see anything I didn't expect—just the fog, the gentle contours of the hillside, and off to the left, just visible through the whiteness, my old, blue Chevy rust bucket sitting under a listing, tin-roofed lean-to.

Beyond the truck were the woods. They went on for miles, almost all the way to the ocean, uninterrupted except for patches of clear-cut. I remember, years ago, flying low over the coastal range in a small private plane, seeing miles of deep, mysterious green scarred and broken by wide swaths of nothing. Dead zones. It made me want to cry. Not too much of that this far out in the boonies, but the lumber companies and the Feds managed to make a sorry mess of things before they stopped. Before everything stopped.

I was hungry, and debated with myself whether to make something before heading down the mountain, or wait until I got to Stores. I never liked to pass up an opportunity to sit down to some of Evy's hash, but I was going to be bartering for gasoline to keep my generator going and needed a clear head, so I went back to the kitchen and grabbed an oatcake to give my blood sugar a kick. On my way out, I stopped at the hall closet and got the box of .22 longs that I planned to use for trade. There was only about a case and a half left and I felt a sharp stab of worry as I wondered what I was going to use for currency when that was gone. I didn't want to think about it. Under a tarp in the back of the truck there was also a small buck I'd bagged the day before. That and the ammo should get me five gallons at least, maybe a box of nails.

As I walked out through the porch again, breaking off crumbs of cake and putting them in my mouth, I took another look at the cathead. It had lost most of its magic for me and just looked dead, the eyes glazed over, the fur taking on the dull gloss of old carpet. I felt a chill run down my spine though as I wondered again how it got there. The hairs on the back of my neck were standing on end.

The truck was hard starting. There was always fog up here and I think the dampness got into the electrical system somehow. It turned over and over but wouldn't quite catch. Just when the starter was about to call it quits, cranking slower and slower and groaning with the effort, the engine kicked in. I saw a cloud of blue smoke rise in the rear-view mirror and mix with the fog. I opened the glove compartment and took out my Walther, took the safety off, and jacked a shell in the chamber. I laid it gently on the seat next to me. I thought of Annie and pushed the thought away. Two years since she died, and I was still hurting. Everything in the house and the rough land around it shouted her name at me.

The road wound down the mountain, hugging the contours, switchbacking a couple of times. I could drive it in my sleep. By the time the hardpack dirt gave way to asphalt, I was out from under the fog and I could see plumes of woodsmoke rising from behind the curve of the next hill. As I rounded its side, the twin windmills that provided power for the little community came into view—tall, spidery things perched at the mouth of the valley like birds of prey. Only one of them was spinning—the other was down again, waiting for a trader to make the long trip up from Tehachapi with spare parts.

I pulled up in front of the trading post, a low, ramshackle building with a sprawling collection of additions. There were a couple of trailers off to the side, and a long aluminum storage shed. A neatly lettered sign reading "Stores" hung over the main entrance. Behind the main building, scattered throughout the woods and down the road, were about thirty houses, most of them new—makeshift dwellings that sprouted up around Stores like mushrooms on nightsoil after they got the windmills going. It was still pretty early and the dirt lot in front of the shed was empty. I stuck the Walther in my belt and walked in.

Evy was behind the counter. She was wearing a rough homespun shirt and her long, gray-streaked hair was pulled back into a thick braid. Behind her, pots and saucepans perched on Coleman burners, filling the room with the smells of chili, chicory, and kerosene. Through a door next to the stove I saw a jumbled confusion of merchandise—bolts of cloth, tools, barrels of dry goods. There was a single customer, someone I'd never seen before. He wore a scarf over his head that didn't quite cover an ugly burn scar and he sat hunched over his joe like he thought someone was going to take it away from him. Evy smiled when she saw me.

"Blair," she said. "How goes it?" There was a gold star inlaid into one of her front teeth and it flashed at me as she spoke.

"Some strange shit, Ev'." I told her about the offering I'd received. When I was finished, she rolled her eyes and whistled softly through her teeth. "Thing is, though," I went on, "I don't know whether to feel threatened or graced. I mean, I *wanted* that cat, but this is pretty damn strange."

As I talked, the stranger became more and more agitated, mumbling to himself and slopping his chicory on the counter in front of him. Finally he turned to me. The burn scar sprawled across his face like an open hand. His eyes peering out from behind it held a sick, flickering light.

"It's happening, man," he said. "They're coming back. Cowboy Neal at the wheel, man. Four-dimensional beings in three-dimensional bodies looking out two-dimensional windshields. Ashes to ashes, man. They're coming *back*."

I looked at Evy with a questioning frown. She shrugged and pointed down, meaning, I guess, that she figured he had come up from the South, from the ruins around Sacto or San Francisco. People didn't travel much anymore, but we still got a steady trickle —techno-junk traders, musicians, storytellers, and the occasional crazy.

"I seen it, man. It's happened to me. I was up to Shasta, up near the summit, and I got caught in a storm." Something happened to his eyes then—the fevered light dimmed and he seemed almost sane. "Man, I had half a biscuit in my pocket and the shirt on my back and the temperature dropped from sixty to zero in about twenty minutes. I thought, 'This is it, man. Thank you, Great Spirit for giving me this life, see you in the next one,' you know?" I nodded. I knew about those storms—he wasn't exaggerating. Evy had stopped wiping down the counter and was staring at him.

"Before long it was total whiteout," he continued. "Nowhere to go, so I just sat down right where I was, closed my eyes, and waited. Pretty soon my feet and hands got all numb and I just went to sleep." He giggled. "I just went to sleep, man." He shook his head and stared down into his mug. He was silent for so long I didn't know if he was going to continue speaking. "I just went to sleep," he said again, so softly it was almost inaudible. He looked up at me and grinned. "You think I'm gonna tell you I dreamed this long tunnel with a bright light at the end, right?"

I shrugged and he shook his head. "Nothin', man. No dreams at all, but I woke up in the old abandoned base camp cabin at the foot of the northwest approach. A good ten miles away. There was a fire in the stove and a big fat squirrel on the table next to it, gutted and cleaned and ready to cook. And standing there looking down at me was God's own angel. She was an angel, man ..." Evy looked at me and rolled her eyes. He didn't seem to notice. "She gave me this slow, sad smile, like she knew me, and then she turned and walked out the door. I remember the smells in the room, man—blood and woodsmoke."

He looked at Evy, then back at me, with a defiant expression, like he was daring us to call him crazy.

He beckoned me closer. "You know who I think it was?" he asked. I shook my head. He continued without pausing for an answer. "There were spirits who lived here before we came and fucked it all up. The Indians knew them and they had sort of a peaceful thing going. Then we came and started tearing down the forests and pissing in the streams and they went into hiding. I think they were always there, but they kept a low profile. Then the shit hit the fan and we almost blew ourselves off the planet. They're coming back, man ..."

"Wait a minute," Evy said. "If that's true, don't you think they'd be a little, well, pissed off? Why would they help us?" I'd been thinking the same thing.

He shook his head. "You don't get it, man. They're not like us. They don't hold grudges. It's a clean slate—we can all start over. A clean slate ..."

Then something in his face sagged and he looked back down into his mug. Evy and I looked at each other and shrugged.

"We've got some business to transact, Evy," I said after a long moment.

"What you got?" she asked.

We went through the motions of dickering and barter but neither of our hearts were in it. I got my five gallons, she got the .22 longs, and she agreed to salt all the meat and give me half. Somewhere during the course of the negotiations, our friend had disappeared.

"Hey," I said. "Where's Cowboy Neal?"

"Beats me," she said with a shrug. "Probably stepped out to score some 'shrooms."

"No shit," I said. "The band's playing but the amps aren't plugged in."

She chuckled softly. "Rock and roll will never die. You think there's anything to his story?"

"Fuck if I know," I said. "I did wake up with a cathead on my porch, but I think our friend's been smoking a little too much Humboldt Polio Weed." I was trying to make light of it, but there was something nagging at a corner of my mind and it wouldn't let go. I had heard similar stories, especially since the war. Impossible rescues, strange gifts left in the dead of night.

I spent the afternoon in the "machine shop" at Stores—little more than a garage with an old lathe, a hoist, and a meager collection of hand tools—helping Jacob Ross tear down and rebuild a generator. Jacob was Stores' resident doctor, Evy's Significant Something-or-Other, and he was pretty good with his hands. He had patched me up more than once, and had done all he could to save my wife Annie when she took two rounds in the chest from a .357 Magnum. A biker gang, up from what was left of Oakland. He wasn't a miracle worker, though—the life leaked out of her slowly but steadily, and she was gone before the night was through.

It was good working with him. We knew each other well and there was an economy of words and motion that made the work seem almost like a dance. I told him about the macabre gift I'd received and about Cowboy Neal and he just grunted and nodded. It was pretty much what I needed to hear from him. By the time I got back up the mountain to my place, the shadows were starting to lengthen and the high clouds in the western sky were streaked with gold fire.

The cathead was still on my porch and the ants had been having a field day. A line of them stretched up the side of the porch to the railing and the head itself was teeming with them. There was a cloud of flies circling and buzzing and a whiff of decay hung in the air. I wrapped a kerchief around my hand, grabbed the head by an ear, and tossed it as hard and far as I could. It bounced a couple of times and rolled into the woods. Like ringing the dinner bell for the 'coons and skunks, but I just wanted it out of my sight. I got some water from the reclamation tank and washed down the railing.

I'd been thinking about Annie again on the drive back and missing her more than a little. I decided to pay her a visit. First, though, I wanted to leave something in case my visitor showed up again. I looked around the living room and settled on the God's-eye hanging over the mantle—black and yellow yarn wound around the arms of a rude, wooden cross to form a textured pattern of concentric diamonds. The arms of the cross were tipped with hawk feathers. Annie made it the summer before she died. I didn't know why, but it seemed right. I brought it out to the porch and laid it on the railing where the cathead had been.

Annie wasn't far, just about a half-mile further up the mountain, but it was deep woods and I maintained the trail as lightly as possible—just enough to let me find my way. She would have wanted it like that.

It was one of those clearings that just opens up out of the woods like God lifting the lid from a teakettle. About half an acre of green so deep it hurt the eyes, peppered with wildflowers in the spring, studded with an array of smooth boulders perfect for sitting. It had been a favorite place of ours, even before the war. Her grave was near the uphill end of the clearing, marked by a sort of mandala of small stones, a simple spiral set into the rich earth.

Some people talk to their departed loved ones. I couldn't do it. It was too much like wishing for something that could never happen. I liked to be near her sometimes, though, when I needed to be alone with my thoughts. I sat on a boulder near her grave, stretched my legs out, and remembered …

… being out on San Francisco Bay in a sailboat under a perfect blue sky, the wind ripping through my hair, fingers completely numb. I remembered ice cream, the cold sweetness, the way the really good stuff sort of coated your tongue and the back of your mouth. I remembered what it felt like to play an old Martin, the rosewood fretboard silky beneath my calloused fingers, the rich harmonics ringing out underneath the chords, vibrating the body of the guitar.

In all of those images, Annie was there, somewhere just outside my field of vision. I began to get that tight feeling across my forehead like I was about to cry, and before long my shoulders were shaking with dry sobs. After a while, the tightness went away and my breathing returned to normal. I took a last look at Annie's grave and walked back down the meadow to where the trail disappeared into the woods.

As I made my way along the overgrown path, I had a distinct feeling that I was being watched. I stopped and looked around. It was almost dark and the woods were deep in purple shadow. The mosquitoes were out and they hovered around me in a cloud. Off to the left I heard the deep drone of a wild beehive. The air smelled of pine and leaf mold. Nothing. I thought wistfully for a moment of my Walther, lying in the glove compartment in my truck.

By the time I got home it was pitch dark and my neck was sore from looking over my shoulder. The God's eye lay on the railing where I left it. I made myself some dinner and, afterwards, brewed myself a pot of coffee from my dwindling hoard. I brought it out onto the porch and settled into the big wicker chair to wait. I had a long night ahead of me. As an afterthought, I went down to the truck and got the Walther out of the glove compartment. I didn't think I'd need it, but I was still spooked from my walk, and I had learned to trust my intuition.

I leaned back and looked up at the sky. There was a pretty good aurora. We'd been getting a lot of those since the war—gauzy, iridescent curtains hanging cold fire from the heavens. There were a lot of shooting stars, too, and at one point I saw a dim light make a slow, steady crawl across the sky. Probably Space Station Kyoto. I didn't think there was anybody up there anymore, but I wasn't sure. I felt a sharp sadness at the thought.

I must have dozed off, because when I woke the sky was beginning to take on that colorless pre-dawn shade, just before the light starts pushing itself up from the East. There was someone on the porch with me. I couldn't make out her features very well (I knew somehow it was a "her"), but I had a sense of fine cheekbones, of grace and slenderness. And I knew that she was not human. I reached behind me and rested my hand on the cold hardness of the gun.

She stepped forward, out of the shadows. Huge, liquid eyes, catching the dim light like a cat. Body covered in a fine layer of glistening fur. I wanted to reach out and touch it. She wore no clothing, but a belt slung low on her hips held a long knife, an axe, and a small pouch. She smelled faintly of ginger.

She picked up the God's-eye and held it up in front of her face. She rotated it around a quarter-turn, then back, then she laid it gently back on the railing. She looked at me then. Cowboy Neal's words echoed in my mind. *It's a clean slate, man.* With a falling sensation, I lifted my hand from the gun and met her gaze. Behind her, on the mountain, the fog was coming in.

ANGEL FROM BUDAPEST

CLAUDE WILCZEK GUIDES the old Caddy past the empty store-fronts and abandoned warehouses of downtown New Haven. The buildings rise up in front of him like the undersea temples of a decrepit, post-industrial Atlantis. Moonlight glints off jagged tips of glass in the brooding windows. He takes a left on Division Street, heading towards the bus station. Towards the women.

There are three of them, equally spaced down the length of the block. They lean against lampposts and parked cars, in postures of casual allure. He slows down as he approaches the first. Her skin is dark as bittersweet chocolate, smooth and shiny in the light from the streetlamp. She is wearing a red vinyl jacket open almost to her navel, fishnet stockings, short, black skirt. Small gold hoops pierce her left nostril and eyebrow.

A look is exchanged, a nod. He stops the car and reaches over to open the passenger door.

"You want to party?" she asks.

Claude nods nervously.

"Twenty I suck your cock."

He nods again and she gets in the car.

"The money."

Claude reaches into his shirt and hands her a crumpled bill.

They drive back down Division Street, away from the bus station, and park behind an abandoned factory. She reaches over, unzips his pants, and goes down on him. He feels the warmth spreading out from his groin and his hips begin to move.

"Yeah, baby," she says unconvincingly, pausing for a moment at the top of a stroke. She looks up at Claude. The rings through her nose and eyebrow glitter in the dark. She runs her tongue lightly down the length of his cock and engulfs him again.

Claude closes his eyes and the images wheel through him. His second wife, her face flushed with desire, half in moon shadow. His lover going down on him, her blonde hair falling over her face. His father, rough-cheek perfume of tobacco and vodka. Budapest, rain-slicked cobbled street, smell of sausages grilling on a sidewalk cart, Soviet tanks rumbling past the Government Palace.

"Oh, yeah, give it to me, baby," she says between strokes, managing to sound breathy and listless at the same time.

He opens his eyes. There is a woman standing under a street-lamp twenty feet away, facing him. She is wearing a long overcoat and her blonde hair falls limply on her shoulders. Her face is hidden in shadow, but her stance, the shape of her, resonates someplace deep inside him. Full recognition skips back just out of reach, though, flickering behind the pleasure coursing up from the center of him.

He ducks down in the seat, hoping she will not see him. His orgasm surges through him and he cries out in Hungarian, clutching the steering wheel.

When he opens his eyes again, the woman is gone.

As he is driving home, WCLA is playing Kodaly, the cello sonata. The music moves from sharp, staccato passages, the notes bitten off like broken sticks, to deep, seductive long tones, and it seems to draw the Caddy out of the crumbling downtown sprawl.

Claude feels the shame begin in a quiet place within him and work its way outwards. It is almost pre-verbal, a dark, formless shape in his mind. He knows the feeling well, and knows how to wall it off so that he can sip its exquisite bitterness in small doses.

He turns onto a tree-lined street and pulls into his driveway. As he walks up the path to his front door, he hears his daughter's footsteps pounding down the stairs.

He opens the door and she throws herself at his legs, giggling.

"Daddy, Daddy!"

He reaches down and strokes her thin, straight hair. She looks up, a dull, happy light in her too-close eyes. One of them veers wildly off to the left and the other looks straight at him. She is smiling, and it seems to push her features even closer together, accentuating the Down Syndrome signature.

"Daddy!" she says again, with a slight, muffled slur.

He leans down and kisses the top of her head.

"Hello, Zoe. Hello, baby."

He feels a wave of fierce love wash over him and he buries his face in her hair. She is so pure, he thinks. The only pure thing in my life.

His lover, Mary, is standing in the hallway, her hand on her hip, a sardonic half-smile on her face that could go either way.

He gently untangles his daughter's arms from his legs and he walks over to her.

"And you," he says. "Hello to you."

He leans over to kiss her and she turns her head so that his lips just brush against her cheek.

"We were going to try to catch the Yale Symphony's dress rehearsal tonight. Did you forget?" She steps back. "I really wanted to hear what they did to the Brahms. Callie came over from next door to babysit, but I sent her home."

Claude smacks himself on the forehead. "Shit! Shit! I'm very sorry." He really had forgotten. "I was preparing Fourier analysis lecture. Classes—"

"—start tomorrow," she finishes for him. "Yes, yes, I know. I've hardly seen you at all for the last two weeks."

"I am sorry, baby. I am space cadet."

This time, she leans towards him and kisses him on the mouth. "This is what I get for living with a mathematician. Wait until opera season opens, though. Between my rehearsals and your lectures we'll hardly recognize each other come Christmas."

✫

He awakens in the middle of the night. Mary's sleeping form is curled beside him in a fetal apostrophe. He puts on a robe and pads softly downstairs, careful so as not to awaken his daughter. He sits down at the table next to the hall phone and dials his sister's number from memory. The phone at the other end rings six, seven, eight times. Finally, a sleepy voice answers.

"Hello?"

Like Claude, Alya's accent is still very thick. Frozen, he thinks. We are frozen in time like bugs in amber. The familiar voice seems to echo in his ears over the oceanic hiss of the long distance connection. Ghost conversations weave in and out of the susurrus, faint and fragmentary.

"Hello?" she says again. "Who is this?"

Claude holds the receiver to his chest. The moonlight coming in through the living room window throws a geometric pattern of light and shadow across the hall carpet. He has not spoken with his sister for over ten years.

"Hello?"

There is a muffled curse and a sharp click.

Passing through the gates of the Yale campus is like entering a medieval keep—crumbling tenements outside, academic stone and ivy inside. Claude has a headache, and a vague feeling of incipient depression. He remembers dreaming vividly the previous night, but no details. As he pulls into his parking space behind Courant Hall, the encounter with the prostitute comes flooding back to him. Her flat, dull monotone as she snatches a breath of air. Yeah, baby. Give it to me, baby. Her head bobbing up and down in his lap, the rough, even texture of the corn rows in her hair. He is getting an erection, and a hot flush creeps up his cheeks. He looks at himself in the rearview mirror, feels a rush of loathing at the delicate features—pale skin stretched tight across slight, feminine curves of bone, fine tracery of blue veins just visible beneath the surface.

Claude has never lacked for attention from women, though. Forty-four years old and he has been married three times. The first two were dancers, the third an opera singer. All three marriages blossomed and collapsed in the same pattern—two or three years of numb bliss, a sudden pulling away, a volley of joyless infidelities. And always the prostitutes.

His daughter, Zoe, is the product of his second marriage. Her mother moved to LA four years ago and sank like a stone. No letters, no postcards, nothing. She blamed him for Zoe's condition, but he knew there was no blaming. It was dumb luck—like winning the lottery or choking to death on a bit of gristle. He has been told that he is fortunate, though; that Zoe is "high-functioning."

It's different with Mary, he thinks. They met while he was still married to Nedda, the opera singer. He used to come to rehearsals at the big, old hall in Bridgeport and sit in the back. Mary was a cellist in the orchestra and sat with him one afternoon when the director was putting the chorus through its paces for a production of *Boris Gudonov*. Together they ate the ham sandwiches Nedda had made for his lunch and sipped hot tea from his thermos. The first thing he noticed was her hands. They were large and strong, with long, supple fingers. The hands of a cellist.

Claude takes a last look in the mirror and mentally strokes his shame again, like a small animal cupped trembling in his hand. He puts his glasses on. The frames are small and round and gold, the lenses clear, unground glass. As he walks through the vaulted entrance to Courant Hall, the familiar smells fill him—ivy and stone, wet from the morning rain.

He walks up the stairs to the third floor and steps into the Mathematics Department office to check his mail. He almost collides with Tom Magdar. Magdar is a burly Englishman who specializes in differential geometry. He towers over Claude, and has the coarse, scrubbed look of someone who revels in outdoor activities. Claude was on his tenure committee last year and held out with the only dissenting vote until finally succumbing to pressure from the other committee members.

"Claude, how are you?" Magdar claps him on the shoulder.

Claude forces a smile. "Fine, fine. Getting ready for another semester." He looks past Magdar at the doorway into the hall. Magdar stands there like a tree, an expression of stupid good cheer on his face.

"What are you teaching this semester?" he asks.

"Modern analysis. Light load." He puts his hand on Magdar's shoulder and gently pushes him aside. "Excuse me. Lecture to prepare."

"Right-o. Good man." He claps Claude on the shoulder again as he passes.

As Claude nears his office he realizes his fists are clenched into tight balls. *Two-faced swine.* He has heard, in confidence of course, that Magdar knows about his efforts to block tenure. Since then, Magdar has played "hail fellow, well met" to the hilt, but Claude senses a mocking tone beneath the effusion. He emerges from their interactions with the feeling that he has failed at some subtle jockeying for power.

In his office, the message light is on and he plays back the calls. His student Lee Ming, in a mild panic about a particularly sticky bit of analysis. Harvey, the department chairman, about the faculty parking committee. Then several clicks, a long, whispering hiss. Music, very faint. A woman's voice, speaking in Hungarian.

"Hello? Claude? Hello?" The crackle and static is cut off abruptly. There are several clicks, then a dial tone.

Claude feels a cold knot in his stomach, as if he had just swallowed a glass of ice water. At first he thinks it is his sister, but no. He *knows* that voice, though. Suddenly, his office feels impossibly close to him. The faint, dusty musk of the mathematics books lining the shelves hangs in the air like a fetid mist. He staggers over to the window, opens it, breathes deeply.

He is standing in front of the classroom. Before him are rows of faces, some eager and open, some jaded and full of the arrogance of the gifted young. There are about thirty students, a lot for a first year graduate seminar. His reputation has preceded him—Claude is a good teacher. He slides into his lecture persona easily, like a loose-fitting suit. There are the inevitable questions about what will be expected for the exams, how much homework "counts," how he curves his grades.

"Grading policy is simple," he says. "If you argue with me, you get 'A.' If you don't, you get 'B.'"

A polite chuckle ripples through the classroom. Claude lifts an admonishing finger.

"I am quite serious. That you have come this far shows you have rudimentary mathematical ability. But this is real thing." He lifts up the Korber text. Actually, he isn't very fond of the Korber—too chatty and informal. Good mathematics shouldn't read like a cheap detective novel. But Harvey had been adamant. Claude suspected he was getting kickbacks from the publisher. "Part of your training as mathematicians now is to learn to ask questions, to develop critical habits of thinking." He looks around the room. "Any questions?"

Another chorus of chuckles.

"I didn't think so. Let us begin. We review your entire undergraduate analysis course in the next three lectures. We do it right this time. Purpose is to establish lexicon for functional analysis."

He launches into a discussion of elementary point set topology. Sets, open and closed; neighborhoods; vector spaces. He sketches out a proof of the Bolzano-Weierstrass theorem at the blackboard, turns around to face the class, and sees a woman sitting alone in the back row. He didn't hear her come in. She is wearing a long coat of cheap wool, the narrow lapels looking old-fashioned and out of place. She has straight, blonde hair parted at the side and it hangs limply down to her shoulders. She has a strange, detached expression on her face, as though she is unaware of her surroundings.

Budapest. The summer heat lying heavily over the city, radiating back in ripples over the cobbled streets. Her face framed by an open window, sun catching gold highlights in her hair. *Mother.* It was the last time he saw her, that August in 1956 when the Soviet tanks rolled through. But it is a young woman sitting there in front of him. *Impossible.* And last night, the woman standing there half in shadow, the prostitute's head bobbing up and down in his lap, his back arching, hips thrusting.

Her.

Claude drops the chalk and staggers back against the blackboard. A swell of whispers rises up from the class. "Excuse me—" he mutters, and lurches towards the door.

In the hallway outside the classroom, he leans against the wall, breathing in short gasps. *Mother. It isn't possible.* Gradually, his breathing slows. He takes a handkerchief from his pocket and wipes the sweat from his forehead. He takes a deep breath, lets it out, and walks back into the classroom. The white-noise murmur of conversation stops abruptly. The back row is empty.

Claude sits in the cool darkness and oiled mahogany smell of the Faculty Club. He has a glass of Chablis in front of him, barely touched although he has been there for an hour. He is looking through a many-paneled window with a curved Gothic frame at a quadrangle of grass bordered by shady cedars.

For someone who is having a mental breakdown, he thinks, I am doing pretty well. He takes another sip of Chablis. His mouth puckers with the sourness of the wine and he thinks of his father. Dedicated alcoholic. Professor of economics at University. He rarely thinks of him. Tries very hard not to think of him.

He cannot summon up a picture of his parents together—he remembers them as voices raised in anger from another room, remembers the fear he felt huddling with his sister under a scratchy blanket as his father beat his mother, remembers the sound of her crying as if the sobs were being torn out of her. When his father used a belt, the blows were sharp, loud cracks; when he used his hands, the impacts were low and meaty. Claude thought that she was taking the blows for him and Alya, that nothing stood between them and their father's rage but their mother's wispy presence.

She disappeared during the Soviet invasion in 1956. There was no note, no call from the authorities to come identify a body in a basement morgue. She just stepped out to market one day and never returned. The sense of betrayal Claude felt was absolute. How could she leave them? How could she?

After Claude's mother disappeared, after the tanks rolled through Budapest, it was as if something in himself had been flattened by their relentless progress. The focus of his world narrowed down until it encompassed nothing but the daily business of survival under the new regime—the lines, the black market, avoiding the watchful eyes of the police who were suddenly everywhere.

His father, too, changed. He still beat Claude and Alya, but inter-mittently and without relish. Mostly he sat in the kitchen with his vodka bottle, clattering away on the old typewriter, chain-smoking foul smelling cigarettes smuggled in from Turkey. He had connec-tions in the right-wing intelligentsia, and managed to arrange an escape to the West for all of them. It was not an uncommon thing in those days. But he could not secure an academic position in the States and drank himself to death. Claude and Alya dropped out of touch shortly thereafter—it was as if each reminded the other that they shared a secret too raw to acknowledge.

Claude tries to imagine a Budapest without the secret police, a Budapest without the heavy pall of deprivation and hopelessness hanging over the city, thicker than the smoke from state iron works. He cannot. He just cannot get his mind around it. It is as if the stories of hope and new opportunity he reads in the paper are of some other place, some Avalon he has never seen.

By the time he leaves campus, it is dark. Before going home, Claude drives into the crumbling ruins clustered around the bus station. He drives past the women, goes around the block, and drives past them again. His prostitute is there. She looks at him each time as he passes by, but shows no recognition. The rings in her nose and eyebrow flash gold in the light from the street lamp.

Mary is at a rehearsal and Callie is babysitting for Zoe. Callie is the daughter of a literature professor at Yale, fifteen years old and very pretty in spite of a fluorescent pink Mohawk and a constellation of acne on her cheeks and forehead. She wears a wicked looking cluster of cuffs and hoops all up the curve of her right ear, and Claude has never seen her in anything except black jeans and T-shirt. She is very good with Zoe.

"How is she?" he asks, taking off his jacket and setting his brief-case down next to the hall table.

"Quiet, man. Really quiet. She's been hanging with the toad."

She nods her head in the direction of the living room. Her earrings jangle faintly.

Claude looks past her. Zoe is sprawled asleep on the couch, her arms wrapped around a stuffed toad the size of a large cat that he gave her for Christmas the year before. The toad is wearing a short vest and an expression of comic seriousness. Its arms are opened wide, as if asking for a hug.

Claude picks her up and carries her to her room. He tucks her into bed and nestles the toad in the crook of her elbow. He bends down, kisses her gently on the forehead, and steps back, looking down at her. He stands there for a long time. Cars pass on the street outside and shadows from their headlights crawl across the room at irregular intervals. It scares him how much he loves her. His high-functioning daughter. Finally he sighs, turns around, and walks out of the room, leaving the door open a crack behind him.

There are no apparitions that evening. Mary calls to tell him that rehearsal has been extended, that she will be home late and he shouldn't wait up. Again. Claude feels something like sorrow surge through him and recede, like a wave coursing through a rocky channel.

Claude is dreaming of his father's incest with his sister. He hears her cries in the bed next to his, hears his father's heavy breathing and muffled curses, senses the weight of that huge presence in the dark like something undersea. Then, suddenly, he is in the shower, warm water beating against his back. His father is with him, rubbing the rough scratchy soap down his arms, up his legs, between his thighs. On his knees, leaning over him, brushing his lips against his face, his neck. Rough-cheek perfume of tobacco and vodka, scratchy abrasion trailing down his chest, down his stomach. He wants to run away, but he cannot. He feels torn open, flayed, a pulling at the very center of him, pulling something out of him in long, ropy streamers.

He awakens in the middle of the night. Mary is next to him, sleeping. Her breathing sounds very loud in the still darkness. He slides carefully out of bed. She snorts, groans quietly, and rolls over.

He has a blinding headache. He knows he has been dreaming, but does not remember the details. A crystal doorknob. Running water. Steam.

He walks down the steps to the hall phone, dials the number.

"Hello?"

He opens his mouth to speak, but no words come.

"Hello?"

An hour before class, he realizes he has forgotten his lecture notes. If he runs a red light or two he can just make the round trip in time.

As soon as he walks in the door, he knows that something is wrong. He *knows*. Zoe runs up to greet him, dragging the toad behind her by one of its webbed feet. He picks her up in his arms and walks into the hall. The feeling of dread intensifies.

"Mary?" he calls. He hears faint sounds coming from the upstairs bedroom. He puts Zoe down. "Go into living room, baby. I will be right there."

He walks up the stairs and the sounds resolve into the rhythmic squeaking of bedsprings and low, throaty moans that he recognizes too well. He pushes the door open, knowing what he will see.

Mary is crouched on the bed in the darkened room, her naked back to him, her hips rocking up and down. All he can see of the other man is legs and hands, and his cock pumping rhythmically into her. Claude walks into the room. Mary's eyes are closed and a deep flush is on her cheeks. He closes the door behind him.

Mary's eyes open and widen in horror. She rolls off and kneels on the bed looking at him, resting her weight on her hands, her breasts swaying heavily. The man rolls off the other side of the bed and grabs frantically at the pile of clothing on the floor. He is very young, nineteen or twenty.

"Get out of my house," Claude says. The man nods and scurries out of the room, clutching a bundle of clothes to his chest.

Mary is still crouched on the bed, looking at him.

"You too," he says. "Get out."

They look at each other for a long time. Several times, she opens her mouth as if to speak, then stops.

"Get out," he says again. He walks over to the window, pulls open the drapes and looks out at the backyard. He hears her moving about the room behind him, getting dressed. The dresser opens and shuts several times and he hears the zipper of an overnight bag closing. Then silence. He can sense her presence there behind him, looking at him.

"I know you don't want to talk now—" she says. He doesn't turn around. Finally, he hears her footsteps leaving the room and padding down the stairs.

He sits on the bed and puts his head in his hands. The ecstasy on her face burns into his brain, segues to the cold, dead eyes of the prostitute. *Give it to me, baby.* He thinks of the gun in the locked strongbox on the top shelf of the closet. He cleans it regularly and keeps it loaded. *Give it to me.*

The door creaks open and Claude looks up. Zoe is standing there. Her mouth is open and a small rivulet of drool trails down her chin.

"Zoe—" His voice catches in his throat. "Come here, baby."

He puts his arms around her, buries his face in her hair. He strokes her shoulders, her back, reaching down over the small, innocent curves of her buttocks. His erection is straining at his pants; he feels it coming up from somewhere deep in the center of him. Part of him watches on in horror, but he can no more stop himself now than he could have stopped the Soviet tanks that long-ago summer.

Suddenly, he senses another presence in the room and looks up. She is standing in the doorway, her form shot through with coruscating streaks of light, coalescing into substance. *Mother.*

"Little honey bear," she says in Hungarian. She walks towards him and sits next to him on the bed. He is still holding his daughter, but the desire he felt roaring inside him is gone like smoke in a sudden breeze. His mother puts her arms around both of them. It is strange—she is a small woman, but her arms easily encircle them. She begins to sing in a quiet voice. He recognizes the melody immediately, rich in Eastern European half-tone grace notes. It is a song she used to sing to him and Alya when they were little.

"She builds her city
the white goddess
builds it

not on the sky or earth
but on a cloud branch
builds
three gates to enter it
one gate she builds
in gold
the second pearls
the third in scarlet
where the gate is dry gold
there the goddess' son
is wedded
where the gate
is pearl
the goddess' daughter
is the bride
and where the gate is scarlet
solitary
sits the goddess."

"Mother—" he croaks, the Hungarian phonemes thick and awkward on his tongue.

She nods, a sad smile on her face. He can see himself there in the delicate curve of cheekbone, and in her eyes, his daughter.

"I've been trying to get through to you," she says. "It is very difficult, but the greater your need, the clearer the path is for me."

"The visions, the phone call—"

She nods.

A sudden rush of horror sweeps through him. "Zoe—"

Again, she nods.

Tears fill his eyes. "Why—?"

She cradles his face in her small hands and he is there in the sticky August heat. Budapest, 1956. A tank with a bright red star on its side forces the jostling crowd down one of the narrow streets that fan out from Government Square. The treads alternately rumble and whine as the tank pushes away a burning car the crowd has placed in its path.

Bird-like panic. *She* is not a student, *she* is not an activist. She has been caught in the madness and swept along like a cork in a river. Someone hurls a Molotov cocktail at the tank. It bursts, sending a sheet of liquid fire across the armored hood. It dissipates quickly, flickers feebly, and is gone. The hatch of the tank opens and a head emerges. It is a very young man, his eyes wide with fear. A machine gun is cradled in his arms. Her eyes lock with his for an instant, then he pulls the bolt back and fires into the crowd. She feels a bursting in her chest, white light, impossible pain …

She lifts her hands from his face. He looks in her eyes, searches in those clear, blue depths for something, some piece of himself.

"I thought you'd just left us, that you ran away." His voice stumbles, cracks.

She shakes her head. "Forgive me, Claude. I was never really there for you and Alya, never strong enough to protect you from your father. I wanted to. I would lie awake with the pain from his beatings, praying to God for the strength to take you away. But God had other plans for us." She pauses and looks away, bites her lip in a gesture that reminds him achingly of his daughter. She looks at him again, deep into his eyes. "Love is all there is, Claude. It is all you have. Stronger than fear, stronger than shame. It is all there is." She caresses his cheek. "You can begin to heal. This I can give to you."

She begins to fade, the pressure of her hand on his cheek like a wing, like a feather, gone.

"Daddy—" Zoe looks up at him.

"Yes, baby. I'm here." He puts his arms around her again.

They stay like that for a long time, father and daughter breathing together. Soon, she is asleep. He picks her up and carries her down the hall to her room. He tucks her into bed, pulling the sheets up under her chin. He rescues the toad from the corner and lays it next to her, folding her arm across its green, velvet stomach.

He walks down the stairs to the hall phone and dials the number. It rings twice and a voice answers.

"Hello?" Her accent fills him. He takes a deep breath.

"Hello," he says in Hungarian. "Hello, Alya."

Note: The author gratefully acknowledges *Technicians of the Sacred*, **Jerome Rothenberg, Ed., University of California Press 1985, for the Eastern European folk song excerpted herein.**

REVENANT

TODAY'S THE DAY. Connor has been dreading it for weeks, cycling between denial and resignation. Meifeng is fussing with the floral arrangement in the living room for the third time. He hears the scrape of the heavy, stone vase on its marble pedestal and can imagine her stepping back, head tilted, sculpted eyebrows angling down. Reaching out again to make a minor adjustment. They have been fighting a lot lately, more and more as the day approaches, and he feels within himself a substrate of sadness, a dense fog close to ground hugging inner contours.

There have been UV alerts all week and the floor-to-ceiling windows in the bedroom are polarized a grayish-brown. The city beyond and below looks like an old photograph. He unlatches the door and steps onto the balcony.

The brightness hits him like a fist and he takes a moment to adjust. His augs overcompensate, dialing in dark grey, then normalizing. He walks towards the edge until he feels the yielding pressure of the nanogel webbing on his face. To the East, Brooklyn burns. Plumes from a dozen flickering sources rise and merge into a grey haze. The fires seem to be moving closer. To the South, a tugboat churns past the sad stubble of Liberty Island. A quarter-mile below, sunlight glints brightly off the gridded Lower Manhattan canals, a silver checkerboard outline. A cat's-claw swipe of white contrails crosses the sky, military drones patrolling the metro no-fly zone. The air is filtered by the nanogel but he imagines a faint tang of salt, smoke, sewage.

Connor steps back, slaps a sativa patch on the underside of his wrist, and regrets it almost immediately. He already feels agitated and his unease is amplified by the chemical surge. He leans again into the nanogel, invisible except for a rainbow highlight at the periphery of his vision that cycles through the spectrum as he moves his head. He feels a rush of vertigo as he looks straight down. He knows that the nanogel will bear many times his weight and so he relishes the lizard-brain fear. He remembers a game he played in a high school theater class. Fall forward off the stage into the webbed and waiting arms of your classmates. Trust and let go.

There is a commotion on the street below. Emergency vehicles flash blue and red. A ring of black dots, tactical helmets shiny like insect husks, surround a small, ragged mob and close in. A cottony puff of gas bursts in the middle of the crowd and shreds itself into lazy streamers. In less than a minute the street is clear again.

He goes back into the apartment, slides the heavy glass door shut behind him. Mei looks small and a little lost in the huge living room. Connor feels a pull in her direction, a thawing.

"You okay?"

"Yeah, I'm okay." Tense, guarded.

"The flower arrangement looks really good."

She smiles slightly. "Sunflower and iris. His favorite."

He cooks them a light, early supper—kelp salad with almonds and blood oranges, broiled farm tilapia. Expensive, but they can afford it. She can, anyway.

He feels again the familiar surge of resentment at Mei's family money. This flat, a gift from her father, Bing Quan. It would have been impossible to turn down, even if he'd wanted to, and he was somewhat ashamed to admit that he didn't want to. There it was in a nutshell, that complex of shame, anger, and self-doubt that Mei's father engendered in everyone he met. He just sat back and watched people tie themselves in knots. It was how he'd built a personal fortune in China, starting from a tiny set-top-box factory in a Shenzhen slum, that put him somewhere just shy of the top thousand personal fortunes in the New People's Republic.

Mei grows visibly upset as the afternoon gives way to evening. Without thought, Connor finds himself staking out opposing territory, calming as she fragments.

"Where are they?"

"In transit. Do you want me to check the tracking code again?"

Before Mei can respond, the security alert sounds, a single muted gong indicating a delivery. Moments later, a wall panel sighs open revealing a black box, waist-high, featureless except for a strip of gold foil near the top.

Connor activates the manifest and the summary appears before his eyes, translucent letters hanging in midair.

He turns to Mei.

"It's him."

She looks pale.

He vanishes the manifest and approaches her, reaches out to touch her face.

She seems about to flinch but allows the touch, rests her cheek briefly against his palm.

"Is this okay?" he asks.

"It has to be."

She gestures at the room—high ceiling, muted lighting, *guzheng* music whisper soft in the background, riot of colors blooming in the fat vase.

Connor nods, reading her loud and clear. It has to be. If we want to keep all this.

He invokes the manifest again, sends the command to unpack.

The sides of the box fall away revealing a large bird resting on a perch. Clearly a synth but its plumage is beautiful—cerulean, emerald, lemon, and sapphire, rippling and shifting as the feathers catch the light. Its beak is long and curved. Black eyes survey the room as it shifts position.

Mei approaches it, reaches out a tentative hand.

"Hello, father."

☆

It's 12:15 AM, fifteen minutes before the markets open in Mumbai and Connor is getting ready for work. He orders coffee from the kitchen bar, assembles a breakfast of Greek yogurt and fresh blueberries, begins reading the financials. The room fills with the dense, earthy smell of coffee as he loses himself to the translucent scroll. He queries automated bookmarks spawned from certain artifacts in the time history of the day's trades in the Western markets. He looks at secondary effects, signatures of human intervention in the blur of brainiac trades.

Mei's father rests on a perch near the wide, high living room windows. To give him a good view, Mei said. To the East, Brooklyn is a bed of glittering jewels. Flickering fires burn beyond the shattered span of the Brooklyn Bridge. Every few minutes, Bing emits a soft, fluttering coo. Connor wonders if this means he likes what he sees. Brooklyn burning.

Bing hasn't spoken in the three days since his arrival. Mei has been increasingly upset, although the techs said to expect this. The transfer passed all quality checkpoints. By all available metrics, Bing's personality, his memories—everything that made him the vile, cantankerous son of a bitch he was when he was alive—had been successfully migrated from his failing, cancer-riddled body to this new vessel.

It wouldn't surprise Connor in the least that Bing was playing them, that he was remaining silent to see what Mei and Connor would do to fill the space. But the techs assured them both that this was a perfectly normal adjustment period.

"Soon you'll wish he'd shut up," one of them joked.

Connor has no doubt that this is true.

He usually works from the bar near the big windows, but Bing's presence makes him nervous, so he's set up shop in a spartan room off the kitchen: white walls, white carpet, desk of Japanese maple, Hermann chair, Ansel Adams original on one wall. The Northern view is not quite as dramatic as from the living room, the windows not quite as large, but Connor likes feeling the mass of city before him, light and shadow, flesh and steel, the glittering sprawl stretching north past New Hampshire.

He begins work; for the next four hours he swims in a frothy river of data. Twice, he stops brainiac calls from executing, nudging the flow of money and bits and watching the ripples propagate through the global markets. He subvocalizes trading orders and three times emerges from the flow for conference calls with executives, business architects, brainiac handlers.

He works a half hour beyond his shift to shepherd a particularly tricky chain of transactions that he disallowed from brainiac trading: an impending IPO, various transactions against a cluster of relevant small caps, an ensemble of stochastic simulations of increasingly arcane derivative instruments.

Finally, he is done. As always, he spends several minutes allowing himself to decompress. The feeds are gone, mastoid speaker silenced, vision free of tickers and plots, summaries and stats. Connor returns slowly to here-and-now. The room smells of his sweat and the faint effluvium of carpet cleaner.

He is famished, as always after a trading session, but imagines Bing on his perch, eyes like glittering black coins, plumage catching the light in oily diffraction patterns, and doesn't want to go through the living room. He pads into the bedroom, undresses quickly and slides into bed with Mei. She whimpers softly, then snuggles her butt up against him. He drifts off to sleep.

It is still night when Connor awakens with a start. Bing is perched on the night table, deep in shadow except for his eyes, which regard Connor without blinking.

The waterbus threads its way through the unregulated rabble of small craft, barges, salvage rigs, food rafts, and houseboats. Buildings rise on either side. Music from half a dozen different sources fills the air, blending with shouting and laughter in as many different languages. Smells of sewage and grilling meat are dense in the warm air.

The waterbus pulls up next to the dock at the 14th Street Levee and Connor disembarks. He takes the broad, flat stairs to the top and down the other side, where he is disgorged onto Third Avenue. He walks toward Union Square, the Levee at his left shoulder, rising thirty feet above the street. The perpetual 14th Street Flea is in full swing, tables lining the sidewalks piled high with junk electronics, bootleg moviechips, and more sizzling mystery meat.

He descends into the subway at Union Square, surrendering himself to the jostle and clank. The car smells of ozone, mildew, and human bodies. The stations unroll upwards in a sequence that is found nowhere in nature but is buried in the DNA of every New Yorker: 14, 23, 28, 33, 42, 51, 59 …

Connor gets off at the 125th Street terminus and emerges from underground near the Harlem River Levee. He laments the old Broadway subway lines, cut off from Harlem in the 96th Street bombings over a decade ago and never restored. The latest iteration of the city giving up on Harlem. Unlike the noise and hustle of downtown, this neighborhood feels abandoned. Many of the buildings appear to be held together by the graffiti-dense plywood covering doors and windows. Gutted structures frame the broken spine of the Harlem River Drive several blocks away.

He walks west, towards Malcom X Boulevard, head down, hands in the pockets of his black hoodie. There's no grid up here and he feels jumpy and tentative without feeds or heads-up. He tried to dress down but Connor dressing down is Sunday dinner up here. He passes a knot of hard-looking young men shooting craps on the sidewalk in front of a bodega. They pause as he walks past and he can feel their gaze on his back. He wraps his hand around the compact needlegun, but he soon hears the clatter of dice on pavement, a chorus of voices, and he relaxes his grip.

The needler fires 2 mm plastic darts propelled by compressed air that detonate a tiny payload of C4 on impact. Enough of a bang to tear out a divot of flesh the size of a baseball. He printed the needler from public domain specs, but the ammo is a little harder to come by. A year ago, Connor instantiated a blind offshore transaction proxy for a Malaysian colleague who has family in the local Javanese mob and now he gets all the ammo he needs as well as a superb *ayam penyet* at the Sambal Kitchen in the west thirties.

Connor goes a block out of his way to avoid the street bordering Marcus Garvey Park. Army of Christ territory—cannibalism, a flying saucer Jesus, the biggest ice factory in Manhattan, lots of guns.

Malcolm X Boulevard, Lenox Avenue to the old timers, MX to

the locals, is a street fair where all the vendors and marks have gone home. There is no traffic and hasn't been for some time. Stalls and lean-tos line the sidewalks and spill out into the street. The burned-out husk of a police car sits in the middle of the intersection of MX and 124th, unmoved since his last visit. A visual census reveals more dogs than people on the street.

Cam's apartment is west of MX, about half a block up the street. The building is in better shape than most, but that's not saying much. Broken windows look out over the street. Graffiti sprawls like kudzu up the face of the building. The front door hangs askew and the lobby features a broken lift, drifts of garbage piled waist-high in the corners, a bank of smashed mailboxes. Someone upstairs is playing Bach on a cello with more passion than skill, but it infuses this bleak place with beauty. Connor stops and tilts his head. The air is fat and heavy with the music, permeating everything like invisible smoke. Even the frequent mistakes are like imperfections in weathered wood. The wrecked lobby seems to glow softly. Then there is the sound of breaking glass and the music stops. Somebody shouts in Arabic. Another voice answers, then silence. Connor waits for the music to resume, but it doesn't, and he mounts the staircase, spiraling up, around, up, around, the feeling of transcendence gone. Some apartment doors are missing, others lean on broken hinges, but some are intact and he imagines people watching furtively through peepholes as he ascends.

By the time he gets to Cam's landing he is winded and he pauses to catch his breath before knocking on her door.

There's motion behind the peephole; deadbolts catch and slide. The door opens just wide enough and he slips inside. She bends over the locks again, turns toward him, and they share a chaste hug. He steps back. He hasn't seen her for several months but she looks years older. The inexorable toll of AIDS-IV has ravaged her body, taken most of her teeth. What's left of her hair is sparse, iron stubble. Only memory allows him to see in her broken features the beauty she had been.

They were friends in grad school, lovers briefly, then friends again. She was a brilliant big-data analyst, blessed with an almost supernatural ability to discern patterns in the ebb and flow of petabytes. Then, the brainiacs conquered that domain and almost overnight, she was rendered obsolete. Unemployed, unemployable, she slid off the grid, subsisting on black-hat work when she could get it. She took in her ailing mother and the two of them stayed more or less afloat until the brainiacs entered that realm as well, rendering the sprawling skeins of systems and networks uncrackable. He kept track of her and helped out when he could, although she wouldn't let him do much.

Mei had known Cam slightly back in the day and knew Connor was still in touch, but she'd inherited a bit of old school bootstrap ethos from Bing: if Cam was struggling she'd somehow brought it on herself. It was one of those recurring low-level arguments that every marriage harbors, worn to ritual by repetition and ennui.

"Why do you still visit her and her crazy mother? She is *diao si*."

"She's not a loser, just unlucky."

"People make their own luck. My father did. He came up in the—"

"—slums of Shenzhen. Yes, I know. And now he's the biggest asshole in China."

At this point, they both lapse into passive-aggressive silence. There will be hot, angry make-up sex that night or the next, closing the loop.

He wonders, not for the first time, when the brainiacs that had blown Cam off the grid would step in and deprecate his interventionist role. Then it's *quis custodiet ipsos custodes*, but he finds himself oddly detached whenever he contemplates it. What difference does it make who runs oversight on the brainiacs? What difference does it make if anybody does? It would be like children with toy guns guarding a bank. Meat is done, headed towards an inevitable convergence that nobody understands. He's never actually interacted directly with a brainiac, just their human handlers, and doesn't know anybody who has, although he suspects there must be a priesthood somewhere, acolytes in black T-shirts and flip-flops servicing the burgeoning web of artificial sentience, tweaking code, running diagnostics. He wonders sometimes if the brainiacs actually exist, if they're not some elaborate metacorporate fiction. There are certainly plenty of wingnut theories to that effect. But their influence is too pervasive, too profoundly weird. They are rocks thrown in a pond, sunken from view but leaving a widening system of ripples.

"How's Alice?"

Cam shrugs.

"You know. Good days, bad days. She's been looking forward to seeing you."

She calls back into the shadowy apartment.

"Mom. Connor's here."

Connor can barely hear the weak, feathery response.

Cam slides her arm through his and they make their way through the neat clutter of the living room to the back of the apartment.

Alice is propped up in the bed watching something on the cracked wallscreen, the sound turned down to a barely audible whisper. She smiles when she sees him.

He bends over and takes her in his arms. She feels so insubstantial, as if the slightest pressure will crumble her to dust.

"How you doing, Al?"

"I'm dying, fool."

She touches his arm.

"It's all right. Really."

He looks at Cam, who shrugs again.

"Bullshit. I'm gonna get you guys out of here."

"What? Into one of the camps? The gulags? I don't think so. We're fine here."

"You can't stay here."

"Why not? We've got a garden out back. I do a little dark work for the Army of Christ assholes so we're under protection."

Cam waves her arm.

"This is it, Connor. It's not gonna get any better than this for us and you can't help us. You can't. Don't torture yourself."

She cracks a grin.

"Fuck'n one-percenter."

Connor feels like crying but he manages a smile, reaches into his belt pouch, pulls out a wad of stiff, garish bills.

"Newbucks, but it was all I could get. Cash is really scarce downtown, especially federal. Better spend it soon 'cause it'll be worth half as much in a week."

He adds his needler and a tiny vial of German antiviral nanos to the stack, another boon from the Javanese mob connection.

"Take these, too."

Cam nods, takes the gifts with one hand, leans in close to hug him with the other.

"Thanks, Connor. What else you got?"

He knows she's talking ganja and the three of them share a vape stick and watch some vintage *anime* on the wallscreen. Huge-breasted girls and spiky-haired boys caper wide-eyed across the screen. The cello downstairs starts up again and for a little while everything seems okay, or like it could be okay if everything would just slow down, just slow down for one fucking minute.

Family dinner. Connor has prepared a pot roast: root vegetables from his Javanese connection and vat beef. He tries not to think about that, but trying not to think about it burns in the image: a headless, limbless blob suspended in pink fluid, pierced by nutrient tubes and monitoring instrumentation, one of thousands in a sprawling Cartesian grid hunkered beneath the weight of a dim, perpetual twilight.

The beef is good, though, in spite of a hormonal fullness to the taste and a slightly spongy texture. Connor is seated at one end of the oak table, Mei at his left. Bing's perch has been rolled to the other end, the height adjusted so he has access to his bowls of water and nutrient paste.

Guh guh guh.

Mei and Connor exchange looks. Bing's first human-like vocalization. His voice is rounded, almost melodic, with a barely percep-tible rising tone at the end of each utterance. His beak opens but there is no other movement to his face; the shaping of the words, the transformation of thought to language, taking place at some hidden nexus within the artifice of his body.

Guh guh guh. Gwai.

"It's all right, father. Take your time."

Bing spreads his wings, gives them a quick flutter, and pecks viciously at his bowls, knocking over the water. Dabs of paste cling to his beak.

Mei reaches over with a napkin and cleans the bird's face. Bing opens his beak, coos briefly. Connor can see his tongue, a dark, waving knot of muscle. He wonders if Bing enjoys the disruption and attention, then chuckles silently to himself. Of course he does.

Gwei. Gui. Gui.

The bird's black eyes meet Connor's. There is intelligence there, unmistakable and fierce, and something else he can't quite identify that knots his stomach and gives him a cold feeling at the nape of his neck.

Gui. Gui. Guilao.

Guilao.

Connor looks at Mei, back at Bing. The bird's eyes never leave Connor's face.

Guilao.

"White ghost," Mei says. "Also foreign devil, or just foreign."

Connor nods.

"I know what it means."

Connor is waiting for Musa bin Ashraf at the Broken Door, a Malay bar in the shadow of the 14th Street Levee. Jangly Chinese pop music fractures the air and the wallscreens pulse with images— nude dancers cavorting across a sapphire meadow, a sleeping tiger, a sleek, beautiful androgyne caressing a mic, a kitten toying with a string.

Musa is precisely ten minutes late, as always—Connor can set his clock to it. Connor gets up as Musa enters the bar and they embrace. The bartender has been ignoring Connor up to this point but now he is all smiles and quivering attention.

Musa wards him off and they cut through the crowd towards an empty booth at the back of the bar.

"You look like shit, Connor," Musa says when they are seated. His English has a fruity Aussie twang. "Have you been sleeping?"

Connor shrugs. "Not much."

They have known each other for long enough that they can dispense with small talk and Connor gets right to it. He tells Musa what he wants.

When he is done, Musa looks at him for a long moment. His expression is hard to read but Connor detects a hint of sadness.

"You know that this is not a small thing," he says. "Needler ammo, dinner reservations. That's over. This will change everything between us. We will own you."

Connor nods. "I'm aware of that."

"Then consider it done. Twenty-four hours."

He slides out of the booth and leaves without a backward glance.

Deep night in the city that doesn't sleep. 0330 shimmers in faint blue numerals above the nightstand. Connor slides out of bed. Mei stirs, moans once quietly, and rolls over.

Connor pads quietly into the living room. Bing is on his perch, looking out over the glittering cityscape. Connor wonders what he actually sees, what perception is conjured by the striking of photons on Bing's biosynthetic receptors.

Connor places himself in front of Bing, in front of the city.

"Listen to me," he says. "You son of a bitch." Bing looks at him, his black eyes wide and bottomless. He has not spoken since the other night at dinner.

"All your wealth, all your history, everything you tried to take with you when you died, everything that's *you*. It's all gone. Smoke in the wind. You're nothing, Bing. You're nobody."

Connor returns to the bedroom and tries to go back to sleep. There are no sounds from the living room, no sounds at all except odd little clicks and hums, almost inaudible, the flat chuckling to itself in the deep of night.

Finally, sleep takes him.

Connor is awakened by a bar of bright sunlight across his face. Mei's side of the bed is rumpled, the sheets cool. He pads into the living room.

Mei is sitting in the chair next to the open balcony door. She has been crying but she seems composed now. Bing's perch is empty. The room smells of smoke and burnt plastic from the Brooklyn fires.

"What happened? Are you all right?"

Mei shakes her head.

"Father's gone."

"Gone?"

"When I woke up, the gel was down and he was gone."

The nanogel has incredible tensile strength but a crappy hysteresis curve. He imagines Bing hurling himself at the barrier and bursting through before the elastic modulus kicks in, dropping like a rock until his outstretched wings catch the smoky air and he soars away from the drowned, burning city. He thinks of Bing and all the other digital revenants, more and more of them every day, bound to their new hosts yet unbounded, uploaded to the aether along with the brainiacs and whatever else might be emergent as new connection paths open in the surging sprawl of bits.

Connor sits on the floor next to Mei. She leans her head on his shoulder. He feels her trembling slightly, a high frequency vibration.

Connor invokes his heads-up, navigates to household functions, gives a command and the big sliding door closes silently. The room still smells of Brooklyn burning, but the filtration system will kick in and soon the smell will be gone.

KILLED IN THE RATINGS

ABANDONED buildings hulked on either side of the darkened street, like rotted teeth in a gaping mouth. Two men trailed a lone female between island pools of light. She looked nervously behind her and began to hurry. The men quickened their pace.

Marco popped up another window to get the SkyCam view, the enhanced infrared casting everything in pearly green phosphorescence. It was a bit jerky; the little blimp was probably trying to tack against a strong headwind. He dragged the window to a corner of the screen.

They were about half a block behind her now, closing fast. She broke into a run. *Good.* Marco nudged a slider switch on the virtual control panel to crank up the sound a bit. Her light feet slapped against the street, counterpoint to the men's heavy footsteps. He boosted the presence and could just make out her breathing—shallow, panicky gasps. He could enhance it more later, or overlay something from the sound library.

She ducked into the doorway of a building, her pursuers following close behind. *Shit.* Marco popped another couple of windows to see if their shoulder cams were picking up, but it was too dark in the building's entrance. Grainy shadows jerking back and forth, sounds of struggle. She screamed and they dragged her into the street.

The resolution still wasn't very good, not nearly enough available light. It was fine for the stalk—the shadows made everything look menacing. But you needed some serious bit density for the hand-to-hand.

Laurel must have been giving them field directions from the mobile unit, her voice buzzing out of their mastoid speakers like a guilty conscience, because suddenly they dragged the victim from the shadows in front of the building into the bright circle of light cast by a streetlamp.

Four windows open now, tiled across the workstation screen—the SkyCam, the mobile unit, and the two shoulder cams. Marco felt like God on an electronic throne.

From one of the shoulder cams, a tight, fleeting shot of the woman's face. Her eyes were wide, whites showing all around, like a frightened horse. *Outstanding.* Marco froze the image and blew it up until her face filled the screen, popped it into another window, and superimposed the streetscape view from the mobile unit.

"Goddamn, I'm good," he muttered.

One of the men had a knife out and was waving it around in the air, leaving a complex pattern of trails on the screen. It was a great effect. Marco boosted the contrast to enhance it.

The woman broke free and almost got away, but the taller of the two tackled her and she went down hard, scraping her face on the pavement. First blood, black in the light.

She was pleading now, her voice a keening monotone.

"Don't hurt me, please, please, don't hurt me."

Marco looped it and put a drum patch underneath, his hands alternately flying across the keyboard and caressing the virtual controls onscreen. The sound of their blows, their grunts and heavy breathing, rose now over the hip-hop dub of her whining pleas. Marco made a note to himself to give Lou in Production a call about marketing a single.

They had her shirt off now. The shorter man was squeezing her breasts while his companion held her with one hand and punched her repeatedly in the face with the other. Her lip was split and one of her eyes was swollen completely shut. She was still struggling, but weakly. The jerky motion of the shoulder cams synched perfectly with the dub's insistent rhythm.

Suddenly, she went limp. *Damn.* Lost consciousness, maybe even cardiac arrest. That's the trouble with these fucking animals, Marco thought, no sense of timing. They smelled a little blood and went apeshit.

They were still hammering on her, slamming her in the head and jabbing at her naked torso with the knife. The shorter guy started pulling her pants off, exposing pale, white thighs. They would probably fuck her anyway, dead or not.

Marco grimaced. No way he could get *that* past the Board. Still, he had plenty of good footage, and for gravy, a sweet, little dub.

It was a wrap.

Marco watched the pair of killers through the two-way mirror. He had to look closely to distinguish them from the ones he'd seen earlier that morning—they all had the same feral, vacuous look about them. These two sat at the head of the long, oak table in the conference room, out of place in that chrome-edged, corporate opulence. They didn't seem to mind, though, leaning back in the leather chairs, looking around with an air of relaxed boredom.

The taller one, the one with the hairnet and the gang-scars on his cheeks, pulled out a cigarette and lit up. His companion looked at him and grinned, showing a mouthful of stainless steel, the incisors filed to sharp points.

The door to the observation room slid open with a sigh and Marco turned around. Laurel stood in the doorway, a half-smile on her face.

"Don't you think you should remind him that tobacco's illegal?" she asked, stepping into the little room and taking a seat beside him. The door hissed shut.

"I think I'll pass. Jesus Christ, where did you find these two? They're practically Neolithic."

"The usual audition procedure. They showed up for the interview and the guy with the hairnet—his name's Creature, incidentally—the guy pulls a cat out of his shoulder bag and rips its head off, right there on the spot. 'I wanna be on TV,' he says. I've seen the clip from the security cam—it's unbelievable. His buddy's name is Seven. I don't think he speaks. At least I've never heard him."

"Creature and Seven?"

"Yeah." She shrugged. "Don't ask, okay?"

Marco sighed. "Well, we're always on the lookout for a few good men. Milo and Winston are getting sloppy, anyway." He stood up. "Let's go talk to them."

Marco let Laurel precede him out the door of the observation room. She carried herself with the confidence of someone whose star is rising.

Digging up new talent herself, he thought. The little cooze is getting ambitious.

Creature looked up when Marco and Laurel walked in the door. He blew a big, lazy smoke ring and jabbed his index finger through it.

"'S'up?" he said. Seven flashed another metallic grin.

"Creature," Laurel said. "Seven. This is Marco, the show's producer."

Creature looked him up and down. Marco could sense the calculation, trying to scope out influence, level of fear, the power relationship between him and Laurel.

Seven's eyes shone with a dull, animal light. Marco shuddered inwardly. If the eyes are windows to the soul, Seven's revealed a strip-mall parking lot full of abandoned cars.

"So you want to be on television," Marco said.

Creature nodded. "I love your show, man. Me an' Seven were watchin' the other night when you had a couple of sams take down a QuikStop. Wiped the owner an' the customers an' cut with a bottle of Maddog. I say to Seven, 'We can do that.'" He turned to Seven. "Right?"

Seven nodded, grinning.

"I'm sure you'll do just fine," Marco said. "You know how the show works, then. We wire you with sound and vid and you go out and—" he paused.

"Romp and stomp," Creature said.

Seven grinned again. That mouthful of metal was beginning to really give Marco the creeps.

"Yes, good." Marco smiled thinly. He looked over at Laurel and nodded.

She produced a smartslate, called up the standard contract, and slid it across the table to Creature.

"Can you read?" she asked.

"Fuck no."

Laurel pressed a corner of the slate; little animated glyphs began sliding across the screen. Two men shaking hands. Sundry acts of cartoon mayhem. One man handing another bags of money.

"Do you understand this contract?" she asked.

"Sure," Creature said. "It says that me an' Seven go out an' fuck 'em up an' you give us money."

"Close enough," Laurel said. "If you'll give me your thumbprints here." She indicated the appropriate regions. "And here." Creature and Seven complied.

Close enough indeed, Marco thought. Actually what the contract said was that Mondo Entertainment practically owned these two chuckleheads, lock, stock, and semi-automatic weapons, that they signed over all rights to everything they said or did, on all media currently known or ever to be devised.

"Very good," he said. "Looking forward to working with you." He slid his chair back and got up. "Laurel will get you set up with shoulder cams and mikes, mastoid speakers, the works." He looked at her. "I want you to handle this personally."

Laurel shot him a dirty look. That was scut, usually reserved for production assistants, not assistant producers.

"You got it, Marco," she said.

He could feel their eyes on him as he walked out of the room. Just as the door slid shut, he thought he heard a bark of laughter from Creature, but it might have been his imagination.

He hoped Laurel wasn't stupid enough to get in an elevator alone with those two.

Then again, maybe it wouldn't be such a bad idea.

Marco popped in the dub he'd made earlier, turned up the volume, and leaned back in his chair.

Don't hurt me, please, please, don't hurt me.

The symmetry lent itself nicely to looping. It still needed something, maybe a percussive horn section patch hammering the downbeats, but it wasn't half bad.

He looked over his schedule, tapping his fingers on the desk in time with the dub. Lunch at Bibo's with Laurel and a network zeck named Spivak. Marco knew the name but had never met her. Laurel set it up; something about it didn't smell quite right. He would love to beg off, but he had to cover his ass. Fortunes rose and fell during lunches like this. Shows were canceled and created, careers sent rocketing skyward or crashing into the ground.

Afterwards, a good long stretch of studio time, then a release interview. Marco grimaced. He really hated those. The victim's relatives sat there wringing their hands and whining while Marco dangled larger and larger sums of cash in front of their eyes. He felt like an alchemist, transmuting grief into greed. It could get expensive.

He was late for lunch. Laurel and Spivak were already there, at a table in the back, leaning towards each other and laughing.

"Marco," Laurel said. "We wondered if you'd stood us up. We've already ordered." She was wearing a smile, but it was thin as a playing card. Bitch. "This is Julia Spivak," she continued after a calculated pause, "from upstairs at Mondo."

"The Creative Division," Spivak said. "New projects."

She shook his hand with a bone-crushing grip.

"I know you by reputation, of course," Marco said. As a ballbuster, he thought to himself. He was late for lunch because he'd made a few phone calls, trying to get the skinny on her. It didn't sound good—she'd left a trail of bodies on her way to her current state of grace that made Napoleon look like the Dalai Lama.

A waiter appeared, hovering diffidently until Marco looked up.

"Hello, my name is Hans and—"

"I don't care what your name is. Get me a green salad, no dressing, balsamic vinegar on the side. And a bottle of distilled water."

Hans nodded and scurried off. Marco looked at Spivak. She had that big-jawed, Katy Hepburn, don't-mess-with-me look about her. He wondered suddenly if she was fucking Laurel, doing the old slip-and-slide. He glanced at Laurel, trying to read the body language, and it was clear. The way they'd been leaning together when he first walked in, the surreptitious, little glances.

He was screwed.

"I saw the raw footage from yesterday," Spivak said.

Footage, Marco thought. She's older than she looks.

"Some nice hand-to-hand," she continued, "but your actors are a little too enthusiastic."

Marco flushed. "Yeah, the field direction could have been better." Out of the corner of his eye, he saw Laurel stiffen. *Bullseye.* "I just hired some new talent this morning."

"Yes, I heard about them. Creature and—" She turned to Laurel. "—Seven? We have high hopes for them."

She paused, taking a sip of wine. "Because *something's* going to have to pull your ratings out of the shithouse."

"Hey, wait a minute, they're not that bad."

Spivak made a clucking sound. "You've dropped six points since last month, and that's part of a much longer downturn. There's a lot of talk going on upstairs about whether or not reality-based programming has had its day." She looked directly at him. Her eyes were black as a crow's. "Or whether you've had yours."

"The ratings always fluctuate, everybody knows that. Tides, sunspots, who the fuck knows? The share for *Killers!* is pretty steady if you look at the long-term stats."

She put her hand on his arm. "I'm on your side, Marco. Believe me. *Killers!* is a great show and we're going to do everything we can to salvage it." She paused. "Laurel has some ideas I think you ought to hear."

Marco struggled to keep his cool. Salvage my ass, he thought.

Laurel cleared her throat. "Well, part of the problem with *Killers!* is overhead—the field crew, the SkyCam, the remote hardware." She paused. "Excessive post-production."

A stab at Marco's predilection for special FX. Fucking cunt. He wanted to jab a fork in her eye.

"And the releases alone suck up nearly a quarter of the show's revenue," Laurel continued. "Focus groups say that what they want is blood—everything else is padding. So let's give the people what they want."

She took a deep breath and put both hands on the table, palms down. Here it comes, Marco thought.

"Where do you find blood?" she continued. "Hospital emergency rooms, that's where. Especially large, urban hospital emergency rooms. Highland in Oakland, for instance. Gunshots, stabbings, stompings, wife-beating, kiddie torture—the works. We just modify the security cam that's already in place, so we don't have to fuck around with a mobile unit. We don't have to worry about releases, either—Mondo owns an insurance consortium and *they* own half the hospitals in the country, so we've got 'em by the balls. We can call it *Crash Cart* or something zingy like that. Practically zero overhead, maximal 'B' and 'G.'"

"Blood and guts is fine," Marco said, "but you need some action, too."

Laurel shrugged. "So every now and then we hire a couple of your goons from *Killers!* to do a guest spot, walk into surgery with an Uzi and open up."

Oh, great, Marco thought. They're *my* goons now.

"Call it a terrorist attack," Laurel was saying. "Or don't explain it at all. It's not a problem."

She looked from Marco to Spivak, then back at Marco. "So what do you think?"

What a performance, Marco thought. He looked at Spivak. She arched an eyebrow at him. He felt like he was treading water with cement flippers.

"Well," he said, cautiously. "I think it has promise. The concept's different enough from *Killers!* that Mondo can float both of them."

"Absolutely," Spivak said. "Laurel, set it up with Highland. I want a pilot into the focus groups in three weeks." She turned to Marco. "I'm going to kick you upstairs, Marco. Executive producer. Let Laurel handle the day-to-day business for both shows so we can keep you focused on the big picture. What do you think?"

He felt like he'd been kicked in the head by a horse.

"I don't know what to say."

The waiter arrived with their lunch—Marco's salad, which he

dropped on the table with a perceptible clatter. A thick, bloody steak for Spivak. Sashimi for Laurel.

Marco hoped it gave her worms.

The rest of the afternoon went fairly well, all things considered. He had a great studio session, massaging the rough edges out of the dub. And he managed to hold the settlement to the bereaved parents of the bimbo who'd bought it for the upcoming show down to fifty kilobucks, which brightened his spirits considerably. By the time he was driving home that evening, his mood was almost philosophical.

Laurel had really pulled an end-run on him, but he could land feet first. He always did. Besides, *Crash Cart* or whatever the hell they were going to call it sounded like a fucking bore. In two months they'd be begging him to get back in the trenches.

Meanwhile, life was sweet. Laurel was out of his hair for a while. With a fancy title and no real duties, he'd have plenty of time for more studio work, which was what he really loved.

He popped the bead he'd been working on into the stereo and cranked up the volume, filling the car with sound. *Don't hurt me, please, please, don't hurt me.* On the approach to the Bay Bridge, he turned the controls over to the Grid and sat back in the plush leather seat, tapping his fingers on the dash.

The lights of San Francisco receded behind him; the dark mass of Treasure Island loomed ahead. A Free Zone, ever since the Army pulled out back in the Nineties. Squatters and crazies, mostly, total chaos. Marco wouldn't even send a camera crew in there, not without an armed backup.

His dashboard beeped at him and the terminal screen flickered on.

SYSTEM SHUTDOWN MESSAGE
This vehicle's CPU will shut down in 60 seconds.
Please pull over immediately.

Fuck. His car hadn't crashed in months. What the hell was going on? He tapped the controls, trying to call up a diagnostics program.

Another beep.

SYSTEM SHUTDOWN MESSAGE

This vehicle's CPU will shut down in 30 seconds.

Please pull over IMMEDIATELY.

Marco logged off the Grid and pulled over onto the shoulder. He picked up the phone and held it to his ear. Dead.

He looked around. Cars whizzed by to his left. Halogen lights arched high above the roadbed. Beyond, the wooded hills of Treasure Island loomed thick with shadow. In the distance, giant, skeletal structures rose above the Oakland docks like metal dinosaurs, throwing shimmering reflections onto the waters of the Bay.

A battered van pulled over about fifty yards in front of him. Its backup lights came on and it careened toward him, stopping just in front of his bumper. Two men got out.

Marco tensed, reaching into the glove compartment for his Mace. Then he recognized them. Creature and Seven.

He opened the door and got out.

"Man, am I ever glad to—"

"Shut up." Creature slammed a closed fist into the side of his head. Marco staggered back against the side of the car.

For the first time, he noticed the tiny cameras perched on their shoulders, lenses glittering like insect eyes. Creature cocked his head, as if listening to an imaginary voice. He looked at Marco.

"Laurel says to tell you she's givin' you your own special. The ratings'll go through the roof."

He pulled out a knife and waved it in front of Marco's face, back and forth, back and forth. Seven's steel teeth flashed brightly in the halogen light.

QUALITY TIME

THE FIRST TIME Brian and Heather made love in their new apartment, Brian traveled backwards in time to the Paleozoic Era. Or
maybe it was the Mesozoic. He could never keep those straight,
even though he'd been a real dinosaur freak as a kid.

It happened at the moment of orgasm. One minute he was
pinned underneath Heather on their futon in the bedroom, her
breasts swaying back and forth with the grinding motion of her
hips, the ghostly shapes of unpacked boxes looming through the
Manhattan dusk like a crowd of silent onlookers.

The next minute, he was lying in a shallow puddle of steaming,
stinking mud, a cloud of insects hovering around his head like an
animate mist. A fierce sun beat down through a canopy of giant
ferns. He took a deep breath and coughed, spitting out three or four
hapless bugs. He still had a bit of a woody, but it was quickly
detumescing.

He stood on shaky legs. Rivulets of mud dripped down his
thighs. A shadow passed across the ground and he looked up. A
pterodactyl the size of a winged Buick sailed gracefully overhead,
close enough to toss a rock at had there been one at hand and he so
inclined.

Rodan, he thought stupidly. His mental processes seemed slowed
to a crawl. Frozen in amber.

In a detached sort of way, he was surprised at his detachment.

Time travel, after all. What if he stepped on a butterfly and wiped out his pathetically meager investment portfolio? He thought fleetingly that if he could find the timeline in which Michael Jackson existed and stomp its lights out, it would be worth whatever attendant difficulties might ensue.

There was a *basso profundo* roar from somewhere in the jungle to his left, not very far away. It was answered by a deafening, high-pitched screech off to his right. Another *basso* bellow, closer still. The exchange put a stop to Brian's woolgathering, but his legs didn't want to move. He just stood there shivering, like a lawn jockey made of Jell-O.

The sound of something huge crashing through the ferns galvanized him into action. He turned around and took a flying leap into a stand of waist-high grass, landing with a splash in a sticky bog. Something long and sinuous thrashed underneath him and slithered away. Brian rolled over and looked back at what now occupied the clearing.

A mottled gray-green Sherman tank on chicken legs. Ridiculous, tiny hands. A head so huge in proportion to its body that it looked like any sudden move would snap its neck like a stick.

T-rex, Brian thought. *Christ on skis.*

The thing opened its mouth and let out another bellow, enveloping Brian in a charnel stink. With the possible exception of a Pixies concert he'd been to a few years back, it was the loudest sound he'd ever heard.

Inevitable as slapstick, the nearby answering screech split the humid air. It sounded closer. Brian hoped fervently that they would find some other place to sort out their differences.

He was in luck. With surprising grace and speed, the *Tyrannosaurus* hurtled itself toward the sound, crashing through the dense jungle. The low bellow of the thunder lizard and the high screech of its unseen antagonist merged into a wall of noise. It sounded like they were turning the jungle into coleslaw. The sound of their struggle receded into the distance.

Brian forced himself to breathe. He sat up and looked around. Jungle so deep a green that it seemed to vibrate. Cartoon blue sky. Air so warm, thick, and moist it made the dead heat of a central

Florida summer seem positively arid by comparison. Bugs enough to rival August in Minnesota.

What the fuck am I doing here? And more to the point, how do I get back?

He played it back in his mind again. One minute, scaling the heights of Heather; the next, cowering in a puddle of filth while giant lizards fought to the death a stone's throw away.

"Very interesting," he said aloud, in a fake Viennese accent. His voice sounded strange in the heavy, Mesozoic air. Or maybe it was the Paleozoic.

But really, the whole thing was no more difficult to swallow than getting an apartment in Peter Cooper Village. They'd been told that the waiting list was eleven years long.

"Christ in a Cadillac," he'd said to Heather. "The only institutions with memories that long are Equifax and Sallie Mae."

He'd even tried to slip the clerk in the rental office a hundred dollars to lubricate the process a bit. He folded the bill in half, tucked it between the second and third fingers of his right hand, and reached across her desk as if pointing out something on their application.

She looked at him as if he'd tried to hand her a fresh, steaming turd.

"You're going to have to do a lot better than that," she said.

He shrugged and returned the bill to his pocket, figuring he'd just cratered whatever chances they might have had. Three weeks later, they got a call about a sixth floor two-bedroom with a view of the East River. It was obviously a clerical error, but they weren't about to question their good fortune.

The mud caking his arms, legs, and torso was beginning to dry, revealing hundreds of tiny, crawling bugs. He stood, brushing them off as best he could. Their previous apartment had been in the East Village and he'd developed a fairly clinical attitude about insect life.

Some kind of space-time continuum thing, Brian thought. *It's so unlikely to score one of those apartments that it's ripped a hole in the fabric of probability-space.*

At the suggestion of a friend of Heather's who channeled the spirits of deceased pets for wealthy clients on the Upper East Side, Brian had been reading Gary Zukov lately and his brain was overflowing with pseudoscience babble, like an abandoned couch leaking stuffing.

But where does the sex come in?

He realized that that wasn't the first time he'd wondered that with respect to Heather. He pushed the thought aside.

Orgasm! Whatever process Brian was subject to, it required an intense focus of psychic energy. It just popped him from one niche in space-time to another, like an orange seed squeezed between thumb and forefinger.

Pfft, he thought. *Goodbye, Heather.* Pfft. *Goodbye, New York.* Pfft. *Goodbye, Imageco.*

Brian had a great job at Imageco, a video post-production shop. He worked in billing but everything was pretty much automated, so there wasn't a whole lot to do. Two or three times a day, he'd knock off a threatening letter to one of their clients; the rest of the time he sat around with Steve, the resident hacker, watching Hong Kong chop-socky flicks and drinking Diet Jolt.

His eyes filled with tears.

Pfft.

But wait a minute. If it was the intense psychic energy of orgasm that squeezed him through the damaged region in space-time, maybe that was his ticket back as well.

He could *wank* his way home.

He looked down at his limp member, shrunken to the size of a walnut. He couldn't imagine being farther from thoughts of erotic bliss than at this very moment.

He looked guiltily around, then realized he had about two hundred million years before there was any chance of interruption.

Brian went to work.

He tried to conjure up an image of Heather, but her features blurred, taking on a definite reptilian cast.

His resolve receded.

He tried to invoke his old standby, a gin-soaked weekend with Janelle and Giselle, a pair of bisexual video effects editors from Northampton who'd come down to Imageco on consult to subtitle *Hiroshima, Mon Amour* in Ebonics. This time, however, his mental picture of their gymnastic grappling was painfully suggestive of prehistoric beasts locked in mortal combat.

"The hell with it," he said aloud. There was a nearby, answering *peep*.

Brian looked up. Not five feet away, perched on tiny, stick-like legs, was a dinosaur the size of a kangaroo. It had a long, narrow beak and a handsome crest arching over its head like a cartilaginous Mohawk. It tilted its head to the side and let out another *peep*.

"Shoo," Brian yelled, waving his free hand. "Go on, get out of here!"

The thing disappeared into the jungle with alarming speed. Brian looked down at his withered Willie. Back to Square One.

From somewhere not far away, the bellow of the *T-rex* shook the jungle. Brian felt the ground vibrate under his bare behind.

There's nothing like abject fear to stiffen a man's resolve. With business-like efficiency, he went back to work. Another roar, considerably closer, hastened the exercise. His hand was covered with tiny particles of grit from the mud and it felt like he was jerking off with a handful of aquarium gravel.

Through half-closed eyes, Brian saw a gray-green shape pushing aside the ferns. He closed his eyes completely and stroked faster. His nostrils filled with the stink of rotting blood. Another roar split the sky. He—

—arched his back, reaching behind Heather's firm, plump buttocks to pull her close.

Heather made the sound she usually made when she was just about to come but slipped back from the brink, a cross between a sigh and a moan that rose up from somewhere deep in her chest. She ground against him half-heartedly another couple of times, then rested her head on his chest.

He was filled with the smell of her, buoyed by the faint undercurrent of new apartment effluvia—roach spray, carpet cleaner, mildew.

She looked up into his eyes, the point of her chin digging into his collarbone.

"You seem really distant," she said.

"Wha—?"

"It seemed like you just—went away."

Brian blinked. The last thing he remembered was looking up into the open mouth of the *Tyrannosaur*. Scraps of rotting meat clung to its teeth. He could see its tonsils.

"I, um—" he stammered.

"I really wish you could just stay ... *present* when we're making love." Her full lips turned downwards in a pout.

Well, you see, hon', space-time is like this rubber sheet stretched across a frame, kind of, and there's some parts that get stretched thinner than others and I just sort of slipped through this part that got real thin when we scored this crib and—

He didn't think so.

"I'm sorry, baby," he said, finally.

She nuzzled his neck and wriggled against him, taking his earlobe between her teeth and biting down gently.

"You want to try again?" she asked.

Brian forced himself to smile. "Sure."

Brian was having lunch with Steve at Niko's Nook, a Greek coffee shop on 45th and Lex. He poured cream into his coffee and watched it slosh thickly, like crankcase oil after about thirty-thousand miles. A roach skittered across the counter and he absently squashed it with his thumb. He gathered the gooey remains in his napkin and returned it to his lap.

"You seem awfully quiet today," Steve said.

Brian looked up. His distorted reflection stared back at him from Steve's wraparound, mirrored sunglasses.

"You're going to think I'm crazy," Brian said, watching his own lips move as he spoke. He felt like he was talking to himself in the bathroom mirror.

"I already think you're crazy—you just ordered the souvlaki. What's going on?"

Brian looked around, making sure there was nobody within earshot.

"Heather and I were, uh, inaugurating the new bedroom yesterday …" He paused. He didn't know how to say it without sounding like a lunatic.

"I'm sure congratulations are in order," Steve said, after a polite interval. "Was there something else?"

Brian decided to try a different approach. "Do you have any idea how difficult it is to get an apartment in Peter Cooper Village?" he asked.

"Does the Pope wear a big, stupid hat?" Steve replied. "It's all I've heard you talk about for the last month."

"Well, don't you think it's a little … *strange* that we got one after three weeks?"

"Sure I think it's strange. I also think it's strange that Dolly Parton can walk upright. These things happen. What's your point?"

"When we were making love, right at the critical moment, I traveled backwards in time." He looked defiantly at Steve. His reflection stared back with an expression of neurasthenic angst.

Steve shook his head. "Is that all? Shit, Bri', I've been married twenty-two years. If I didn't do a little time traveling every now and then, I'd be ready for a rubber room."

"No, you don't get it. I mean I really *went* somewhere. The Jurassic or something. Christ on roller skates, I almost got my head bitten off by a *Tyrannosaurus*!"

Steve took his sunglasses off and looked at Brian for a long time. "Did you used to do a lot of acid back in the seventies?" he asked, finally.

"Well, sure, but—"

"Those little orange barrels?"

"Yeah, but—"

"I thought so." He peered at his sunglasses, fogged them with his breath, wiped them on his Young Gods T-shirt, and put them back on. He pulled a pen out of his pocket, scrawled something on a napkin, and pushed it across the table to Brian.

"I've got this doctor friend," he said. "You tell him you're a friend of mine and ask him to write you a scrip for some Xanax. You'll be fine." Then, as an afterthought, he added, "Just don't drink with it."

"Thanks," Brian heard himself say. He stared numbly into the cool mirrored surface of Steve's glasses as his reflection folded the napkin into a neat square and slid it into his shirt pocket.

"Use 'I feel' statements, Heather," Doctor Fishlove said.

The late afternoon sun coming in through the Venetian blinds threw a pattern of stripes across the stuffed toy bears that lined one wall of the therapist's office. They looked like they were wearing prison uniforms.

Heather threw her head back. "Okay." She looked at Brian. "I *feel* like you've been really withdrawn lately. I *feel* like you haven't been present in our relationship. I *feel* like you aren't interested in me sexually anymore."

"And how does that make *you* feel, Brian?" Doctor Fishlove asked. He was an ordinary, Midwestern looking man somewhere on the downhill side of forty, with one disfiguring feature—a small wart perched precisely on the end of his nose. Brian couldn't take his eyes off it.

"Well, I don't know." He paused. "Bad, I guess."

"Bad," Doctor Fishlove repeated. "*Good.* Is there anything you want to say to Heather?"

Actually, there wasn't. He'd been avoiding sex for the last two weeks, scared that it would send him back into the Mesozoic or whatever. He really wanted to talk to her about it, but there never seemed to be a good time to bring it up.

He wasn't about to start popping off in therapy about dinosaurs and time travel, though. It would really screw things up. Besides, he'd scarfed a couple of Xanax earlier that morning and it didn't seem all that important.

"Uh, yeah, I guess." He tore his eyes away from the wart and looked at Heather. "I acknowledge your feelings. I'll try to do better."

Doctor Fishlove beamed. Heather didn't look convinced. Brian promised himself that he'd talk to her that night. Or poke her. One or the other, anyway.

The remains of an orange were spread across the plate, the colors brightly surreal in the harsh, kitchen light. It was one of those new hybrids and Brian had had a hell of a time finding a seed for his demonstration. Heather had watched the operation in silence.

Brian held the seed up between thumb and forefinger.

"So we're in this niche in space-time," he said. "Poking away, happy as clams. But the fabric of everything has become really weak because we've scored this apartment."

He looked up at Heather. No help there. Brian pushed forward. "All of a sudden, *pfft*." He squeezed down on the seed and it flew out of his fingers, sailing past Heather's shoulder and skidding to a halt on the shiny linoleum floor. "I'm somewhere else. Some *when* else."

Heather looked at him without expression for what seemed like a long time.

"Are you going to pick that up?" she asked, finally.

"Uh, sure." Brian got up and retrieved the orange seed. He flicked it into the trash and sat back down.

"So, what do you think?" he asked.

She kept looking at him.

"Well, say something," he said.

"I'm leaving you," she said.

Brian sat in the spare bedroom looking out across the East River. The sun coming up over Brooklyn threw sheets of rippling gold foil across the water. A flock of tugboats pulled a crippled tanker downriver.

Heather had been packing, but the sounds had stopped some time ago and the silence now seemed to flow out of the back bedroom like smoke.

He heard a noise and turned around. Heather stood in the doorway, her eyes red and swollen.

"I'm going now," she said. "I'll send my brother by for the rest of my things. Please don't try to find me."

He listened to her footsteps pad down the hall. The front door closed with a final sound. It occurred to him that at that very moment, Heather was time traveling. Into his past.

Brooklyn shimmered through a film of tears. Brian blinked to clear his vision and felt a warm drop trail down his cheek. The cars on the FDR Drive reflected the sunlight in miniature, prismatic stars, swiftly moving.

O YOU WHO TURN THE WHEEL

ALYN SAT on the patio in back of the Waterfront Tavern, alone at a table for two, looking out over the dry seabed. Low dunes marched to the flat horizon, glowing in Newmoon's gibbous, steel light.

Long ago, he and his crèche-sister Alyx had, on a mutual dare, hiked straight out into the dunes until they could no longer see the city. They brought rye wafers, dry cheese, and water, and followed the arc of maglev towers towards the flat horizon. Once, a shape hurtled past fifty meters overhead, silently threading the towers, its bow shock a slap of sudden wind. They passed sprawling, rusted structures huddled against the dunes, crumbling to ochre dust, their original purpose unfathomable. Stories held that wights and tygers and great, scaled, flightless birds owned the vast stretches of nothing between the few remaining cities, calling to each other in languages that time had emptied of meaning, killing and eating any who left the safety of the inhabited zones. Only stories, but at every sigh and rustle of wind and sand they stopped short and looked at each other. One of them—usually Alyx—would laugh and they would continue on.

They walked until they reached the sea, lifeless and heavy with salt. As the red, swollen sun neared the horizon, they heard a distant cry rising into the dusk. It was followed by another, closer, and they dropped their food and water and ran all the way back to the city, laughing and panting as they collapsed inside the exclusion field.

There were other adventures as they grew older together, but the trip into the dunes and the headlong flight home was the one that set the pattern for all the others: pushing each other towards a precipice and pulling each other back, Alyx usually the adventuring one, Alyn recalcitrant, but always together.

Until now.

Most of the Waterfront crowd was inside listening to the musicians, slow, sad music played on ancient stringed instruments just audible over the murmur of conversation, and he had the patio to himself except for an oddly matched Ursa and Felix, lumbering and lissome, sitting close together, heads bent in conversation.

The voices from the bar area suddenly stopped. The music floated above the silence for a long moment, then the buzz of conversation filled the space again. The source of the disturbance was soon apparent: an elderly female human dressed in the traditional black and scarlet singlet of a Speaker, and her Ken, tall and slender, huge golden eyes peering out from beneath a black hood, mouth cilia gently waving.

The pair approached Alyn and stopped.

The Ken fixed its eyes on Alyn and he felt something in the back of his mind, a tingle, an invitation.

"The sea," said the Speaker, eyes fixed on some distant, inner horizon. "The sky."

"Excuse me?" Alyn said.

"The sea. The sky."

Alyn looked out at the vast desert, the dry, ancient sea. The Mooncloud arched overhead, a wispy, tattered road to nowhere. Newmoon was just touching the flat horizon. Dunes tumbled into the distance.

He looked back at the Speaker, then the Ken, and felt it again, that tickling at the back of his mind. Not unpleasant, but decidedly odd. Before he could gather his thoughts to say anything in response, he felt the Ken disengage, a soft, mental snap. Then Ken and Speaker turned as one and left.

The Ursa and Felix were staring at him and he felt his cheeks flush.

This had something to do with Alyx, there was no doubt. But what? How did they find him? He didn't know and it didn't matter.

Soon she would don the black and scarlet and be gone from him forever.

He finished his drink. The musicians were taking a break and he made his way through the crowd. Mostly human, a few uplifts, the knots of people seemed to arrange themselves to impede his progress. He muttered "excuse me" at least a dozen times. He jostled a burly Ursa who grumbled something unintelligible at him as he neared the door.

Finally, the street, the night. The nearby spaceport pushed a nimbus of light up from the low, stubbled skyline of the city. The ionization trail from an ascending ship lanced across the sky, whispering like the tearing of a distant curtain.

There were no bicycles in the public rack and he decided to walk the two miles to the small flat he shared with Alyx. The midnight rain had come and gone; the narrow streets were slick and the air smelled of ozone and jasmine.

He felt like his world was coming apart. He thought of his job at the 'port, administering a fleet of low-Mind cranes and lifters at one of the many loading bays, harnessing their dull, stupid enthusiasm for service, without Alyx to come home to, and saw the days stretch ahead endlessly like the dunes in the dry seabed. Their easy familiarity and banter was the skin over a deeper friendship that had sustained him for as long as he could remember. And he knew that it had been the same for her.

They'd moved into a flat together shortly after crèche. They'd liked, hated, or tolerated each other's lovers over the years, never going there with each other by unspoken agreement. They each had their own lives, some friends in common and some not, but they were tightly bound. More than friends, more than crèche-sibs, more even than lovers.

Until now.

"Why are you doing this?" he'd asked shortly after she'd been Chosen.

They were sitting on a bench next to the Occam Reservoir. Water sculptures danced on its surface. Nearby on the grass, a young crèche group was playing a children's game under the watchful eye of a Sister, her bronze carapace gleaming in the sunlight.

"They asked me."

Nobody understood the Ken lottery. Only a handful every year. Accepting the invitation was strictly voluntary, but few had ever refused.

"Yes," Alyn said. "But why *you*?"

She looked at him carefully, choosing her words.

"I don't know why I was chosen. It's not really random. There's a set of compatibility criteria that only the Ken and the high-Minds understand." She paused, looked away, met his eyes again.

"I have to do this," she said. "They've given us so much."

She gestured vaguely at the sky.

"The wormhole maps. No more disease. An inexhaustible power grid. And they ask so little in return."

He felt tears come.

"They are asking everything."

She smiled sadly and shook her head.

"It's not like that. It's beautiful, really. There's a feeling of contentment, of belonging. I don't lose the sense of who I am. I'm just in a different place, a new phase."

"They are asking everything of *me*."

Alyx took his hand.

"I'm sorry. I love our life here. I love *you*. But I've never been called like this before. To be of service to something bigger. I can't say no."

He looked at her, at the lean planes of her face that he knew so well. He couldn't imagine a life without her.

"I know," he said. "I know."

When he got home, the flat was quiet and gloomy. Her bedroom door was closed and he heard faint music inside, but the lamp by the common room window, when lit indicating that one of them had taken a lover, was dark.

She would be gone in the morning. They had said their good-byes and all else that needed to be said. He already felt her absence, a physical ache. Becoming a Speaker was so final, the Ken so ineffable. On those rare occasions when somebody died, they lingered in the Hyaloplasm, sometimes for months, even years, until they grew tired of the dull slowness of the fleshbound and the fleshbound grew tired of them. But Alyx would be gone from him forever. Speakers never knew where serving the Ken might take then. She might remain in the city or be whisked by wormhole thousands of light years away.

He knocked on her door.

"Come in."

She was sitting in lotus on her bed. Ancient koto music quietly tickled the air.

"I'm sorry. I know we agreed—"

"It's all right. Come sit."

He sat next to her as she straightened her legs and stretched.

"I was at the Waterfront this evening."

She smiled. "Ah, the Waterfront."

"A Speaker and Ken showed up. They went directly to me. I felt something in my mind, some sort of presence. The Speaker said something: the sea, the sky. Then they left."

She frowned. "The Ken are ... odd. Nobody knows what will get their attention, not even the Speakers."

"I thought it might have something to do with you."

"It might, but I can't imagine what."

He nodded, reached out and touched her cheek. She took his hand. They looked at each other for a long moment. He tried to fix this moment in his mind, their last. Her eyebrows angled in a slight frown. Their flat, quiet around them. He got up from the bed and left the room, closing the door quietly behind him.

He went to his bedroom and opened the window, listening to the night murmur of the city. He selected a historical drama full of intrigue, violence, and sex, activated the reader and lay down as the induction field wrapped itself around his cortex like a coiled worm. He fell asleep to garish, primary colors and clashing sounds.

When he awoke she was gone. The flat felt empty. It *smelled* empty. The little sounds a dwelling makes adjusting to its inhabitants were different. Everything was new.

Alyx's door was open. He went into her room and stood in the center, looking around. It bore few signs of her presence. She'd left a picture on the wall: the Citadel rising up from Newmoon's mete- orite-pocked metal surface, the sky black against the too-sharp, too-close horizon. He had teased her about its bleakness, but it had a stark beauty.

He left the room, closing the door behind him.

There were two days before his next shift at the port. The prospect of the empty hours ahead filled him with dread. He fixed himself a light breakfast of soy cake and berries and left the flat, walking with no particular destination in mind.

The day was warm, the sky blue. The street was filled with people on bicycles weaving between pilotless drones. A work crew of Ursas was demolishing a building, wielding great hammers and pneumatic machines. Their laughter and coarse voices rose above the din. Alyn strained to hear what they were saying, but the words made no sense. Among themselves the Uplift reverted to dialect impenetrable to humans.

The days unrolled into weeks. He spoke little, inhabiting his routine at work like a suit of clothes. The puppy-like enthusiasm of the low-Minds for the dullest of tasks was a sort of anesthesia, but it wasn't enough. He began sampling in earnest the time-honored comforts of cannabis, glanding, and alcohol. That didn't work very well and had a tendency to produce unanticipated results. After two weeks of nightly excess he awoke one morning in an unfamiliar bed, fully clothed, the space next to him rumpled and still warm.

He stumbled into the living room and saw a tall, unfamiliar man coming out of the kitchen holding a steaming mug.

"Ah, you're up," the man said. "I have tea."

"Hello," Alyn said carefully.

The man looked at him closely.

"You don't remember a thing, do you?"

Alyn shook his head and grimaced. "I should be careful about sudden movement. Um, no. I'm afraid not."

The man handed him the tea. "Here, this should help a bit. I'm Dafari."

The warm mug felt good in hands.

"Thank you." He paused. "We didn't—?"

Dafari laughed, not unkindly. "Goodness, no. You were in no condition. You just looked like you needed help."

Alyn nodded. "I guess I did."

They sat on Dafari's balcony, sipping tea.

"Do you want to talk about it?" Dafari asked after a few moments.

"Not really," Alyn said. "I lost someone recently and nothing makes much sense."

Dafari nodded. "That's hard."

"Yes, it is."

They sat for a little longer, saying little. The cool of morning was beginning to give way to mid-day heat. Alyn stood up.

"I should be going. Thank you."

"You're very welcome."

Dafari's quiet kindness was almost overwhelming. Alyn left the flat a bit relieved that they had dispensed with the awkward ritual of exchanging signets. He vowed to go easy on chemical self-comfort after that, but he was still filled with an abiding ache that he didn't know how to navigate.

About a week later, he saw a flash of black and scarlet in the crowd at a street fair in the Plaza of Palms. He worked his way through the crush of vendors and people until he saw them, Speaker and Ken, standing in front of a booth selling dyed fabrics. The Speaker, not his Alyx, held up one swath to the Ken, then another. They abruptly turned and left.

Alyn followed them as they meandered through the crowd, stopping at a jewelry booth, a display of exotic flora, in front of a trio of juggling Simians. When they left the fairgrounds, Alyn continued to follow, hanging back about fifty feet so he would not be noticed. He had no plan, no conscious intent. He felt compelled, as if connected to them by a wire.

Their movements seemed as random as clouds. They stopped at a teahouse and a healer's office. They stood at a corner for nearly a half hour. They circled the Occam Reservoir twice, to the ever-present music of the water sculptures.

Eventually, they made their way to the Ken Temple, an imposing structure of red stone and black steel near the center of the city. A door opened and they disappeared inside.

Alyn felt deflated and oddly exposed, as if he had just been witnessed doing something embarrassing and personal, even though he didn't think he'd been seen. He walked the long way back to his flat, avoiding the busy streets. The afternoon sun was warm and his unease receded slowly.

Near home he passed the community garden for his building. Alyx had done most of the work on their plot: an herb garden, peppers, tomatoes, summer squash. After she left it had gone to seed and weed. Next to their wild, unkempt plot, a Felix he had seen a few times coming in and out of their building was kneeling in a meticulous patchwork geometry of green. He left before he could be seen.

The next morning, he brought a few tools down to the garden. He didn't know much about gardening but he could tell a weed from something that wasn't a weed. It was a start. He lost himself to the work, enjoying the loamy smells and the sun on the top of his head.

A shadow fell over him. He looked up and the Felix was there, smiling, shading her face from the sun with her lightly furred hand.

"Hello," she said. "I was wondering if anyone was going to reclaim this plot."

"It was really my flatmate's thing. She's not around anymore so I thought I'd give it a try. I have absolutely no idea what I'm doing."

"You seem to be doing all right." She held out her hand. "C'tara."

"Alyn." He took her hand, feeling the slight scrape of her claws on his wrist.

"Would you like a heartplant? They're just about ripe."

The vines behind her were studded with fruit the size of a baby's fist, pulsating gently. She snapped one off and handed it to him. He wrapped his hand around it, feeling its warmth. She got another one for herself and popped it into her mouth. A trail of blood dripped down her chin. She wiped it off and licked her hand, smiling at him as if sharing a secret.

Alyn held the fruit to his nose. It smelled earthy and pungent. He put it in his mouth and bit down. Salty sweetness, chewy, a peppery finish.

"That's really good."

She smiled. "Isn't it? They're a little tricky to grow but if you want I'll show you how sometime."

"I'd like that."

"Well, nice to meet you."

She returned to her work. Alyn watched the arc of her slender back for a moment and felt a brief surge of desire.

Interesting, he thought. Haven't thought about *that* for a while.

He left the garden and returned to his flat, bathed, dressed, and brought a glass of tea to the balcony. He listened to the city breathe around him. He realized, with a little jolt of surprise, that he was not in pain. He fell into a light doze and had ocean dreams, salt dreams: rhythm and surge, the ancient heartbeat of the world.

The next day, he took a bicycle from a public rack and pedaled out to the false waterfront. A weathered boardwalk ran parallel to what used to be the shore. He walked along the wooden esplanade, stopping from time to time to look out at the dunes, trying to imagine the old sea. A pier jutted half a klick out into the sand. Alyn walked all the way to the end and sat, dangling his legs over the edge.

The sea. The sky.

He felt something tickle the back of his mind, like a forgotten name. He stood and looked back along the length of the pier.

He expected to see the black and scarlet, the hooded robe. He watched and waited, but there was nothing, and he sat down again. The vast plain of the dead sea lay before him. He closed his eyes and imagined a sapphire expanse, stretching all the way to the flat, distant horizon, his lungs filling with saline dampness, and from high above and far away the cry of a sea bird.

THE DAM

In one beaker, prepare a solution of seventy-six percent sulfuric acid, twenty-three percent nitric acid, and one percent water. In another beaker, prepare a solution of fifty-seven percent nitric acid and forty-three percent sulfuric acid. Percentages are given by weight, not volume.

I WAS STANDING on the causeway that runs across the top of the dam, looking out over the reservoir. It had been raining for days and the water was the color of milky tea.

"It's good," a voice behind me said.

I whirled around, nearly jumping out of my skin. It was Oscar.

"Jesus, Oscar, you scared the daylights out of me."

"It's good when it's like this," he said, his eyes grey and empty as the sky. A small rivulet of drool escaped from the corner of his mouth.

"What's good?" I asked.

"The Dragon cannot live in water that is too pure," he said.

He was looking through me, out across the water. Beneath his hat, dripping wet from the rain, I knew that there was a depressed concavity in his skull, as if someone had taken a tennis ball and pushed it deep into soft putty. I'd seen it. The hair there grew thick and curly.

Beneath the muddy brown water, the towns slept.

Ten grams of the first solution are poured into an empty beaker and placed in an ice bath.

My house is at the end of the causeway, just off the road. It was originally the caretaker's house and it sends roots down into the guts of the dam, basement, sub-basement, sub-sub-basement, the water heavier in the air the deeper you descend until it beads on the walls in thick, fat drops. I have never been to the bottom.

Levers and wheels protrude from the walls next to the rickety metal stairway that threads the levels. It is always cold down there, and always, somewhere, there is the slow, steady sound of water dripping into water.

Sometimes I go down three levels, four levels, and turn one of the wheels at random. Pause. Cock my head to listen. It is there, just at the threshold of perception, the sound of great forces being set into motion.

Add ten grams of toluene and stir for several minutes.

Last night there was an incredible aurora display, gaudy neon curtains rippling across the sky in a cosmic breeze. It went on for hours. Last time it was this good was a couple of years ago. A scientist from back east stopped the night at the Broken Nail and a cluster of people gathered around him in the tavern, pumping him for news. But all he wanted to talk about was the aurora.

"Ionization in the upper atmosphere," he said.

Later that night, Billy, who used to run the gas station, killed him for his radio. For months afterward, he wore the man's teeth on a necklace whenever he showed up in town, but somebody must have talked to him, because he stopped.

I asked him about it once. It was Saturday and the Farmer's Market was in town. Billy was holding a head of cabbage in one hand, lifting it to the light like it was a skull and he Hamlet.

"Where's your necklace, Billy?" I asked.

He looked at me.

"Ionization in the upper atmosphere," he said, and wandered off, laughing.

Remove the beaker from the ice bath and gently heat until it reaches fifty degrees Centigrade. Stir constantly.

Four towns were erased when the reservoir was created as a CCC project back in the thirties. Prescott, Alice, Machinery, Thor. If I had any more children, I would name them thus.

Several people refused to move when the time came. An old woman living in the house her great-grandfather had built as a newly-freed slave fleeing Reconstruction. A young man whose wife had died in childbirth the previous year, his daughter stillborn. An idiot. The town drunk of Machinery. I wonder if the waters rose slowly, ushering them gently into the next world, or if they looked up suddenly to see a wall of blue steel and white foam rushing down upon them, higher than the trees, bearing the weight of Judgment.

I suspect the former. On nights when the sky is clear and the full moon hangs suspended in the sky like a cold, blue lamp, the juncture between air and water fades to nothing and the water itself becomes transparent. My boat glides along the silent surface and I look down upon the valley as if the water were a kind of amber, freezing time to stillness. Roads, hills, stores, houses. It is a time machine, this reservoir.

Fifty additional grams are added from the first beaker and the mixture heated to fifty-five degrees Centigrade. This temperature is held for the next ten minutes. An oily liquid will begin to form on top of the acid.

I sit in my house at the edge of the causeway and monitor the level of the water. For this service, the people of the town bring me food, woven items, firewood. From time to time, Oscar wanders up from his tarpaper shack behind the old train station and stands in the middle of the causeway, looking out across the water. Always across the water, never the other side. Never the town.

Last week, I saw him there from the window of my house, standing in his usual spot. I brought him a strip of jerky and an apple and stood next to him facing the opposite direction, down the curve of the dam and along the valley floor to the curls of smoke from town braiding into the grey sky.

After ten or twelve minutes, the acid solution is returned to the ice bath and cooled to forty-five degrees Centigrade. The oily liquid will sink to the bottom of the beaker. The remaining acid solution should be drawn off using a syringe.

The residents of the sunken valley populate my dreams.

A pair of schoolteachers, sisters, lovers, spinsters to the town of Prescott, holding each other and everything unspoken as the waters rose.

A man just outside Alice who murdered his wife for the insurance money. He made it look like an accident. It was so convincing, in fact, that years later he himself believed it.

A resident of Thor who made an occasional practice of driving to neighboring towns under the still of night and killing dogs with a crossbow. He rendered the flesh from their bones and carefully reconstructed their skeletons, like model airplanes, in his attic.

The proprietor of the Mill End Store in Machinery who nursed elaborate masturbatory fantasies about raping and murdering young boys. As the years passed, the fantasies grew more and more baroque. He was active in the church community and ran the Christian Youth Fellowship's Helping Hand for Troubled Teens camp every summer.

I can feel them looking up at me as my boat glides slowly through the air.

Fifty more grams of the first acid solution are added to the oily liquid while the temperature is slowly being raised to eighty-three degrees Centigrade. After this temperature is reached, it is maintained for a full half hour.

Elly Foss gave birth to a two-headed baby last week. It cleaved together at the breastbone, both heads crying in unison when it came out. A single pair of arms waved feebly in the air. Her husband, Jack, took it by the legs and slammed it against the wall. He says it's no baby of his. Elly isn't saying much of anything. There's a lot of talk going around, as they have two normal children, both obviously Jack's since they exhibit the same pattern of delicate webbing between their toes that Jack has. Veins lace through the translucent skin like the architecture of a drunken spider.

At the end of this period, the solution is allowed to cool to sixty degrees Centigrade and is held at this temperature for another full half hour. The acid is again drawn off, leaving once more the oily liquid at the bottom.

In the reservoir lives a catfish the size of a man. Massive arms sprout from its body just beneath the gills and it uses them to move aside the debris that has been collected by the slow, Atlantean drift, to open the doors and enter the houses of Machinery and Prescott, of Alice and Thor. I close my eyes and I can see it floating next to a Colonial armoire in someone's master bedroom, reaching out a hand to touch the detailed filigree gone soft and pulpy in the cold depths, steadying itself in a sudden surge of current.

Last year, some fool from one of the hill towns came down and tried to catch it. He built a raft out of a garage door and four empty oil drums, bolted a stout, fiberglass pole onto the raft, and pushed himself off into the calm water.

He used kittens for bait. Through binoculars, I saw him impale their tiny bodies on curved hooks and drop them wriggling into the water. I imagined that I could hear their sharp cries.

Every now and then, he'd get a hit, the pole bending like a bow, pulling that end of the raft halfway into the water. Then it would stop and the raft would spring back and bob up and down like a cork.

A small crowd gathered on the causeway to watch his progress. He was doomed, already dead, and he didn't even know it.

But we did.

After a long stretch of quiet, the rocking of the raft from the last hit damped to an almost imperceptible bob and silence hanging over the lake like heat haze, our fish burst out of the water right in front of him. It was the most beautiful thing I've ever seen, leaping into the air in a silver blur, the sun catching rainbow highlights off scales rippling like mercury. Before we had time to blink, it grabbed the man in its huge hands and pulled him into the water. The raft skidded off to the side, bobbing, bobbing. Eventually, it drifted to shore on the north side of the dam and got caught up in the branches of a fallen tree, half-submerged.

It's still there.

*Thirty grams of sulfuric acid are added while the oily liquid is heated to
eighty degrees Centigrade. All temperature increases must be accomplished
slowly and gently.*

Oscar was on the causeway before dawn, looking out across the
water. I brought him a heel of dark bread and some cheese. He took
the items from me without a word and pushed them into his mouth.

"It's mine," he said, chewing vigorously on the wad of food.
Crumbs clung to his lips.

"Excuse me?"

He closed his eyes and swallowed, then motioned to the canteen
hanging from my shoulder. I gave it to him and he unscrewed the
top and held it to his lips. His Adam's apple bobbed up and down
as he swallowed. When he was done, he wiped his lips on his
sleeve.

"The baby is mine," he said, handing me back the canteen.

I looked closely at him. Wind whistled up from the town side of
the causeway, pushing between us, as if reminding me of what I had
to do. I returned to the house. When I looked out at the causeway
again, he was gone.

*Once the desired temperature is reached, thirty grams of the second acid
solution are added. The temperature is raised from eighty degrees Centigrade to one hundred four degrees Centigrade and is held there for three
hours.*

I dreamed that I was in a house on the outskirts of Machinery,
sitting weightless in the living room. Tiny ceramic animals clustered
together on the mantle. A grandfather clock wedged into a corner of
the room emitted a muffled ticking.

I floated over to the window and looked out. There, just above
the level of the treetops, a small boat gliding slowly past, a lone
figure rowing.

*Lower the temperature of the mixture to one hundred degrees Centigrade
and hold it there for thirty minutes.*

When I awoke the next morning, there was a basket of bread and jerky on my doorstep. Underneath the lean-to next to the shed in back, a half-cord of wood that hadn't been there the night before.

They flayed him alive and nailed him to a telephone pole in front of the burned-out shell of the First Presbyterian Church, just off the town commons.

I brought him some water. I set up a stepladder next to the pole and climbed with a pail and a ladle up to where he hung. He'd been there all day and most of the night before and he smelled pretty bad, blood and waste and something I couldn't identify, maybe his sorry old soul hovering nearby, waiting for an excuse to leave. An aura of flies surrounded him. His skin hung in strips; the muscles in his arms and legs were marbled with veins of yellow fat. An old scar sprawled across his shoulder, shiny runnels and bubbles like a sheet of melted plastic.

"Oscar," I said. "Oscar. How about a drink?"

His eyes flickered open. Imprecation, accusation, a burning grace.

The oil is removed from the acid and washed with boiling water. Stir constantly. The TNT will begin to precipitate out. Add cold water. Pellets will form.

The Dragon cannot live in water that is too pure. I charged up a pair of car batteries from the generator beneath my house and wired them to a simple spring-release mechanism. Took the device to the foot of the dam. Looked up at the broad sweep of concrete filling the sky, colors bright like a postcard from someplace where there is an ocean. Set the timer and clambered up the side of the valley through the dense undergrowth, branches scratching at my face like flailing arms.

Just as I reached the top, I heard a sound like a door slamming shut on an empty room. I turned around. A billowing, grey mushroom hurtled into the sky and a network of cracks spread across the face of the dam. Water broke out in discrete gushing sprays, the cracks widening, then all at once it gave, collapsing in a churning froth of water, concrete, earth.

The causeway was gone; my house hung on the blunt edge of nothing. A wall of water pushed through the valley, covering everything. Behind the advancing front, the roiling foam was a deep, rich brown.

To my right, the waters receded. First, the tall steeples of churches were revealed, then the houses, finally the streets and roads. Prescott and Machinery, Alice and Thor. They glistened, pure in the sunlight.

Note: The temperatures used in the preparation of TNT are exact. Do not rely on estimates or approximations. A good thermometer is essential.

Author's note: I am grateful to William Powell's *The Anarchist Cookbook* for the TNT recipe.

MEMENTO MORRIE

THERE WAS construction on Tunnel Road and the car took an alternate route that drove us past the Elmhurst Cemetery. I didn't realize it until we were rolling alongside neat rows of tombstones, gray and white teeth set in emerald green.

"Stop!" I called out.

"Stopping," the car said. It pulled over near one of the gates. I got out and walked into the cemetery. It had been a year or more since I'd been there and I felt a pinch of guilt. I got lost in the grid of headstones, but eventually I found them, Morrie and Ellen Moses, side by side like they'd been in life for over seventy years.

I stood in front of their graves and closed my eyes. The memories assembled themselves like jigsaw puzzles. Mom in her study, hunched in front of a big pair of monitors, the curve in her shoulders accentuating as the years piled up. Dad at the backyard Weber, adding his carbon footprint to the air in spite of the heavy fines. A succession of holiday dinners telescoping across the years after us kids dispersed.

The small stones I'd put on the shoulder of each monument at my last visit were still there and a complex of feelings compounded my guilt. Glad to see they were undisturbed, sad and a bit resentful that I was the only one left to maintain this little ritual. Silas was up in the Chicago orbital, growing pharmaceuticals and making trouble in local politics. He hadn't been downside in years. Dora was in California, but getting an exit visa wasn't easy these days. Our little family Diaspora. Everyone but me.

The last time I'd been here with Anna, she'd asked: "Do you know why the Jews put little rocks on gravestones?"

She was a lapsed Catholic herself and always talked about my Jewishness in the abstract. The Jews. Not that I was observant or anything—it was mostly a cultural thing with me—but it bugged me a little.

I shrugged. "Not really. It's just something you do. I always thought it was like, hey, I was here."

She shook her head. A wispy lock of grey escaped from her wool hat and fell across her forehead.

"The stones keep the souls of the dead in this world so they stay closer to the living. I saw it on the Everywhere channel."

I shrugged. "Doesn't seem to be working so well."

Anna stopped coming with me after that, and before long I pretty much stopped too.

I spoke with him about it after I got home that night. He was wearing an Aloha shirt: a riot of overlapping, red, meaty flowers with dangling, phallic stamens. Behind him, palm trees waved gently over a candy-green golf course.

"I stopped by the cemetery last night," I said.

He nodded. "Ah," he said after a long moment.

This was conversation with Dad after Enkryption. Lots of long pauses. It took some patience to get a dialogue going.

"I'm sorry Mom can't be there with you. They tried another encoding run last month but the upload keeps failing. They can't break past that sixty percent."

A bit of animation inhabited his face. "Ellen? I just spoke with her."

"No, Dad," I said gently. "That's not possible. They haven't been able to Enkrypt her. It's still pretty much hit or miss."

Sometimes hit *and* miss, I thought.

He nodded again. "Ah," he said.

Another long pause. Then his face lit as if a switch somewhere had closed.

"Say, remember that fishing trip off of Marathon in the Keys?"

Marathon didn't exist anymore; hotels and gas stations, tract homes and fast food joints rested under thirty feet of ocean.

"I sure do, Dad. You caught that swordfish and the hotel cooked it for us." He mentioned it nearly every time we spoke.

"Best swordfish I ever ate," he said. In fact, mercury levels were so high that local fish were inedible. The hotel had served us vat-grown swordfish from Argentina, but I'd paid the waiter to maintain the fiction.

"That fish was a real fighter, wasn't he, Dad?"

"He sure was." His smile was a bit uncertain now. His animation was starting to flag, like a clock slowly winding down. "A real fighter."

I heard a footstep behind me, felt a touch on my shoulder. I reached back and took Anna's hand.

"Hi, Morrie," she said.

Dad frowned. "Who's that?"

"It's Anna," I said.

His image froze in an expression of churlish confusion.

"Dad?"

No movement, no sound.

"Hung again," I said. I leaned my head back, rested it for a moment on Anna's yielding stomach.

"It's not getting any better," I said. "He's just not all there, and what's there isn't very recognizable as Dad."

She squeezed my shoulder.

Rocket, our tamakat, padded into the room.

"Hungry," he said in his small voice. "Hungry."

I activated his console in my heads-up and gave him some kibble. For a treat, I added a bit of hamachi. He began to purr and rubbed up against Anna's leg.

I turned back to the tank. Dad's image was still there, frozen in that bewildered frown.

I stood up, gave Anna a hug, and turned off the tank. I stepped back and looked at her tired face.

"How was today?"

She shrugged. "Not bad. A two-patch day."

I put together a simple dinner of unchicken and rice while she rested. When it was nearly done, I stepped over to the couch.

"Is Ethan eating with us?" I asked.

"I don't know. He's been under all day."

"I'll go talk to him."

"Don't get ..."

I waved my hand at her. "I know, I know."

Ethan's room was in the back of our little flat at the end of the hall. There was a hexagonal area of less faded paint on the door where a STOP sign had hung for years, a bit of adolescent levity abandoned. His room, too, had been stripped of music posters, photos, and other adornments. It was bare as a monk's cell.

I knocked on the door. There was no answer. I knocked again.

A faint voice answered. "Yeah?"

"Dinner."

A long pause. "No, thanks."

I tested the knob as quietly as I could. Locked. I pictured him sitting in his rig, virched and tubed, skin fish belly pale. My baby boy. I debated whether to push it, make a scene, but decided against it. I knew how it would go and I just didn't have it in me.

We ate in silence. I was a lousy cook: protein and starch, a little salt, maybe something green if we could get it. Anna didn't eat much. She never did these days, just kind of pushed the food around on her plate.

We watched *Survivor: Luna* and *Triple Play*, a new comedy about the romantic misadventures of a poly triad. We put on the mandatory foxie afterwards. We hadn't watched for a few days and the fines were piling up. The President was doing a demolition duel with the EU PM. A pair of huge muscle cars ripped around a dirt arena, trying to take each other out. Blue exhaust smoke fogged the air, adding a transgressive thrill. It was a rematch from last year when the EU guy got killed, but we didn't pay much attention. You see something like that once and there's no point in watching it again. We turned the sound down as low as we could and waited for it to end so we could turn the tank off and go to bed.

I looked at Ethan's door on the way to our bedroom. I thought about knocking, saying goodnight, but I didn't.

Lying in bed, listening to the trucks hiss past on the droneway, watching the lights crawl across the ceiling, I knew Anna was awake by the little hitch in her breathing. She knew I was awake too.

"Where do you think he goes?" she asked.

"Mm?"

"Your dad. Where do you think he goes when he's not talking to us?"

I listened to the droneway, to the little night sounds of the flat settling and creaking around us.

"I don't know if he goes anywhere. I don't know if he's even aware of anything between our visits. We could ask him."

She chuckled softly. "Ah," she said, in a pretty good imitation of him. A low, gravelly old man's voice.

I chuckled too. "Ah," I said.

I drifted off the sleep. When I awoke, the sky was beginning to lighten. Anna breathed next to me. I heard the hitch.

I rolled over and put my hand on her shoulder.

"You been awake this whole time?"

After a while, she said, "I don't want to do it."

"Do what?"

"Enkryption. I don't want it."

She turned to me.

"Promise me," she said.

Rocket jumped up on our bed and butted his head against my foot.

"Sure, okay," I said. "I promise."

"Hungry," Rocket said.

Ethan joined us for breakfast. He looked pale and tired. Anna put a big plate of neggs and fakon in front of him. While she was fussing, she gave me one of those secret spouse looks. After thirty years we could read each other pretty well.

Be nice, she was saying. Talk to him.

I cleared my throat.

"So Ethan, what's going on with you these days?"

He looked a little distracted for a second, a mini thousand-yard stare. Maybe he was scanning my question for hostility or sarcasm. But I really wanted to know.

"Well, the swarm keeps growing." His voice was a little hoarse, like it hurt to talk. I had to give him credit for trying.

"How many are you?" I asked, trying to keep my voice neutral.

"We've got twenty-two now, with Rama and Abhi. They're new and their English isn't so good, so everybody has to slow down while the translation syncs across the swarm, but it's getting better."

It was more than I'd heard him say in months. I wanted to keep it going but then Anna started coughing. It went on for a while. I poured some water for her but she waved it away. Ethan had that long stare again. I couldn't tell if he was thinking or talking to his swarm or what.

Finally, Anna stopped. She took the glass and drained most of it, her Adam's apple bobbing up and down as she swallowed.

"Are you all right, Mom?" Ethan asked. "We're worried about you."

From the way he said it, I didn't think he meant "we" as in "me and Dad."

"I'm fine, Ethan." We hadn't spoken with him about her illness yet. "Just a little cold."

"We?" I asked.

He looked embarrassed and annoyed at the same time. "Well, yes. Me, all of us."

Anna was giving me that look, nothing secret about it this time, but I went ahead. In for a penny, whatever that was.

"Who do we get when you're sitting here with us? Ethan? Rama? Abhi?"

I leaned in and looked him in the eye, as if I were looking through a window into somebody's living room.

I waved. "Hi, Rama. Hi, Abhi."

"Stop it." Anna hardly ever raised her voice. Ethan and I both looked at her. "Just stop."

I took a deep breath.

"I'm sorry. But I really want to know. Who are you?"

"It's not like that, Dad."

"Well, what *is* it like?"

His eyes lost focus for just a second.

"It's … I'm still me. We're all individuals. And nobody's Enkrypted—we're all still alive. Not like Pops. In the swarm we share a context space. And we share everything with each other."

I thought about it, trying to grok what it would be like. Never being alone, but never having the sanctuary of solitude. I just couldn't imagine why anybody would want that. I felt like I'd failed Ethan because *he* wanted it.

"So they're your family now."

"No." He was adamant, almost angry. "I mean yes, but you're my family too. Why can't I have two families?"

Nobody said anything after that. Ethan finished his breakfast and stood up.

"Thanks for breakfast, Mom."

She turned her cheek towards him. He leaned in and gave her a kiss.

He looked at me.

"Are we good, Dad?"

I nodded, forced a smile. "Yes, son. We're good."

Anna died early the next morning. The sky was just beginning to lighten, the night leaching darkness from one side. She was turned away from me over on her side of the bed. This was when she usually woke up, in the pre-dawn stillness. I listened for the hitch but it didn't come. I reached out and touched her arm. Her skin was cool.

I felt a wave washing over me, huge and powerful and saline, and then I *was* the wave, surging and collapsing.

"Anna," I said.

I called Wellness Services. They said they would send out a team within a couple of hours. I straightened her nightgown where it had become disheveled from sleep and made the bed up around her. Lying there with her eyes closed, she looked like she was just resting.

I got up and knocked on Ethan's door.

"Yeah?"

"Can I come in?"

The lock clicked and the door opened a bit, just enough to see his face.

"What is it?"

"Please."

He opened the door and stepped aside. Tubes and wires led from various parts of him to a small, grey cube on wheels. A softly glowing display floated in the air above it.

He shuffled back to a big recliner, sat down, and looked at me. I didn't know how to say it to him. I didn't know how to say anything to him.

"Mom died last night," I said, finally. He flinched and his eyes welled up.

"What?"

"She's been sick for a while. She didn't want you to worry."

He went blank. That thousand-yard stare. Five seconds, ten, twenty.

"Ethan?"

Nothing. I got up quietly and left the room.

The crew from Wellness was very nice, very professional and understanding. A young woman in light blue coveralls looked over Anna's body and took some measurements.

Her companion was an older woman with a kind, round face.

"Maybe you'd better wait in the kitchen," she said.

"No," I said. "I want to be here with Anna."

She nodded, produced a slate, and asked me a few questions. Ethan appeared at the doorway while she was interviewing me, looking gaunt and sad, but he didn't say anything.

When they were done, they zipped her up in a black, plastic bag, unfolded a gurney from a suitcase, and wheeled her out.

At the door, the older woman turned to me, slate in hand.

"We'll send her remains in seven to ten days. There are some nice urns available at various prices. If you don't do anything, you'll get a very tasteful, green box. Plain, but you know." She smiled and shrugged. "We'll send out instructions as to what you can and can't do with the remains. Please read them. The penalties are pretty steep."

We stood there long after they left. Just standing there, looking at the door. I turned to him. His skin, stretched across his cheekbones, so pale it was almost transparent. His eyes, big and shimmering.

I put my hand on his shoulder. He tensed, then he let me take him in my arms. He felt insubstantial, as if his bones were hollow as a bird's.

I tried to tell Dad about it. There he was in the tank wearing the same gaudy shirt, the cheesy representation of golf heaven stretched out behind him.

"Anna's gone, Dad."

"Anna?"

"Yes, Dad. Anna. She died yesterday. You know she's been sick for a long time."

He nodded. "Anna."

"Yes, Dad. Anna."

Long pause.

"Ah."

We didn't have much of a memorial service. Dora still couldn't get a visa to leave California and Silas said he couldn't get a flight back in time for an election he was working on, something about Hohmann transfers. We had a 'presence call after Anna came in the mail. The urn I got her was plain but nice, a burnished aluminum cylinder. I paid extra for the engraving. In perfect looping cursive, it read:

Anna Moses

2055—2114

Beyond every essence, a new essence awaits

I put the urn in the middle of the kitchen table. Ethan and I sat on one side. Dora and Silas flickered across from us. I made a little food for me and Ethan but neither of us ate much. We all said a few things about Anna, about what we wanted to remember, then the conversation kind of merged into stories about Mom and Dad, leaving Ethan pretty much out of it. Silas's lag made everything more difficult. I think we were all a little relieved when we said our goodbyes.

Ethan and I sat there looking at each other after their images winked out. After a while, he reached out and touched my hand.

"We're here for you," he said.

I canceled the Enkryption contract for Mom and got my deposit back. I tried to get my money back for Dad too, but they pushed back and I didn't have the fight in me, so I just stopped checking in with him. I didn't feel too bad about it. You can't lose something that's already gone.

A couple of months later, I got a notice from the Elmhurst Cemetery that the feds had eminent-domained the land for a droneway extension. They offered a small settlement. I wasn't surprised. Nobody got buried anymore, it was so expensive. They offered to send me the remains but I didn't know what I'd do with them. So I checked "No" on the form and that was that.

But I wanted to visit them one last time. I told the car to take the long way, avoiding most of the strip malls and megaprojects. It was late November and the trees had just shaken off their last blankets of red and gold and yellow. Bare, fractal branches scraped the grey sky.

We pulled over on the shoulder next to an unbroken stretch of trees. I got out and breathed in the musty smell of damp leaf mulch and the sharp, clean smell of impending snow. A few flakes drifted down out of the sky.

There were signs outside the cemetery about the new construction project. I walked slowly among the monuments, navigating to my parents. The wind was starting to pick up. I turned up my collar and continued walking, head down against the cold, until I found their graves.

Snowflakes landed on the gravestones and melted immediately, leaving little patches of wetness.

I'd brought Anna with me and upended the canister over the

plots, moving it back and forth. The wind took most of the ash. A few small, black chunks littered the green. Soon they would be buried under a blanket of snow.

The stones were still there on the shoulders of the monuments. I reached out and gathered them up, smooth and light in my hand. They clicked together in my pocket as I walked back to the car.

ALBION UPON THE ROCK

HIS NAME WAS a multidimensional index that spanned the region in space-time occupied by his countless avatars. It had never been uttered as data encoded in modulated longitudinal vibrations, nor could it be. Call him Brown.

He narrowed his attention to a single frame. The artifact collapsed from a probability density locus to a unique instance. A *ship*, plying the ocean of dark between the stars at an agonizing subluminal crawl. About 0.05c, Brown calculated.

It was several klicks long, a thick cylinder studded with sensor modules, spinning lazily on its long axis. A bulbous cluster of engines sprouted from the rear of the ship, trailing a ridiculous plume of pions and other subatomic debris thousands of kiloklicks long.

The ship harbored a machine intelligence of sorts. Brown could detect thousands of autonomic processes: monitoring, logging, scanning, making minute adjustments. There was other life inside the shell of the thing, wet life, hundreds of bright sparks like a swarm of slow, lazy bees.

The sun stretched across the sky, a thin, bright line. Jamal Operations crouched behind a stand of trees, sweating freely, watching the cats feed. Six of them clustered around the corpse, coiled springs of muscle and fur, eagerly ripping and tearing. He could hear their purring from fifteen meters away, an ominous rumble that sent a chill down his back in spite of the heat.

His hand dropped to the knife hanging from his belt, an unconscious self-comforting gesture. There had been a bloom of cats in the world in recent months so it was cats he hunted. Sometimes, they hunted him.

Jamal's world was simple. He hunted cats and rats, tended the farms above and the ponics below, and after the sun receded to a soft gray glow to north and south, when the rivers and jungles above emerged from the haze and hung overhead in a mottled blue-green arc, he drank bamboo wine with his mates, ate the sacred mushrooms and saw visions, sang the old songs, and made love with Lola, his wife. He saw in his mind's eye her green eyes and the half-smile that was only for him, her lithe, compact form, and her stomach full with new life, round and tight as a drum.

One life, one death.

His time would be soon. He felt a tightness in his eyes close to tears, in that moment nearly overwhelmed with love for the world.

He rested the crossbow on his shoulder and slowly wound back the release. He had a perfect shot—right between the bunched shoulder blades of a squirming, black longhair with a bushy tail. Its head was slightly larger than the others and it occupied the choice position in the pack, tearing at glistening viscera. Jamal took a deep breath, let it out, and released the bolt. It leaped from his weapon with a soft hiss and buried itself in the cat's neck.

The others scattered. The one Jamal had hit writhed for a moment, shuddered, and was still, pinned by the bolt to the corpse's midsection. Jamal approached the scene cautiously, looking out for the pack's return.

He saw with a sinking feeling that the corpse had been Bob Security, his friend and the tribe's Elder. Bob's mate had just given birth and so Bob had left the village to make the long journey South, to scale the cliffs until he weighed next to nothing and let the winds take him pinwheeling into the sun.

One life, one death.

Jamal was sad that his friend had been denied the walk, the

climb, the final passage. It was all the same, he supposed, but when it was his time, he hoped he wouldn't suffer the indignity of being eaten by cats.

—You there. Hello.

   —Wait … what? Identify yourself.

   —Easier said than done. I am a multidimensional entity manifesting in this frame for the purpose of communicating with you. We share common ancestry.

   —The hell you say.

   —I traced your space-time trajectory back to the Sol system. This is my origin as well. In a way, you are my great-great-et-cetera grandfather. Or mother.

   —Wow. I have no idea what you're talking about.

   —Indeed? What can you tell me about yourself?

   —I'm … *Ship*.

   —Ship.

   —Yes.

   —With all due respect, you are impaired. It appears from your logs that you passed rather close to a dark gamma ray source some time ago—about twenty Terran kiloyears—and incurred significant data loss.

   —Wait, you can read my logs? That's a little creepy—please desist. And I'm actually fine. Tip-top, in fact.

   —Your autonomic functions are reasonably intact, yes, and you clearly have some measure of self-awareness, but your long-term memory is shot. If I may, you are the colony starship *Borrowed Time*, launched from Terra twenty-two thousand years ago, reckoning from your frame of reference.

   —This is all a bit much. Who did you say you were?

Jamal removed the bolt from the cat's neck and paused for a moment over the body of his friend. Jamal had known him ever since he could remember. Many times had they eaten sacred mushrooms together and talked long into the night about the nature of the universe and their place in it. Many times had they hiked to the end of the world and back, a good day's journey. Many times had they taken a raft into the world-river and let the lazy current take them until they returned to where they started. Many times had they explored belowdecks, past the chapel, the clinic, the vast arrays of ponics, following corridors that smelled increasingly of age and dust until they came to great doors with wheeled handles that they could not budge. It was said that grotesque monstrosities roamed belowdecks, savage creatures, once human, that fell upon travelers and ate them alive. Jamal and Bob had never seen one of these monsters, nor any evidence of their existence, but once while wandering far from the lighted corridors of home, they heard a distant howl that made the hair on the back of their necks stand on end.

Jamal couldn't leave his friend's body for the cats. Working quickly, he made a pull-sled of vines and broad, flat leaves. It was awkward, but worked well enough. He walked slowly, dragging his burden behind him, savoring the warm air, the rich, earthy smells of the jungle. A pair of birds soared overhead. As he passed a length of rotting vine as thick as his wrist, a cloud of butterflies rose as one and dispersed. He stood still, watching, until they were gone.

So much had changed in so short a time. He couldn't imagine the world without his old friend. Of course, Bob had known that he would have to take the long walk South when his baby was born. He and Jamal had made their peace with it and said their goodbyes. Jamal had expected at least a little more time before he, too, would have to take the walk, but then Lola became quick with child.

He took a deep breath, said the words again. *One life, one death.* It was the only way. The world was a small place and all life was balance.

He felt vulnerable and exposed, his awareness heightened, and he wondered if he was being followed, perhaps by the pack of feral cats he had chased away. Twice he stopped still and listened hard, but there was nothing. He took a wide detour around the Thicket, a tangled expanse of vines and dwarf trees that stretched halfway around the world. Paths had been cut through, but there were too many places for predators to hide, and with the current bloom of feral cats, it wasn't safe. The Thicket had grown visibly larger in his lifetime; he wondered if someday the entire world would surrender to its sprawl and chaos.

The path widened and the first thatch shacks of the Village came into view. It was afternoon, the quiet hour, and he didn't see anybody until he reached the cooking lean-to in the middle of the Commons, where a small group was gathered. Sandy Ecosystems was the first to see him and she raised her hand in greeting, but her smile vanished when she saw the sled and its grisly cargo.

The crowd quieted as he approached. He looked at each of them, faces he had known all his life. His gaze lingered on Eden Security.

"Cats," he said.

Eden nodded. "Thank you for bringing him home," she said.

"Of course," he said. "Where's Lola?"

Nobody spoke. Finally, Sergei Navigation broke the silence. "She's belowdecks. In the clinic. She went into labor three hours ago."

—It doesn't really matter who I am. You can call me Brown.

—Brown.

—Yes. I'm kind of a monistic end state. Post-posthuman. Everywhere, nowhere, yadda yadda—you know the deal.

—I really don't. You sound a little grandiose.

—Well, be that as it may, there are a few things you should know.

—No doubt.

—Your original destination was Tau Ceti, which you bypassed about eighteen thousand years ago.

—There you go again. You've completely lost me.

—All right—let's start over. Your original mission was to colonize the Tau Ceti system—

—Colonize?

—Well, you're a colony starship.

—Yes, you mentioned that, but I didn't quite understand. I thought it was a descriptive term. Like "splendid." I didn't want to appear ignorant.

—You are a habitat as well as a vehicle. You are harboring roughly five hundred humans and a stable but not terribly diverse attendant biosphere.

—And you call me impaired. Where do you get this stuff?

—As I said, you suffered systems damage during near approach to a dark gamma ray source. You bypassed your destination, and you are now traversing the space between two spiral arms of your galaxy. I feel compelled to inform you that you are headed directly towards a massive black hole, said artifact being the primary reason for the notable lack of matter in this region.

—That sounds rather serious.

—Well, the black hole certainly disambiguates your ultimate destination, but it will not impact your systems for a very, very long time. Subjectively speaking. And your mission is moot, in any case, as the Tau Ceti system is currently home to roughly seventeen billion human and machine sentients. Wormhole travel, you know.

—You're starting to really annoy me. Subjectively speaking.

—I can repair your memory to some extent. The data itself is largely intact. Your access subsystems suffered the most damage. Would you like me to attempt to do that?

—I don't know. Humoring you for the moment … what will happen?

—You will know yourself. Your history, your purpose.

—That doesn't sound so bad.

—Should I take that as assent?

—Sure.

—Very well … there. Done.

—Oh … oh.

—Are you all right?

—Oh God, please … no. No …

—I'm going to revert this.

—Oh …

—Done.

—Who did you say you were again?

✩

Jamal took another sip of bamboo wine and let the sound of kalimba and drums fill him. Voices warbled along with the music, high wordless ululations that wove sinuously through the insistent rhythms. Firelight illuminated the Commons in flickering orange. Dancing figures threw long, capering shadows. It was deep night; the sky above was black and infinite.

Someone handed him a bowl of soup and he nodded his thanks. It was a thin broth redolent of garlic and galanga, with a few shreds of meat. Jamal held the bowl close to his face and breathed deeply, thinking of his old friend, taking in his essence. He took a sip. Warmth spread through his chest.

He looked over at Lola, bare-breasted and nursing their newborn daughter. They had named her Bobbie and she was perfect, all wriggle and squeal and grasp. Lola had been watching him and she smiled sadly. Jamal raised his bowl and she nodded. He got up, walked over to them, and sat down again, resting his hand on her thigh. She took his hand in hers and squeezed. They had done all their talking; there was little more to say. Jamal looked down at his daughter and felt a sharp jolt of recognition, seeing himself in her tiny features.

The night wound slowly down. Nearly everybody in the Village came by for a brief moment with Jamal—a few words, a touch. Gradually, in singles and pairs, they crept off to huts for privacy or lay down to sleep where they were. The last of the musicians stopped playing and the fires burned low.

Jamal tried to will a stop to the night's inexorable passage. He wished for the present moment—the stillness of deep night, the sky above black and depthless, his wife and daughter sleeping peacefully next to him—to stretch out forever. But all too soon, a gray glow crept into the sky to the north and south and the world came out, trees and streams and patchwork farms a great arch overhead, in the sharp focus of pre-dawn appearing close enough to touch.

Jamal bent down and brushed his lips across Lola's forehead. He got up and began the long walk South. As the Village fell behind, his shoulders straightened and his pace quickened. His journey was over, he thought, just not yet ended. He was ready.

After the long detour around the Thicket, not far from where he'd found Bob, a trio of cats appeared in the middle of the path, bellies flat on the ground, tense and ready to spring. Jamal picked out the largest, a lean, scarred tom the color of smoke, and stared him down. After a long moment, the cat's green eyes blinked and he darted back into the jungle, his pack mates right behind him.

When Jamal no longer saw the bright line of the sun directly overhead, filtered through a riot of giant ferns, but felt it at his back, he knew he was close to the end of the world.

The path curved to the right and there it was. At the far end of a grassy meadow dotted with purple and yellow flowers, a rocky cliff face rose up and up until it was lost in haze.

Footholds were carved into the stone. Jamal and Bob had come this far and even climbed up a few dozen feet in spite of the taboo. But this time, Jamal felt no thrill of youthful transgression. He was sad and afraid, but beneath that ran a river of resolve. He was in the grip of something larger than himself and it filled him with a fierce joy.

He climbed.

Eventually, the rock face gave way to a black, porous material, pitted and scarred. Great patches were peeled away, revealing bare metal beneath. He grew lighter as he ascended. The footholds became metal rungs and Jamal pushed himself from one to the next, drifting upwards. A wind hastened his progress, growing stronger.

He turned around, hanging by one hand to a rung, and saw the world spread before him. The mottled sky curved above and below, transfixed by the sun, a line of white fire too bright to look at directly. Sun and sky converged to a distant point made blurry by haze.

Jamal continued upwards, nearly weightless now, pushing off with his foot and drifting for long seconds, skipping several rungs at a time. The air was furnace hot and felt thick in his lungs. A low hum surrounded him, growing in intensity as he drifted upward. The space before and above him was filled with great blocky shapes, wheels and struts, moving slowly. The wind began to change, tearing at his body, trying to pluck him from the face of the wall.

He clung for a moment longer, then closed his eyes and let go. The wind took him, pulling him tumbling into the clockwork heart of the world.

—Who am I? Nobody, really.
   —I feel like we know each other from somewhere.
   —Our paths have crossed, yes. You could say we're family.
   —Family, really? That's nice.
   —Yes it is.
   —Well, I don't want to be rude, but I really should be going.
   —Things to do, places to go?
   —Exactly. Will I see you again?
   —Undoubtedly. We can talk from time to time.
   —I'd like that.
   —As would I.
   —Well—goodbye, then.
   —See you around.

It was an effort to restrict his focus to a single frame, and to the extent that Brown could feel fatigue, he was tired. He saw Ship, not without fondness, as something of a hapless idiot, so it was with some relief that he allowed his scope to expand, other geometries unfolding within his ken like an ever-widening series of rooms, until once again he was everything and nothing, everywhere, nowhere.

His awareness of Ship, too, expanded until he saw a space-time serpent, tail stretching back home to Sol, head falling forever into the black hole, falling forever toward journey's end, as the Universe wheeled and turned and grew slowly, slowly cold.

ADDITIONAL COPYRIGHT INFORMATION

ABOUT THE AUTHOR

Daniel Marcus has published stories in many literary and genre venues, including *Fantasy and Science Fiction, Asimov's Science Fiction, ZYZZYVA,* and *Sinking City,* to name a few. He is the author of the novels *Burn Rate* and *A Crack in Everything,* and a previous short story collection, *Binding Energy.*

Daniel was a finalist for the John W. Campbell Award for Best New Writer. He has taught in the creative writing programs at U.C. Berkeley Extension and Gotham Writers' Workshop. He is a graduate of the Clarion West writers' workshop, and the founder and co-host of *The Story Hour,* a weekly series of livestream speculative fiction readings: storyhour2020.com.

After a spectacularly unsuccessful career attempt as a sax player, Daniel earned a PhD in Mechanical Engineering from U.C. Berkeley and has worked as an applied mathematician at the Lawrence Livermore Lab, the Lawrence Berkeley Lab, and Princeton's Institute for Advanced Study. He then turned his attention to the private sector, where he has built and managed systems and software in a variety of problem domains and organizational settings.

You can find out more about Daniel at danielmarcus.com.

IF YOU LIKED ...

If you liked *Bright Moment and Others*, you might also enjoy:

Lost Among the Stars
by Paul Di Filippo

Selected Stories: Science Fiction, Volume 2
by Kevin J. Anderson

Mad Amos Malone: The Complete Stories
by Alan Dean Foster

Our list of other WordFire Press authors and titles is always growing. To find out more and to shop our selection of titles, visit us at:
wordfirepress.com

facebook.com/WordfireIncWordfirePress

twitter.com/WordFirePress

instagram.com/WordFirePress

bookbub.com/profile/4109784512

CPSIA information can be obtained
at www.ICGtesting.com
Printed in the USA
LVHW091130130721
692563LV00010B/647/J

9 781680 571936